THE GIRL FROM MARS

A Starstruck Novel

BRENDA HIATT

dolphin star
PRESS

THE GIRL FROM MARS

A Starstruck Novel

Dolphin Star Press
ISBN: 1-940618-50-9
ISBN-13: 978-1-940618-50-0

DEDICATION
For everyone who has ever doubted they would find their happy ending

THE STARSTRUCK SERIES BY BRENDA HIATT
Starstruck
Starcrossed
Starbound
Starfall
Fractured Jewel: A Starstruck Novella
The Girl From Mars

Contents

Preface

AN INTRODUCTION TO NUATHAN HISTORY, 83RD EDITION

(BASIC CURRICULUM TEXT—USE IN PLACE OF PREVIOUS EDITIONS)

OVERVIEW

Nuath's true origins have been lost in the mists of time. However, it is generally believed that nearly three thousand years ago, a technologically advanced alien race created the underground cavern on Mars with its Earth-like environment. The aliens then transplanted the inhabitants of a small Earth village to this cavern, in order to conduct genetic and social experiments on their captives. As the human population increased from a few hundred to many thousands, the habitat was gradually expanded to its present size. Then, approximately one thousand years after establishing this underground Martian laboratory, the aliens departed for reasons unknown, leaving no record of their nature or their future plans.

Without their alien overlords, the abandoned community, by then known as Nuath, continued to evolve on its own. By necessity, a system of government emerged, the earliest leaders chosen from among the most gifted colonists. This led to the formation of the first *fine*, or bloodline, which divided a few generations later into the Royal and Science *fines*. Most of Nuath's governing body is still drawn from those two groups. Meanwhile, increasing specialization of various skill-sets led to the rise of numerous other *fines*. There are currently no fewer than ten major *fines*, most further divided into several sub-*fines*.

As the colonists learned to use and adapt technology left behind by their alien abductors, they were able to advance scientifically to the point of building and launching spacecraft of their own. 523 years ago, under Sovereign Arturo, Nuathans first visited their nearest neighbor, Earth, and discovered it was their planet of origin. More expeditions followed, with small groups of Nuathans occasionally emigrating to Earth despite the harsher conditions found there. Those earliest *Echtrans,* or expatriate Martians, are believed to have sparked Earth's Renaissance period. To facilitate communication, Nuath eventually adopted the calendar and measurement system of Earth's Ireland, home of the first real *Echtran* outpost. Because the planet remained socially and techno-logically backward by Nuathan standards, it was early decided to keep emigrants' origins and abilities secret from their Earth (or *Duchas*) neighbors.

Safely concealed on Mars, Nuath remained peaceful and prosperous, if not perfect, until fifteen years ago, when the ambitious upstart Faxon began sowing discord, stirring up resentment in the less-prestigious *fines* against the Royals and Scientists. Over a two-year period, Faxon gath-ered enough support to stage a coup, deposing and then assassinating Sovereign Leontine and his wife. A general purge of the Royal bloodline followed, though some survived Faxon's depredations by fleeing to Earth. Among those were Leontine's son, Mikal, with his wife and infant daughter.

The majority of Nuathans, even those who had helped Faxon rise to power, were horrified by his excesses. As his support waned, Faxon resorted to intimidation and repression to maintain control. Fearing Mikal and his family could become a rallying point for the fledgling Resistance movement, Faxon sent a few still-loyal adherents to Earth with orders to eliminate them. When word came back that the last of the Sovereign line had been killed, most Nuathans were thrown into despair. Rebellion having been largely bred out of the early colonists, the Resistance faltered and would have failed but for the efforts of a few Royals, most notably the O'Gara family, who obscured their origins to remain on Mars and rally their people's spirits, restoring to them a measure of hope.

This hope was greatly bolstered when Nuathans learned that the last of Sovereign Leontine's line had not, in fact, perished. The news that his granddaughter, Princess Emileia, had been discovered alive on Earth galvanized the Resistance, allowing them to finally cast off the yoke of Faxon's oppression and remove him from power. Since then, Nuathan society has begun to rebuild itself, striving for an eventual return to its former prosperity and security. It is hoped that the recent return of the Princess, lately Acclaimed Sovereign Emileia, will hasten that recovery.

PART I

Kira of Nuath

Caidpel

CAIDPEL (KAYD-PEL): *predominant sport played in Nuath, combining elements of the Irish sports of hurling and Gaelic football*

"Kira! I'm open!" My teammate Brady's call comes from across the *caidpel* field as two opposing players box me in.

Whirling to face him, I toss the ball from my hand to my *camman*, then use the stick to flick it his way over my opponents' heads. Brady barely has to stretch to catch the *schlitur* on a dead run toward the other team's goal. My way no longer blocked, I'm free to assist. As I streak down the *caidpel* pitch, the opposing goalposts loom up like a giant letter "A" with two crossbars, one above the other.

Brady lobs the ball toward the middle goal, between the two crossbars, five feet above the goalie's head. Not high enough. She extends her stick and jumps, deflecting it at the last second, but now I'm in position.

I leap in front of the man she's aiming for, knocking his *camman* aside with my left hand as I snag the ball in my right. Two quick steps, then I hurl the ball twice as high as Brady did. The *schlitur* sails through the small, triangular goal at the top, between the short upper crossbar and the pointed peak where the two posts converge twenty feet above the ground.

Five points! Seconds later the final chime sounds, ending the game with our team up 12-10 over the Healers.

My teammates converge on me, cheering wildly. "You did it, Kira!" screams Leitis, our goalie and my best friend on the team.

"Again," adds Brady, grinning at me over the top of Leitis's head. "Was a good day for the Ags when you joined us, Kira. Glad now I didn't make that three-pointer and throw us into overtime. Gave you a chance to go for the win. Well done!"

"Thanks." I grin back at him.

This is only my second season in the elite Senior *Caidpel* League, though I started playing on Hollydoon's girls' team when I turned twelve, nearly five years ago. Playing *caidpel,* even becoming one of Nuath's top players, might not be as world-changing as helping the Resistance was, but I still love it. Especially at moments like this, when I've just helped advance the Agricultural *fine*'s team into the playoffs.

Our green-clad fans start streaming onto the pitch to congratulate the players—especially me. Though I enjoy the adulation, seeing so many of my teammates being hugged by their families is a sharp reminder that my own didn't come. Never come.

Dad claims it's because the crowds spook Mum so much. Maybe it's true. She's never quite been herself since Faxon's goons arrested her last year, two weeks before the dictator was overthrown. I should probably cut her more slack.

Retrieving my smile, I turn to a few younger fans thrusting their tablets toward me. I'm autographing the last one when I spot my little sister making her way through the crowd. Scanning the area behind her, I see no sign of our parents.

"Hey, Adina. Did you come by yourself?"

"I came with Bronwyn's family. They figured I wouldn't want to miss your big game and they were right—you were awesome!"

I return her hug, absurdly touched. "Thanks, Sprout. You want to stick around and celebrate with the team? Coach said something about Sheelah's."

Adina's amber eyes widen at the name of the best restaurant in Newlyn—one of the best in Nuath, in fact. "Oh, wow, Sheelah's! I'd…no, I'd better not. The water dispenser in the sheep pen has been glitching lately and Mum never remembers to check it. Besides, I said I'd be home for dinner."

"You and your sheep." I ruffle my sister's short blonde hair.

While my parents and I have the skills with plants typical of most

Ags, Adina has always had a special affinity for animals. Dad sometimes teases that Adina is a throwback to the time before Horticulture and Husbandry split into separate Agricultural sub-*fines*, five or six hundred years ago.

"I'll see you later then, okay?" I say. "Tell Mum and Dad not to wait dinner. And thank Bronwyn's folks for bringing you."

When the happy crowd finally disperses a little while later, our team heads to Sheelah's for our celebratory dinner. Coach assures us he called ahead to reserve their party room, but when we arrive the owner tells him it's already taken.

"But...I just called to confirm fifteen minutes ago," Coach protests. "You said you were holding that room for us."

The man, both shorter and noticeably pudgier than the average Nuathan, shrugs apologetically. "Sorry about that. They arrived just ahead of you, so what could I do?"

He jerks a thumb over his shoulder toward the archway leading into the room in question—the only one large enough to accommodate our whole team. Looking, I spot the unmistakeable tall, copper-headed figure of Sean O'Gara, the Sovereign's future Consort, laughing and talking with a dozen other guys around the same age. They all look pleased with themselves for pulling rank to snag the best room—the room that was *supposed* to be ours.

Even as I watch, Sean O'Gara turns his head and spots our team, still hovering by the door. Nudging a couple of his buddies, he grins widely and gives us a cocky thumbs-up. Gloating. Arrogant, Royal *twilly*.

"Seriously?" I say to our coach. "They bumped us for the Sovereign's lapdog and his Royal friends? They don't even need a room that big!"

"Shh!" Coach hisses at me. "Do you want to get us all in trouble?" Then, more loudly, "C'mon, everybody, we'll celebrate with fish and chips next door instead. My treat."

There's quite a bit of grumbling as we file back out, but no one dares protest too loudly. I glance back over my shoulder as I leave the restaurant and see Consort Sean still grinning at us, like he's daring us to try to oust him and his gang of Royals from the room *we* reserved.

"Jerks," I mutter. "They're as bad as Faxon's favorites used to be, lording it over everyone else."

The only one close enough to overhear is Brady, who immediately falls into step beside me. "You still miss it, don't you?" He slants a glance down at me with those dark blue eyes that make all the girls swoon.

I look up at him, startled. "Miss—? You mean...when we were still working to change things and *caidpel* was more than just a game?"

Brady is the only other member of our team who used the sport as cover to help the Resistance last year, when Faxon was still making everyone miserable. Our matches and practices take us all over Nuath, so it was easy to pass messages without Faxon's *bullochts*—who were everywhere—getting suspicious.

He nods. "I'm not criticizing, you're playing better than ever this season. But I can tell you don't have quite the same fire you did then. Am I wrong?"

For a second I don't answer, then I shake my head. "Not wrong. But we're supposed to be happy about it, right? The Resistance did what it set out to do—got rid of Faxon. Brought back the Sovereign." I can't quite keep the bitterness out of my voice on that last word.

Brady keeps watching me, not saying anything else until the team is busy placing their orders at the fish and chips counter. Then, softly, "What if I told you there are still ways to make a difference?"

"What do you mean?" I whisper back. "How?"

"Ask me tomorrow, after our practice in Monaru. 'K?"

I nod eagerly and he moves off. Leitis immediately takes his place at my side.

"Ooh, that looked a bit intense, Kira. You and Brady, eh?"

"Nah, just talking game strategy." I can't claim I'm not attracted to him. But so is every other girl on the team, along with half the female population of Nuath, drooling over him on the feeds.

Leitis sighs, looking over her shoulder after Brady. "He can talk strategy to *me* any time he wants, whether it's to do with *caidpel* or not," she says with a wink.

If I'm honest with myself, I feel the same way. But handsome as Brady is, at the moment I'm more interested in hearing whatever he's going to tell me tomorrow than in starting a romance.

"C'mon," I say to Leitis. "We'd better get our orders in before they run out of fresh chips."

Riding the zipper home to Hollydoon an hour later, I puzzle over Brady's cryptic words: *make a difference*. How?

Sure, there are things I'd change if I could. Because, no matter what my mother says, Nuath is nothing like I thought it would be once Faxon was gone.

Okay, maybe things aren't as bad as when people got hauled from their homes in the dead of night never to be seen again. And Faxon's *bullochts* are no longer roaming around taking whatever—or whoever— they want while supposedly "protecting" our villages. But while everything might have improved for those in the upper *fines*, not a whole lot has changed for the rest of us, other than feeling a little safer.

For instance, there's still no direct zipper from Newlyn to Hollydoon, which means I have to change in Thiaraway. Slinging my school bag over my shoulder, I get off my *tapacarr* and head across the main terminal to catch the next one home. As I swing by the big screen to check departure times, slightly raised voices off to my left catch my attention.

"How do we know you don't have anything good in there if you don't let us look?" I hear a male voice saying in a hectoring tone.

"Yeah," says another. "Open it up. Let's see what you've got."

Frowning, I glance over and see two guys about my age picking on someone much smaller than they are—with short, blond hair.

"Adina?" Outraged and furious, I barrel toward the group but realize halfway there that the blond kid is a boy, not my sister. Even so, I don't slacken my pace.

"What's the problem here?" I yell in the same voice I use to shout out plays on the *caidpel* pitch.

The two bigger boys whip around to glare at me. "None of your business, Ag," the taller one sneers, eyeing the green uniform I'm still wearing. "Just move along."

"I don't think so." I keep moving forward. "Not until you tell me why you're hassling this kid."

"He's got something we want," says the stockier boy. "Don't you, kid?"

"No!" The younger boy sounds scared. "I told you, all I have in here is my school stuff. Those omnis you saw earlier weren't mine, they were ones my dad repaired for their owners. I already delivered them."

"Then you won't mind if we take a look." The tall boy reaches for the kid's pack.

I push right up between them. "Let me guess, your dads used to work for Faxon and you think it's still okay to bully people? It's not. Knock it off unless you want everyone to know your families are still sympathizers."

There were penalties in place for that now, though I wasn't sure how strictly they were enforced.

"Shows what you know." The shorter, heavier set boy smirks at me. "My dad happens to be the Acting Under-Minister of Culture, not some filthy Faxon holdover."

"That's right," the skinny dark-haired one affirms. "So an Ag like you can't touch us. Playing on some stupid sports team doesn't make you *that* special."

Royals. I should have guessed. If anything, my opinion of them sinks lower.

"How do you think your parents will feel if word gets out their sons are shaking kids down right here in Thiaraway? That'll play great on the feeds. They love scandals like that."

I'm totally ready to get physical if that threat doesn't work...but it does.

"C'mon, Zach." The stocky one puts an urgent hand on his friend's shoulder.

The taller one glares at me for a second, then shrugs. "Yeah. This kid's not worth our time anyway. You both better watch your step, though. We'll be watching."

"So will the media," I call after them as they hurry off. Then I turn to the blond boy. "You okay?"

He nods. "Thanks. Those two are the biggest bullies in school. Dunno what they'd have done if you—" Breaking off, he stares at me, apparently taking in my uniform, my face, for the first time. "Whoa! You're...are you Kira Morain?"

"Um, yeah. Why?"

"I caught the last half of tonight's game on the feeds," he says excitedly, his eyes shining now. "That last goal was brilliant! My family's Maintenance *fine,* Mechanics. No *caidpel* team, so we've always supported the Ags. Wait till I tell them I met you in person! Boy, will my brother be jealous."

I have to stifle a laugh. At least he seems to be over his fright. "You want me to autograph something so you can prove it?" I ask, half teasing.

"Oh, wow, would you? Yeah! Just a sec." He rummages in his pack, then pulls out a tablet that looks even older than mine. Grinning ear to ear now, he pulls up a blank screen and hands me a stylus.

"What's your name?"

"Jareth."

Smiling to myself, I write, "To Jareth, a cool kid. Nice meeting you! - Kira Morain #19."

"Awesome," he breathes, reading it. "Thanks! Again!"

"You're welcome. Can you get home all right?"

His head bobs up and down. "Sure, no prob—in fact, that's my zipper now. See ya!" With a last, adoring grin, he sprints for his platform.

I head for my own, still smiling—until I notice *my* zipper just left and the next one's not for twenty-five minutes. "*Flach,*" I mutter, glad Mum can't hear me. With a sigh, I pull my own tablet out of my pack. Might as well get a start on tonight's homework while I wait.

When I finally reach Hollydoon's *tapacarr* station, I have to walk nearly a mile to our house, since our supposedly amazing new Sovereign still hasn't gotten around to turning on the antigrav grids outside the village center. Faxon turned them off a few years back to make it easier to monitor people's movements, sidelining the little local zips and rendering my old hovercycle useless.

Now, with the Sovereign's calls to conserve power, I wonder if that'll ever change. I cut through the village center at a brisk pace, trying to make up for lost time.

"Hey, Kira! Great job tonight!"

I turn to see a family of four waving to me from their front porch. Grinning, I wave back. "Thanks!"

"We watched the game, too," a woman calls out of a window of the house next door. "That last goal was amazing!"

Hollydoon is nearly three-quarters Agricultural *fine* so it's not surprising most of the village follows our matches. Still, it's cool to be cheered by my own neighbors.

"We have a great team this year," I call back as more people start waving from windows and doorways. "Be sure to watch our first playoff game in two weeks!"

There are a few cheers and shouts of, "We will!"

I continue on my way, no longer bummed about being so late. The houses get smaller as I move out of Hollydoon's center toward the narrow track that leads across the fields to our farmhouse.

Low stone walls loom past as I leave the village proper, my path lit only by the thick tapestry of stars overhead. I love walking at night now that it's so much safer. Slowing, I gaze up at the constellations. Holographic, of course, but they supposedly look exactly as they would from the surface of Mars. Fake or not, they're pretty.

By the time I reach our farm I'm hoping there's something left from dinner since I'm already hungry again. My post-game fish and chips were more than two hours ago—and nowhere near as filling as a meal at Sheelah's would have been. My parents are watching something on our little living room vidscreen when I come in.

"Oh, Kira, you're home!" Mum greets me with a smile. "We were just discussing the wonderful news."

Pleased and a little surprised, I grin back. They rarely pay attention to my games but this *was* an important one. "Yeah, it was a great match, got us into the playoffs. I guess you saw it on the feeds?"

Mum gives me that vague look she wears way too often these days. "What? Oh, yes, Adina did mention earlier that your team won. I was so excited about Sovereign Emileia's visit to Hollydoon tomorrow, I'm afraid I barely heard her."

"I understand you scored the winning goal?" Dad gets up and gives me a quick hug. "Well done. We'll have to watch the highlights before bed."

"Um, sure." I turn away, hiding my hurt. The villagers and kids at school treat me like a minor celebrity but my own parents can't even be bothered to watch me live on the feeds. "Is there anything left over from dinner? I'm starving."

"I believe so." Mum's gaze has already drifted back to the vidscreen and some other story about the Sovereign. "Why don't you check the recombinator?"

I go into the kitchen to see what my options are. Looks like it was broccoli and synth salmon for dinner again, not exactly my favorites. Probably means that's what there was most of when Mum went to the marketplace this morning, meaning it was cheapest. Ags, especially less prominent ones like us, never get first pick but there's usually synth salmon and broccoli left over—which means we have it a lot. I quickly scroll through the recombinator menu to see if anything better is stocked. There's not.

Figuring I might as well grab a shower first, I head back through the living room where Mum has reverted to the previous topic.

"I can hardly wait to see her in person," she's saying to Dad. "Consort Galena, her mother, was always so very kind to me when I worked in the Palace gardens..." She trails off, gazing dreamily into space, like she does whenever anything reminds her of the "good old days" before Faxon. Shaking my head, I enter the bedroom I share with my sister.

Adina looks up from her homework when I come in. "Hey. You're home sooner than I thought you'd be. I figured you guys would be partying for hours."

"We couldn't get the party room at Sheelah's after all—had to settle for fish and chips from the place next door." I shrug, my earlier ebullient mood souring further at the memory. "We'll manage a better celebration if we win our first playoff game, though."

Heading into the bathroom, I strip off my *caidpel* uniform, hang it in the ionic cylinder in the corner, then step in myself. In less than two minutes, the dirt and sweat from the game is gone from both my body and the uniform. Pulling on a faded blue tunic and black pants, I go back to the kitchen, where the rest of the family is now gathered.

"—all of us," Mum is saying cheerfully as my sister fills a glass with milk from the chiller that supplies the recombinator. "Won't that be nice?"

"What will be nice?" I ask, crossing to the recombinator myself.

"For us to go as a family to see the Sovereign tomorrow. I'd love for you and Adina to actually meet her," Mum replies. "Especially as she's just about your age."

I try to hide my involuntary grimace. "Younger than me. By at least six months. Anyway, I can't go. I have practice in Monaru tomorrow."

As a member of one of the top *caidpel* teams in Nuath, I have practice six days a week and I *never* skip, unlike some of the others on my team. The coaches are actually fairly flexible if we let them know about conflicts ahead of time, but I've never told my parents that.

"Can't you leave early?" Dad asks with a glance at Mum. "The Sovereign isn't scheduled to start speaking in the square until six."

"Sorry, I really can't. Now that the Ags have made the playoffs, the coaches will be doubling down on us." Which my parents would *know* if they bothered to follow our schedule.

Clearly disappointed, Mum frowns at me. "There *are* more important things than sports, you know, Kira." Not the first time she's said that.

"Your mother is right." At least Dad sounds apologetic. "It was different last season, when you were doing your part for the Resistance, but now that our goals have been achieved, *caidpel* is simply a game, no matter how obsessed some of our citizens may be with it."

"The way some are obsessed with the new Sovereign?" The words are out before I can stop them. "Anyway, what about the crowds? I'll bet most of Hollydoon will be crammed into the village square tomorrow evening."

At that, Mum presses her lips together stubbornly. "I've been doing much better at the Evening Sing the past few weeks. I'm...I'm sure I'll be fine."

Oh, sure, she'll make the effort for those archaic Group Sings most villages resumed once Faxon was out. Or for her beloved Sovereign. But not for my games.

"You know it'll be the same speech as always," I grumble. "The one we've seen on the feeds at least a dozen times." *Those* my parents always remember to watch. "I don't see much point missing practice to hear the same thing again in person. It's not like she writes her own material anyway."

"Kira!" Mum exclaims. "You don't know that."

I roll my eyes. "Seriously? She's only sixteen—and didn't even know Nuath existed until last year. It's not like she's spent her life training for this, like all the previous Sovereigns did."

Mum shakes her head at me sadly. "I don't understand why you're so antagonistic toward Sovereign Emileia, Kira. Most Nuathans understand that she's exactly what we need after the horrors Faxon put us through. Governor Nels did his best, but he was too indecisive to be an effective leader. I truly believe Emileia will become just that. Already, she's beginning to grow into her new role. I think she's shown a great deal of maturity so far, under very trying circumstances."

A laugh escapes me. "Maturity? Like getting caught on camera making out with her Bodyguard, then letting him into her bedroom on their way to Mars? Oh, yeah, that's *exactly* the mature judgment a Sovereign needs."

Dad shoots a concerned glance Mum's way. "Since her Acclamation she's been working closely with Regent Shim to get a properly elected legislature in place, among other things," he points out to me. "Isn't that one of the things you feel strongly about?"

I barely restrain a snort. "I've heard their promises to open up elections to all the *fines*, but who's going to hold them to that? You watch, we'll still end up with nothing but Royals and Scientists in the legislature. They'll never let somebody from Mining or Agriculture bump a Royal out of the *Eodain*, not without a fight."

A fight I fully intend to be a part of, even if all I can use is words.

"They'll have to," Dad insists. "There are barely enough Royals left in Nuath to fill even the *Riogain* these days."

I've heard that on the feeds, too, but I'm not convinced. "The first general election is still a month away," I remind him. "A lot can change by then. Every week more cowardly Royals are coming back from Earth, where they stayed nice and safe while the rest of us had to—"

At Dad's warning glance I break off. He's been more protective of Mum than ever since she got home from that Mind Healing facility in Pryderi a few weeks ago. Even if he's not as big a fan of the Sovereign as Mum, he always shuts me down when I argue politics for fear I'll upset her.

"I'll admit Sovereign Emileia made a few missteps early on, but she's still young," he says. "Give her time."

Shaking my head in frustration, I turn back to the recombinator and punch up a plate of macaroni and cheese. "At least Shim isn't a Royal. If the Sovereign goes back to Earth like she says she will, maybe he'll do a decent job. Though we'd be better off with someone who's actually *lived* here recently, like Crevan Erc. He was planning to—"

"That's enough, Kira," Dad snaps. My parents have never been fans of Crevan or his Populist Party, but I thought he had the right idea.

Mum looks worriedly from Dad to me. "Why don't you bring your plate into the living room, Kira, and we can watch your game highlights together?"

By now, my earlier triumphant mood has been totally ruined. "I don't need to see the highlights, I was there. Besides, it's just a game, right?"

I hate watching myself on the feeds anyway. My hair always looks more red than auburn on the vid. And though I wear it in a messy knot on top of my head when I play, to keep it out of my eyes, it's not a particularly attractive look. Pulling out a fork, I thunk my plate onto the kitchen table and sit down.

Throwing Dad's words back at him only reminded me how much less rewarding my life is these days, without the Resistance. Another reason I have no intention of missing tomorrow's practice. If Brady knows a way I can still make a difference, I absolutely want to hear it.

2

Sean O'Gara

SEAN O'GARA (SHAWN OH-GAYR-UH): *Son of Quinn and Lily O'Gara; destined Cheile Rioga (Royal Consort) to Princess Emileia*

Sean

"Hurry up, Sean," Dad calls to me as I finish dressing. "I don't want to keep the Sovereign waiting."

She only recently asked Dad to resume handling her schedule—even officially appointed him Royal Secretary—so he's more determined than ever to work his way back into her good graces. Somehow, I doubt being on time for breakfast is likely to make her forget it was his idea to erase Rigel's memory several weeks back. Still, I try to be quick as I slip on my shoes and fasten my tunic belt.

"Okay, let's go."

Dad and I leave the quarters we share in the Royal Palace and walk the short distance down a corridor and around the corner to the Sovereign's suite of rooms. Cormac, her personal Bodyguard, conducts us to the dining chamber, where my sister Molly is busy setting out food and plates on the big dining table.

"Morning, Dad, morning, Sean." Since she serves as the Sovereign's

Chomseireach or Handmaid, Molly has a room right here in the sumptuous Royal Apartments.

M—better known in Nuath as Sovereign Emileia—smiles up at us from her place at the table. "Did you have fun last night?" she asks me.

As her "future Consort," I went absolutely everywhere with her before she got Acclaimed and for the first week or two afterward. Now, not so much—though Molly still does. Not that I'm bitter. Much.

"Um, yeah, I did." Forcing a smile, I take my usual place on M's left while my dad moves to sit on her other side. "You guys missed a great game—the Ags made the playoffs! Our whole group went to Sheelah's in Newlyn afterward to celebrate."

"Oh, wow, now I wish I'd gone after all." Molly's not nearly as big a *caidpel* fan as I am, though we both supported the Ags while growing up in Glenamuir.

Dad grins widely, for a second looking like he did before politics took over his life. "Hey, that's great. We should get tickets for their first playoff game."

Molly puts the last dish on the table and sits down next to me, since M refuses to follow Nuathan tradition and make her stand when it's just us.

"Who all went to the game with you?" Molly asks.

"Most of the old gang from Glenamuir. You know, Doyle, Brian, Floyd, plus a few others. Floyd, of course, couldn't resist using my status to insist on the best room at Sheelah's. Most of the Ag team showed up right after we did. I wanted to invite them to join us—that would have been cool—but they left before I got a chance. Anyway, it was fun, though I, um, probably stayed out later than I should have."

I glance at Dad, who gave me a hard time when I got in, but he turns to M, his mind obviously back on business. "Do you feel prepared for this evening's speech, Excellency, or would you like to go over the key points again?"

"I think by now I can recite them all in my sleep," she replies with a wry smile.

I frown, a forkful of scrambled eggs halfway to my mouth. "You're doing another in-person speech tonight? I thought you were cutting back on those. Isn't that why you've been recording all those vids?" That's what she was doing last night, in fact, while I was at the game.

"Shim thinks actually visiting the villages, talking to people face-to-face, is more effective," she says with a cute little shrug. "We're not getting as many bookings as we need yet. And now he's hinting that if I can't convince enough people to sign up for the next few Earth-bound ships, I might need to delay my departure till the next launch window—which I'm *totally* not going to do."

I examine her face—the most beautiful face in the universe to me—with concern. She doesn't look nearly as wrung out as she did while campaigning to get Acclaimed two months ago, but she does look tired.

"Would that be such a terrible thing, really?" I say, though I know it's pointless. "With another two years to change people's minds, you'd be able to slow down, not push yourself quite so hard. You don't want to get sick again, do you?"

She glares across her plate at me with those amazing green eyes. "Of course it would be a terrible thing. Why would you even ask that, Sean? If there's *any* chance I can help Rigel get his memory back—get his *life* back—I have to try. As soon as I possibly can. One of those Mind Healer reports said the longer we wait, the harder it will be."

"And nearly *all* of those reports say it can't be done at all. Look at Elana. She's been under continuous care from the Mind Healers for months now and still hasn't improved enough to be released. And she just had some memories extracted, not completely erased, like—"

"That's totally different!" she interrupts. "I'm really sorry about your sister, Sean, I am. But unlike Rigel, her mind was tampered with by Faxon's people, who didn't know what they were doing."

She averts her gaze from me but the anguish pinching her face proves she knows, deep down, I'm right. It also, unfortunately, shows how much Rigel still means to her, no matter how hard I try to fill that void. Dad, I notice, stays completely out of the discussion. Not surprising, considering *his* role in what happened to Rigel—and that M hasn't exactly forgiven him yet.

"The fact that his memory wipe was done by the head Mind Healer herself just means it was a lot more thorough." Though it never works, I can't help trying again to make her face facts. "You told me yourself that she didn't—"

"I know, okay?" she snaps. "I still have to try. Which means filling up as many ships as I can as quickly as I can, so Shim can convince the Legislature it'll be okay for me to leave—that there'll be enough Nuathans on Earth by the end of the launch window to justify *me* going back there, too."

"But think how much more good you could do here! I know if you—"

Molly puts a hand on my arm, stopping me. "Don't, Sean. You're only making it worse." Then, to M, "When you finish eating, you and I can go pick out what you'll wear tonight, okay? Hollydoon is only a couple miles from Glenamuir and pretty similar, mostly Ags, so I already have some ideas."

Molly's right, of course. Arguing with M, especially about this, only pushes her further away from me. Which is the last thing I want to do, since she'll need me more than ever when...if...we get to Earth and she realizes the Healers—and I—were right about Rigel all along.

3

Populists

POPULISTS: *a minority movement among Nuathans advocating equal rights and representation for all* fines. *(Sometimes referred to as "Anti-Royals")*

At school the next day, the two main topics of conversation between classes are yesterday's *caidpel* game and the Sovereign's impending visit to Hollydoon. Being congratulated about the first one helps me ignore the second, and mostly restores my good mood from our win last night.

"I replayed that maneuver you and Doona pulled off in the first half about six times," Alan Dempsey tells me at lunchtime. A year older than me, he plays wing back on the Ag *fine*'s all-male *caidpel* team—not as prestigious as the co-ed league I'm in, but a bigger deal than the village teams. "Did you two practice that cool over-under thing in advance?"

"Sort of. We have a drill like that, so when we saw our opening yesterday, we took it. Luckily, it worked." Our relay down the field, fast-pitching the larger ball back and forth, high, then low, set up the goal that ended the first half.

"Luck? I don't think so." Shaking his head admiringly, he leans closer but just then Eileen, a classmate who plays on Hollydoon's girls' team, joins us to ask questions of her own.

Which is fine with me. Most girls consider Alan handsome, with his thick, white-blond hair and silvery blue eyes, but he's not really my type —and I know Eileen has a bit of a crush on him. I let the two of them carry the conversation, already thinking ahead to this afternoon's practice—and whatever Brady plans to tell me.

On the zipper to Monaru later, it's all I can think about—until practice actually starts. Then, as always, I'm completely sucked into the intricacies of *caidpel*.

"That relay Kira and Doona ran yesterday got a lot of attention on the feeds," Coach says as we gather around him behind one of the goals. "Since that means we can't use it again anytime soon, we'll work on some other passing drills."

We form two lines of ten down the middle of the pitch, twenty meters apart, one side starting with the *pell* and the other with the smaller *schlitur*. On the coach's instructions, we alternate passing the two balls diagonally down the line using our feet and open palms for the bigger ball and sticks for the little one. As always, it takes a few minutes to get into a groove but by our third time sending the balls down the line we look like a well-oiled machine.

After twenty minutes we move on to scoring drills, running up and down the field balancing the *schlitur* on our sticks or dribbling the *pell* with feet and hands—occasionally both at once, if we get lucky. Twice I send the larger *pell* through the topmost, smallest section of the A-shaped goalposts, worth seven points in a real game.

Practice runs a little over, leaving me exhausted, but in a good way—and more eager than ever for our next match. Only when Coach wraps up his post-practice strategy talk do I remember the main reason I was looking forward to this afternoon.

"You looked good out there today," Brady comments as we head to the equipment bins. "I can't believe how much you've improved over the past year or so."

"Thanks."

I try to think of a way to broach the topic he hinted at after yesterday's game as we return our sticks to the rack. Under Faxon we weren't allowed to carry our *camman* on the zippers—or anything else that might be used as weapons in the uprising he increasingly feared. That rule was abolished, of course, but by then we were used to the coaches storing them between games and practices. Four-foot poly sticks *are* kind of awkward to deal with off the field.

"Still interested in hearing what some of us are doing post-Resistance?" Brady murmurs before I have a chance to bring up the subject.

"Absolutely," I whisper back. "You said there's still a way I can make a difference?"

He nods. "What do you know about the Populist movement?"

"Crevan Erc's party? I caught some of his speeches when he was vying for Acclamation back in April. If my dad came into the room, he always switched to a different feed but I thought Crevan had better ideas than any of the others. Didn't his party mostly fall apart after the Sovereign got Acclaimed?"

"Nope. It's not only still around, it's growing. They have more support now than most people realize, they're just not as public these days. Crevan's being more careful—says trusting the wrong people is what undermined his campaign for Acclamation."

I remember Crevan was banned from that final debate between the then-Princess and her top contenders, just because he wasn't Royal. "Yeah, that sucked. Everyone kept talking about how great it would be to have a proper Sovereign again, but to end up with an inexperienced teenager who's practically a *Duchas* besides..."

"Believe me, you're not the only one who's less than impressed by our new Sovereign." He lowers his voice even more, though we're now well away from our other teammates, walking slowly toward the nearest zipper station.

Out of the corner of my eye, I see Leitis giving me a thumbs-up, but I ignore her. "Do you mean the Populists actually want to *do* something about it? What?"

I barely breathe the words, which could be construed as treasonous. But I'm dying to hear more.

Brady clearly notices my sudden nervousness because he hastens to reassure me. "Nothing violent. Information gathering, spreading the word about what we uncover—a lot like what we did in the Resistance, actually."

"But what are they—you?—hoping to achieve, exactly?"

Glancing quickly around, he angles away from another group headed for the same zipper platform.

"A fully elected, truly representative government, though we know we'll have to take it in stages. We're definitely not looking to stage a coup, if that's what you're worried about. The idea is to build up more grassroots support, do plenty of research into— Oops, that's your *tapacarr*, isn't it? I...guess I should let you go." His reluctance is flattering.

I shrug, trying to play it cool. "I can catch the next one. I'm in no hurry. My parents plan to spend the evening fawning over you-know-who. She's giving a speech in Hollydoon."

Brady looks at me, a speculative gleam in his eyes. I'm struck again by how incredibly handsome he is. His fervor for such a worthy cause makes him doubly appealing.

"There, ah, happens to be a meeting tonight, right here in Monaru," he says after a moment. "If you don't have to get home right away, maybe you'd be interested in coming? I can message ahead to vouch for you so they know you're okay."

My breath catches. "Tonight? Sure! I—" I break off, glancing down at myself. "I'm kind of a sweaty mess, though. I've got my school clothes in my bag, but—"

"No problem." He gives me an easy grin. "You can clean up at my place. I need to change before the meeting myself."

"Really? Thanks, that would be great." What would Leitis say if she knew about this? Not that I plan to tell her. Anyway, it's not like I'm excited for the same reason she would be—mostly.

"C'mon, it's not far. We can take the local zip."

Monaru is Nuath's biggest city, twice the size of Thiaraway and more than fifty times larger than Hollydoon, population-wise. Though it's only fifteen minutes away by zipper, I've only visited it for games and practices.

"So, what kinds of things do you talk about at these meetings?" I ask as we board one of the smaller, local *tapacarrs*.

"Too impatient to wait?" He slants an amused glance down at me. "Information updates, strategy...potential new operatives."

Excitement fills me at the idea of being an *operative* again, working for a cause greater than myself. As we pass through sections of Monaru I haven't seen before, I examine the city. Unlike Thiaraway, with its soaring spires of pink crystal, Monaru's buildings of gray and dark red stone appear more prosaic, more functional. More real. I decide I like it better than the capital city's glittering facade, the pretty face masking oppression—whether by Faxon or the Royals.

"Our stop." Standing, Brady extends a hand to me.

Startled, I take it—and feel myself flushing, which is ridiculous. His almost-grin shows he noticed. The moment I'm on my feet, I pull my hand away, not wanting him to think I'm like all those silly girls crushing on him. Because I'm not. At all.

We step off the zipper at the intersection of two streets choked with hovercar traffic. The walkways bordering the streets are also thronged, people moving purposefully about their business between tall cliffs of gray stone punctuated by occasional windows.

"I live just down here." Brady leads the way to a lane too narrow for zippers or any but the smallest hovercars. "My place...it's not much, but it's close to the aquaponics testing center where I work." He sounds almost apologetic.

"Hey, as long as the shower works. I don't exactly live in a mansion either."

"Yeah, don't know many Ags that do." His voice holds a trace of the same bitterness I feel myself every time I'm reminded of the various perks enjoyed by Royals and most Scientists—especially those in government.

Just ahead, I notice a man in a ragged tunic hunched up on the ground next to a trash receptacle. He looks half-asleep, or maybe sick, but Brady doesn't slow his stride as we pass him.

"Should we try to help that guy?" I glance over my shoulder.

"Wouldn't do any good. He's just drunk or high on *gloraigh*. Probably lost his job and doesn't have anything better to do. We get some of those here in Monaru. Guess the villages mostly don't?"

"Um, not that I've noticed." I look back again, but the man hasn't moved. "There isn't enough work here for everyone? What about food and stuff?"

Brady shrugs. "The markets give away whatever's left over at the end of the day, if people make the effort to go. Some don't bother, though, just scavenge on the streets or hope for handouts. Of course, if you're Maintenance or Mining—or even Ag—you never get the best stuff, even with a few *sochar* to spend."

"I thought that was supposed to get better after we got rid of Faxon?"

"So they said. Though there were plenty of inequities under Leontine, too."

I look up at him curiously. "Can you remember what it was like before Faxon? You can't be that much older than me."

A corner of his mouth quirks up. "I'm twenty-three. You're what? Sixteen?"

"Almost seventeen." I sound defensive, even to myself. "What do you remember from that time?"

"Not a lot. I was only eight when Faxon started decimating the Royals. Early on, I remember my parents and some of their friends, Ags and Mechanicals mostly, talking about how much better things would be getting. They'd bought into his promises, like most people did—until it became obvious they were all lies. This is my building."

It looks like all the others—tall, gray, hardly any windows. Brady leads me through a narrow doorway, up three flights of stairs and down a long hallway before palming open a door.

"Like I said, it's not much." He stands back to let me enter first.

The living area is less than half the size of ours, the only furniture a table, four straight-backed chairs and a small couch. The recombinator in one corner looks even more basic than the one at home.

"The shower's off the bedroom." He points at the only other door. "You can go first. I'll message Crevan to let him know I'm bringing you."

I blink. "Crevan Erc *himself* will be at this meeting?"

"Sure. Most of our meetings are in Monaru because he lives here. He likes to stay fairly hands-on, especially about what we put out for public consumption. Doesn't want to give the media another chance to spin things the wrong way, you know?"

That makes sense. "Cool. Okay, I'll be quick."

"No rush. There'll be food at the meeting, so we won't have to stop on the way." He pulls out his omni as I head into the bedroom.

Brady's bedroom. Nope, not thinking along those lines. Not. He seems to think he's too old for me anyway.

This room is as spartan as the main living area, with just a bed, nightstand and small desk with drawers down one side. Tunics and other clothes hang on hooks along one wall.

His ionic shower is almost identical to ours at home. I takes me less than five minutes to strip, get myself clean and put my school tunic and leggings back on. Wishing I had something nicer to wear, I exit the bedroom.

"Your turn."

Brady clicks off his omni. "That *was* fast. I won't take long either. You can watch the vid if you want." He hands me the omni on his way to the bedroom.

I'm half-tempted to check his message history to see what he told Crevan Erc about me, but I resist. Flicking on the vidscreen, I click to the latest news on the feeds. As usual, the focus is mainly on the new

Sovereign—which means today they're talking about her visit to Hollydoon.

"Sovereign Emileia is expected momentarily and as you can see, Moya, the residents of Hollydoon have come out in force to hear her speak." Gaynor, one of the lead reporters on the Nuathan News Network, sweeps a hand toward the packed village square. "Most of the villages she's visited over the past few weeks have reacted just as enthusiastically, which has to be gratifying for her and her team, given the rocky path she had to Acclamation only two months ago."

The camera pans across the crowd and I lean forward, trying to spot my parents and Adina. Is that them, off to the left? Before I'm sure, the camera switches back to Gaynor.

"It's expected she'll again focus on the recently-discovered power shortage and continue to press her campaign for—"

"Ready to go?" Brady's voice cuts across the reporter's, startling me.

"Oh. Um, sure." I switch off the feed and scramble to my feet. "You were even quicker than I was."

Grinning, he moves forward. "You want a snack before we leave? The meeting's on the far side of Monaru and there's no direct local zip. I don't have much in the recombinator right now, but—"

"No, I'm fine. I don't want to be late to my first meeting."

He touches my shoulder lightly as he ushers me out of the apartment ahead of him. My heart speeds up a little but I'm sure—nearly sure—that's only because I can't wait to meet Crevan Erc in person and learn how I can help make Nuath better.

The Populist meeting is in an older section of Monaru only served by one local zip line. Half an hour and two local connections later, Brady and I are standing in front of a door in a big warehouse-type building that looks partly abandoned.

"Ready?" he asks, the amusement back in his eyes—probably because I haven't stopped whispering excited questions the whole way here. The more he tells me about what the Populist movement hopes to accomplish, the more eager I am to be a part of it.

"Of course." I resist a ridiculous urge to stick my tongue out at him. The last thing I want to do is remind him how much younger I am.

With a half-concealed grin, Brady touches the chime. To my surprise, Crevan Erc himself answers the door.

"Ah, Miss Morain," he greets me with a smile. "Please come in."

Crevan's impassioned rhetoric always impressed me on the news feeds during the campaign. In person he positively radiates confidence and charisma, which explains how someone from the lowly Maintenance *fine* became the primary spokesman for the Populist party.

"Thank you for letting me come." It takes all my self-control not to gush. "I hope there'll be some way I can help your cause."

"That is my hope as well, Miss Morain. Brady here tells me you were active in the Resistance last year?"

I nod eagerly. "I carried messages for them, too, when we traveled for *caidpel*. I…I like to think it made at least a little bit of a difference."

"I have no doubt it did. Feel free to go in and join the others. We'll begin as soon as the last few— Ah, here they come now."

Three more people follow us inside and we all go into a large room that appears to be used for storage, judging by all the poly containers stacked in the corners. A dozen straight-backed poly chairs, similar to the ones in Brady's apartment, form a rough circle in the middle of the room, most of them already filled. I notice the others are a lot older than me or even Brady. Though I feel a little out of place, I try to hide it, determined to make myself useful somehow.

"Thank you all for making the time to be here," Crevan says once the last person is seated. "As we have two newcomers with us tonight, I'll begin with a brief overview of the Populist Party's goals and progress to date."

He goes on to outline the main tenets of the movement, which include a restructuring of Nuath's traditional government to allow truly equal representation for every citizen of Nuath, regardless of *fine* or status, something I thoroughly approve of.

"As the media is fond of pointing out, our goals are not dissimilar to those Faxon originally proclaimed before later perverting them into a naked power grab. We, on the other hand, sincerely do hope to improve conditions for all Nuathans. While we of course deplore Faxon's atrocities against the Royal *fine*, his horrific depredations have provided us with a unique opportunity to bring about the very changes he, and a majority of our population, once clamored for.

"The Legislature is only now beginning to rebuild itself. Even small departures from its traditional composition could influence how Nuath is governed for generations to come. We must not let this opportunity pass! However, we must be cautious. Already we've seen how easily our good intentions can be misconstrued by the media. All of our hard-won support will quickly evaporate if we give them the slightest ammunition to portray us as secret Faxon sympathizers. That is why we cannot be too careful when it comes to admitting newcomers to this, our inner circle."

I shoot Brady a startled glance, but he doesn't seem to notice. He made it sound like this was just a regular gathering of people interested in the movement, not some highly restricted meeting for its leaders. How did he convince them to let *me* attend?

While I'm still puzzling over that, Crevan turns to the other newcomer, an older man. "Porter is already known to some of you. He has proven useful to our cause on numerous occasions, organizing rallies in Thiaraway and elsewhere. I therefore felt it was time to allow him a greater say in our ongoing operations."

Porter stands and bows, murmuring a few words of thanks. As soon as he sits, Crevan turns to me.

"And this is Kira Morain. Many of you will recognize her from the sports feeds, but she also comes to us highly recommended by Brady. She worked with him during the Resistance and is likely to prove an asset to us as well, particularly in getting word of our true goals out to the youth of Nuath, our people's future."

The smile he gives me is overpowering, making me feel for a moment as though I'm the only other person in the room. "Am I correct that you have frequently expressed dissatisfaction with our new Sovereign, finding her ill-prepared for such an important role?"

"Yes, sir. I probably haven't been as discreet about that as I—"

"No, please don't worry about that. Your youth allows you far greater freedom to express your views than we of more mature years enjoy, while your status as a sports figure provides you a platform to share them more widely. You have a reader with you?"

I nod, gesturing at my bag. "I went straight to *caidpel* practice from school," I explain.

"Good. Before you leave I'll give you a file that will contain a great deal of, ah, ammunition you can use to better inform the opinions you share with your fellow students and athletes. Everyone needs to fully understand the dangers of entrusting the future of Martians everywhere to an untried girl."

Which is *exactly* what I've been telling people all along. I listen attentively as he turns back to the others.

"This recent news that the Sovereign intends to return to Earth before the end of the current launch window gives us yet another opportunity. Shim Stuart, Nuath's first non-Royal Regent in centuries, is likely to be more open to well-reasoned arguments in favor of our cause than any Royal Regent would be. It will be safest, however, to wait until Sovereign Emileia has actually left Mars to begin that campaign. Unfortunately, we can't be certain she won't change her mind, as she so frequently seems to do."

The rest of the brief meeting focuses on what strategies they should use to persuade Regent Shim and other highly-placed non-Royals to embrace the most important tenets of the Populist movement. Afterward, while the others linger to socialize and eat, Crevan takes me aside to load the promised file onto my tablet. I immediately encrypt it, which seems to please him.

"I have a feeling you may prove even more valuable to our cause than I previously believed, Miss Morain. Thank you again for joining us."

I start to ask the obvious question, but stop myself. "I should get home if I don't want my parents asking too many questions," I say instead.

But as soon as Brady and I are alone outside a few minutes later, I turn to him curiously. "What did Crevan mean by 'previously believed'? It sounded like he was expecting me to come even before today."

Brady hesitates for a second, then gives me a half-rueful grin. "Well, yeah. He kind of did. I've been talking you up for a while now."

"You have?" I blink. "Then why didn't you—?"

"He only agreed I could invite you a couple of days ago. I didn't want to get your hopes up by saying anything sooner. You're not mad, are you?"

Though do I feel kind of gullible now, I shake my head. "Not mad, no. But I wish you'd told me before the meeting. I might not have been so nervous."

"You've got nothing to be nervous about, now or ever. I wouldn't have recommended you if I didn't know you were up to the challenge."

Though I'm flattered by his confidence, I'm not sure how to respond as we continue on to the station where I can catch a direct zipper to

Hollydoon. I'm about to board when I ask, "Why me, though? Why not someone more—?"

He stops me with a touch on my cheek that feels almost as intimate as a kiss. "You're pretty special, Kira. I thought you'd figured that out by now." Stepping back, he winks. "See you at practice tomorrow."

4

Hollydoon

HOLLYDOON (HOL-ly DOON) (POP. 1,677): *largely Agricultural village in northwest Nuath; suffered particularly harsh ravages by Faxon's forces*

I spend the zipper ride to Hollydoon reading the file Crevan Erc gave me—a much better use of my time than replaying that brush of Brady's fingers along my cheek.

The file contains a complete rundown of the Populist Party's long and short-term goals, along with loads of carefully reasoned arguments that Populist supporters can use to convince the unconverted. Like:

"Point out the absurdity of an intellectually superior race clinging to an antiquated system of hereditary rulers. Though Nuathans claim to be more rational and enlightened than the *Duchas,* they are well ahead of us in this area. All historically important Earth monarchies were abolished generations ago in favor of representative governments elected by their people."

I'll use that one the first chance I get—maybe tonight, to my parents. My mother acts like the girl singlehandedly brought Faxon down, but the Populists claim what I've believed all along: that it was simply the *idea* of an heir to Sovereign Leontine, not Emileia herself, that motivated the Resistance to finally throw off Faxon's yoke. A paper cutout would have been as effective if enough people rallied around it.

When the zipper pulls into Hollydoon, I reluctantly put my reader away. I plan to cut through the main square again until I hear cheering. The Sovereign must still be here. Quickly adjusting my trajectory, I make a wide loop around the village center. If my parents spot me, they'll expect me to join the adoring crowd, which is the *last* thing I want to do.

Thinking back over everything I learned tonight as I walk home, I experience the same excitement I used to feel last year, carrying messages for the Resistance. Knowing I was doing my part to undermine Faxon. That proves I'm doing the right thing, joining the Populists. And to think that Brady's been talking me up to Crevan Erc for weeks! Is it possible I mean more to him than I've dared to—?

A sound from the sheep byre interrupts that interesting speculation. Peeking inside, I see Adina frantically scooping water out of an overly full trough and pouring it back into the receptacle above her head.

"Hey, Sprout, whatcha doing?"

She turns to me in obvious alarm, then relaxes slightly. "Kira, can you help me? I taught Nelly to open the water valve herself because the timer keeps glitching but she must have done it over and over! If Mum and Dad find out she wasted water, I'm afraid they'll get rid of the whole flock."

Not a baseless fear, given how strictly rationed that precious commodity is. If we run short of our own drinking and cooking water because of the sheep, our parents will be furious.

"It only overflowed a little." She points to a patch of damp straw beneath the trough. "So if we can just put most of this back in the supply tank…"

I pick up a second empty container and start helping. With two of us scooping, it doesn't take long to restore the trough to its usual level.

"I can't believe you managed to train a sheep to do something like that." I glance at the long lever she'd attached to the release valve. "I thought they were really stupid?"

"Not as smart as I hoped, obviously." Adina quickly unfastens the lever from the valve. "There. Now Nelly can't do it again. You won't tell Mum and Dad, will you?"

"No," I promise. "Why didn't you go with them into the village to listen to you-know-who?"

"I did, but when it got so late I asked if I could go home early to check on the sheep. Good thing, too."

A shaft of alarm goes through me. "You walked back all by yourself? In the dark?"

"You do it all the time," Adina points out. "What's the big deal?"

"You're a lot—" I break off. Because not only did I do the same when I was thirteen, it was a lot more dangerous back then, with Faxon's goons still roaming around.

"Sorry." I force a lighter tone. "Guess I still think of you as younger than you really are now. Probably always will. Big sister privilege."

She laughs. "It's good to know you've got my back, Kira, whether I need it or not. Guess we should go in and figure out dinner, huh? You want first shower tonight?"

"Oh, I got one at...um, after practice." To cover my near-slip, I quickly add, "Anyway, you'd better get yours before Mum and Dad get back or they'll want to know how you got so wet."

Once inside, Adina goes to shower and change while I check the recombinator to see what our dinner options are. Not many, but more than last night. I'm heading toward our bedroom to ask Adina what she's in the mood for when Mum and Dad walk in.

"Oh, Kira, you should have been there!" my mother gushes. "Sovereign Emileia is even more charming in person than in her vids. I can't get over how much she looks like her mother, Galena. And she has the same remarkable green eyes as Sovereign Leontine."

I fake a smile. "That's nice. I guess the crowd didn't bother you too much?"

Dad gives her shoulder a little squeeze. "She did extremely well, didn't you, dear?"

"Yes, I was fine," she agrees happily. Which means she'd be fine attending my games, too—if she really wanted to come.

"So, did the Sovereign say anything worth hearing, or did she just look pretty and act charming?" I blurt without thinking, everything I heard at the meeting and read afterward still fresh in my mind.

Mum's smile evaporates and Dad gives me a quick, quelling head shake.

"Perhaps if you had come with us this evening, you'd feel differently about her now," he suggests. "I thought she expressed herself extremely well." He glances at the screen I've pulled up on the recombinator. "I take it you haven't eaten either? Why don't you put something together for all of us?"

I select a vegetable and synth chicken casserole I like but when I start to program it in, Mum stops me.

"I know it's late, but let's make dinner the old-fashioned way tonight."

"What? Why?" I turn to look at her in surprise. "It's been great having a working recombinator again after the way Faxon randomly cut our power. Things were finally starting to get back to normal before—"

At Dad's frown I break off but Mum's already wearing her stubborn look. "Sovereign Emileia has good reason to ask everyone to conserve while our Scientists look for a solution to our energy shortage. We should do our part. A food recombinator is a luxury, and one we can comfortably live without."

"I doubt cooking the old-fashioned way uses any less power—and it takes forever," I argue. I'm starving, what with *caidpel* practice, then being too excited after the meeting to eat anything.

"It will be good practice," Dad says. "Recombinators are only one of the conveniences we'll have to learn to do without."

I blink at him, confused. "Huh? Why?"

"We have some rather, ah, exciting news. We'd planned to tell you and Adina over dinner."

"News?" I ask suspiciously. "What kind of news?"

Mum puts a gentle hand on my shoulder, her eyes pleading—which doesn't reassure me at all. "Please don't be angry, Kira, but...the Sovereign was extremely persuasive tonight. She told us such wonderful things about Earth, and about her own hometown of Jewel, in a place called Indiana. I'm sure you and Adina will love it there. Why, you might even become friends with the Sovereign herself!"

I jump backwards, feeling as if she just slapped me in the face. "*What?*" I shriek so loudly the people in the next farmhouse over probably hear me. "You're crazy! I'm not leaving Nuath! And I sure as *efrin* don't want to become *friends* with that presumptuous little child-Queen."

"Now, Kira," Mum cautions me, "you know you mustn't say things like that. And there's no guarantee we'll be allowed to live in Jewel itself. Still—"

"No!" I shake my head fiercely. "We can't go. At least, I can't! Our team just made the playoffs, remember? They need me. Believe it or not, I'm actually an important player. They...they don't even play *caidpel* on Earth!"

But Mum's looking stubborn again. "Conserving Nuath's power for future generations is far more important than winning games, Kira. You need to reexamine your priorities."

"*My* priorities? What about yours? I'm starting to think those Mind Healers did worse things to your brain than Faxon did. How—?"

"Kira!" With two quick steps, Dad gets in my face. "Don't you *dare* speak to your mother like that, after what she's been through. You've seen the statistics on the feeds, we all have. Nuath's power can only be extended if we start the emigration process now, during this launch window. When the Sovereign called for volunteers, your mother and I agreed it was our patriotic duty to step forward. We booked berths on the *Horizon* for all four of us."

"Patriotic—!"

Adina hurries into the kitchen, still tying the top of her tunic. "What's all the shouting about?"

"Mum and Dad want to haul us off to Earth!" I tell her before they can answer. "We don't even get a say, apparently."

"Really?" She looks to Mum and Dad for confirmation. "We're all going to Earth? Cool!"

I glare at her. "It's *not* cool! Do you really want to leave all your friends? The farm? The sheep?"

That last word finally dims Adina's smile. Determined to at least get my sister on my side, I press my point.

"This won't be some sightseeing trip, like a school visit to the Central Pillar. This would be permanent. We'd have to say goodbye to everything and everyone we know—our whole world. Pretend to be *Duchas* for the rest of our lives. And for what?" I demand, turning back to my father. "As a favor to the new Sovereign? Mum may believe everything will be better with the Royals in charge again, even for us lowly Ags, but that doesn't make it true. She's stuck in the past and you know it."

Mum lets out a little gasp but I'm too upset at the idea of leaving to think how insensitive I sound. Then I notice Dad's expression. Even before he speaks, I know I've crossed an invisible line.

"To your room, Kira. Now."

"Fine."

Tears of fury pricking my eyelids, I stride from the kitchen. If the door to my room were slammable, like the ones I've seen on Earth television feeds, I'd slam it. The little hiss as it slides shut doesn't make nearly as strong a statement. Probably the *only* thing I'd like about Earth.

Not that I plan to go. If I can't talk my parents out of this ridiculous idea, I'll find another way to stay on Mars. Everything I care about is here. Especially now.

Five minutes later, Mum taps on the bedroom door. "Kira? Dinner's ready. I realized you must be very hungry, so I had the recombinator make that casserole you selected. I'm sorry you're upset, but please join the rest of us so we can talk."

I want to refuse, but it would be stupid to waste this opportunity to convince them they're making the wrong decision while there's still time to change it. Besides, I'm starving.

"Fine. I'll be out in a minute." I take several deep breaths, tamping down my totally-justified outrage so I can argue—rationally—why moving to Earth would be a terrible idea for all of us.

Which I do, all through dinner.

"What will happen to our farm if we leave?" I ask at one point. "It's been more productive these past few months than I can ever remember."

"That's why I expect the Murraghs will be happy to add it to their own holdings, as their farm shares a border with ours," Dad replies. "We plan to talk to them tomorrow."

Mum nods and I glower at both of them before launching my next volley. "Did you know my first playoff game will earn me—us—fifty *sochar*? If we win, the next one will pay twice that. Only last month Dad mentioned wanting an aquaponic agbot to speed up the harvest. Those extra credits would more than pay for one. We'd be able to eat a lot better, too. Maybe add more crops to our rotation."

But my parents don't budge. Mum is a hundred percent convinced they're doing the right thing and Dad will do *anything* to make her happy these days.

By morning, I'm no less determined to stay in Nuath than I was last night. The moment I wake up I start rehearsing more arguments, like how it will affect Adina's education to attend a massively inferior *Duchas* school instead of her current one here. I'll bring up *caidpel* again, too, and how rewarding it's been for me—though not the Populist angle, obviously.

"*Efrin*," I mutter, spotting my school tunic crumpled in the corner of the bedroom. "I totally forgot to clean this last night." My dirty *caidpel* uniform is still stuffed in my bag, too.

"Do it now," Adina suggests, yawning. "There's time before school."

Throwing on my tattered old robe, I hang my burgundy tunic and leggings for school and my green and yellow *caidpel* uniform in the ionic shower on our way to the kitchen for breakfast. When my sister and I leave for school half an hour later, my class outfit is as clean and wrinkle-free as Adina's pale peach one and my *caidpel* uniform is neatly folded in my bag.

"Is it true they don't have ionic sanitizers or food recombinators on Earth?" she asks as we walk the half mile to the village school.

I refrain from snapping that it doesn't matter since I have no intention of going there. "Not outside the *Echtran* compounds, according to my Earth Studies class last year. No anti-grav transport, either. The *Duchas* are centuries behind us, technologically. Practically primitives. Why Mum and Dad—"

"Maybe it won't be so bad." Adina, ever the optimist, grins up at me. "There are supposed to be thousands and *thousands* of different kinds of animals there. I can't wait to see some of them. Ooh! Do you think Mum and Dad will let us get a...a dog, I think they're called? Some *Duchas* keep them as pets."

"Let some animal live right in the house with us? Ew. I hope not." I've read about that weird *Duchas* custom. It sounds totally unsanitary to me.

"I think it would be great."

I slant a skeptical look at my sister. "Do you honestly want to move to Earth? What about your friends here? What about the sheep?"

"Okay, yeah, I'll miss my friends. And the sheep, but it's not like they let me keep more than a few at a time anyway, and never for very long. If I could have my own dog, though..."

Watching the animation in her face as she continues to chatter about what an adventure it will be, my spirits sink further. If I can't even convince my little sister we'd be better off staying in Nuath, what possible chance will I have with our parents?

I don't mention our potential move to any of my friends at school, though I'm sure Adina's telling everyone she knows. Maybe, if I can't talk my parents out of this crazy idea, I can convince my *caidpel* coach, or Brady, or even Crevan Erc himself to come up with a way to keep me in

Nuath. I refuse to assume I'm leaving until I've exhausted *all* of my options.

At lunch, I briefly consider messaging Brady. Then, remembering his almost-tender goodbye last night, I worry that might seem clingy, since I've never messaged him directly before. Better to wait till I see him at practice.

Today's is in Bailecuinn, northeast of Hollydoon. About twenty minutes in, Brady and I happen to be next to each other between drills so I grab my chance to tell him about my parents' horrible surprise last night.

He quirks an eyebrow at me, which weirdly makes him look even more handsome than usual. "Did they buy into the Sovereign's whole 'Nuath's running out of power' bit? We suspect she—or her handlers—are just using that as a scare tactic to manipulate people and concentrate power further. Same kind of stuff Faxon used to do, so everyone would be afraid to oppose him."

"You mean the power reserves aren't really that low? They're faking all that data?"

"Crevan thinks they might be. He says it's too coincidental that the very groups he hopes to benefit most are the first ones signing up for Earth. I saw the first two Earth-bound manifests myself—not a single Royal on them."

I didn't realize the Sovereign's new campaign was mainly targeting the lower *fines*, but it makes sense. They'd be the easiest ones to convince they'll be better off on Earth.

"Do you think—?" I begin, but Coach's shout cuts me off.

"Kira! Brady! We're not here to socialize, we've got a playoff to prepare for. Take your positions!"

We don't get another chance to talk until after practice ends.

"You were right earlier," I tell him as the team heads for the zipper station after turning in our sticks. "My folks are convinced it's our patriotic duty to emigrate to Earth—but I totally don't want to go. Do you... do you think Crevan Erc might be willing to help me stay in Nuath? He seems to think I can be useful here."

"I'll talk to him," Brady promises softly. "He has a lot of connections —more than most people realize. Bet he can manage something."

His confidence is contagious. During my short zipper ride home, my spirits are higher than they've been all day.

5

Cannarc

CANNARC (KAN-ark): *rebellion; mutiny; resistance*

The following day, I discover—no surprise—that everyone at school has now heard about my family leaving Nuath. My friends are about evenly divided between sympathy and envy.

"Oh, wow, I've always wanted to see Earth," Brigid bubbles before Astrophysics class. "The cities are huge compared to ours—so many people! And the planet's more than half water—can you imagine? Do you think you'll get to see an ocean?"

I scowl at her. "If it was just a *visit*, I wouldn't mind so much. And I doubt we'll be in an actual city. Mum wants us to move to the same village where the Sovereign grew up. It's barely bigger than Hollydoon and nowhere near any oceans."

"Yeah, that'll suck," my friend Ros agrees. "You might as well move to a *teachneaglis* village like Keary if you have to give up recombinators and everything. At least in the cities there'd be cool stuff to see and do, but even those are primitive by our standards." She shudders.

"The whole *dabhal* planet is primitive," I say loudly enough to earn a glare from the teacher. Not only aren't we supposed to be talking in class, anything we *do* say in school is supposed to be in Martian—not just the curse words.

Alan is the most understanding, coming over to sit with me at lunch again. "Hey, I just heard. You, too?"

I frown at him. "What do you mean?"

"My folks signed up for Earth, too—I think after talking to yours. Can't say I'm happy about it, but you—! How can your parents expect you to leave when the Ags are finally in the playoffs?"

"Trust me, I've asked them that at least a dozen times. Unfortunately, they've never really been into *caidpel*."

"Even so." He shakes his head gloomily. "The Ags won't have any shot at all at the championship without you. At least I won't be here to watch us lose. We're on the *Horizon*, too, and it launches the same day as our first playoff game."

Rather than risk him hearing it from someone else, I reluctantly tell Coach the bad news at practice that afternoon.

"What? This close to the playoffs? They can't do that!"

His outrage gives me a shred of hope. "That's what I tried to tell them! Can *you* try to talk them out of it?"

"I'll do better than that, I'll take it up with the League. You're one of my best players—and almost as big an attendance magnet as Brady. At the very least, we need to delay your departure until after the playoffs. Don't worry, Kira, I'll take care of it."

A surge of relief rushes through me. If anyone can talk my parents around, Coach can—especially if he has the Nuathan Caidpel League's support.

Near the end of practice my hopes are buoyed further. Between drills, Brady whispers, "I talked to Crevan last night. He definitely wants to keep you on board, says you're too valuable to lose."

"Yeah? That's great! Coach promised to help, too."

"It'll be fine, Kira. You'll see." He gives my shoulder a little squeeze, then sprints off, leaving my spirits even higher than they were after yesterday's practice.

I'm still feeling upbeat at dinner that night, even when Dad starts talking about all the reading we're supposed to do before leaving, to prepare us for life on Earth.

"I just took Earth Studies last year," I remind him. "Nothing will have changed since then, so I shouldn't need to—"

"I, ah, imagine this will go well beyond what they taught you in school," Mum says warily—probably because I've blown up at her and Dad so many times over the past two days. "We'll need quite a lot more than basic facts and history to actually live there."

Not that I expect to need any of it myself. Clinging to the two assurances I received during today's practice, I just smile and nod. My parents should hear from either Coach or the League tonight or tomorrow.

"Do we get to skip school?" Adina asks. "Reading up on Earth will be way more interesting than dumb Chemistry, and Nuathan history won't do us much good once we leave."

"Sorry," Dad tells her, though with a smile. "You'll both continue with school until the last few days before launch, though your teachers may allow you to use class time for the reading. There is an orientation session tomorrow afternoon in Cleirach that we're all expected to attend, but not until the end of your school day."

"Just the one, right?" I try to keep the alarm out of my voice at the thought of missing a single *caidpel* practice this close to the playoffs. Especially for some stupid Earth class I won't even need.

Dad glances at the info on his omni. "There'll be another the day before we board, then a full training program once we reach Earth. I'm copying the schedule to each of you now, including a link to all of the reading materials."

My momentary panic subsides. Unless Coach and Crevan Erc *both* flake out on me, I should have permission to stay in Nuath before that second class.

Since there's no getting out of that first orientation session, before school the next day I message Coach I'll be missing practice—and why. I hope it'll also remind him to follow through on his promise.

I'm not allowed to check my omni again until after school—a rule going back to the Great Unplugging a couple of generations ago—but when I do I'm elated by Coach's reply.

On it.

Renewed hope makes me almost cheerful when I join my parents and Adina at the zipper station an hour later. Almost.

"Ready to learn about our new home?" Dad's joviality seems slightly forced but Adina nods eagerly.

"Will we be allowed to ask questions? I want to know what kinds of animals they have in Dun Cloch—that's where we're going first, right? That's what it said in the file."

Mum smiles at her enthusiasm. "Good for you, Adina, getting a head start. I'm sure they'll allow questions at the end. I wonder if they can tell us how many will be accepted for Jewel? Maire heard they've already received more requests than the *Echtran* Council is likely to approve."

"I messaged to ask about that, as I know it's so important to you, Deirdra," Dad says. "I was told there will be a selection process, though the specifics are still being worked out."

"We must all be on our very *best* behavior, then." Mum glances pointedly at me.

I shrug. "Hey, I'm more than willing to stay behind if that will improve your odds of being chosen."

Though she mutters, "Don't be silly, Kira," she still looks worried.

Cleirach is just two zipper stops from Hollydoon, so we don't even bother to find seats. Dad leads the way to the Aquaponic Engineering building, where a large lecture hall has been set aside for the hundred-plus Nuathans expected to board the *Horizon* six days from now.

"Welcome, everyone," a tall, thin, redheaded man greets us with what I consider unnecessary enthusiasm. "I'm Willis, under-secretary to the Minister of Terran Relations. On behalf of Sovereign Emileia, allow me to congratulate you all on the exceptional bravery and patriotism you've shown by volunteering to emigrate to Earth. Today I'll be sharing a few basics that we hope will make your transition not only easier, but downright enjoyable."

I manage not to snicker and roll my eyes, limiting myself to a barely-audible huff that's still enough to earn me a quick glare and head-shake from Dad. Mum and Adina, hanging on the instructor's every word, don't notice.

"Now, if you'll all open your readers to the first file in your emigration packet, the one titled "Earth Basics," we'll begin."

Half an hour later, it's all I can do to stay awake. Nothing this guy is telling us goes beyond what I learned last year. I can't believe I'm missing *caidpel* practice for this. To console myself, I angle my reader so neither of my parents can see it and pull up this season's playbook, since this class is clearly intended for people who've either never taken or completely forgotten Earth Studies.

I look up occasionally, paying just enough attention to be sure I'm not missing anything important. I'm not. But from the way Mum and Adina chatter as we leave the lecture hall two hours later, you'd think Willis had just unlocked the mysteries of the universe.

"Did you hear what he said about all the different animals Earth farmers raise?" Adina's practically squirming with excitement. "Not just sheep and chickens, like here, but cows, pigs, geese, even rabbits! I've never even SEEN a goose or a rabbit."

"You know they're mostly raised for slaughter, right?" I tell her, stifling a twinge of guilt when her face falls. "They haven't figured out how to synthesize meat yet, so they have to kill it themselves."

"Kira!" Mum admonishes me, though she has to know I'm right. "It's not the *Duchas'* fault they're behind us technologically. Our ancestors on Mars did the same, as you know perfectly well."

I lift a shoulder. "But *we* evolved beyond it. Adina might as well know the truth now—better than being blindsided once there's no turning back."

"We...we won't have to kill any animals ourselves, will we?" My sister still looks distressed.

"Of course not." Dad shoots me a frown. "Jewel, where we're hoping to settle, specializes in crops, not animals. It should be a good fit for Agriculturals like us."

"That's right." Mum smiles reassuringly at Adina. "Corn, mostly, and soybeans. I've been reading up on Jewel. If you prefer, you can become a vegetarian once we move to Earth—it's not that uncommon."

Adina relaxes. "I...I think I might be okay eating fish, at least. They're not very smart, and not cuddly at all."

The moment we and our classmates step outside the Aquaponic Engineering building, we're pounced on by three different news crews from the feeds.

"Excuse me, ma'am," a reporter asks the woman in front of us. "Can you tell us what prompted you to heed the Sovereign's call for emigration? Was it a difficult decision to make?"

The woman starts to stammer an answer while the other reporters converge on the rest of us.

"Sir, will this be your family's first trip Earth?" a woman asks my father. It's Moya, from the Nuathan News Network.

"Yes. We're all very excited." I notice he carefully doesn't look at me as he says that.

"And how do they—?" she begins, turning toward Adina and me, then does a little double-take. "Isn't this... Aren't you Kira Morain, the *caidpel* player?"

I nod cautiously. "These are my parents."

Now her eyes positively gleam at having stumbled onto a bigger story than she expected. "*Are* they? You both must be very proud of your daughter and her team. Is Kira going with you?"

"Yes. Yes, she is," Dad says firmly before I can so much as hint otherwise.

"I see. Kira, surely you must have a few qualms about leaving Nuath just as the playoffs begin?"

Again, Dad replies before I can. "Our whole family feels strongly that our duty to Nuath outweighs any mere sporting event. Don't we?"

He pins me with a stern look until I reluctantly give a grudging nod. I don't dare open my mouth for fear of what might spill out.

"How very commendable," Moya gushes, favoring us all with a brilliant smile. "I'm sure your example will motivate others to step up as well. The Sovereign must be very pleased."

She moves on then, but before we even reach the zipper station Dad gets a message from Moya asking if she can contact him later for a few follow-up questions. After a quick consultation with Mum, he says that will be fine.

Efrin, I think as we board the zipper back to Hollydoon. If the feeds run that story, it'll be harder than ever to convince my parents to let me stay on Mars. They'll claim our whole family will look bad if I don't go to Earth with them now.

Sure enough, Moya's interview with my dad is already playing on the news by the time we finish dinner that night. When I arrive for practice the next afternoon, Coach gets in my face before I even reach the equipment bins.

"I thought you wanted to help us win the playoffs?" he practically snarls. "Now it's all over the feeds you're emigrating to Earth. They're making you look like some kind of hero for leaving us in the lurch!"

"That wasn't my fault!" I protest, stung. "I didn't say anything at all to that reporter, it was just my dad. I guess you never called him, like you said you would?"

That stops Coach in mid-tirade. "I...was going to do it tomorrow," he grumbles. "I've been busy. Then I saw that story on the feeds and—"

"You'll still talk to them, won't you, Coach?" I try not to sound as desperate as I feel. "Please?"

"I'll never get the League behind me now." He glares at me from under his heavy brows, then shrugs. "I...guess I can look up a few things tonight. Maybe come up with an argument for keeping you here that won't make me sound like a traitor."

But I can tell he really doesn't want to now. "That's a great idea, Coach!" I force more enthusiasm than I feel into my voice. "I'll keep talking to them, too. I promise the last thing I want to do is hurt the team's chances of winning!"

He just nods morosely and waves me onto the field. Grabbing my *camman* from the rack, I sprint off, trying to ignore the heavy knot in my stomach.

Instead of drills, Coach has us play twelve-a-side against each other, like a real match, so we can practice various plays in sequence. I'm glad now I took that time yesterday to review the playbook instead of paying attention in that stupid class.

"You played great today," Leitis says with a grin when the final whistle blows. "I sure hope Coach can keep you around."

"I guess everyone knows now?"

She nods. "Coach told us after yesterday's practice, then there was that bit on the news. Coach was..." She hesitates. "I'm sure he'll be able to fix it so you can stay, though. I mean, this would be an *awful* time for you to leave, with the playoffs so close. Especially now that you and Brady are—" Breaking off, Leitis glances behind me. "Oops. Later!"

Sure enough, when I turn around, Brady is approaching. "Hey."

"Hey."

"Missed you at practice yesterday."

He's not specific whether *he* missed me or everyone did. I don't ask. "Yeah. My family had to go to a stupid class for emigrants. You wouldn't believe how lame it was. I mostly studied the playbook instead."

"It showed." He grins down at me. "You looked good today. Anyway, I wanted to tell you Crevan might be contacting you in a day or two."

I huff out a cautiously relieved breath. "Does that mean he's figured out a way to keep me here? Coach said he'd take care of it, but...now I'm not so sure."

"Hey, it'll work out one way or another. Try not to worry, okay?"

Not quite the reassurance I was hoping for. "Okay."

"Good girl."

I half expect him to touch me again, like he did last practice, and at the zipper station in Monaru, but he doesn't. He just gives me another bracing grin before going to turn in his equipment. I wait several seconds before following.

I don't sleep well that night. In the morning, I ask Dad over breakfast if he's heard anything from my *caidpel* coach.

"Yes, I had a message from him late last night, saying what a loss you'll be to the team. He also sent links to some articles extolling the virtues of the sport, but I haven't had time to read them yet."

I have trouble swallowing the bite of scrambled egg I just put in my mouth. "He didn't...didn't say anything about me staying in Nuath through the playoffs? I thought—"

"Oh, I'm sure he'd prefer that, but he must know it's impossible at this point. Really, Kira, you need to start looking forward, not back. Our futures lie on Earth—not only ours, but nearly all Nuathans. You're a smart enough girl to understand it's the only way for our people to survive."

That afternoon I make the mistake of stopping by home to drop off my school bag and change before practice, which gives Mum a chance to waylay me before I can leave again.

"You should spend the afternoon sorting through your things, Kira," she tells me. "We can only bring two bags apiece, you know, and we leave in just five days."

"I know. I'll do it when I get back."

Mum's still frowning, though. "I don't understand why you need to practice anyway. You've said yourself that no one plays *caidpel* on Earth, and we'll be gone before your next game."

I huff out a breath. "Yeah, thanks for reminding me. You do realize that besides the fifty *sochar* I get for the first playoff game, they pay us a whole lot more if the Ags win the tournament. Isn't that worth waiting for, even if you're determined to move us all to Earth after—"

"We've been through this, Kira." She sounds exasperated now. "Nuathan *sochar* won't be of any benefit on Earth anyway."

They'll sure benefit *me* if I stay behind, though. "Right. Okay. Just... let me play while I can, okay?"

Immediately, Mum's expression becomes sympathetic. "Of course, dear. Go have fun."

But fun is the last thing on my mind when I head to Newlyn for practice. With time getting so short, I'm absolutely determined to pin down both Coach *and* Brady before I leave today.

Unfortunately, thanks to Mum, practice has already started when I arrive. The coach just waves me to my position, giving me no chance to ask again about him talking to my parents. Then he spends our one break deep in conversation with the two assistant coaches. At that point I look around for Brady, hoping maybe I can get info from him, at least, but he's joking around with several other guys on the team, not even looking my way.

The moment practice ends, I hurry over to the coach. Before I reach him, he motions to me and I break into a trot.

"You have news for me?" I ask breathlessly...hopefully.

His sad smile answers me even before he speaks. "Sorry, Kira. I was hoping to keep you but with the playoffs looming I couldn't afford to gamble on that. We've just recruited Bailecuinn's top all-male player and I'm promoting Kinnard to your position. He's not as good as you are, of course, but...I had no choice. I really am sorry."

He seems to mean it, but it doesn't lighten the weight that just landed in my stomach. Using every ounce of my will, I hold back the tears threatening to spill over.

"I...I understand." I can't keep my voice from breaking a little. "Thanks, Coach." I turn quickly away, not sure how much longer my control will last. Brady, I notice, is already turning in his equipment. Like earlier, he doesn't look my way.

Which must mean he doesn't have any good news for me, either.

Feeling empty and useless, I head for the zippers.

6

Launch window

LAUNCH WINDOW: *period occurring approximately every 26 Earth months and lasting approximately four months, when the distance between Earth and Mars is small enough to allow travel between the two planets*

Sean

"Whoa, Shim just sent me the passenger numbers for the next three Earth-bound ships," M exclaims, showing her omni screen to my dad. We're all in her quarters again, getting ready to leave for a formal dinner meeting. "I guess he was right about in-person visits making a difference."

Dad leans over to look at the figures. "Certainly a noticeable improvement. And I see the *Quintessence* is already at 78% capacity. There's a chance it could be full as well by the time it launches in another two weeks."

"Shim says if we can keep filling the ships at this rate, he'll be okay with me leaving for Earth myself before this launch window closes at the end of July."

She grins around at us, but Molly's the only one who immediately grins back. "That's great! You must be so relieved!"

M nods happily.

I wish I could be happy for her, too, but I was raised from birth to put our people's welfare ahead of everything else—and I honestly feel M leaving Mars that soon will set back the progress Nuath has made over the past few months.

"That's, um, really good news." I hope my smile doesn't look *too* fake. I can tell Dad's no more enthusiastic about her leaving than I am, though we've both been careful to avoid the topic of M staying put, after the way she reacted last time. He shares an understanding glance with me, then clears his throat.

"Oh, Sean, I meant to tell you earlier that I've arranged for us to attend the Agricultural team's first playoff game. Molly and the Sovereign as well, if they care to join us."

Though I'm sure he's saying it to cheer me up, it has almost the opposite effect. "It may not be that great a game," I tell him with a shrug. "I saw on one of the sports feeds that the Ag team is losing their best forward."

"Oh? That's a shame," Dad says. "This was their first time making the playoffs in several years, wasn't it?"

"What happened?" Molly asks. "Is he hurt?"

"She. And no, she and her family booked berths on the *Horizon*, which leaves the same day as the first playoff game. Guess you were a little *too* convincing when you visited Hollydoon last week," I add to M, though it's really not her fault, of course.

M looks sincerely apologetic. "Sorry, Sean. I mean, we all knew getting this many people to emigrate in one launch window would cause some disruptions, since nearly everyone is filling a necessary role somewhere. I hadn't even thought about sports teams, though."

"What will this do to their chances?" Dad asks. He knows I've been obsessing a little about sports lately—mainly to keep my focus off things I'd rather not think about.

"Not sure. They still have Brady, their star midfielder, but they're definitely not expected to dominate now, like they were before this news hit. But hey, this is minor stuff in the greater scheme of things, right? It only makes sense the less advantaged *fines*, like Agriculture, would be among the first to leave. They probably *will* have more opportunities on Earth, just like you've been telling them. Of course, if too many leave, it's going to be hard to get good people for that balanced Legislature you're wanting to set up, won't it?"

"I hope not," M says worriedly. "Shim says he's convinced a few people from non-Royal or Science *fines* to stand for various positions, but not enough yet. I was sure we'd have at least set a date for the first election by now."

Yet another reason I don't think she should be leaving Nuath anytime soon. Shim's fairly popular with the people, especially the non-Royals, but nowhere near as popular as M. She'd have a much better chance than Shim of talking people into entering public service, which is what I think she should do once this launch window closes. I don't want to risk saying so directly, though.

"What do you think, Dad? Will Shim get enough people to stand for election that one can be held within the next month or two?"

But Dad's even less willing than I am to say anything M doesn't want to hear—though in private he's told me he agrees strongly it's a bad idea for her to leave so soon.

"It's...possible," he says carefully. "Though it might not be a bad idea for you to record a vid or two in support of what Shim is trying to do, Excellency. Oops, we'd better go or we'll be late for that dinner."

7

Doolegar

DOOLEGAR (DOO-luh-GAHR): *despondency; depression*

I'm too depressed to say much over dinner that night, but nobody seems to notice. Mum, Dad and Adina are all talking about what they've read about the various types of Earth villages, towns and cities and the occupations likely to be most needed in them.

"With our farming experience, we'll certainly be well suited for Jewel." Mum beams around at us. "Though I suppose I can be happy elsewhere if we're not selected. According to today's vid update, there will be even more competition than I'd anticipated."

"Our chances should still be good, Deirdra," Dad assures her. "We're well known as staunch Royalists and the fact you knew Consort Galena personally is bound to weigh in your favor. But as you say, either way we'll find a place to make home—and we'll still be able to visit Jewel. There are hundreds of farming towns in that region. We'll settle in one of those, if not in Jewel itself."

I know I should start paying attention now that my fate is sealed, but at the moment I can't bring myself to care.

Not until I'm getting ready for bed do I bother to check my messages —and nearly drop my omni when I see one from Crevan Erc. Heart pounding with renewed hope, I pull it up—only to have my hopes dashed again.

Sorry to hear you won't be remaining in Nuath, as you would have been a valuable advocate for us. We will consider an alternate role for you on Earth if a significant portion of our people emigrate there. Should such an opportunity arise, you will hear from one of our Echtran operatives. Best of luck in the future, Kira Morain.

—CE

I wonder if Brady told him how bummed I was tonight about Coach cutting me from the team. *Efrin,* he probably *asked* Crevan to message me, thinking I'd feel better if I thought I might still be useful to their cause somehow. Someday. Maybe.

Feeling dismissed, patronized and more depressed than ever, I crawl into bed and quietly cry myself to sleep.

Our last few days in Nuath are a blur as our preparations ramp up to a frenetic pace. The Murraghs agree to take over our farming operations and another family from the village comes to look at our house. We have to leave almost everything behind, of course. Among the hardest things to part with are my numerous *caidpel* trophies.

Just two days after being cut from the team, I have my last day of school. All my friends gather at lunchtime to say their goodbyes.

"I'm going to miss you so much, Kira." Eileen has tears in her eyes. "Who else can I talk *caidpel* with at school and get pointers from? Nobody else gets it like you do. Now I'll never make the co-ed team."

"Sure you will. You're really good." I return her fierce hug with a lump in my throat, then turn to Ros and Bridgid, both waiting to say their own tearful goodbyes. The only thing that keeps me from crying, too, is pride. Because I never cry in front of anyone. Ever.

I have to remind myself of that again when Coach invites me to a post-practice party just outside Thiaraway, so my teammates can say their farewells. Though I'm pretty sure it was Leitis's idea, I still appreciate it. Especially when Brady makes a point of walking with me to the zipper station afterward for a private goodbye.

"The team won't be the same without you, you know." That devastating grin that makes all the girls crush on him has a sad edge. "There's no way Kinnard will improve to your level before next season. But I'm betting you end up doing something on Earth that's a lot more important than *caidpel.*"

"What? Did Crevan say?"

He shakes his head. "I just told him you'd be better than anyone I can think of for any assignment, anywhere, now or in the future. But... I'll miss you, Kira. A lot."

"Um, yeah. Me, too."

Brady leans in and for a second I think he's going to kiss me. Instead, just like on the zipper platform in Monaru, he brushes my cheek with his fingertips. Sudden tears threaten—again—and I turn quickly away.

"Bye, Brady. Keep in touch, okay?"

"I'll try. Take care of yourself, Kira."

Two hectic days later my family takes the zipper to Arregaith, where we'll board the *Horizon* to leave Nuath forever. I spot Alan and his family near the back of our car and give a halfhearted wave. He enthusiastically waves back, grinning.

"Wow, look at how tall the buildings are," Adina exclaims as we move into the outskirts of the town housing Nuath's space port and support facilities. "I didn't know Arregaith was this big."

I realize Adina has never been this far from home before. Because I travel—traveled—so much for *caidpel*, I tend to forget that my family, like most Nuathans, hasn't seen as much of the colony as I have.

"You should see Monaru, just a little farther south." The zipper slows as it nears our station. "It's twice the size of Thiaraway, though not as clean."

"Even around the stadium?" Mum sounds surprised.

Oops. I never mentioned to them that I went into the city that day, for obvious reasons. "Oh, um, some of us went downtown after practice once for a bite to eat."

To my relief the zipper stops then, sparing me the need to elaborate. I hate lying, even for a good cause—almost as much as I hate being lied to.

A uniformed woman near the edge of the platform steps forward as we all carry our bags off. "Those who have booked passage for this evening's launch, please follow me."

She holds her omni aloft and it projects a brilliant turquoise sphere above her head. That makes her easy to follow through a winding, maze-like path that finally opens out into an enormous open area at least a quarter of a mile across, ringed by an almost solid wall of towering, pinkish-gray buildings. Crouching in the very center is the *Horizon,* looking for all the world like an enormous black rock.

"Cool, huh?" Alan asks from just behind me.

I nod. I've only visited Arregaith for *caidpel,* never the actual space port, so this is my first time seeing one of our interplanetary ships, outside of pictures. It's even bigger than I imagined.

"Please proceed to the processing center." Our guide indicates a building a short distance away marked Main Passenger Terminal. "Good journey, everyone!" Her turquoise sphere winks off and she departs with a wave.

Official-looking hover vehicles of various types and sizes criss-cross the huge courtyard as we make our way to the terminal. Adina's head whips from side to side as she tries to take everything in. As we enter the building, we're greeted by a man in a silvery bodysuit and gray tunic.

"This way, please. We're on a rather tight schedule." He points across the large, high-ceilinged room to a long counter staffed by a dozen red-uniformed people.

Our group joins those already in line. With the *Horizon* booked almost to capacity, it takes the better part of an hour to process everyone. Everyone's bags are electronically tagged and the larger ones loaded onto hover-carts to be taken directly to the ship. We keep our smaller bags with us.

My family finds four chairs together in the waiting area. At the far end, there's a vidscreen streaming the Nuathan News Network's main feed. I watch, hoping they'll flash up the score of today's playoff game in the sidebar. When they finally do, I groan. A week ago, the Ags were predicted to beat the Miners easily, but we're currently trailing them 10-8. Even if we win, we won't stand a chance against the Engineers next week. Because of me—not that I had a choice.

A chime sounds, then two more, in quick succession. "First call for boarding," a pleasant voice announces from invisible speakers. "Passengers in A Group please proceed to embarkation area."

My family is in D Group, the last one, which isn't announced for another twenty minutes. "Come on, everyone." Dad springs to his feet, his face now alight with an excitement that rivals Adina's. "Time for our first space flight!"

When we're finally shown to our quarters on the *Horizon*, I'm appalled. Families from the more prestigious *fines*—or with enough *sochar* to upgrade—have private cabins on the upper levels of the ship. Those at the bottom of the pecking order, like us, are consigned to Steerage, just above the engine room.

"Seriously? We're sharing this one room with a dozen other families?" I drop my small bag next to the bigger one that's already sitting on my assigned bunk. Between them, they contain everything I'm allowed to bring for a whole new life on Earth.

Dad frowns. "I don't know why you're surprised, Kira. We've known our accommodation assignment for days. The ship's configuration was covered in the reading, complete with diagrams."

"Guess I skimmed that bit," I mumble.

I never did do any of the required reading. Until four days ago, I was still convinced I could get out of this trip. When I was finally forced to relinquish that hope, there'd been a million other time-sensitive things to do. Oh, well, I should have plenty of time to read on the way to Earth.

"It's only four nights," Adina reminds me, tossing her little duffel onto the bunk above mine. "It'll be fun. Like a big sleepover."

Trust Adina to find the *fun* in any situation, no matter how depressing.

"Yeah, right. All it'll take is one or two snorers—"

"Come along, girls," Mum interrupts. "We have less than fifteen minutes before we need to be seated and belted in for launch."

Already a line is forming in front of the single lift to take people up one level to the Commons. I look around for stairs, but don't see any.

Adina, practically bouncing with excitement, chatters nonstop. "Pol told me there's a huge screen in the Commons so we can watch the take-off. And we'll be able to see Earth two whole days before we get there! I wonder if we'll be able to tell the difference between the land and the oceans from space? In pictures, it looks really different from the surface of Mars…"

We manage to squeeze into the lift for its third trip up. It spits us out into a room twice the size of Steerage, filled with rows of chairs. The huge vidscreen Adina mentioned shows the launch area we left half an hour ago.

"File in, file in," drones a bored-looking crewmember, gesturing us toward a row of chairs. "Find a seat and belt yourselves in. Liftoff in zero minus eight minutes."

I follow Adina and our parents to the next open seats. Those of us from Steerage are way in the back, but at least we're near the middle of our row. An announcement over the speakers instructs us all to fasten our safety harnesses. On the vidscreen, the friends and families of those traveling start frantically waving goodbye from the edges of the launch area.

No one from Hollydoon has come to see us off but Adina waves back anyway, too excited to sit still. When excitement at the prospect of my first space flight starts to well up inside me, too, I ruthlessly tamp it down. Because I am *not* okay with what we're doing. Not by a long shot.

Shortly after the last passengers have belted themselves in, liftoff is announced. Though I can't feel the ship moving, everything on the vidscreen slowly drops away. For a moment we're looking at the smooth, crystalline walls of the shaft instead of people and buildings, then the vid switches to a camera below us and we see the launch area from above, rapidly growing smaller.

Abruptly, we emerge from the shaft and the outer surface of Mars appears below us. Up close, it looks even more hostile and lifeless than in pictures and news feeds. But then it's not so close. The ship gathers speed and in barely a minute the curve of the horizon is visible...and then the whole planet.

Though it's a well-known fact that the whole underground colony of Nuath is less than one one-hundred millionth of Mars's volume, this vantage point forces a true understanding of how very insignificant a speck that is in the vastness of space. I stare at the slowly retreating, reddish-brown sphere, already aching for the small cavity inside that's the only world I've ever known. That's when it finally hits me, once and for all, that this is for real.

Like it or not, I'm on my way to Earth.

8

Horizon

HORIZON: one of four Nuathan transport ships traveling between Mars and Earth during biennial launch windows

"You may now unfasten your harnesses," a voice from the speakers informs us. "Please leave the Commons quickly so it can be converted for other use."

"I guess we should go settle in, eh?" Dad's cheerfulness sounds slightly forced. I wonder if he's as rattled as I am by the enormity of what we've just done.

A glance at Adina proves she doesn't share my weakness, which is both embarrassing and irritating. Of course, she's been excited about this trip from the start, viewing it as a grand adventure. Maybe I'd feel the same if I hadn't been forced to give up everything that's ever been important to me.

By the time we file back out of our row, dozens of people are already lined up at the lifts.

"Why do we always have to be last?" I mutter.

Mum hears me. "We're not last, Kira. There are quite a few people behind us. I do hope you don't intend to complain for the entire trip and spoil things for Adina and the rest of us."

It's the most sharply she's spoken to me since my initial blowup about being forced to move to Earth. I nearly snap back at her before I notice she looks paler than usual.

"Mum? Are you okay?"

She nods. "Just a tiny touch of motion sickness. I'm sure it will pass quickly."

I haven't noticed any motion at all, but Dad immediately puts a protective arm around her.

"Why didn't you mention you weren't feeling well?"

Mum forces a little smile. "It's nothing, Aidan, really. You know I've always tended to get a bit queasy on long zipper rides. Apparently space travel has a similar effect. I imagine I'll be fine in an hour or two."

Still concerned, Dad politely asks the people in front of us if he can move Mum up the line to get her to her bunk sooner and they obligingly move aside. When Adina and I reach Steerage several lift trips later, he's already tucked her into bed.

"I feel silly being such a bother," she tells us all with a wan smile.

"Nonsense." Dad pats her hand. "According to the schedule, the Commons will reopen for dinner in half an hour. Would you like something brought down for you? Some soup or tea?"

She agrees to that, apologizing again.

"Adina and I can bring meals down for both of you, if you don't want to leave her alone, Dad," I offer, feeling slightly guilty for all my grumbling since boarding.

"Thank you, Kira."

Dad's obvious surprise underscores what a pain I've been ever since they told us about this trip. Justifiably. I still believe they had no right to yank me off Mars without my permission, but now it's done, complaining won't change it. While Mum's feeling so poorly, I can at least try to keep my gripes to myself.

That resolve gets tested as soon as Adina and I go to wash up before dinner.

"Seriously?" Wrinkling my nose, I gaze around the Steerage bathroom. "Just three shower cylinders and four elimination booths for all these people?"

"The guys have their own. This one's just for women," Adina points out. "And we'll have to start calling them 'toilets' on Earth, remember? Anyway, it'll be fine. There are plenty of cleansing stations." She points at half a dozen ionic sanitizing units spaced along a counter beneath the mirrored wall.

Shrugging, I move to one of the units to sanitize my hands. "Toilets. Right." I really do need to catch up on that reading or I'll sound like an idiot when we reach Dun Cloch. "I don't know if I can get used to wasting so much water."

"Earth is mostly made of it," Adina reminds me—a fact known to every Nuathan over the age of five. "Just think, we'll never have to worry about using up our monthly ration again."

She always finds a bright side to anything, but I know this will be only one of a thousand things that will be strange and different about our new home.

When we return to the Commons a few minutes later, Adina gasps. "How did they do this so fast? It's like...like magic!"

"Not magic, technology." But I'm also amazed by how quickly they transformed the space where we were so recently strapped in for liftoff into something completely different.

Dining tables now take up one half of the room while the other is clearly a recreation area, with small tables for games, mats for exercising and various pieces of athletic equipment. Only two rows of chairs now face the vidscreen, still displaying Mars as it continues to retreat behind us. I stare at the image for a long moment, a lump forming in my throat.

"C'mon." Swallowing, I turn my attention back to the dining side. "Let's get food for Mum and Dad, then we can come back up here to eat."

The recombinators along the far wall have ten times as many options as we've ever had at home, even more than the ones at school. I order up tea, toast and vegetable soup for Mum while Adina gets roast beef, mashed potatoes, steamed spinach, and a glass of lemonade for Dad.

Mum's color is noticeably better by the time we carry the food trays down to Steerage. She thanks us, then shoos us back upstairs. "This will be your first chance to make friends with the other young people aboard."

By now there's a line at the lift again, but not a long one. A couple minutes later my sister and I are back in the Commons. This time, I avoid looking at the vidscreen.

"Where do you want to sit?" Adina asks, looking around. "Should we get food first, or—?"

"Kira! Over here." Alan Dempsey waves to us from a nearby table where a few other teens are already seated. "You want to sit with us?"

We both head that way. "Hey, Alan." I force a tiny bit of cheerfulness into my voice. "Have you met my sister? Adina's still in Basic so you might not have seen her at school. Alan's from Hollydoon, too," I tell her.

He grins at both of us. "Exciting stuff, huh, space ship to Earth and all?" Then, to the other teens, "See? Told you Kira Morain was on this ship. I don't think Wade believed me." He gives me a wink and a ginger-haired boy on the other side of the table shrugs sheepishly.

"That reminds me," I say to Alan, "did you catch the final score of the Ags' playoff game?"

"Yeah, just before we came down to dinner. The Ags won, but by just one point. They obviously missed you at forward."

There's a chorus of agreement from several of the others, who start introducing themselves. Two of the guys seem embarrassingly excited to meet me.

"Hey, Adina, it's me, Jana!" A girl about Adina's age hurries over from the far end of the table. "This is going to be so fun!" I've never seen the girl before, so I'm startled when they hug.

"Kira, this is Jana, from Einion," Adina says then. "We've been chatting in the under-fifteen emigrant forum online since finding out we'd both be on the *Horizon*."

Jana's pretty, with a thick brown braid and wide greenish eyes. She looks up at me now in apparent delight. "Yeah, but you never mentioned your big sister is Kira Morain! I've seen you on the feeds, playing *caidpel*—you're, like, famous!" She lowers her voice conspiratorially. "Tell me, is Brady as yummy-looking up close as he is on the vids?"

Thinking about Brady—and *caidpel*—makes my heart hurt but I force out a little laugh. "Yeah, I guess he is. Come on, Adina. We still need to get our food."

As we head to the recombinators again, Adina glances at me, wide-eyed. "Wow, you're a bigger deal than I realized."

"Was." I emphasize the past tense. "And only to people who follow *caidpel*."

"Which Mum and Dad never did. No wonder you didn't want to leave. I'm sorry, Kira."

I shrug. "Nothing we can do about it now." My throat still tight, I avoid her sympathetic gaze and face the recombinators. "So, what are you in the mood for? Looks like they have everything."

I'm curious to try non-synth chicken or beef but suspect that would upset Adina. Instead I punch up synth-beef stew and applesauce while she gets some kind of fish and fried potatoes. We carry our trays back to the table of teens where Alan has saved me a seat next to him. Adina goes to the other end to sit with Jana.

Unfortunately, the first thing the others want to talk about is *caidpel*. I try to be polite since we'll all be together for the next four days on the *Horizon* plus however long our Orientation takes in Dun Cloch. Besides, it's not *their* fault I'm here.

When conversation finally moves on, it's some comfort to discover I'm not the only one who was reluctant to leave Mars. Some lament leaving their friends, while others are clearly anxious about adjusting to life on Earth.

"Dun Cloch shouldn't be that different from Nuath, at least," says Mattie, a blonde girl a year or so younger than me. "It's so isolated, they can use all kinds of Martian technology without the *Duchas* noticing."

The ginger guy, Wade, nods. "Yeah, did you see in the reading that Dun Cloch is over a *hundred* miles from the nearest village? A hundred miles! I'll bet we don't see a single *Duchas* before we get to the towns we'll be living in. We've asked for Denver, in the mountains, where my dad's sister lives."

That starts them all talking about where their families plan to live after our orientation period ends. Fully half of the dozen teens at the table say their parents requested Jewel, including Alan, and Adina's friend Jana.

"We put down two alternate places, too, so it won't be a big deal if we don't get it," Peter, a dark-haired boy Alan's age, says philosophically.

"So did we," an older boy volunteers. "New York and Los Angeles. My dad's always been fascinated by *Duchas*, and those places have more of them than anywhere else in North America."

As the conversation goes on, the others sound increasingly eager to reach Earth...while I idly wonder if I can stow away aboard the *Horizon* until it returns to Nuath.

"I'm going to go check on Mum," I tell Adina as soon as I finish eating, feeling out of sorts again. At least the food was good.

She glances up. "Oh. Um, I'll be down in a little while, okay?"

"Sure, that's fine." She should be perfectly safe with so many people around. "G'night, everyone."

Mum is dozing when I get back to Steerage, despite the incessant hum of the gravity drive right below us and the chatter of everybody coming back from dinner. Dad motions me a short way away from their bunk.

"She said she was feeling much better, but I'm sure the best thing for her is sleep."

"You don't think she's really sick, do you?" My earlier concern rushes back.

To my relief, he shakes his head. "Mostly exhausted, I think. It's been a busy, stressful week for all of us, but especially for her." Partly because of me, I know, though Dad doesn't say that. He doesn't have to.

"I'll try not to be such a grump around her."

"Thanks, Kira. I know this isn't what you wanted, but I hope you can find a way to be as happy on Earth as on Mars—or even happier."

I don't see how, without *caidpel*, friends or purpose, but I give him a quick, fake smile. "I hope so, too." Grabbing my small bag off my bunk, I head to the bathroom for a pre-bedtime shower.

Adina's back from dinner when I come out. She and her new friend Jana have their heads together, giggling over something, so I climb up to my bunk and settle down with my reader. I spend half an hour on the required reading about Earth before flipping to my encrypted files from Crevan Erc.

Though he didn't promise me a mission, I'm determined not to lose my passion for social justice. If the Sovereign convinces a majority of Nuathans to emigrate to Earth over the next few decades, the Populists are bound to need operatives there eventually. If called into action, I plan to be ready.

Meanwhile, I should devote myself to persuading as many *Echtrans* as possible to the Populist cause. It's the only thing I can think of that might give my life on Earth meaning.

Mum feels well enough to go up to the Commons for breakfast the next morning. Once we all get our food, she and Dad join another couple from Hollydoon and urge Adina and me to seek out people our own age as well. We head to another table where a few of the kids we met last night are already sitting. A moment later Jana and Adina are whispering and giggling together as they eat.

Alan's not here yet but Peter greets me eagerly. "After you left last night, Alan talked about playing some *caidpel* in Dun Cloch if we have time in our schedules. He thought you'd maybe be willing to coach us?"

"Oh, um, maybe." Training a bunch of amateurs who'll never be able to play *caidpel* again once we leave the compound would be kind of lame, but better than sitting around studying every day.

When Alan shows up a couple minutes later, he immediately floats the same idea, obviously expecting me to be excited—and impressed that he thought of it.

"I know how much you're going to miss it, Kira," he says with a smile that's a little too intimate. "Me, too. I figure this will help. And hey, if we both end up in Jewel, or some other town together, maybe we can start a *caidpel* club, even teach the *Duchas* how to play—though they probably won't be much good at it."

"Probably?" My laugh has a bitter edge. I wish they'd stop talking about *caidpel*. "And how do we explain being into a sport nobody on Earth has even heard of?"

He shrugs. "They're supposed to give us all fake Earth histories, right? We'll just say the game was invented wherever we supposedly came from and hope it'll catch on."

"That should work," Peter agrees. "The *Duchas* are supposed to be really gullible."

Mattie had been pointedly ignoring the *caidpel* conversation but at that she says, "Don't count on it, guys. My mum told me the *Echtran* Council, the ones who call the shots on Earth, are super-obsessed with keeping us secret from the *Duchas*. She's worried they might not let minors like us leave Dun Cloch at all."

Peter shakes his head. "The Council's just seven people. Once the Sovereign gets to Earth, she's going to put together a proper *Echtran* government."

I seize that opening. "A truly representative government? That's the only way those of us in the lower *fines* will get any say in what the rules are."

"The Sovereign plans to do that eventually," Alan says. "When she gave that speech in Hollydoon—"

"Exactly." Peter nods vigorously. "According to my folks, we'll have tons more freedom then. We just have to pretend to be *Duchas*—and how hard can that be?"

"Pretending to be weaker, dumber and slower than we really are? Yeah, that'll be fun." I can't keep the acid out of my tone.

"It will," Peter insists. "Think about it. We'll be the best at almost anything we want to do—sports, academics, you name it."

Mattie shakes her head darkly. "If we're allowed to."

But Peter is unfazed and continues to talk about all the cool stuff he plans to do once his family moves to their permanent destination.

After breakfast there's a brief orientation session in the Commons for those who've never been on a ship before, which is nearly everyone. I spend most of it gazing longingly at the little reddish circle on the vidscreen.

"Might as well relax while we can," Wade comments when it ends, heading for the recreation area. "Sounds like we won't have much spare time once we get to Dun Cloch."

Which reminds me I still have lots of reading to do, so I take my tablet to a relatively quiet corner of the Commons. Unfortunately, Peter and Alan aren't the only ones who want to talk sports. At least half the *Horizon* passengers recognize me from the feeds and come over to talk *caidpel* or gush about how selfless I was to leave Nuath right when I was making such a name for myself. Though it feels dishonest, I don't admit I'm here against my will.

Though I've barely made a dent in my reading backlog, when I finally get a break from all the interruptions I'm too restless to sit still, I'm so used to daily physical activity. Three more days cooped up on this ship followed by weeks of sitting in classrooms is sure to make me crazy, fat or both.

Setting my reader aside, I head to the other side of the Commons to join an aerobics class just starting.

That afternoon the vidscreen view abruptly switches from Mars to Earth —a bigger image, even though it's farther away. The pang of loss I feel from losing even that picture of Mars completely wipes out the brief high I got from exercise. When Alan again brings up the idea of a Dun Cloch *caidpel* club at dinner, I immediately change the subject.

"So, what makes you guys think our new Sovereign's going to be able to put a decent government together on Earth when she hasn't managed it on Mars yet?"

"Are you kidding?" Alan says. "Look how much better things already are in Nuath, only two months after she was Installed. Why shouldn't she be able to?"

I can't help rolling my eyes. "Gee, maybe because she's no older than most of us here? Not to mention she's basically lived her whole life as a *Duchas*. How can she possibly live up to everything people expect of her?"

"She has lots of experienced advisors to help her," Alan points out, shifting uncomfortably now.

"Advisors or handlers?" I retort.

Alan makes a shushing motion and looks nervously over his shoulder.

Mattie, on his other side, whispers, "You shouldn't say things like that, Kira!"

"Why not? I thought one of the things that's supposed to be better now is that we're allowed to express our real opinions?"

Now Wade joins in. "Technically, yeah. I mean, it's not illegal anymore. But do you want people to think you're one of *them*?" He nods toward a nearby table.

I follow his gaze and see a group who seem to be deliberately keeping apart from the other passengers. Some of them look almost furtive.

"Who are they?"

"Former Faxon supporters, Dad says." He curls his lip in distaste. "Must not have done anything bad enough to get arrested or maybe they just weren't caught. Not surprised they don't want to stick around Nuath now there's a Sovereign in power again."

Alan snorts. "Traitors. Good riddance. Remember the ones we had in Hollydoon? Lorded it over everyone while Faxon was in power, then practically went into hiding once he was overthrown. Nobody would have anything to do with them. Wade's right, Kira. Criticizing the Sovereign just isn't…"

"Sorry," I say, even though I'm not. "I'm sure she's a perfectly nice girl, but it's pretty obvious that ever since she arrived in Nuath everything she's said or done has been dictated by either Quinn O'Gara or Regent Shim. Which only makes sense, I guess."

"What…what do you mean?" Wade's still frowning.

I lower my voice slightly. "You can't pretend she's exactly shown great judgment since finding out who she is. We all know what happened during her trip to Nuath, with that Bodyguard—then she totally let him take the fall for it."

"That's not fair," Peter protests. "That was his choice, according to—"

"Sure, that's what we were told after the fact, but how do we know? They say it's no coincidence our new Regent just happens to be Rigel Stuart's grandfather," I add, dropping my voice to a whisper. "Haven't you heard the rumors?"

Shaking their heads, matching expressions of horrified fascination on their faces, Alan, Wade, Peter and Mattie all lean in.

"They *say* the Sovereign's people made a deal—a compromise—that she'd appoint Shim Regent in return for his family agreeing to have the kid's memory wiped and then sending him back to Earth. To get him out of the way and leave a clear path for Sean O'Gara."

The others exchange glances.

"She...she seems happy with Sean these days," Mattie says after an uncomfortable silence. "But a girl at my school lived in Bailerealta for a while, then came back to Nuath on the same ship as the Sovereign. Brenna claimed Sean and Rigel Stuart seemed *jealous* of each other. And...and that Emileia kept flirting with both of them."

I nod, trying not to look smug. "Like I said, not great judgment. I also heard—"

"Hey, what are you guys whispering about?" calls Jana from the other end of the table.

Immediately, all the others straighten and start eating again, avoiding each other's eyes.

"Nothing much." I'd rather my sister not report back to our parents what I've been saying. "You guys know what movie they're showing tonight? The schedule didn't say."

My answer seems to satisfy the younger girls. They put their heads back together and a moment later they're both giggling again.

When conversation at our end of the table finally resumes, everyone is careful to stick to safe topics, like who has relatives on Earth. But a little later, when we're all taking our trays back to the drop, Alan sidles close enough to whisper.

"You want to be careful saying the kind of stuff you did earlier, Kira. If the higher-ups hear about it, you could hurt your family's chances of being selected for Jewel—and you don't want that, do you?"

I stop myself from saying that would be fine with me. The truth is, no matter how badly my mother wants to live there, the last place I want to end up is Jewel, encountering Sovereign Emileia on a regular basis. I'd almost certainly blurt out what I really think of her, which probably *would* get my parents in trouble.

Especially since Crevan Erc was apparently right that some people already equate the Populists' goals with Faxon's. The last thing I want to do is betray Crevan's trust in me—which means even here on the *Horizon* I shouldn't be so blatant about trying to sway people to the Populist way of thinking.

"I guess you have a point," I agree after a moment. "Thanks, Alan."

Over the next two days I try to couch my opinions a little more diplomatically. I guess it makes sense there are so many staunch supporters of the Sovereign on the *Horizon,* since it's one of the earlier emigration ships. But hearing her praises sung without pointing out how little she's actually done tests my self-control to the limit.

To avoid further arguments, I do a lot of reading—but the more I read, the more convinced I am that life on Earth will be anything but fun. Dun Cloch, at least, has basic Nuathan conveniences, but none of the *Duchas* communities will. Then there's that whole bizarre weather thing, which sounds downright dangerous.

Every time I start feeling anxious about the future I flip back to the Populist stuff on my reader, though by now I've practically got it memorized. If I can put that to good use, all the sacrifices I'm making will at least be worthwhile.

Our final night on the ship, Adina and Jana are the last ones to join the teen table. As usual, they're giggling.

"What have you two been up to?" I ask, half amused. They share a conspiratorial glance.

"Exploring," Jana says with a shrug—and another giggle.

Adina nods excitedly. "You should see how big the first class cabins are. And the cushy lounges on all the upper levels."

"What?" I say, surprised. "When did you—?"

"See that cute guy over there? He's Science *fine*—Chemistry. Jana was talking with him—okay, maybe flirting a little." More snickers from both girls. "Anyway, he offered to show us his family's quarters as soon as his parents left for dinner."

I frown, mostly at the reminder of all the perks Scientists and Royals get that we Ags never do. Maybe if my parents had let me participate in the playoffs, we'd have been able to afford a private family cabin, too, if not first class.

"I'm sure Steerage passengers aren't allowed up there," I finally tell them. "You're lucky you didn't get caught."

They just giggle again.

The next morning, the excitement—and nervousness—among the *Horizon* passengers is palpable. Looks like I'm not the only one worried we're all committed to something we'll regret. Mum and Adina, however, seem as enthusiastic as ever when the announcement comes shortly after breakfast for everyone to report to the Commons to prepare for landing.

"Ready for your first sight of our new home, girls?" Mum asks as we strap ourselves in just like we did for takeoff and for the gravity reversal two days ago.

Adina grins, nodding vigorously, but I'm determined to remain—or at least appear—calm.

"First sight? It's been up there for more than two days." I glance at the blue and white sphere that now fills the vidscreen.

"You know what she means," Dad says. "It's one thing to look at pictures—even a live one—and another to take our first steps on a new planet, breathe its air, feel its non-artificial gravity..." He swallows and I realize he's not as calm as he pretends, either.

Adina points at the screen. "Look! You can see continents now."

She's right. Where the surface isn't obscured by clouds—real clouds, not the holo ones in Nuath's sky—land masses are distinguishable from the dark blue of Earth's oceans. I squint, trying to identify them from the maps I've seen, but already we're too close for me to tell what we're looking at.

We're moving so quickly, surface features flash past in dizzying succession, blue, green and brown, punctuated by the dazzling white of clouds in the atmosphere. Then we slow perceptibly, the vivid colors fading to shades of gray as we move to the opposite side of the planet from the Sun. I wonder how long it'll be before we're back on the lighted side when I remember we have to land at night, so the ship isn't spotted by any *Duchas*.

"What time is it in Dun Cloch?" Adina asks. "Nuath's on Bailerealta time, right?"

Dad nods. "Montana is seven hours earlier, so it's just two hours after midnight there. We should adjust to the time change fairly quickly, based on what I've heard from people coming the other way."

I doubt that, but my attention is again absorbed by the vidscreen now that we're low enough to discern landscape features even in the dark. Something that has to be a mountain looms up, then is replaced by an enormous flat expanse. It bears no resemblance whatsoever to Nuath.

As we continue to slow, our view is suddenly obscured by a swirling gray darkness. Finally it clears enough to show we're hovering over a brightly lit landing area surrounded by dark structures of various sizes, the buildings and houses of Dun Cloch. Then, with an almost imperceptible bump, we touch down and the vidscreen switches off.

We're here.

9

Dun Cloch

Dun Cloch (Dun Klok) (pop. 1,247+): *founded 1933 in north-central Montana; largest Echtran compound on Earth; main production hub for Martian technology*

The Captain's voice comes over the speakers, welcoming us to Earth and informing us that our luggage will be taken directly to our accommodations in Dun Cloch. "You will leave the ship according to level, so please remain seated until your section is called."

Steerage is the very last group allowed to leave, of course. As we're waiting in the long line to exit the ship, I hear occasional exclamations from those ahead of us—probably excitement at seeing Earth for the first time.

Finally, I follow my parents through the outer portal for my first breath of Earth air—then gasp when something cold and wet slaps me in the face. "What the *efrin*?"

"Oh, wow!" Adina sounds thrilled. "I was hoping to see rain once we got to Earth, but I didn't expect it to be happening when we landed. Isn't it amazing?"

"Amazing," I echo. "That's one word for it."

"Move along, please," comes the first officer's voice from behind us. "You'll only get wetter if you dawdle. The shield starts at the edge of the launch area."

Our family hurries after the others down the ramp and across the brightly lit square around the ship. I'm doing my best not to cringe at the unfamiliar feel of water lashing my face and arms, especially since my sister seems to be positively reveling in it, actually turning her face up to the bizarre torrent from above.

I break into a trot and a moment later the deluge abruptly stops. Glancing back at the still-cascading rain, I realize I've reached the force shield, which apparently protects everything but the landing site from assaults by the open sky.

Adina follows more slowly, clearly enjoying this, our first Earth adventure. On joining us under the shield, she grins and shakes her head violently, sending water drops flying in every direction—including into my face.

"Hey! I'm wet enough without that."

"Aw, lighten up, Kira," she teases. "You're not afraid of a little rainstorm, are you?"

Before I can answer, there's a blinding flash of light, followed almost immediately by an ear-splitting explosion. I instinctively drop to the ground, covering my head with my arms. Most of those around me do the same. Maybe, if we all lie low...

Nearby laughter interrupts my panicked thoughts. Laughter? When we're clearly under attack?

Cautiously, I raise my head to look in that direction and see a crowd of people watching the Horizon's passengers disembark. Are they all Faxon supporters? Did they set off that explosion?

"It's all right, it's all right." A tall woman shoulders her way through the crowd and hurries toward us. "You lot, stop laughing!" she calls to the amused spectators. "Most of you were no better during your first thunderstorm."

She turns back to the frightened group of new arrivals. "That was a rather rude greeting for you all, fresh from Nuath. Sorry about that. I'm Fianna, Dun Cloch's chief immigration officer. We'd have delayed your landing until after the storm if it were possible, but of course it wasn't. Really, though, it's nothing to worry about, just a bit of thunder and lightning."

Those of us who dove for cover begin clambering sheepishly to our feet even as another flash occurs, followed by another tooth-rattling boom. Adina, I notice, remained standing—brat—but Mum and Dad look nearly as shaken as I am.

"Of...of course," Mum manages after a moment. "How silly of us. They did warn us about weather. I just didn't expect so... so *much* of it immediately upon our arrival."

Dad chuckles. "I'm sure none of us did. Are you all right, Kira?"

Feeling totally stupid now, I nod. "I'm fine. It just startled me, that's all. Reminded me of that time Faxon's goons blew up the—" Mum flinches and I break off. "Sorry."

It was during that series of reprisals against Hollydoon's protests that Mum was captured. Scary for all of us, but much worse for her.

"We should be able to dry off soon enough," Dad says with forced joviality. "Where are we supposed to be?" he asks the woman who greeted us.

"Follow me." She touches a button on her collar. "This way, every-one." Her voice is now magnified enough to be heard over the babble of voices and the hissing rain. "Our agents will check you in as quickly as possible, then let you go to your lodgings. Your luggage has already been taken there."

There's no gleaming terminal like the one in Arregaith. Instead, several people wearing official-looking sashes move among us, verifying our identities with retinal scans and thumbprints and checking our names off their lists.

Once we're in the system, our agent loads a map of Dun Cloch to Dad's omni with our assigned lodging highlighted. "Any of your thumbprints should open the door. Enjoy your stay in Dun Cloch."

Even as Dad thanks the man, he's already turning to the next group, probably eager to finish and get to bed.

"Looks like we go this way," Dad says, consulting the holographic map. We follow him away from the landing area, past several large buildings that appear to be single-family homes.

"Wow, will we be staying in one of these?" Adina points at one on our right. "These are really nice houses."

Glancing again at the map, Dad shakes his head. "Looks like we're in one of the new housing units they've built to handle the influx of immigrants."

We keep walking, passing progressively smaller houses. Suddenly, we're getting wet again.

"Hey! What happened to the shield?" I shake my head to get the water out of my eyes.

"I imagine it only protects the central area," Mum says. "It would take far too much energy to climate control the entire compound, considering Dun Cloch is larger than Hollydoon."

We walk faster. To my disgust, I continue to flinch every time another flash of lightning and its resulting thunder occur. For the past year I've tended to think of myself as the strong one in the family, so it's galling to discover my little sister is braver than I am.

"Here we are." Dad stops in front of a short set of metal stairs leading to a door labeled "C-153."

Peering through the still-driving rain, I see it's one of dozens of doors spaced along a low metal structure that stretches away into the dark in both directions. Not very inviting.

Hoisting his small bag higher on his shoulder, Dad mounts the three steps and presses his thumb against the pad by the door. It slides open with a reassuring hiss and lights come on inside. We all crowd through the door, eager to get out of the rain, then look around.

"Ew." I eye the tiny gray room with distaste. There are bunk beds on one wall and a pair of desks on the other, with a vidscreen on the wall above them. Two open doors at the back reveal a bathroom and a second bedroom. "I guess it's better than Steerage, but…"

"It's only temporary. Soon we'll leave here for Jewel, where I'm sure things will be much nicer." Mum's cheerfulness sounds a little forced.

Even Adina looks dubious as she stares around. "Just the one bathroom, huh? At least there will only be four of us sharing it now."

"It will be fine," Dad says firmly. "Look, they've provided us with towels, that's nice. Let's dry off and try to get a bit of sleep before breakfast, as we'll be facing a full day tomorrow. If it's still raining, I'll see if I can add a shield app to my omni before we venture out."

He grabs a couple of towels from the bathroom, then he and Mum disappear into the back bedroom, where their bags are waiting by the foot of the bed. Just like on the *Horizon*, my larger bag is on the top bunk, Adina's on the bottom one.

My sister goes into the bathroom and comes out with two more towels, handing one to me. "Until I read those chapters on Dun Cloch, I was hoping we'd have hot showers and stuff here," she says, "but at least we got to experience getting completely wet. I didn't expect rain to be so cold, though."

Unlike Adina, I was relieved to learn we'd still have Martian technology here. Not only are we ridiculously far from the nearest Earth community, the compound generates its own energy using solar and wind power, making Dun Cloch nearly undetectable by the *Duchas*. So at least we don't have to give up conveniences like ionic showers yet.

Towels are a novelty, though. We get out of our wet things and dry off, then put on nightgowns even though we only woke up on the *Horizon* a few hours ago.

"Let's unpack," I suggest.

While Mum and Dad each take a quick turn in the bathroom, Adina and I stow our few belongings into the four drawers beneath the bottom bunk, then take our own turns in the bathroom.

Embarrassingly aware that my little sister is handling this transition a lot better than I am so far, I turn off the light and climb into bed. The rain is hammering more loudly than ever on the metal roof, less than four feet over my head. No way will I ever fall asleep.

Next thing I know, it's morning.

"Wake up, sleepyheads."

At the sound of Mum's voice, I open my eyes and blink, momentarily confused by the unfamiliar ceiling above me. Then memory returns and I sit up. The rain seems to have stopped, and light is filtering through a narrow, curtained window I didn't notice last night.

"What time is it?" Adina asks sleepily from the bottom bunk. "I feel like I just fell asleep a minute ago."

"Past eight-thirty, Montana time," Dad says from behind Mum. "They'll stop serving breakfast in less than an hour, so we should hurry if we want to eat."

We had breakfast on the *Horizon* an hour or two before landing in Montana, but it's way past lunchtime in Nuath by now. My stomach growls and I scramble out of my bunk.

It's surprisingly chilly when we step outside—cooler than I've ever experienced in Nuath, though the bright morning sun warms us quickly as we walk. I squint up at it but only for a moment. The brilliance hurts my eyes.

"Check out our shadows," Adina says excitedly, pointing.

The dark silhouette moving along with me is both creepy and kind of cool. The only shadows in Nuath are those cast by unusually intense lights at night, like at some *caidpel* games.

In sunshine, Dun Cloch seems more welcoming than it did last night in the rain, but the rows of metal buildings housing the new immigrants look uglier than ever. Dad leads us to a nearby dining facility, where we're greeted by the enticing odor of bacon and scrambled eggs. My stomach rumbles again, the prospect of food lightening my mood further. We carry our filled plates to one of the long tables, where several of our fellow travelers cheerfully wish us good morning.

"Where is your family staying?" Jana moves her tray to sit next to Adina. "Is your place as lame as ours?"

"Building C, unit 153," Adina tells her. "And yeah, it's small, but way better than Steerage. Where are you?"

Jana wrinkles her nose. "D-72, next building over. I guess it's okay since we'll mostly only be there to sleep. Wonder when we find out who gets to go to Jewel?"

I let everyone's chatter flow over me at first, totally focused on my breakfast. Not until I've taken the edge off my hunger do I notice Alan and a couple other teens from the *Horizon* at the next table. He sees me looking and motions me over. I'm just getting up to join them when an announcement booms through the dining hall.

"Good morning. Our newest arrivals are asked to move to the western end of the room for a newcomers' meeting, which will begin in ten minutes. Everyone else, please proceed to your assigned classes."

As soon as the hundred-odd *Horizon* passengers are seated, Fianna, the same woman who greeted us last night, stands up in front of us.

"Hello again, everyone. I hope most of you managed to get a bit of sleep despite last night's thunderstorm. Though we'd prefer to give you a few days to accustom yourselves to the time change and your new surroundings, circumstances require us to begin your training immediately. Due to the unprecedented arrival of so many Nuathans during a single launch window, we have compressed the traditional three-month orientation program into half that, in order to make room for later arrivals as earlier ones complete their training and leave."

While she's talking, two men and a woman start handing out clunky-looking tablets to everyone.

"These tablets will be yours to keep," Fianna explains, "as they are designed to look like ordinary *Duchas* technology despite a few special enhancements. Once everyone has one, I'll show you how to access your personal orientation schedules. Those will vary somewhat, depending on which town or city you are bound for. In addition to the facts and training specific to your destinations, each of you will be assigned a

Duchas identity complete with personal histories. It is imperative that you learn every detail of those identities. That will minimize your likelihood of arousing *Duchas* suspicions that could risk exposure of our true origins. The importance of maintaining absolute secrecy on that point should be obvious."

A woman off to our right raises her hand.

"Yes?"

"What if we haven't requested a permanent location yet? I thought we'd be able to learn more about our choices before deciding."

Fianna nods. "Not to worry. The first ten days of your orientation are applicable to any location. After that, however, you will need to either submit a settlement request or confirm that you are willing to allow the administrators to assign you to a location they consider appropriate. Your tablets contain information on numerous acceptable towns and cities, or you may research others on your own. Those of you with children below the age of twelve are asked to limit your choices to primarily *Echtran* communities, though you will be free to relocate once they are older. Please note that while we will do our best to honor your selections, in some cases that may not be possible."

Another hand goes up. "Yes?"

"Why not?" a man asks. "You won't split up families, will you?"

"Not nuclear families, of course not," Fianna assures him. "In fact, we'll do our best to keep extended families and friends together, if you've noted that in your preferences. However, we must take into account how many newcomers a particular community can reasonably accommodate. For example, if you request Jewel, Indiana, as many have already done, we strongly recommend you indicate at least one alternate choice."

There's some muttering at this and I notice a few people exchanging concerned glances.

Fianna holds up a hand and the murmuring subsides. "You must understand that with only five thousand *Duchas* inhabitants, Jewel cannot possibly absorb several hundred new *Echtrans* at once. It hasn't the space or the resources. While the *Echtran* Council is taking steps to maximize the number Jewel can accommodate, it is unlikely that more than a few dozen from the current launch window will be cleared to move there. However, a great number of Earth communities share many features in common with Jewel. I encourage you to look into those."

A woman from behind us speaks up without being called on. "But when the Sovereign came to our village she said—"

"Yes, the Sovereign did tout the attractions of her hometown in her efforts to overcome your understandable resistance to emigrating, but no specific promises were made as to who would be allowed to live there."

"When will we *know*?" another woman asks plaintively.

"Shortly after the current launch window closes, six weeks from now," Fianna replies. "Before that time, everyone who insists on keeping Jewel as their first choice will undergo extremely thorough background checks. The results will be taken into account when making final selections."

More muttering. Clearly no one had counted on this, though it does make sense.

"In addition," Fianna continues, "those who *are* selected will require at least two weeks of additional instruction before relocating to Jewel. Needless to say, choosing a different town will almost certainly mean an earlier release from Dun Cloch to your permanent Earth homes. Something to keep in mind. Now, if you will all activate your tablets..."

For the next hour, she walks us through the accelerated Orientation schedule. Along with intimately familiarizing ourselves with Earth culture, those of us still in school will study age-appropriate academics before being sorted into *Duchas* grade levels. Everyone over the age of sixteen will also be taught how to operate the primitive gas-powered automobiles used by Earth humans.

As settlement assignments are made, we'll be given fake personal histories, along with corresponding identification and supporting documents. Later, we'll be tested on those false backgrounds and our accents will be fine-tuned for believability.

Most evenings we'll be expected to view popular films and television shows, followed by discussion groups and/or online quizzes on the material. In other words, the next six weeks will be scheduled almost to the minute. Though at first we'll follow the Nuathan tradition of taking every third afternoon off, later we'll switch to the *Duchas* seven-day work week.

"Lunch won't be served for another hour," Fianna finishes at last. "I recommend you use that time to settle in and familiarize yourselves with your schedules for the next few days. After lunch, your instruction will begin in earnest."

Alan Dempsey catches up with me as we all file out of the dining hall to head back to our quarters. "Sounds like we won't have much time for *caidpel* after all, huh?"

"Guess not." I don't really care, though I hope I'll have time for *some* kind of exercise. "Maybe we can at least find a place for speed drills. Wonder if they have standard conditioning equipment here somewhere?"

"I'll look into it and let you know," he promises. "We can be running buddies, at least. This is going to be great, Kira, you'll see. And even better once we both get to Jewel."

With a parting grin, he follows his parents off to the right while my family goes left. I wait till his back is turned to grimace. Because I'm not seeing the great myself, unless it's that I'll be too busy to dwell on everything I've lost.

10

Threoirach

THREOIRACH (TRO-ROK): *instruction; orientation; guidance*

Sure enough, my schedule is so full over the next few weeks I don't have much time to dwell on the gnawing emptiness *caidpel* and the Resistance used to fill. Even my supposedly "free" afternoons often have extra classes wedged in. Then there are brief Evening Sings before dinner on those days, like in Nuath. That makes Mum happy, though I'm not really into them, since Group Sings were banned by Faxon most of my life.

Every few days, another batch of immigrants arrives to begin their Earth Orientation, making mealtimes progressively more crowded. Our classes progress from basic *Duchas* culture to more complicated things. One I find easier than expected is cultivating a so-called "typical American" accent, though Adina has some trouble with it. After a week or two, I even find myself thinking and dreaming in that accent instead of my old Nuathan one, which is unsettling.

Soon after our arrival, Alan talks my parents into letting me go running with him on nights when nothing else is scheduled. I appreciate the chance to work up a sweat a few days a week, but the price is Alan's increasingly obvious flirting. No matter how many times I make it clear I'm not interested, he simply refuses to take the hint.

On one of our late-night runs, we pass the compound's central square as a ship—the *Luminosity*—is being prepared for launch. Seized by a sudden, fierce longing to be aboard, to be heading back to Mars, I stop to stare at it. Which lucky people—?

"Um, we'd better keep going." Alan interrupts my musing. "I promised my folks I'd be back by eleven."

"Oh. Yeah. Sorry."

Busy as I am, I try to keep an eye on Adina and Jana, who still spend a lot of time together. One evening when our parents are in the central square for Group Sing, I follow them when they sneak off to Dun Cloch's industrial complex, where nearly all the Martian technology on Earth is produced.

"I heard them again last night," I overhear Adina saying to Jana. "If Gaelen is busy tonight, can we try to find them? They must be somewhere nearby."

"So watching the birds isn't enough for you anymore?" Jana teases her. "Gaelen has had this shift the past two times, but...okay. If he's not there, or too busy to talk to us, we can spend a little time looking for them. As long as we don't miss dinner."

Frowning, I tail them to the communications factory, where a handsome boy my age or possibly older is standing near the entrance looking bored. When he spots the two girls, he straightens, grinning and brushing a hand through his dark hair in a gesture that reminds me uncomfortably of Brady, back in Nuath.

"Hi, Gaelen," Jana sings out. "We can't stay long but I was hoping you'd be here."

I stay out of sight until Jana's done flirting with the guy and both girls head back for dinner. Then I approach Gaelen myself, who now eyes *me* with obvious interest.

"What the *efrin* is wrong with you?" I demand.

He blinks, then frowns. "What do you—?"

"Do you know how young those girls are? I'd better not catch you sniffing around my sister again—or any other girls her age."

"I didn't...I wasn't..." he stammers, blanching now.

I just shake my head in disgust and stalk off, while he continues to splutter behind me. I don't say anything to Adina or Jana when I see them at dinner a little later, not wanting them to know I saw them. I'm fairly sure I scared Gaelen enough to put a stop to that particular bit of mischief. Of course, now I have to worry about whatever Adina was trying to persuade Jana to do instead.

Pulling my attention away from the girls, I notice Alan moving from table to table, talking to other teens and a few slightly older immigrants. I wonder what he's doing until he catches up with me as we're leaving the dining hall.

"Guess what?" Alan says excitedly. "I've been asking around over the past few days and just now reconfirmed with some folks... Anyway, counting you and me, there are almost twenty people interested in playing some *caidpel* here!"

I regard him dubiously. "Yeah? So?"

"So, that means we can at least play eight-a-side. Peter even managed to find enough *camman* and a few balls in one of the storage buildings near the old *caidpel* field. You know where it is, right?"

"Um, yeah." Soon after we got here I noticed the weed-filled clearing to the west of the temp lodgings, with its rickety goalposts. It obviously hasn't been used in years.

His grin fades slightly at the lack of enthusiasm in my tone. "Anyway, we're going to meet there right after classes next half-day. Isn't that great?"

"Yeah, it is."

Though I suspect he's mostly doing this to score points with me, and lame as playing with a bunch of amateurs will be, at least it's something to look forward to. Forcing a bit more eagerness into my voice, I say, "Thanks, Alan."

"I knew you'd be excited. See you later, Kira!"

Three days later, I'm glad I didn't expect much as I survey the motley group of young people Alan scraped together for our first attempt at a game. The ten boys and six girls range from roughly fourteen to twenty-five years old. Judging by the way they hold the *camman* Peter is handing out, most have never handled one before. Several, I notice, are darting furtive glances my way.

"Thanks for coming, everybody." Alan moves to face the rest of us. "This is going to be a great way to get some exercise after all that class-work and to improve our skills at the same time. I've brought along Kira Morain, the Nuathan League star, just like I promised. You'll be willing to give everyone else pointers as we go, won't you, Kira?"

He starts to put a proprietary hand on my shoulder but I step away. Quickly, but nonchalantly enough that I hope it doesn't look like a snub.

"I'll do my best." I summon a smile. "How many of you have played *caidpel* before?"

To my dismay, only half raise their hands. At Alan's prompting, they introduce themselves and relate their prior *caidpel* experience—or lack thereof. One girl spent time on a junior team in Ballytadhg, but the others have only played for fun.

"I guess we'd better start with the basics." I try for an encouraging smile. "Even if you've only watched it on the feeds, you already know *caidpel* is played with two balls. This is the *schlitur*." I hold up the smaller one. "And this is the *pell*." I toss the larger, softer ball into the air with my other hand. "Each player has a *camman*—" I nod toward the stick Alan is holding— "but it's only used on the *schlitur*. Hands and feet can be used on both balls but you can't carry either one more than two steps before tossing it to either a teammate or your own foot or *camman*. Following me so far?"

I wait for everyone to nod before continuing. "Okay. See the goalposts? Sending either ball below the first crossbar is worth one point. Between the two crossbars, three points. If you can get it through the triangle at the top, above the second crossbar, it's five points for the *schlitur*, seven for the *pell*. That takes good aim, since the *pell* is nearly as big as the gap. Got it?"

Though they all nod again, one or two wear puzzled frowns. Seriously? Why are they here if they haven't even *watched* enough *caidpel* to know how the scoring works? I'd figured it out before I was six.

"There aren't enough of us to field two full teams of twelve, so we'll play eight-a-side. That means each team will have a goalkeeper, three forwards, three backs and a midfielder."

I make them all run down the field and back, then assign positions based on relative speed and size, figuring I can make changes once I have a better idea of their skills. I decide Alan and I should man the goals, so we can both watch the whole field. Since there's no referee, I toss the two balls into the center myself to start play, then sprint to defend my goal.

Turns out, I didn't need to hurry. Ten minutes later, neither team has progressed either ball down the field. Mostly, they're just trying to avoid each other's flailing sticks and feet. It takes a lot of yelling to make them stop running into each other long enough for me to change up the positions and give them a more thorough explanation of what each of them should be doing.

Things improve slightly after that...but only slightly. By the time we stop so we can all shower before dinner, most have collected a few bruises but none have come close to scoring a goal.

"Not bad for our first practice," I lie as they gather around me. "I recommend watching a few *caidpel* vids so you'll have a better idea how to play your positions next time."

As we all head back toward our temp lodgings, several of them shyly approach me to ask what it was like being famous and, in a couple of cases, for my autograph. Sighing inwardly, I sign the proffered tablets and try to answer their questions. When I send Alan an accusatory glare, he just shrugs apologetically.

"Didn't realize so many of them hadn't ever played before," he whispers once the others have dispersed. "I figured anyone really interested—"

"In playing? Or in meeting 'famous' Kira Morain?" I demand.

"Um...I might have played up that angle a little to get some to commit. But it was still fun, wasn't it? I know how much you've missed it..."

I keep glaring for a few seconds, then relent with a shrug. "It'll be good exercise, I guess, once we give up playing goalkeeper to be more hands-on. You don't worry this will make it harder than ever once we leave here and never get to play again?"

He shrugs. "Maybe not, if we both end up in Jewel and—what?"

I'm laughing and shaking my head. "If you think this was bad, can you imagine trying to teach *Duchas* how to play? Thanks, though, Alan. It was nice of you to set this up—and I did sort of have fun."

"I was hoping you would." He clears his throat. "I was thinking maybe later, instead of running, we could just go for a walk. Look at the stars." He takes a half-step toward me, one of his hands drifting toward one of mine.

I jerk my hand away, then try to cover by combing my fingers through my messy hair. "I, ah, need to get some studying in tonight, sorry. Guess we should hurry and shower or we'll be late to dinner. See you, Alan!"

"Oh, um, sure." He appears crestfallen, but only for a moment. Quickly summoning an engaging grin, he winks and says, "Later!"

Turning away from him, I can only shake my head at his willful self-delusion. I'll just have to work harder at discouraging him.

When I get back to our quarters, I'm not surprised to find Mum, Dad and Adina have already gone to dinner.

I spend less than five minutes in the bathroom, taking an ionic shower and dressing in a fresh tunic and leggings. So I'm startled to come out and discover Adina is already back, fussing with something on her bunk.

"Hey, Sprout, you haven't already eaten, have you?"

She whirls about, her face going red. "Kira! I didn't know you were here. I, uh…"

Because she seems to be trying to screen whatever is on her bunk from my sight, I step past her to see what it is—then jump backwards with a gasp.

"Where—? What—?" I point a shaking finger at the creature looking back at me. Four-legged, with rough, yellowish-gray fur, the thing is curled on Adina's bed, regarding both of us with eerie-looking yellow eyes.

"Do you think Mum and Dad will let me keep him?" my sister asks, turning an adoring gaze on the animal. "He's *almost* a dog, right?"

I manage to find my voice. "No! Adina, that's *not* a dog and you know it. Is that a…a wolf?"

She laughs. "Of course not. Just a coyote. They're not nearly as big as wolves. You've heard them howling some nights, right? I was dying to see one, so I talked Jana into exploring those hills to the north with me, since that's where the sounds always seem to come from. Most of them ran away—so did Jana—but this one stopped when I called after them, then he followed me back. I grabbed a bit of synth beef from the dining hall to coax him in here. He seemed to like it."

"I'll bet." I'm still staring at the thing, half-expecting it to lunge at one of us any second. "You need to get it out of here, Adina, now. Seriously. You may be good with sheep and other domesticated animals, but this one is wild. There's no knowing what it might do."

Adina argues, but when I threaten to go get Mum and Dad she realizes I'm serious. Reluctantly, with many an injured look my way, she opens the outer door of our quarters.

"Go on, then," she says to the coyote. In two smooth bounds, it leaps from her bed and out the door. Then, with just one backward glance from those weird yellow eyes, it lopes off northward. Adina heaves a sigh.

"You should check your bunk for vermin before you sleep in it again," I tell her, still shuddering. "Sanitize your hands—thoroughly!—and then let's go to dinner."

She begs me not to tell our parents, so I don't—though I do make her promise not to bring any more animals into our quarters.

By the time we've been in Dun Cloch a month, everyone who traveled on the *Horizon* with us has chosen at least one preferred community, and those who picked Jewel have named backups—except my parents. Mum refuses to name an alternate, convinced that could hurt our chances, even when Dad points out that could mean staying in Dun Cloch permanently—a choice quite a few people have already made.

"I wouldn't mind staying here," Adina pipes up. "Especially if we can live in one of those nice houses closer to all the shops and stuff. I think Jana's family put it down as their second choice."

Though I haven't completely given up my dream of somehow getting onto a Mars-bound ship before the launch window closes, I have to admit living in Dun Cloch *would* be the next best thing to going home. Way better than Jewel, anyway. Here, we'd still get to use all the Martian conveniences we're used to. Plus I could continue playing *caidpel*—sort of.

By now, several of those who showed up that first night have dropped out, but at least as many others have joined us, some of them permanent Dun Cloch residents who got wind of what we were doing. Gradually, our fledgling team has started to improve.

I can't avoid spending time with Alan during those occasional *caidpel* practices, but other than that I've been doing my best to steer clear of him. For example, I no longer coordinate my evening runs with him, going out alone more often than not, though my parents don't know that. They also don't know how often I hang around the launch area. Unless it's—shudder—raining, I swing by there almost every night, especially when a ship is getting ready to leave for Mars.

Eventually I strike up a slight acquaintance with one of the women working there and casually ask if they ever take on new crew members.

To my embarrassment, she chuckles. "You're not the first to ask, but no—certainly never this late in a launch window. Nor would someone your age be eligible. Sorry. And please don't get any ideas about getting aboard any other way. Last week a young man attempted to stow away—hid inside one of the supply trolleys before it went in. The pre-launch sensor sweep found him, of course, but I'm afraid the incident was rather embarrassing for his family."

That effectively squelches every scheme I've considered for returning home. Still, I keep watching the ships and hoping against hope until the very last one leaves at the end of the current, extended launch window. At that point, I abandon my nighttime running regimen altogether, finally, painfully forced to accept that I'm stuck on Earth for at least two years.

11

Emileia

EMILEIA (EM-I-LAY-AH): *current Thiarna (Sovereign), granddaughter to Sovereign Leontine; sole heir to the Nuathan monarchy*

Two days before our six-week Orientation period ends, we arrive for breakfast to see a dozen uniformed men sweeping the dining hall with sensors.

"What's going on?" Dad whispers to a man at a nearby table.

"Something to do with the Sovereign's visit later today," he replies. "Standard security measures, they said."

I regard the nearest uniformed guy dubiously—they all have energy weapons, just like the ones Faxon's soldiers used to carry, holstered at their hips.

Mum brightens, however. "Oh, I can't wait to see Sovereign Emileia again! I'm pleased they're not taking her safety lightly after those Nuathan protests we used to see on the feeds."

I'm a lot less pleased by all the extra security. For one thing, there are only half the usual selections available for breakfast, probably because of disruptions in the kitchen. And the uniformed detail is paying way too much attention to private conversations among the diners, which leads to lots of awkward silences. When we leave, more security people posted at the exits sweep us with sensors—I assume looking for hidden weapons.

"It's like living under Faxon again," I mutter as we head toward the instruction area.

"Oh, Kira, don't be silly," Mum admonishes me. "It's only for today. They published the Sovereign's schedule shortly after she landed in Bail-erealta. She has half a dozen stops to make before finally returning to Jewel next week. I wonder if it will be possible to speak to her person-ally? I must ask about that."

A few minutes later we find out all of today's classes have been canceled to allow everyone to get ready for the Sovereign's visit.

"What, are we supposed to dress up or something?" I wonder aloud to Adina.

"I hope not. I didn't bring anything very fancy. What do you think, Mum?"

She just smiles. "I imagine as long as we're well-groomed and presentable, it will be fine. Oh!" She looks at the screen of her omni. "I have a reply. It says if I'm willing to undergo some additional screening, I may have a chance to speak with the Sovereign after her speech. I'll go do that now."

"I'll come with you," Dad offers. "We'll see you girls back at the lodging."

"If I'd known they'd be canceling classes, I'd have scheduled *caidpel* for this morning," I grumble once our parents are out of earshot.

Only a couple of the original players are still here, other than Alan and me, but with the addition of those permanent Dun Cloch folks, our level of play has continued—slowly—to improve. Those *caidpel* sessions are the only thing I look forward to, since I quit pushing Populist ideals at mealtimes after a few people overheard me and got upset. One called me a "Neo-Faxist" to my face and another actually told my parents. Needless to say, they were pretty upset.

Over lunch—where we're again subjected to heightened security—Mum ecstatically tells us that she's been cleared to speak with the Sovereign later. "I'd love for you girls to meet her, too, if that's allowed."

I hope not. I'd be way too tempted to tell her to her face that it's all her fault my life went from awesome to awful in less than two months. Bet *that* would keep us from having to move to Jewel...

As we're leaving the dining hall, there's a compound-wide announcement that the Sovereign has just arrived and will give an address in the central square in twenty minutes. Before I can slip away, Mum herds us ahead of her, making our family among the first to arrive.

Nearly beside herself with excitement, she leads us to a spot just behind the barriers that have been set up around three sides of the square—the same place the *Horizon* landed.

Ten minutes later a black *Duchas* vehicle with darkened windows rolls into the open side of the square. A uniformed man gets out, followed by the Sovereign, then another uniformed man. Flanked by the men, she proceeds to a dais in the center of the square and steps up to a raised podium to face the still-gathering crowd.

"Hello, everyone," she begins, but I doubt anyone but those up front can hear her. Hardly the voice of a commander. But then she touches something on her collar and her next words ring out across the square.

"Sorry about that. Hello, everyone," she says again. "I'm here to personally thank you all for your willingness to spearhead our necessary emigration to Earth. Your bravery and initiative will almost certainly help to extend the life of our colony on Mars, giving our Scientists additional time to find a more permanent solution to Nuath's power shortage."

As she continues to spout platitudes, I examine her critically. In person, she looks even younger than on the feeds—no wonder she can't project the kind of authority a leader should. Like Crevan Erc does, for example. Surely the savior of Nuath, as people like my mother consider her, shouldn't have to amplify her voice to get her ideas across—ideas almost certainly written by someone else for her to memorize.

"I'll be here for two more hours and hope to speak with as many of you as possible during that time. Please don't hesitate to come to me with any questions or concerns you might have about adapting to life here on Earth."

Please don't hesitate? When my parents had to be specially screened just to get close to her? Her hypocrisy sours my stomach.

As she steps off the dais, those who've received clearance are directed to line up to have their passes verified. Mum motions for Adina and me to join her and Dad, but when we step forward, the man checking credentials frowns.

"Were these two properly screened?"

"Er, no," Mum says, "but they are our daughters, and minors. I thought it would be nice for them to meet the Sovereign. My husband and I—"

"Sorry. Only those with official clearance are allowed access. They'll have to wait here, behind the barriers."

Mum hesitates, then she nods. "I'll at least point you out to her," she tells us apologetically as she steps through the gap in the barricade.

Won't that be special. I keep my instinctively snarky comment to myself.

My parents join the line forming to speak with the girl-Sovereign. One of her Bodyguards shepherds people forward, then away, making sure no one monopolizes her for more than a minute or two. When it's Mum and Dad's turn, they bow deeply to her, right fists over their hearts —deeper bows than anyone else so far.

"Such an honor, Excellency." I can just make out Mum's breathless gushing. "I am Deirdra Morain and this is my husband, Aidan. I...I knew your mother, years before you were born, when I worked at the Royal Palace. She was always extremely kind to me. You look remarkably like her."

The girl smiles, though from here it looks fake. "Thank you. I've been told that. What did you do at the Palace?"

"I tended the Royal gardens." Mum bobs her head obsequiously, making me wish I could shake her, snap her out of it. "Not just me, of course, but Consort Galena often complimented my work. I'm hoping— that is, my family is hoping—" She glances toward my sister and me and I quickly look away before the Sovereign can see the disgust on my face.

"Ma'am," interrupts the Bodyguard, "it's time to move along so everyone else has a chance to meet the Sovereign. If there's time, you may get another chance to speak with her before she leaves."

"Oh! Of...of course." Mum backs away, bowing again, but when she and Dad rejoin us a moment later, she's smiling ear to ear. "She was so gracious! Did you see? Could you hear?"

Gracious? Seriously? "Um, yeah. She sounded very...polite." That earns me a quick frown from Dad.

"I'm sorry I wasn't able to bring you to her attention," Mum continues, still bubbling. "But her guard said there might be a chance later. Why don't we go see if we can get proper clearance for you two before she leaves? Then perhaps—"

"No, really, Mum, it's okay. If we end up going to Jewel, we'll have plenty of chances to meet her. And if we don't...it won't matter, will it?" I glance at Dad.

His frown softens. "Kira's right, Deirdra. We shouldn't get too invested until we know for sure. I still think— " He breaks off. "Never mind. Let's get you out of this crowd."

Not that Mum is acting especially nervous, despite the press of people around us. I suppress a twinge of annoyance remembering how she always begged off my games back in Nuath.

Two days later we finally finish Orientation. Everyone in our group is issued the various pieces of identification we'll need to pass as *Duchas*. Those include fake utility bills from our supposedly previous residences, birth certificates, and drivers' licenses for Mum, Dad and me. By now we all have a rudimentary *Duchas* wardrobe, as well, so we can theoretically blend in wherever we end up.

Those who aren't staying in Dun Cloch are now required to turn in all Martian tech except our new tablets. This causes a lot of grumbling, even though everyone over the age of twelve is also given a "mobile phone," a sort of primitive *Duchas* omni. They're simplistic things, can't even send or receive off-planet messages. At least they can receive important MARSTAR communications, though we'll have to input a special code to read them.

Giving up my old tablet with its encrypted files of Populist hurts. Even worse, I realize if Crevan Erc or his people ever *do* want to contact me, they won't be able to. Not unless we stay in Dun Cloch, and I get another omni. But...surely there's a decent chance of that? Only last night, while in the bathroom getting ready for bed, I overheard part of an argument between Mum and Dad on the other side of the flimsy wall.

"It's already August, Deirdra. Everyone's preparing to leave Dun Cloch except those of us still holding out for Jewel—only a few hundred at this point. And even those have named alternate communities so that they can leave as soon as the list is posted."

"But don't you see? That means our odds of being chosen keep improving." Mum sounds as cheerful about the prospect as ever.

There's a pause, then Dad says, "I've done a bit of research, and the schools Adina and Kira would attend in Jewel begin classes in just three days. If we *are* selected, we'll all be required to take at least two weeks of additional classes before moving there. This transition will be challenging enough for our girls without the additional stress of arriving for school well after the start of the term."

"Many other towns' schools have already begun," Mum points out. "Honestly, Aidan, don't you think the advantages to our girls of attending school with the Sovereign outweigh the disadvantages of waiting?"

"Perhaps. But unless you're willing to remain in Dun Cloch, we should find out which communities' schools begin latest—say, another town in Indiana."

"I suppose," Mum says. "But I'm still confident we'll end up in Jewel. You'll see."

Remembering that now, I shake my head at Mum's blind faith—which I devoutly hope is misplaced. Seeing the Sovereign frequently but having to hide the way I really feel about her would suck. Like being forced to lie constantly. I doubt I could do it, which means my whole family could end up in trouble.

Maybe I can convince Dad to put Dun Cloch down as an alternate without telling Mum.

Over the next week, the dining hall becomes noticeably less crowded as more and more people leave Dun Cloch. With Orientation over, I have plenty of time for *caidpel*—but not enough players. Nearly all of those we started with have left by now. Of those remaining, everyone but the locals are too busy finishing up their own Orientations to make time for it.

"Bummer, huh?" Alan says when we cancel yet another session because only seven people showed up. "Maybe just as well, though. My mum is hounding me to finish packing so we'll be ready to leave as soon as they announce the Jewel selections. We finally put down Branson, Missouri, as our alternate, though I pushed for Dun Cloch instead."

I've done the same, pointing out to Dad that nearly twenty percent of emigrants are opting to stay here. But he refuses to go behind Mum's back and she's still totally, irrationally convinced we'll be picked for Jewel.

After Alan heads back to the lodgings to pack, I run a few speed drills with the local *caidpel* enthusiasts so I can at least work up a good sweat. If we *do* end up staying here, maybe we can eventually convince enough other people to play to start having games again. Lame ones, but at this point I'll take what I can get.

One week after the Sovereign's visit, I'm awakened by a happy squeal from Mum. "I knew it! I knew it! Girls! Girls! Wake up and check your tablets—we're going to Jewel! Haven't I said all along we were meant to live there, Aidan? Haven't I?"

I roll over with a groan to see Mum brandishing her tablet.

"You have indeed," Dad says with an indulgent smile, though he sounds pleased, too. "I never should have doubted your intuition."

"Hey, look!" my sister exclaims from the bottom bunk. "They sent the whole list of who's going and…yay! Jana's family is on it, too!"

I grab my own tablet off its little shelf behind my head and sure enough, there's a notice congratulating me on the main screen. I click the link to the complete list and see close to two hundred names displayed —about twice as many as they told us to expect.

"Wow, looks like we're going to be awfully busy again," Adina says then. "Check out the new course schedules they've sent us."

She's right. According to this, the next two and a half weeks will be even crazier than our first month in Dun Cloch. Not only will we be drilled on how to behave around the Sovereign and everyone who knows her, we'll be required to learn reams of information about NuAgra, a corporation the *Echtran* Council has apparently established in Jewel as cover for so many *Echtrans* moving there at once.

I go back to the list of those going and start scrolling through the names, which are in alphabetical order by surname, the three Blairs up near the top. A little further down I see Alan Dempsey and his parents listed, so naming an alternate didn't hurt their chances after all.

At breakfast, Adina and Jana greet each other with squeals of delight, hugging and jumping up and down. I'm so far from sharing their happiness I turn away, wondering sourly how much more mischief they'll get into in Jewel than they have here.

"Awesome that both our families got picked, huh?" Alan comes up from behind me to clap a hand on my shoulder. "I figured our odds were almost nil. Sounds like this NuAgra place will need a fair number of Ags, though, so I guess it makes sense. We should start getting to know everyone else around our age who's going, don't you think?"

Rather than being contagious, his enthusiasm just irritates me. "Sure, I guess. How many are there, do you know?"

"Not many—seems to mostly be singles and childless couples going. Including you, your sister and me, I only counted eleven school-age kids and some aren't in Dun Cloch, yet. On the schedule it said they'll be coming here for the final training, so they'll probably arrive soon."

The next day is filled with goodbyes, some tearful, as the Jewel hopefuls who weren't selected finally leave for their alternate destinations. Adina and Jana are especially upset that Clarisse, another girl they've hung out with, wasn't on the list. Mum and Dad also seem sorry to bid farewell to two or three couples they've gotten to know since our arrival.

I never bothered to get particularly close to anyone here, so I don't have anything to get choked up about except losing even my lame version of *caidpel*. There's never been any hint of that "alternate role" Crevan Erc mentioned and I'm virtually certain there won't be any Populists in Jewel to work with.

The eighty-odd others selected for Jewel arrive the following day from Bailerealta, Ireland, where they did their regular Orientation. Among them are three more teens, who Alan drags me over to meet at dinner that evening.

"Hi, everyone! Welcome to Dun Cloch. Looks like we'll all be attending Jewel High School together, huh? I'm—"

Before he can finish, one of the boys, a tall guy with dark hair, jumps to his feet. "Kira Morain! I couldn't believe it when I saw your name on the Jewel list—I was a huge *caidpel* fan back on Mars. You must have been so bummed to leave right before the playoffs."

The sympathy in his blue eyes takes some of the sting out of that reminder. "Yeah, moving to Earth definitely wasn't my idea, but I couldn't do much about it once my folks committed us."

"Especially after they started holding you up as an example on the feeds, I'll bet. But even if your leaving let my team—the Engineers—make it to the finals, it still seemed wrong for the sport to lose a player like you. Do you think—?"

"Um, as I was about to say," Alan interrupts, edging closer to me, "I'm Alan Dempsey and this, obviously, is Kira Morain."

The boy who greeted me so enthusiastically flushes slightly. "Oh, er, yeah, sorry. Liam Walsh." He shakes Alan's extended hand. "And this is—"

"Lucas Walsh." A boy so similar to Liam he must be his twin steps forward. "We'll both be juniors at Jewel High."

"Nice to meet you, Lucas, Liam." Alan turns to the other newcomer, a girl with bright red hair who hasn't spoken yet.

Blushing deeply, she gives us both a tentative smile. "I'm...I'm Erin Campbell. I'm supposed to be a sophomore—tenth grade."

"Then you'll want to meet Grady," Alan says. "He's going to be a sophomore, too. Hey, Grady, come here!"

A similarly shy boy with dark blond hair and brown eyes looks up from a nearby table and Alan motions him over. A moment later Adina and Jana join us, as do three younger kids who'll be attending Jewel Middle School with Adina.

Soon all eleven of us are clustered around the table, sharing stories about our lives in Nuath and comparing Dun Cloch and Bailerealta. To my relief and mild surprise, I find myself liking these people I'll be getting to know a lot better in the weeks and months to come. Maybe, just maybe, leaving Dun Cloch won't be *quite* the nightmare I expect.

The new arrivals spend the next morning settling into temporary lodgings recently vacated by others. After lunch, the future Jewel residents are directed to the same end of the dining hall where we had our initial briefing almost two months ago. A tall blond man, handsome even by our standards, moves to the front and flashes a wide smile.

"Hello, everyone. I'm Connor, the *Echtran* Council member tasked with overseeing your resettlement on Earth." One of the four Council Royals, I recall. "Congratulations to all of you on being chosen to live in Jewel, Indiana, our Sovereign's hometown. That honor was reserved for the very cream of our newest immigrants from Nuath.

"As you may have been told already, most of you will be working at the NuAgra facility in Jewel. NuAgra's stated purpose is one of agricultural research, which is why so many of you here are from the Agricultural *fine*. Of course, there will be jobs there for those of you from other *fines*, as well."

He goes on to explain the history of the company and the Council's future plans for it, which include it eventually doubling as a center for *Echtran* government as more and more Nuathans emigrate to Earth over the next decade or two.

"As the vanguard of what will become an important focal point for our people, you will all have vital parts to play, apart from the valuable Agricultural research you will be doing there. As our numbers continue to grow, keeping the secret of our origins will become progressively more difficult. Therefore, we must begin carefully preparing the ground now for the eventual dissemination of the truth to the *Duchas* population at large. Much of that preparation will fall to you, as members of what will become the largest integrated community of *Duchas* and *Echtrans* on Earth."

After a few more platitudes, he introduces Ida Lunn, Head Researcher at NuAgra, who gives us an overview of the research going on there and the sorts of jobs the adults, at least, will have once we arrive in Jewel.

Finally, Fianna, the same woman who gave us our initial Orientation briefing, comes forward.

"Over the next two and a half weeks, you will receive initial training on your NuAgra duties along with instruction on how to behave once in Jewel. It will be particularly important to prepare for encounters with the Sovereign, her future Consort, Sean O'Gara, and the other illustrious persons living there, to include four members of the *Echtran* Council. You will practice striking the right balance between showing proper respect and maintaining the illusion that you and they are all ordinary, Earth-born humans.

"Those of you still in school will be assigned your final grade placements and given additional opportunities to role-play interacting with the Sovereign and others in classroom settings, surrounded by unsuspecting *Duchas*. With so many *Echtrans* concentrated in one small town, maintaining secrecy will be as difficult as it is imperative, but I have no doubt you will all rise admirably to the challenge. Questions?"

Dad's hand is the first in the air. "Where will we all live once we get there?"

"Housing arrangements are already being made," Fianna assures him. "Families and couples will be given priority for larger homes and apartments, which will be underwritten by the *Echtran* treasury with repayment coming from your NuAgra wages. Most singles will be given quarters at NuAgra itself until more apartment units and houses can be built in Jewel to accommodate them. You'll have an opportunity to look over your housing options and submit requests as your training proceeds."

She answers a few more questions that show how nervous some people are, now that they've been chosen. Mum, I notice, doesn't look the least bit worried. Neither does Adina—though that might be because she's so busy whispering with Jana.

Finally, Fianna dismisses us with what I consider an unnecessarily bright smile. "Be sure to get a good night's sleep so you'll be fresh for your first day of Jewel training tomorrow."

Won't that be special.

12

Rundacht

RUNDACHT (ROON-DAHCT): *extreme secrecy; classified information*

The next day we're all issued new identification and bios consistent with the story that we're moving to Jewel from another NuAgra facility in Upstate New York.

Other than memorizing our new background info, the special "Jewel training" mostly consists of stupidly obvious rules. Like—don't bow to the Sovereign or call her "Excellency" where any *Duchas* could possibly notice, don't be too cliquish with the other *Echtrans* in town, adhere to local fashions except inside the NuAgra complex... Sheesh.

Role-playing how we'll act if we run into the Sovereign or one of the O'Garas on the street is a lot more challenging, though—at least for me. I quickly realize my safest course will be to simply avoid anybody "important." Otherwise I'm bound to say or do *something* that will get me—and maybe my parents—in trouble.

Over the next week I grow more and more dejected and resentful, what with the collapse of our *caidpel* group and knowing I'll be forced to lie constantly once we reach Jewel. Then, just as we're leaving the dining hall after lunch one day, the phone in my tunic pocket vibrates.

I pull it out with a sigh, anticipating yet another message from Alan asking me to spend the evening with him. Instead, I discover a cryptic text from a number I don't recognize.

Still committed to CE's cause? #11 Alban, 9pm.

Heart pounding, I stuff the phone back in my pocket, trying not to let my sudden excitement show.

But Adina, ever-observant, asks me, "What's wrong? Did you forget something?"

"Um, no. I just noticed my tunic is stained." I cover the nonexistent spot with my hand. "Save me a seat while I go change, okay?"

Stifling a twinge of guilt for lying to my sister, I hurry to our lodging. The moment I'm safely inside, away from prying eyes, I send a message back.

Still committed. I'll be there.

To preserve my cover story, I yank off my perfectly clean tunic and replace it with the one I wore yesterday. Then, smiling for the first time in days, I head to the lecture hall.

It's harder than ever to keep my mind on the training that afternoon, or the conversations around me during dinner. Back in our quarters, Mum, Dad and Adina settle down to watch yet more *Duchas* TV. I pretend to pay attention but my mind is seething with curiosity about that text and who sent it.

When one of the silly sitcoms ends at 8:30, I stand up. "Oh, I almost forgot I, uh, promised Alan I'd go running with him tonight, if that's okay?"

Mum glances up with a smile. "Of course. It's nice that you and Adina will already have friends your age when we get to Jewel. That should make the transition easier for you both."

"Yeah, I'm sure it will." I barely know what I'm saying, I'm so eager to get to my rendezvous to find out what they want me to do.

I walk quickly toward the central area of Dun Cloch, shivering slightly in the chilly evening air despite my light jacket. After our last *caidpel* session, the permanent residents insisted the evening chill was a mere taste of what's coming, weather-wise. I had to look it up before I'd believe temperatures in Dun Cloch stay below the freezing point of water for much of the year. Brr.

Even so, I'd much rather stay here than move to Jewel. Especially since the whole center of town and all the houses are climate-controlled. Shoot, I might even lower myself to playing *chas pell* indoors during the months when it's too cold and snowy for *caidpel*.

Alban Street contains some of the biggest, fanciest houses in the compound, which strikes me as an odd place for a Populist to live. I'm early, so I find a discreet place to wait, where I mentally review the material from Crevan Erc I had on my old tablet.

At one minute till nine, I tentatively ring the bell of number eleven—not the biggest house on the street, but by no means the smallest, either. The door opens and two men I don't recognize usher me inside, then quickly close the door again.

"You weren't seen coming here, were you?" asks the taller and younger of the two.

"I...I don't think so. I tried to be careful."

"Good." He smiles now. "Thank you for coming, Miss Morain. I am Lach Lennox, former Governor of Dun Cloch, and this is Allister Adair, previously of the *Echtran* Council."

I take a quick step backward, trying to conceal my sudden panic. "Why did you—? I haven't done anything wrong, I swear! Whatever you've been told about me, I only—"

The older, stockier man holds up a hand, stopping me. "Please calm down, Kira. May I call you Kira? Governor Lennox and I haven't asked you here to accuse you of anything. In fact, we're very much hoping you can help us."

"Help you?" Still suspicious, I regard them both warily. "Help you do what? I don't know anything, if that's what you're thinking. I only ever met Crevan Erc once, on Mars, and haven't had any contact with him since leaving."

Governor Lennox puts a hand on my shoulder and I feel a strange calm flow from his touch. "Not to worry, Kira. We're not asking you to betray Crevan or his followers. Quite the reverse. Over the past year Allister and I have realized he's absolutely correct that the hereditary monarchy has outlived its usefulness. We've agreed to do our part toward a fairer, more egalitarian future for our people."

I blink in confusion. "But...you're Royals. Aren't you?"

"A mere accident of birth." Allister waves a hand dismissively. "Much like that which resulted in the elevation of a foolish teenaged girl to the role of Sovereign. Believe me, I know better than most how woefully inadequate she is to the task. At the Council's request, I attempted to instruct her in her duties once her lineage was proved, putting a very successful *Duchas* career on hold to do so. Unfortunately, she proved both disinclined and ill-equipped to learn. She then had the effrontery to blame *me* for her lack of progress, despite my personal sacrifices on her behalf."

Disgust twists Lennox's handsome face. "I also experienced both her appalling lack of judgment and her vindictiveness firsthand. It was well hushed up at the time, but the very day Faxon was overthrown, when our people most needed her as a symbol to rally around, she was persuaded to an elopement by a boy she had been cautioned to avoid. They clearly realized that with Faxon gone, she would be expected to take on more duties, making their clandestine relationship untenable."

"An elopement? Seriously?" *That* wasn't mentioned in Crevan's reading material! "And no one heard about it?"

Allister smiles grimly. "No, we on the Council went to great efforts to hush it up."

"But...she was just fifteen then!"

"And Rigel Stuart barely sixteen," Allister confirms. "Not that their youth excuses what they did. Governor Lennox and I did everything we could to mitigate the damage when they were located. We returned her safely to Jewel and brought the Stuart boy here to Dun Cloch, as he was clearly a bad influence. She repaid our efforts on her behalf by having us removed from our positions and placed under virtual house arrest."

Lennox nods. "Had our warnings been heeded, their flouting of tradition during their voyage to Mars last spring never could have happened."

"That was really stupid of her," I agree eagerly. "There was no hushing it up, either, once that kiss caught on camera was all over the feeds. My parents were worried it might be enough to keep her from getting Acclaimed. Too bad it wasn't."

"Indeed," Lennox agrees. "We had hopes that the Council might see reason after that, for it proved we'd been right all along about the Sovereign's tendency to put personal and emotional considerations above the good of our people."

"Yes, that incident should have proved beyond all doubt that she is not fit to lead, yet the people of Nuath still voted for her Acclamation." Allister sadly shakes his head.

I barely suppress a snort. "All because of a stupid power glitch. It scared enough people—including her two main contenders for leadership—that everyone was willing to overlook her obvious shortcomings just to have a Sovereign again. Like *she* had the skills to somehow fix the problem?"

That blackout rattled me, too, at the time, but not so much I'd have voted for Emileia the Upstart if I'd been old enough. Bile rises in my throat remembering how disgusted I was by the short-sightedness of the Nuathan people—including my own parents. "What is it you want me to do?"

Smiling now, Allister exchanges a quick glance with Lennox before replying. "For now, we simply needed to confirm that you share our goal of removing the Sovereign from power."

"I do," I fervently assure him. "The more I learn about her, the more I realize she's the worst person possible to lead our people. Crevan Erc—"

"Precisely." Lennox is also smiling now. "We'll contact you again before you leave Dun Cloch to fully explain your mission. Until then, we recommend you learn all you can so you will be well-equipped to play your role when the time comes. You will not, of course, mention tonight's meeting to anyone else."

I shake my head vigorously. "Of course not, sir. Not to anyone."

"Good. It appears Crevan's faith in you was well justified." Though he doesn't *quite* have Crevan Erc's overpowering charisma, the approval in his tone warms me, reassuring me that I'm doing the right thing.

Allister opens the door and looks up and down the street to make certain there are no observers, then both men bid me goodnight.

Heading back to our lodgings, my spirits are higher than they've been since leaving Nuath. Crevan Erc didn't forget about me after all! I wonder if Brady—? I quickly cut off that thought. There was never anything between us but the slightest of flirtations and now we're literally worlds apart. Time to focus on the future instead of the past.

With a renewed sense of purpose, I pay close attention in our remaining Jewel classes so I'll be better prepared for whatever mission I'm given. Our fake identities have been tweaked to show us all being brought to Jewel by NuAgra, which involves relearning a few details. I still don't like the idea of pretending to be *Duchas*, but if doing so believably will make me a more effective operative, that's what I intend to do.

I'm beyond eager to hear from Lennox and Allister again, but a full week passes before I receive another message, this time as I'm getting ready for bed.

Tomorrow night, 9pm. Same location. Don't be seen.

Of course, I immediately message them I'll be there—then I'm too excited to fall asleep until well after midnight.

The next night, I again use running as my excuse to skip another evening of American television—this time a movie set in the approximate region we'll be moving to. Adina grins over at me.

"With Alan again? Are things between you heating back up now that you're both going to Jewel?"

"Of course not. We're just friends." Though Alan still makes it obvious he'd like that to change. "I've also spent plenty of time with the Walsh twins, and with you and Jana. It's no big deal."

Escaping before I'm forced to lie, I really do go running—as far as Alban Street. Making sure it's completely deserted, I again approach the house and ring the bell. Like before, I'm whisked into the foyer and the door shut quickly behind me, but this time I'm shown into a plush living room.

"Please have a seat, Kira," Allister says. "I imagine you've been curious to know exactly what mission we have in mind for you?"

Gingerly sitting on the edge of the fanciest chair I've ever touched, I nod. "Yes sir. I am."

"As Crevan may have mentioned back in Nuath, one thing the Populist movement has lacked is someone on the inside, so to speak—someone with frequent access to the Sovereign and those around her. The information such a person can collect will help us craft our strategy to dismantle the monarchy, paving the way for a truly representative government. We are all agreed that you, Kira, are our best choice for that role."

I stare at him. "M-me?"

He and Lennox both nod.

"I…I'm honored, of course, but shouldn't someone more experienced have such an important mission? Someone older? I mean, I only just turned seventeen—"

"On the contrary," Lennox interrupts. "Once in Jewel, you'll attend the same school as the Sovereign, giving you daily opportunities to observe her in unguarded moments and to converse with those who've known her longest."

My surprise gives way to distaste. "So I…what? Have to make *friends* with her?" Ew.

"You needn't go that far," Allister assures me. "Just close enough to discover any weaknesses we can exploit, while at the same time learning how the *Echtrans* relocating to Jewel regard the Sovereign and her abilities. Not the traditional pablum they had to spout to be selected, but their true feelings. Though it might be safest to avoid *directly* speaking out against her, feel free to subtly help along any signs of discord or discontent that may arise."

"Very subtly," Lennox cautions. "First, you must gain the trust of those in a position to provide evidence we can use to discredit the Sovereign—anything with the potential to undermine her current level of support. Obviously, the more evidence you can gather, the better."

So I'll be a spy. Though I don't much like the idea of making nice with the Sovereign and her friends, I'm still pumped to be entrusted with such a vital mission.

"How will I let you know what I find out? I only have this *Duchas teachtok* now." I pull out my mobile phone.

"With this." Lennox takes my phone and hands me another, identical one. "It has quite a few, ah, *special* features added. It is shielded, allowing us to contact you without raising alerts either here or in Jewel. It's also encrypted, so you'll be able to securely send us any information you discover."

I turn it over and over in my hand. It doesn't *look* any different. "How do I—?"

Lennox calls out, "Enid, will you join us?" and a wiry-looking woman with cropped hair immediately enters the living room from the rear of the house.

"Enid has a real gift with technology," Lennox explains. "She was able to circumvent the excessive monitoring of our communications, making our virtual incarceration in Dun Cloch far more bearable."

The woman turns to me. "I was a member of the security detail that foiled the Sovereign's ill-advised elopement and brought young Stuart here to face an inquiry. Needless to say, I was exceedingly disappointed when he was allowed to escape punishment for such an egregious act, despite Governor Lennox's utmost efforts to ensure justice." She sends a fatuous smile his way.

"Will you please show Miss Morain how to use the special features you added to her phone?"

"Of course."

She helps me set up a retinal identification scan and passwords, so no one else can access the modifications. Then she spends another few minutes pointing out cool things like an aural dampening field and a holo generator.

When she's done, Allister says, "Once in Jewel, you should keep this device with you at all times. As an added safety precaution, we'd also like to implant a tracker just under your skin. Should your mission become compromised, it will allow us to extract you from Jewel more quickly."

"Oh, okay, sure." Hearing my mission could put me in danger makes it seem somehow more noble. "How will you know if I need help?"

"Touch the emergency app on your phone," Enid tells me. "That will alert us to monitor the chip remotely. If we detect an adrenalin spike, we will attempt to contact you. If you are unable to answer, a rescue party will be dispatched."

Lennox gives me an almost fatherly smile. "We would be no better than Faxon if we allowed you to risk yourself on our behalf without a contingency plan for your safety."

"Thank you." I'm touched that he cares.

Enid pulls a tiny syringe from the vest pocket of her tunic. "If you'll turn around, Miss Morain?"

I do. She pushes my hair aside and I feel a tiny prick on the back of my neck.

"There. We should run a brief test." Enid punches something into her omni's holo-display, watches it for a few seconds, then nods. "Signal strength is good, monitor readouts are within expected norms. If you will run in place for two minutes, I can calibrate the receiver to your metabolism."

Feeling a little silly, I jog on the spot until she tells me to stop.

"That will do. Thank you, Miss Morain."

Allister then sees me to the front door. "Don't risk suspicion by contacting us too frequently, but do report back with anything of interest you learn after reaching Jewel."

"Of course."

Like last time, he makes sure the street outside is deserted before wishing me good night.

Over the next week, I take advantage of every private moment to explore the spiffy new stuff on my phone. Along with the various apps I find text files similar to those Crevan Erc previously gave me, but with more examples of why our new Sovereign is such bad news for Nuath.

Reading those files convinces me further that Emileia has never been more than a puppet, a spineless figurehead swayed this way and that by the adults around her. In Nuath, her every step and word was orchestrated by others—first Quinn O'Gara, then Regent Shim. No wonder, considering her numerous lapses in judgment when she's attempted to act on her own initiative.

Some of those, like that kiss aboard the *Quintessence*, made the feeds, but now I learn about goofs that were kept from the media, like that attempted elopement when she was only fifteen. There are others, too, like starting a public brawl with a *Duchas* girl at her school right before leaving for Mars. It makes me wonder what kind of behind-the-scenes dealing was involved in allowing Rigel Stuart to accompany her.

Meanwhile, we're wrapping up the last of our coursework and finishing touches are being made to where everyone will live and what they'll do once in Jewel.

"Can I request to be put in ninth grade instead of eighth?" Adina asks over lunch the day before our grade levels will be finalized. "We're allowed to request the next grade up if we do well enough on the tests and if it's okay with our parents."

My parents exchange a concerned glance. "They don't feel that could look suspicious?" Dad asks.

Adina shakes her head. "Jana says it would be *more* suspicious for me to still be in eighth, since they let really smart *Duchas* kids skip grades sometimes, and we're pretty much all smarter than they are. Jana's going to be in ninth for sure, and the kids going to Jewel Middle School are all younger than me. Please?"

"Actually, I think that's a good idea," I offer when our parents still hesitate. "That way Adina and I will be at the same school and I can keep an eye on her. Protect her if I have to."

"Protect her?" Dad frowns. "Why should that be necessary?"

I shrug. "Even with all this training, there's still stuff we don't know about the *Duchas*—specific ones, anyway. From the Earth news I've read, bullying is way more common among the *Duchas* than they've told us in our courses."

Probably why the Sovereign didn't get in trouble for attacking that girl last spring. If she suspects how much I hate her and goes after *me*, I can defend myself. Adina, I'm not so sure about.

"I suppose so," Mum says at last. "If you do well enough on all of your tests."

"I will!" Adina beams at her. "I've been studying extra hard."

The next day, I'm offered the option of signing up for twelfth grade rather than eleventh because I'm already seventeen. I take it. Being a year ahead of the Sovereign should mean seeing less of her.

That seems a lot safer to me, mission or no mission.

13

Moill

MOILL (MAHL): *delay; postponement.*

It's early September by the time we finish our special Jewel classes. The next evening, Fianna calls another after-dinner meeting to congratulate us.

"I've looked over the results of your final evaluations and you all seem well prepared to make the transition to Jewel. You'll be traveling by charter bus in four groups of about fifty each. The first group will leave day after tomorrow, with the rest following over the next few days. Check your tablets for your departure times."

Mum immediately does so. "Oh, no, it looks as though we're in the last group. Not surprising, I suppose, as the work your father and I will be doing can't begin until a few other things are in place, but—"

"It'll be fine, Deirdra." Dad pats her hand. "They told us all the kids will start school on the same day, so our girls won't be any further behind than the others. We've waited this long. What's a few more days?"

"You're right." She relaxes into a smile. "I'm just eager to be there."

I pull out my own tablet. Alan will be on the first bus, I see, and the Walsh twins and Erin Campbell on the second. Ours won't leave for nearly a week. Jana and her family will be on our bus, to Adina's delight.

"That means we have time for some fun here before we go," Jana whispers. The two of them immediately put their heads together, no doubt plotting some last-minute mischief. I'd like to think they'll get it all out of their systems before we get to Jewel, but I'm not optimistic.

The following night, Alan walks back to the lodgings with me after dinner. "We leave super early tomorrow, but I'll see you in a few days. Try not to get bored once I'm gone, okay?"

"I'll do my best." I keep my voice light, wanting no part of some romantic goodbye. "Use your *Duchas* phone to take pictures along the way and post a report to the forum so us latecomers will know what to expect."

"Oh. Sure, okay. Well, um, goodbye for now, Kira."

"Bye, Alan. See you soon!" With a cheery wave, I go inside before he can attempt the farewell kiss I suspect he's angling for.

Five days later, it's finally our turn to leave. A few minutes before sunrise, the last forty-two Jewel-bound immigrants gather in Dun Cloch's central square to begin our two-day trip to Jewel. The driver is still loading our luggage into a big hold beneath the bus when an announcement blares over the speakers positioned around the square.

"Everyone, please retrieve your belongings and return to your quarters. We've just received word from the *Echtran* Council that all relocations have been put on hold until further notice. More information will be shared with you as we receive it. Thank you."

Startled and baffled, we all stand staring at each other for a moment before a worried babble breaks out.

"Do you think something has happened?" Mum asks. "Something...bad?"

Dad shrugs. "We won't know until they find out more. For now, I guess we may as well get our bags and head back."

Everyone else starts doing the same, though not without a fair bit of grumbling. We were already going to be the very last group. How much longer will we have to wait now?

As for myself, I have a whole separate worry—that someone, somehow, found out about my mission and *that's* why they stopped my whole group from getting on the bus. I can't imagine how, but the thought still niggles at me as we return to the lodgings I'd hoped never to see again.

By lunchtime we still haven't been given any reason for the delay and people are getting understandably antsy.

"What about the children starting school?" Jana's mother says worriedly as their family joins ours at one of the big tables. "Weren't they all supposed to be registering for their classes by the end of this week?"

"Looks like that will be pushed back, too," her husband replies, pulling out his *Duchas*-style mobile phone. "Michael Walsh texted me an hour ago saying their bus driver was told to stop just south of Chicago instead of continuing on to Jewel. They're all staying in a hotel until they hear otherwise."

That makes everyone more curious than ever but I'm mostly relieved. If other buses are being held up, too, the delay must not have anything to do with me or my mission.

"Ooh, this week's *Echtran Enquirer* is out!" Jana exclaims when we're all nearly done eating. "And whoa, check out the headline! '*Sovereign Emileia Rekindles Forbidden Romance,*'" she reads aloud.

Everyone else at the table scrambles for their own tablets. Though the *Enquirer* tends toward sensationalism and gossip, it's been our only regular source of *Echtran* and Nuathan news. Well, unless you count MARSTAR Bulletins from the *Echtran* Council, but there have only been two of those all summer.

From that headline, it sounds like this article might play right into my hands, so I don't waste any time opening it on my own tablet.

"Rigel Stuart's memory returned?" Dad glances at Mum, next to him. "I thought that was supposed to be impossible."

"It says here that Gordon Nolan doesn't think it was ever erased in the first place." Jana's mother nods at her tablet. "It was all a ploy to play on the Sovereign's sympathies—which apparently worked. The Council needs to take that young man into custody before he can cause any more damage! He has no right to toy with Sovereign Emileia's affections like that."

Mum nods her emphatic agreement. "I can't imagine why he was permitted to continue associating with her once Sean O'Gara moved to Jewel. I suppose she and the Council were grateful for the role he and his family played in protecting her from Faxon's assassins, but they were allowed far too much familiarity given the difference in their stations."

I barely suppress a snort. That sort of blind acceptance of the Royal *fine*'s superiority is the first thing the Populists—and I—want to do away with. If this new development starts to undermine confidence in the Sovereign's new government, like the reporter predicts, it will be all to the good.

"Poor Sean!" Adina says when she finishes reading the article.

"Yeah, he must feel awful!" Jana agrees. "Ooh, maybe we can help take his mind off it when we get to Jewel, you think?"

Though I can't summon any real sympathy for arrogant Royal Sean O'Gara, the girls' comments prompt another, more thoughtful look at the article. My eyes linger on the next-to-last line: "*Our sympathies, of course, are with Sean, who is again a victim of the Sovereign's poor judgment in dallying with a non-Royal."*

Hmm. If everything in this article is true, Sean should be more motivated to work against the Sovereign than anyone in Jewel. Can I maybe use that to the Populists' advantage?

That night after dinner, I discover I'm not the only one with that thought. When my special phone vibrates in my tunic pocket, I hurriedly duck into the bathroom to check it.

New developments in Jewel. Recommend you cultivate Sean O'Gara once established there. May be excellent source of information and valuable ally for our cause. Do what you must to win his confidence, then contact us for further instructions.

The idea of getting close to Sean O'Gara doesn't particularly appeal to me. Since that incident at Sheelah's, I've had more contempt for him than ever. But if that's what it will take to bring about a truly representative government, it's a sacrifice I'm willing to make.

Sean's mother, I've learned, is not just a member of the *Echtran* Council, but Allister Adair's sister. As Sean's uncle, Allister should be able to give me tips along the way to help me influence Sean, if necessary. For my bedtime reading, I call up everything I can find on Sean O'Gara.

"I can't believe they *still* won't tell us what's going on," Grady Quinlan's father complains at lunch the following day.

Because Grady's the only other Jewel High-bound student left in Dun Cloch, his parents have made a point of joining our family and Jana's for the past few meals—though Grady's too shy to say much.

"Maybe they haven't been told themselves, yet," Dad suggests.

Jana's dad snorts. *"Someone* knows. But apparently *we're* not allowed to."

The adults are still throwing out theories on what the problem might be when we all leave the dining hall. I wish I dared believe the ones that involve the Sovereign disappearing—or worse.

"C'mon, Kira, Grady, let's go see what arrived from Bailerealta for the shops this morning," Jana says. "They should be unloading everything right about now."

I suspect she and Adina really want to flirt with a couple of the younger stock boys but since I have nothing better to do, I go along to keep them out of trouble. Grady begs off, saying he'd rather read.

Once everything is off the truck, the three of us spend the rest of the afternoon browsing in Dun Cloch's two clothing stores, even though none of us have any money to spend. Our parents claim we will after they start their jobs at NuAgra, in Jewel.

I'm longingly fingering a pretty shawl the exact green of my old Ag *caidpel* team's logo when a compound-wide announcement instructs everyone to gather in the main square. Exchanging curious glances, the girls and I start moving that way.

"Maybe they finally plan to tell us what's going on," Jana suggests.

That's my guess, too. "Hope so. Come on."

The square is already full to overflowing when we get there. Before the recent launch window, Dun Cloch was already the biggest *Echtran* settlement, with over a thousand residents. Now, with so many newcomers opting to stay here permanently, its population has roughly doubled. The excited chatter of two thousand voices creates a dull roar reminiscent of what I used to hear at my matches. I scan the crowd for Mum, wondering how she's handling it.

A voice from the speakers cuts across the rumble of voices. "Everyone, please turn your attention to the surrounding vidscreens for a statement from Sovereign Emileia."

Sudden silence falls over the square, then the four huge vidscreens simultaneously show the Sovereign's face. She looks nervous.

"Hello, everyone," her voice booms across us. "What I have to tell you may sound like a history lesson at first, but please bear with me. As most of you know, Nuath was originally created well over two thousand years ago when an alien race transplanted the inhabitants of a small Irish village to a prepared habitat under the surface of Mars."

That's what they taught us in school, anyway, though I always wondered…

"Most of Nuath's earliest history has been lost in the mists of time," the Sovereign continues, "but we know that our alien abductors remained for less than a thousand years before inexplicably disappearing. They left a lot of their technology behind, though, and over the centuries Nuathans put most of it to good use. For example, by adapting alien technology for space travel nearly six hundred years ago, we discovered that our nearest neighbor, Earth, was our species' home of origin. But while we figured out many ways to use their technology, we never did figure out who those early aliens were—until now."

The silence around me becomes profound as every single person in the square holds their breath, riveted. I certainly am.

"I have recently been contacted by those aliens—they call themselves the Grentl—and have learned that they are worried about what humans, particularly Earth humans, are evolving into. They feel partly responsible for what they consider some wrong turns by our race, and now plan to undo as much of our modern progress as possible.

"By now, some of you may have heard about the satellites taking up positions around the Earth. The Grentl plan to use them to generate a massive electromagnetic pulse with the intention of disrupting all Earth communications and technology. This is expected to occur this coming Saturday at 12:47am Eastern time on Earth, or 5:47am Nuathan time. While Nuath itself should not be directly affected by this pulse, Earth is likely to experience a complete loss of power, and possibly much worse."

A frightened murmur runs through the crowd but quickly subsides as the Sovereign continues speaking. We're all hanging on her every word now.

"The *Echtran* Council and our most qualified Scientists recommend that everyone living on Earth shut down and disconnect *all* electronics before midnight Friday night. This includes car and other batteries and anything else that could be affected by an EMP. If you can, please urge your *Duchas* neighbors to do the same. A story is already being sent to *Duchas* media worldwide, warning of unusual sunspot activity and encouraging them to take exactly these precautions.

"If enough of us do this, we may weather the Grentl's assault with minimal damage or casualties. I'm sure you have a lot of questions. You can direct them to Regent Shim Stuart on Nuath and to Kyna Nuallan of the *Echtran* Council on Earth. Above all, please don't panic. We are a resilient people and I have every confidence that we'll all come through this challenge stronger than ever. Thank you, and God bless you all."

The vidscreens go dark. We all stand frozen for several tense, silent heartbeats, then everyone starts talking at once.

Cries of, "Can it be true?" and "*How* can it be true?" break out from every direction before another announcement cuts across the frightened jabber.

"Everyone, please return to your homes in an orderly fashion. We will evaluate how best to comply with the Sovereign's requests and tell you all how to prepare for what's coming. Meanwhile, please heed the Sovereign's final admonition and do not panic. We have every confidence that our Scientists can avert a large-scale catastrophe."

Slowly, dazedly, people move to obey, breaking into smaller groups to continue discussing what we just heard. Despite all the assurances, nearly everyone seems on the verge of panic. Off to my left, I hear a woman crying hysterically that she wants to go back to Nuath and somewhere behind me a man loudly declares he doesn't believe a word of it.

"The old religion was true after all!" I hear someone wail. "We ignored our gods all these centuries and now they're angry!"

"I think it's Faxon's doing!" another shouts. "His parting shot, to do away with us all."

"I told you coming here was a terrible idea!"

The frightened babble swirls around us.

Adina and Jana seem more excited at the moment than scared, to my relief. I keep them both close as we move through the crowd. Finally I see our parents up ahead and hurry the younger girls toward them.

"Thank goodness you're all safe!" Mum exclaims as soon as she sees us. She's clearly distressed, despite Dad's protective arm around her shoulders.

"Come on, Deirdra, let's get you out of this mob. We can talk once we're back in our quarters."

Jana's parents also look thoroughly shaken as they silently shepherd their daughter away from the square.

Mum and Dad don't say anything else as we make our way back to our lodgings. Meanwhile, I consider the possible ramifications of what we heard.

If what the Sovereign says is true, the entire planet could devolve into chaos over the next few days. An EMP of that magnitude will almost certainly take out all communication satellites and every active power grid on Earth. The *Duchas* are practically savages already—what will they become once the trappings of civilization are stripped away? Will even *Echtrans* be able to survive on such a world?

It crosses my mind that the complete breakdown of society might be a shortcut to the Populists' goals—but at what cost? All I can do—all any of us can do—is wait and see what happens.

"Please don't worry, Deirdra," Dad says as soon as we're back indoors. "Dun Cloch is self-sufficient, so we'll be perfectly safe here. They'll simply turn off the generators and restart them once the EMP passes."

Mum nods, sending Adina and me what she clearly intends as a bracing smile. "Yes, I'm sure we'll all be fine. It turns out to be a very good thing they kept us here, doesn't it? I hope everyone who already left for Jewel—and who moved to other cities around the country—will be all right. They must be so frightened right now! Do you think they'll hear the news in time to protect themselves?"

"The Sovereign said the *Duchas* news outlets are urging precautions as well," he reminds her. "That should give everyone plenty of time to prepare, especially given that an EMP won't *directly* harm anyone, just disrupt power and scramble circuitry."

"You're right, of course, Aidan. I just wish…we could *do* something."

That sense of helplessness is expressed repeatedly over the next two days, even as we're assured that every safety measure has been taken and all we can do now is wait.

Friday night, as the time of the predicted attack draws near, no one even considers going to bed. Everyone from the temp lodgings gathers just outside the dining hall as the minutes tick past on an old wind-up clock someone found.

"Two minutes." Dad double checks the time on a non-electronic wrist timepiece he bought specifically for this occasion.

"Maybe our Scientists figured out a way to keep it from happening," Jana's mom responds hopefully.

We all watch the sky, though there's no particular reason to think the attack, when it comes, will be visible.

"Ten forty-seven," Dad and two others with mechanical chronometers announce simultaneously.

It's time. I can hear my heart beating as I stare at the star-encrusted canopy above us.

The entire crowd gasps when a brilliant point of light abruptly appears over our heads, then spreads outward in all directions, taking on every color I've ever imagined as it advances across the sky. It's both terrifying and breathtaking—literally.

Gradually, the multi-hued cascade of light fades, until the sky looks just as it did before. I'm not the only one still holding my breath.

"Did...did it happen?" Adina finally asks, a quaver in her voice.

Dad pulls out his mobile phone and powers it on. "It must not have," he says after a moment, "or this shouldn't be working. I don't suppose—"

"Attention, everyone," an announcement blares across the compound. "Dun Cloch appears to have escaped the worst effects of the expected EMP, though we are just now restarting all systems and running tests. We'll have more information for you after we have made a full assessment, probably in the morning. Meanwhile, you can all relax."

"Well, that was anticlimactic," I mutter. So much for shaking up the status quo.

Unfortunately, Adina overhears me. "Seriously? You thought that incredible light show was anticlimactic? I've never seen anything like it! You sound like you're *disappointed* everything didn't get fried!"

"What? No! Of course not. It just...seems like we were all worried for nothing."

"And thank goodness for that!" Mum fervently exclaims. "I'm sure we'll all sleep better tonight. I certainly will. Let's go back."

But as we return to our quarters, I can't suppress a niggling suspicion that everything the Sovereign told us three days ago was a lie.

The next morning there's a notice on our tablets, repeated at breakfast, that Dun Cloch did indeed come through the events of last night unscathed. More than that, preliminary reports from around the world indicate the expected EMP never happened at all—though what exactly *did* happen is unclear.

Not until that evening do we get an explanation, when another MARSTAR bulletin from the *Echtran* Council appears on everyone's tablets. I quickly read through the brief statement confirming that the EMP never reached Earth. Our Scientists apparently used a positron beam somehow, to turn what would have been an EMP into last night's light show. The *Duchas* media are being informed it was an exceptional display of Northern Lights because of the fictitious sunspots previously mentioned.

The bulletin also gives the Sovereign some credit for "communicating" with the Grentl and making them leave. I consider it far more likely they simply left in embarrassment when their EMP fizzled—assuming they were ever in orbit at all. Either way, the so-called threat is apparently over.

Though I hear cheering from around the compound as others read the report, I suspect more strongly than ever the whole thing was fabricated. Maybe to promote unity among all the new immigrants and ensure their continued allegiance to the Sovereign? Seems like the sort of thing Royals might do.

I wonder if I'll ever know for sure.

PART II

Jewel

14

Away game

Two DAYS after being assured that the so-called crisis was supposedly averted, our bus to Jewel is finally allowed to leave, nearly a week later than originally scheduled.

All through the first long day of our trip, as we trundle through Montana and most of South Dakota, everyone keeps exclaiming about the miles—and miles—of nothing. For someone born and raised in Nuath, where you can't go a quarter of a mile without seeing buildings and people, it goes beyond freaky to downright creepy.

Early on the second day, though, I start to see more signs of civilization. More traffic, for one thing. At least by now I'm used to how fast those gravity-bound *Duchas* cars can go, which was startling at first. Signs and buildings sprout up, thicker and thicker, as we cross from Minnesota into Iowa, then Illinois.

It's full dark by the time we reach the Indiana border. An hour and a half later the driver announces we'll arrive at the NuAgra facility in ten minutes. We start gathering up our belongings. Peering past Adina out the window, at first I just see a lot more nothing, punctuated by an occasional building. Then a long metal fence looms up in the darkness and a moment later the bus pulls to a halt in front of a tall gate of the same material.

The driver speaks briefly to a guard, then the gate slides open and we continue on to a building bigger than anything I saw in Dun Cloch, not to mention Nuath.

"Everyone, please make sure you have everything you brought on board as you leave the bus," we hear over the speaker. "There will be a short briefing indoors before you're taken to your individual residences. Thank you for your patience during this long drive. I wish you all the best in your new lives here."

Mum is beside herself with excitement as people start to file off the bus. "We're here! We're actually in Jewel! I can't wait to see what our new home will look like!"

Though Dad's smile is indulgent, he looks almost as excited as Mum. Adina, who slept the last two hours, is yawning.

"Have you seen my—? Oh, there it is." She retrieves the stylus for her tablet from her seat, where she was apparently sitting on it.

Once off the bus, we're directed into the central building, then down a corridor to a huge room full of desks and chairs, like a classroom. As soon as we're all seated, a woman steps up to the podium at the front of the room.

"Welcome to Jewel, everyone. I am Breann, one of four Jewel-based members of the *Echtran* Council. You've had a long journey from Dun Cloch and I'm sure you're all tired, so I won't keep you long."

She goes on to explain that we'll have a day or two to settle in before training begins at the NuAgra facility. "Those of you with school-age children, however, will want to get them registered tomorrow so they can begin attending their *Duchas* classes the following day. Please consult the informational files you were given before leaving Dun Cloch.

"Given the lateness of the hour, the first to be taken to their new residences will be families with underage children. Please follow Rory, there, who will take you and your luggage in the van. For those few of you who will be living here at the NuAgra facility for the present, Maddy will show you to your quarters. We should have the rest of you settled within the next hour or so."

My parents, Adina and I head back outside the building. Those of us who'll be living at the Diamond View Terrace Apartments—us, Jana, Erin and their parents—are directed to the middle of three waiting vehicles. The others fill the other two vans, depending on where they're headed. The van seats aren't nearly as roomy as the ones on the bus, but this drive only lasts fifteen minutes.

"Here we are," our driver announces cheerfully. "I hear your apartments have all been recently refurbished, so you should be comfortable here."

He helps us unload our bags, then escorts us to a tiny office staffed by a woman who looks as tired as I feel.

"If you'll just sign your leases, you can fill out the rest of your paperwork tomorrow." She stifles a yawn. "NuAgra paid your deposits yesterday, so you can move right in. Here's a map of the complex." She hands each family a sheet of paper along with their keys. "Sleep well, everyone."

Our apartment is on the second floor. Because of our luggage we take the little lift—elevator, I remind myself—though I'm glad to see there are also stairs we can use. After two days on a bus, I feel as much in need of exercise as I did on the ship.

Dad fits the key into the lock. It clicks, but nothing else happens. After a moment, he tries the round metal knob just below the keyhole and the door opens.

"I'd nearly forgotten they still use doorknobs on Earth," he comments, stepping inside. "Oh, and these." He gropes along the wall just inside the door and light floods the interior.

"Cool!" Adina exclaims as we follow him into what will be our home for at least the next year or two. "I can't wait to try out all the Earth gadgets!"

"Sshh!" Dad hastily closes the door. "Remember, we need to be extremely careful if there's a chance we could be overheard by *Duchas*."

The need for absolute secrecy about our origins was drummed into us over and over, but I worry Adina—especially with Jana's influence —might blurt something out she shouldn't when completely surrounded by non-Martians. It'll be ironic if my sister accidentally gets us booted back to Dun Cloch before I can even begin my mission here.

Unabashed, she starts exploring. "Look, we have our own bathroom again, Kira. Ooh, with a real Earth toilet and a *water* sink and shower! Can I take a shower before I go to bed, Mum? Please?"

"It's awfully late," Mum begins, but Dad shrugs.

"I don't see why not. You don't have school tomorrow, except to register, which we don't have to do first thing. We can all sleep in a bit in the morning. I believe I'll take a water shower myself."

He and Mum head for their room and I follow Adina into ours. The apartment is furnished but looking around, I'm not impressed by whoever did the furnishing. Two twin beds with matching plain blue spreads, a nightstand between them under the single window, two tiny desks and a chest of drawers. All made of actual wood, which would be prohibitively expensive on Mars.

"You can have first shower if you want," Adina says, opening her larger bag. "I'm going to unpack. We have a lot more drawer space here than we did in Dun Cloch—ooh, and a closet, too!"

I do feel grubby after two days on that bus, so I pull out my night-gown and go into the bathroom—then stare around at the unfamiliar fixtures. I never did finish that chapter in the reading we were given back on Mars, but I figure if the *Duchas* use this stuff, it can't possibly be too complicated.

In place of the usual ionic cylinder, there's an oblong trough with two pipes sticking out of the wall above it, one up high and one lower. The elimination device is different, too, with water in a white bowl below the seat.

Hoping it works basically the same way, I close the bathroom door and sit down. When I'm done, it takes me a few seconds to figure out that I need to turn the silvery lever on the shiny white box behind the seat. The bowl empties with a startling whoosh, then refills. Efficient, I suppose, but a terrible waste of water.

Where a sanitizing unit would normally be, there's a sink with a pipe over it and two handles. Gingerly, I turn the handle on the left and water gushes out, quickly becoming hot. Alarmed, I turn it back off, then try the other handle. This one produces cold water. By turning them both at the same time, I manage to produce water that's comfortably warm.

The shower works similarly, though at first I can only get water from the big, lower pipe. Will I have to *sit* in water to get clean? Ew. I tug experimentally on a little knob atop the pipe and a jet of wet hits me in the back of the head. Cursing, I jump backwards to glare at the upper pipe, now raining into the trough.

Feeling stupid now, I strip and step into the trough to let the water wash over me for a minute or two. No way this is getting me as clean as an ionic shower, but I guess it's better than nothing. Disliking Earth more than ever, I turn off the water and pull a towel off the rack.

"You were in there a long time for such a short shower," Adina says when I rejoin her. She's tucking the last of her things into a drawer.

"Took me a minute to figure out the knobs and stuff," I admit sheepishly, opening my bag to put my things away, too.

Adina frowns at me in apparent confusion. "Why? They look exactly like they told us, plus you took Earth Studies."

I lift a shoulder. "Earth Studies didn't cover day-to-day stuff like that. It was more about Earth's history, geography, culture, that sort of thing. And I, um, kind of skimmed that part of the reading." Because I was still in denial about coming here at all.

Mum is already bustling around the kitchen when I make my way out of the bedroom the next morning. "I don't guess there's anything for breakfast?"

"There certainly is," she says brightly. "They were nice enough to stock the cooler, er, refrigerator with enough food for our first day or two as we've no way to get to a grocery store yet. Your father and I plan to buy an automobile today—we've been offered a ride to a market here in Jewel that sells them. Then we can drive you and Adina to the high school to register for your classes and do a bit of shopping."

Adina comes out of the bedroom still yawning. "What smells so good?"

"*Real* eggs, scrambled up with fresh vegetables," Mum happily informs her, dishing some onto a plate. "We have orange juice as well— it's apparently quite easy to come by here."

Only the upper *fines* can afford citrus anything in Nuath, those fruits are so tricky to grow hydroponically. My mood lightens slightly as Adina pours each of us a generous glassful.

I'm less cheerful three hours later, when Mum and Dad show us the "new" vehicle they just bought—a small blue contraption with noticeable scratches and dents. Our old hovercar was in better shape than this thing.

"It's, um, nice," Adina offers.

"I know it's not much," Dad says, "but it was the best we could afford from the selection available."

Mum nods, clearly delighted with it. "Tell them the best part, Aidan! Guess who sold it to us, girls? Louie Truitt!"

We both stare at her blankly.

"You know," she prompts. "The Sovereign's adoptive uncle. Not only that, while we were signing the paperwork, Mona and Brad Gilroy stopped in to invite him and his family to dinner this coming weekend. They arrived here last week and had already purchased a car from him. As soon as they left, we did the same—and he accepted! We'll be hosting the Sovereign herself for dinner next week, can you believe it? Of course, we'll need to make the apartment more presentable first. Perhaps some new curtains..."

She chatters on about other things she wants to buy—stuff we probably can't afford and the Sovereign won't even notice, she's so used to luxurious surroundings. Finally, Dad reminds her that they still need to get us registered at school, so we all climb into the little blue car.

After ten minutes driving past enormous fields of corn and not much else, we pull up in front of Jewel High, a long, single story building of yellowish stone. The only other thing within sight is a smaller, similar building across the street labeled Jewel Middle School. And more corn.

"How can anyone eat this much corn?" I comment as we get out of the car.

"A lot of it is for animal feed," Adina knowledgeably informs me. "The whole Midwest grows mostly corn—well, that and soybeans. They use it in all kinds of food products you'd never expect."

All of which I'd know if I hadn't zoned out so often in our early classes.

Once inside, we're directed to the school office, where a woman behind the counter immediately pulls out all the papers we and our parents need to sign. We're obviously not the first newcomers to register today.

"I'm sure you're both going to just love it here," the woman gushes as we fill out our schedules. "This is an excellent school, and Jewel is such a friendly town, you'll find it easy to get involved and meet people. Our sports teams have improved enormously over the past year, too."

Mum thanks her profusely but I'm doubtful. Even Adina wouldn't be challenged by the 12th grade classes I'll be taking, while her subjects cover things she learned in her third or fourth year of school back on Mars. The only ones likely to be remotely demanding are U.S. Government, for me, and World Geography, for Adina. And compared to *caidpel*, their stupid *Duchas* sports will look like kid games. Which is exactly what basketball is back in Nuath, only we call it *chas pell*.

The rest of the day is spent shopping and prettying up our new apartment. When I wonder aloud if we can really afford all we're buying, Dad waves my concern aside.

"It may be a bit of a stretch just now, but we'll be fine. They've advanced us a nice sum for the work your mother and I will be doing at NuAgra, to help us get established. In another month or two we'll be drawing good salaries there."

By bedtime even I have to admit the apartment looks better than it did last night. I'm less pleased by the notice we all receive on our tablets about a mandatory meeting at NuAgra tomorrow night.

Mum, of course, thinks that's great. "It says the Sovereign wants to personally welcome us all to Jewel. Isn't that wonderful?"

———

To my secret relief, Mum and Dad offer to drive us to school the next morning, even though we learned yesterday that a school bus will stop right in front of our apartment complex. Once we've met a few *Duchas*, I probably won't mind riding with dozens of them. But on our very first day...

"Can Jana come with us?" Adina asks. "She and her family live in Diamond View Terrace, too. She told me she'd have to take the bus today since her mum has to be at NuAgra super early, but I could tell she was a little nervous about it."

They have no objection and a short time later Dad drops all three of us off in front of the school. "Make friends and pay attention in your classes," Mum calls to us through the window.

"We will," Adina calls back.

"Speak for yourself," I mutter under my breath, but she and Jana are chatting excitedly as we go inside and don't hear me.

We're surrounded by *Duchas* students as we walk through the big central area with windows in the ceiling to let in sunlight. I try to ignore their curious stares.

"My locker and Adina's are both down here." I made a point of memorizing the map of the school last night so I wouldn't look like an idiot trying to find my way around.

Jana pulls her map out and looks at it. "Mine's the other way. See you in class, Adina." With a wave she moves off, already smiling at every boy she passes.

Heads continue to turn as my sister and I head down the right-hand corridor. I refuse to be intimidated, telling myself it's natural they're curious about all these new students showing up a month after the start of school.

"You have World History first period, right?" I say to Adina, mostly to give me an excuse not to make eye contact with anyone else.

She nods. "With Jana. We have almost all the same classes, isn't that great?"

"Um, yeah. Just don't talk in class when you're supposed to be paying attention—especially about you-know-what. Okay?"

But Adina isn't listening. She's staring down the hall ahead, her eyes widening.

Even as I follow her gaze, a familiar voice says, "Hey, welcome to Jewel. I'm Marsha Truitt, but most people call me M. And this is Rigel Stuart."

It's the Sovereign. Adina, clearly overwhelmed by the sudden meeting, starts to stammer. I elbow her before she blurts out anything she shouldn't.

"Nice to meet you," I reply automatically, grudgingly noticing the Sovereign is a little prettier up close. "And thanks. I'm Kira Morain and this is my sister, Adina."

Rigel, the boy who's caused so much trouble, says, "I hope you'll both like it here. Let us know if we can help with anything while you're still, y'know, getting used to the place."

Like I'd ask either of *them* for help? I attempt something I hope looks like a smile. "I'm sure we'll be fine, but thanks anyway."

With a hand on Adina's arm, I hurry her toward our lockers, silently cursing myself for handling the encounter so poorly.

"That was kind of rude, Kira." Adina glances worriedly over her shoulder. "Mum wants us to make friends with the, er, with her."

I shrug. "Sorry. I just…wanted to get away before you blurted anything out by accident."

Now she looks sheepish. "Yeah, maybe you're right. Next time I see her I won't be so nervous. I just wasn't expecting to see her so soon!"

"Neither was I." But that's no excuse for being caught so off-guard. Especially since I *knew* it was likely I'd see the Sovereign today. I just didn't think she'd be the very first person at Jewel High to talk to me.

15

Rejected

Sean

"D~ID~ you see any of the new kids registering yesterday?" Pete Griffin asks as we get out of his truck in the school parking lot. Everyone at school is curious about them, though not for the same reasons I am.

"Not yet. You?"

"Nope, but Matt said one of the girls is a real looker. Hard to believe we're getting eight at one time—getting *three* last year was a huge deal."

Last year—when Rigel, then Molly and I, started attending Jewel High.

"Should be interesting." I'm not sure if I'm looking forward to having so many more *Echtrans* here or dreading it. Guess I won't know till I meet them.

The warning bell for first period has already rung before I feel my first twinge of *brath*—that vibe we all feel when another Martian is nearby. A second later I see a boy with dark blond hair, younger than me, heading my way.

"Hey, you're new, aren't you?" I smile and stick out my hand. "I'm Sean, Sean O'Gara."

The boy swallows visibly, his eyes going wide. "Er...hi. Grady Quinlan." He belatedly shakes my hand. "I just met your...I mean the, um—" He glances nervously over his shoulder, where I see M's and Rigel's retreating backs.

Mindful of all the other people—*Duchas*—around, I cut him off before he says anything dumb. "Yeah, it's a friendly school. I imagine lots of people will be introducing themselves today."

Swallowing again, he nods. "I won't— I mean I'll try—"

"You'll be fine," I quickly assure him. "Just be yourself."

At his worried frown, I add, "Just try to think before you speak, okay?"

"O-okay. I will. Thanks. Um… See ya!" Still looking way more nervous than a new *Duchas* student ought to, he scampers off.

Sighing, I shake my head. M told us these kids got extra coaching before coming here. Maybe not enough?

When I reach Physics, I glance around the classroom before joining Paul Jackson at our lab table. No new *Echtrans* here yet, though yesterday the teacher said we'd be getting a couple.

"I was wondering, Sean, are you and Missy Gillespie like, a thing now?" Paul asks as I stuff my backpack under the lab table.

I shrug. "Not really. We just went out the once."

Missy was voted Homecoming Queen and I was King, so it made sense to go to the dance with her. Especially since M and Rigel got back together, taking my preferred option off the table. And because I promised M I'd try to move on. Missy is pretty for a *Duchas* girl but I don't see anything happening there.

"So…you'd be okay with it if I asked her out? Not that she'll probably—"

"Sure, go for it."

I barely notice what I'm saying because right at that moment the two new students walk in—a blond guy nearly as tall as I am and a gorgeous girl with dark auburn hair. Weirdly, they both look a little familiar. I swear the girl looks almost like— Nah, must be a coincidence. M would have mentioned it if—

"Ah, you must be Alan and Kira." The teacher confirms my startled guess. "Welcome to Jewel High. You can share that lab table if you'd like, or I can pair you each with an existing student who can help you catch up."

Nearly every guy and girl in the classroom looks suddenly hopeful until Alan says, "We'll share. Thanks."

The two of them move to an empty table near the back of the room. I try not to stare but I'm privately geeking out over Kira Morain, the big *caidpel* star, joining my Physics class. I figured she was already out of school, but up close she looks younger than on the Nuathan sports feeds —and a lot more gorgeous. I didn't know the elite coed league even *took* players less than eighteen years old! She must've been even better than I realized, to be accepted so young.

"Whoa," Paul whispers as she slides into her seat without making eye contact with anyone. "Maybe you can have Missy after all."

I stifle a snort. "Fickle, much?" I whisper back, forcing a grin. The idea of Paul asking out Kira Morain somehow bothers me more than the thought of him with Missy. Because she's *Echtran*, of course. It could risk him finding out more than he should.

Grinning back, he just shrugs.

I'm too distracted to pay much attention in class, but I'm by no means the only one. Nor, I discover when the bell rings, am I the only one eager to introduce myself. Both newcomers are surrounded before they can get to their feet.

Not surprisingly, the guys seem more interested in meeting Kira, while the girls are practically shouldering each other out of the way to say hi to Alan. I wait until people are leaving for next period before stepping forward myself.

"Hey, welcome to Jewel, both of you." I'm determined not to *only* pay attention to Kira, like most of the other guys did. "Let me know if I can, y'know, answer any questions or help out while you get used to the place."

They both clearly catch the added meaning behind my words but only Alan seems appreciative.

"Hey, thanks, man. You probably don't— Er, we'll talk later, okay?"

I nod. I still haven't placed where I've seen him before, but it sounds like he remembers me, too. Maybe one of those village visits in Nuath, when I was still accompanying M everywhere?

"Yeah, thanks," Kira echoes without enthusiasm. Then, with barely a glance at me, she gathers up her books and heads for the door.

To cover my disappointment, I turn back to Alan. "So, um, you know where you're going next?"

He pulls out a sheet of paper and glances at it. "AP Calculus. Next hallway over?"

"Yeah, I'm in there, too. I'll show you."

As we walk, we're careful to limit our conversation to things like his first impressions of Jewel—nothing anyone overhearing us would find suspicious. Unlike that younger kid I met earlier, Alan seems well-prepared, even makes offhand comments about upstate New York, where he supposedly lived before moving here.

We reach the classroom and find another newcomer already there. Lucas, a junior, seems only slightly startled when I introduce myself.

"Hey, nice to meet you. I'll have to introduce you to my brother, Liam, when we get a chance. He's all about sports. I know he'll want to talk basketball with you."

Which suddenly reminds me where I know Alan from. "Hey, did you play any, um, basketball when you were younger?"

"I did, actually." His knowing look says I'm right. "Though it's been a few years."

At least four—before my family had to flee Nuath, at the start of the previous launch window. I grin to let him know I remember now, too. "You should try out for our Jewel team next month. They always need good players. And it's fun."

"I'll, ah, think about it."

I go to my desk satisfied I'm doing my part to make the new *Echtrans* feel welcome. Grady and Alan, anyway. With luck, I'll get another chance with Kira Morain...as well as all the others.

Turns out Kira's also in my AP Lit class. Like in Physics, all the boys and some of the girls are eager to meet her. She again seems a little stand-offish, saying barely enough to avoid being outright rude, so at least it's not just me she doesn't want to talk to.

Maybe, as big a deal as she was back in Nuath, she's used to keeping people at a distance? Hope she can get over that. No one here knows she's a star, so they might assume she's just stuck up.

After class, I try again to talk to her.

"So, what do you think of Jewel so far?" A totally innocuous question. I want to ask about her *caidpel* career and how she feels about giving it up, but can't very well do that here.

"It's...okay." Her voice is lower than M's, but pleasant. "I haven't seen much of it yet."

"I'd be happy to show you around sometime, if you want."

She quirks an eyebrow and I immediately feel like an idiot. Back on Mars, even in Dun Cloch, people probably cornered her all the time to talk *caidpel* and gush. I don't want her to think I'm just another starstruck fan. Even if I am.

"Or not." I shrug, like I don't care either way. "Up to you."

For another long moment she just looks at me, her expression unreadable. I notice, irrelevantly, what interesting eyes she has, brown with flecks of gold, like little sparks. Never noticed that on the feeds.

She finally gives me a slight smile, though it seems to cost her an effort. "Sure. That'd be great."

Then she's gone, leaving me to wonder what she's really like under that frosty exterior. Hope I get to find out.

16

Unsportsmanlike conduct

I WALK QUICKLY toward the school cafeteria, silently cursing myself. I've nearly sabotaged my mission from the outset because I suck so badly at hiding my feelings! First the Sovereign, and now this.

Most Martian girls would be so honored the illustrious Sean O'Gara noticed them, they'd fall all over themselves. Instead, I nearly shot him down, so revolted by the idea of being shown around Jewel by His High and Mightiness, I temporarily forgot I'm supposed to cultivate him to the Populist cause.

If he follows through on his offer, it'll be a perfect opportunity— though, arrogant as he is, I doubt he will. If he does, though, I'll have to play nice. Much as I hate pretending to be something I'm not, I need to get a whole lot better at it, and fast, if I want to become an effective operative.

All eight of us newcomers get a table together at lunch, eager to share our first impressions of Jewel High, but we're immediately surrounded by curious *Duchas* students, just like in every one of my classes so far.

"Hi, everyone!" A blonde girl, a little prettier than the average *Duchas* and clearly not lacking in confidence, encompasses our table with a wide smile. "I'm Trina Squires. My fellow cheerleaders and I want to officially welcome you to Jewel High. Amber, Donna, everyone, introduce yourselves."

The other girls obediently do so, then Trina takes over again. "We're the ones to ask if you need any help finding your way around or have questions about anything at all!" Another bright smile that reminds me of Moya from the Nuathan News Network back home—like she's on camera or something.

The cheerleaders hang around for half the lunch period giving unsolicited advice on everything from the best places in Jewel to shop to which students we should get to know and which ones we should avoid. Interestingly, Trina repeatedly mentions Marsha Truitt among the latter.

"She's a total player, so you can bet she'll start chatting up you new guys. That innocent girl-next-door act she puts on works with some boys, but you all look too smart to fall for it."

Though Trina doesn't strike me as someone to trust too far, I make a mental note to have a private talk with her soon. Maybe I can make use of her antipathy toward the Sovereign.

Several students pepper us with questions about NuAgra. We're careful to only say what we've been told to, but some of them clearly aren't satisfied, especially when it comes to NuAgra's hiring plans. Not until the lunch period is nearly over do they finally leave us to our now-cold lunches.

"They seriously want us to act like these *Duchas*?" Alan whispers as soon as we're alone. "That's going to be harder than I thought."

Most of us agree, though Liam is pumped at the idea of getting involved in sports here. "Bummer that it's too late to try for the football team. There's basketball, though, then baseball and track in the spring."

Jana brings up the story in last week's *Echtran Enquirer*. "I have to admit, Rigel Stuart is awfully good looking. But my parents say he's a total traitor and ought to be locked up before he can cause any more damage."

"I figured it was just gossip, but apparently not." Erin glances over at the table where he and the Sovereign are sitting together.

"I dunno," Lucas says. "I had him—had them both—in two of my classes this morning and he seems like a nice enough guy. Whatever the real story is between him and the Sovereign, I can't believe he's a Faxon sympathizer."

Alan shakes his head. "Maybe not, but he's still way crossing the line. Look at him, sitting right next to her over there. You'd think O'Gara would have something to say about it, wouldn't you? I used to play *chas pell*, um, basketball with him when we were kids, before his family left

Nuath. He didn't seem like the type who'd just roll over without a fight."

"Yeah, poor Sean." Slanting a look at where he's sitting several tables away, Jana heaves a dramatic sigh. "Maybe one of us should console him, you think?" She, Adina and Erin all giggle together.

The bell for next period rings, startling us. Hurriedly, we gather up our trays like the *Duchas* students are doing, then drop them off before heading to our afternoon classes.

"I didn't know you and Sean O'Gara knew each other back in Nuath," I whisper to Alan as we walk together to U.S. Government. Most Jewel seniors would have taken that class already, but we were told our Orientation crash course wasn't thorough enough for a subject so important—and so unfamiliar.

"Not very well. It was years ago, when his family was still calling themselves Mulgrew and pretending to be Ags because, well, you know."

I nod. The O'Garas were the highest-ranking Royals still in Nuath by then. Faxon almost certainly would have had them executed if he'd known who they were. My parents considered Sean's parents heroes, taking such a risk so they could help the Resistance. So did I—though I never heard about Sean himself doing anything particularly heroic.

Alan and I have U.S. Government next. So do Sean, his sister, the Sovereign and Rigel Stuart. That makes the class almost a quarter *Echtran*, which strikes me as mildly hilarious, given the subject.

The others have apparently spent the past few weeks working on some assignment they have to turn in tomorrow. Since it's obviously too late for Alan and me to start it now, the teacher suggests we sit near the back and read our textbooks while the others break into pairs to finish up their projects.

Alan and I wait till the others start talking together before beginning a conversation the *Duchas*, with their lame hearing, won't even notice.

"Huh, check it out," Alan breathes to me as soon as the volume in the room is sufficient to mask his words. "Stuart and Sean are partners. Weird."

"The teacher said the projects were assigned almost a month ago, so they must have teamed up before Rigel got his memory back. Before he and the Sov—um, M—got back together." Even using a sub-whisper, I need to get out of the habit of referring to her as "the Sovereign" in school.

"Must have. Gotta be awkward now, though."

With my mission in mind, I keep a surreptitious eye on the two boys after that. They don't quite act like best buddies, but if Sean hates Rigel as much as I'd expect, he hides it awfully well. Which means if he's acting, he's a lot better at it than I am—though that's not saying much.

My next class is Economics, which seemed like a good idea since that sort of thing is so different here than in Nuath, or even Dun Cloch. Plus it's required.

The Sovereign happens to be in this class, too. So is Trina, that cheerleader from lunch. She grabs my arm the moment she sees me.

"Hey, Carrie!" Trina leads me to the far side of the room—away from the Sovereign, which is fine with me.

"Um, Kira," I correct her.

"Oh, right, Kira, sorry! You remember Amber, don't you? And Donna? How is your first day going? Move over one, Donna, so Kira can sit here."

The dark-haired girl obediently goes to a different desk. Does everyone at this school let Trina order them around? Is she, like, the head teen *Duchas*?

"So, Kira," she says to me in a slightly lower voice, "tell me about Alan." No trouble remembering *his* name, I notice. "Have you known each other long?"

"A few years, I guess. Our parents worked together at NuAgra, back East."

She eyes me speculatively. "So are you two, like, a thing?"

"Alan and me? No. Definitely not a thing. Why?" Though that's obvious, given how pleased she seems by my answer.

"No reason. It's just..." Trina looks over her shoulder in the direction of the Sovereign. "If you *were*, I was going to warn you to watch out for Marsha Truitt over there. She's got a bad habit of stealing other girls' boyfriends. Who knows what they see in her, it's not like she's even pretty. She must be really easy, is all I can figure."

She snickers and her adherents Amber and Donna join in. I almost do, too, I so enjoy hearing her bad-mouth the Sovereign—something *nobody* in "my" world would do. But with her Martian hearing, I'm sure the subject of Trina's spite can hear everything we're saying perfectly well.

Sure, most people who know me—including Alan and my own family—also know my opinion of the Sovereign. But I'd be stupid to antagonize her so soon after getting here. Especially since I'm supposed to win her trust. Or at least that of her friends.

"Anyway, I hope you'll consider going out for cheerleading. It'll be a perfect opportunity to get to know the people who really matter in this school."

"I'll, um...try," I say noncommittally as the teacher calls for quiet.

The lesson is even more simplistic than I feared, so I spend most of the class concocting ways I might turn Trina's animosity against the Sovereign to my advantage.

"What do you have next?" Trina asks when the bell rings forty-five minutes later.

"Work study."

"Huh?"

I explain that Alan and I and the Walsh twins will be spending three afternoons a week at NuAgra, learning various jobs there. "Kind of an apprenticeship—and we get school credit for it."

"Oh, interesting. But since it's not *every* day, you should totally stop by cheerleading practice after school on one of your off-days and try out. I think you'd be a great addition to the squad."

Mindful that Trina might be useful, I don't refuse—though yelling cheers from the sidelines during sporting events sounds lame. "Thanks. Maybe I will."

"Cool! Hey, do you think I can come out to NuAgra sometime, too? You or Alan could show me around. I'll bet it's fascinating."

"I'll, ah, ask about that." Of course the answer will be no, since no *Duchas* are allowed inside the NuAgra campus. Too big a risk they'll see or hear something they shouldn't.

The Sovereign smiles at me as I pass her and I give her my friendliest smile in return, trying to make up, at least a little, for the way I acted toward her earlier today. She looks like she's about to say something to me, but then glances over my shoulder at Trina and apparently changes her mind.

Huh. Looks like even the Sovereign is afraid to cross Trina. Interesting.

I stop by the front office to sign myself out, as I was told to do, then go outside where Liam, Lucas and Alan are already waiting. A moment later a maroon minivan pulls up.

"Hop in."

To my surprise, the driver is Quinn O'Gara, Sean's father—the man who escorted the Sovereign all over Nuath when she was trying to get Acclaimed, then afterward, during her campaign to convince people to emigrate. Now he's been demoted to chauffeur duty?

"They haven't lined up your regular ride yet," he explains once we're all in the van, "so I offered to fill in until they do. How was your first day of school?"

He chats pleasantly all the way out to NuAgra. Not at all like I'd expect a high-ranking Royal to act toward non-Royals, especially minors. Maybe those in charge hope if they make us comfortable enough, we'll be less likely to slip up around the *Duchas*? He must have *some* motive for being so...nice.

NuAgra looks even bigger in daylight. That first night I only noticed the main, central building but there are three others at least as large set further back from the road. A huge area is fenced off for the research fields, something else I couldn't see last night.

If they plan to use the complex for both agricultural research and as the eventual headquarters for *Echtran* government, I guess it would have to be large, but it's still a little overwhelming.

After the guard at the gate waves us through, Quinn parks in the big lot and escorts us to the main entrance. We all scan in our handprints and the doors open to the big, softly lit reception area I saw last night.

"Do you all know where you're supposed to go?" Quinn asks us. "Agricultural research is straight back and the Engineering offices are in the building to our left, which you can reach through that corridor." He points it out to the Walsh twins. "Your parents will take you home at the end of their shifts. I hope you'll find your time here educational."

"Thank you, Qu—er, Mr. O'Gara." I belatedly remember they use last names a lot more on Earth than in Nuath, especially for adults and people in authority. The others echo my thanks, spared by my example from making slips of their own.

"Quinn is fine here, but it's safest to stick to the local custom around the townsfolk. I'll see you all at tonight's meeting, if not before." With a farewell smile, he exits the complex.

Liam and Lucas head to Engineering and Alan and I walk down the central corridor. The Agricultural Research area takes up the entire back half of the main building, then extends well behind it into a collection of greenhouses, the fourth big building, and the fields beyond. I'm still gazing around in awe when my mum hurries up.

"Kira! You're here, good. How was your first day of school?"

"Fine," I say automatically, just like I have the other dozen or more times I've been asked that question today. "What are we supposed to be doing?"

She describes her current project, which involves genetically improving various types of leafy green vegetables—spinach, arugula and kale, mostly. "Your father has been assigned to root vegetables, in greenhouse six. Alan, I believe your parents are both in greenhouse two, working with fruits."

Alan goes off to join them and I start examining Mum's subjects, reading labels and synopses of what genetic modifications have been tried so far. Soon I'm absorbed in sorting butter lettuce seeds for the next round of testing.

Almost before I know it, a chime signals the end of the work day. Checking my phone, I'm startled to see I've been here two hours. Dad joins us from greenhouse six and we all walk through the enormous building to the parking lot.

"Did Adina take the bus back to our apartment?" I forgot to ask earlier.

"No, Jana's mother gave them a ride," Dad replies. "She works an earlier shift than we do, so she'll be home in the afternoons to keep an eye on the girls. I can drive you to school again tomorrow, if you'd like, though after that you should take the bus."

I nod absently, wondering if it's worth reporting back to Allister and Lennox that I've now met all the other *Echtrans* in school. Probably not, since I haven't learned anything yet.

"We'd best get dinner started right away," Mum says when we get home. "The meeting begins at eight o'clock and I'd like to be there early."

My sister and I compare notes about our first day of school while helping Mum put together a tuna casserole and salads.

"Everyone was so *nice*," Adina keeps saying. "The Sovereign wasn't kidding that it's a friendly town and school."

"M," I remind her. "That's what she told us to call her. If we get in the habit of that even when it's just us, we'll be less likely to slip up at school." The nickname also makes her seem less intimidating…not that *I'm* intimidated, of course.

Mum turns a curious and slightly alarmed look our way. "M? Is that really what people call her at school?"

"They told us that in Dun Cloch, Mum, remember?"

She looks slightly confused for a moment, then nods. "Oh, yes, of course. It just sounds so…disrespectful."

Dad looks up from his tablet. "I doubt she finds it disrespectful, as it's the name she grew up with. It's all part of maintaining secrecy, Deirdra."

"You're right, Aidan, of course. Ah, there's the timer for the casserole. Let's eat."

A little over an hour later, we're in the same huge lecture hall at NuAgra where we were first welcomed last night. It's still mostly empty, since we're among the first to arrive.

"Let's sit right up front," Mum suggests eagerly. "We'll be able to see and hear better there."

We follow her down the central aisle to discover the first row has a cord stretched across the seats. Reserved for the so-called important people, I assume. Undeterred, Mum ushers us into the second row, right behind them.

Over the next fifteen minutes the big room slowly fills, mostly from the front. Apparently Mum isn't the only one who wants to sit as close to the Sovereign as possible. Right at eight o'clock she enters through a door at the front of the room, accompanied by the whole O'Gara family.

Sean, Molly and their mother move to sit in the front row, where the cord is hastily removed for them. Sean flashes me a smile and I make myself smile back, startled to realize he's at least as handsome as Alan. He sits directly in front of me.

"Good first day?" he whispers over his shoulder.

Mum's eyes go wide at what she undoubtedly considers a huge honor, but I ignore her. "Fine," I whisper back.

Just then, a sort of tremor seems to run through the assembled crowd. Heads turn and a low, indignant murmur breaks out as Rigel Stuart and two people I assume are his parents walk down the center aisle and take the remaining seats in the front row.

I don't get it. If he and the…M…are really back together, why did she come here with the O'Garas instead? Politics? It seems hypocritical, even underhanded, for her to spend all her time with Rigel at school, then barely acknowledge him here. For the first time, I feel a faint stirring of sympathy for Sean, having to go along with all this for appearance's sake.

Sean's father introduces the Sovereign—*he* doesn't call her M, I notice—and she takes his place at the podium. Cheers break out, and chants of "Long live Sovereign Emileia," in Martian. I guess here at NuAgra we're supposed to observe all the forms? The inconsistency irritates me.

After a moment the Sovereign begins what's clearly a prepared speech, thanking us for coming, saluting our courage, and talking up the town of Jewel.

"While the people here are not as sophisticated or technologically advanced as we are, they do have valuable qualities of their own that I hope you will learn to appreciate as you get to know them better," she says at one point. From what I've seen so far, I'm skeptical.

She goes on to remind us—again—how important secrecy is. We're also admonished to be extra friendly to the locals, so they don't start resenting us. To dumb ourselves down, in other words. After warning those of us attending Jewel High that the school newspaper plans to interview each of us over the next week or so, she continues in a slightly different vein.

"As you settle in, please feel free to reach out to the O'Garas, the Stuarts, our local *Echtran* Council members, or to me through them, with any questions or issues you might have. However, I must ask that you *not* approach me by way of my adoptive aunt or uncle or any of my non-*Echtran* friends. While I appreciate the thought behind them, surely you must understand that gifts and dinner invitations extended to my uncle at work are completely inappropriate and cannot be accepted."

Next to me, Mum goes scarlet and she and Dad exchange a guilty glance—which pisses me off. How dare this girl embarrass my parents like that when they were just trying to be nice?

She finishes her speech, then invites the O'Garas and Stuarts to join her up front to help answer questions from the audience. Hands go up and people start asking stuff—mostly about Rigel Stuart—but I don't pay much attention. I'm still seething over the way she singled out my parents. Mum is practically her biggest fan, and this is how she repays her?

The question and answer period goes on past nine o'clock, even though almost every question is about something we were already told before we got here. Apparently these people paid even less attention than I did to our special Jewel classes in Dun Cloch.

Finally, Mr. O'Gara calls a halt. "I believe that will do for tonight, as it's either a work night or a school night for most of us. Further questions can be directed to me or to any other *Echtrans* who have resided in Jewel for a while."

The Sovereign thanks everyone again and closes the meeting. The second people start to stand up, Mum and Dad startle me by making a beeline for the Sovereign. So do a lot of other people but because we're right down front, my parents get to her first. Right fists over their hearts, they both bow—more deeply than necessary, in my opinion.

"Excellency, please allow us to apologize!" Mum says as she straightens up. "You were right, of course, that inviting you to dinner through your uncle was inappropriate. But when Mona and Brad came up while we—"

Then she stops, going bright red again. "Oh! I'm so sorry, Excellency! I should have introduced myself at once. I'm Deirdra Morain and this is my husband, Aidan. And these—"

She turns toward Adina and me but no way I'm going up there. Adina takes a step forward but I put a hand on her arm to stop her. I don't want my sister bowing and scraping like that, either.

The Sovereign looks more amused than upset. That only pisses me off more, after the way she made my parents squirm. She says something condescending about remembering Mum from Dun Cloch, and basically admits she shouldn't have made such a big deal about a simple dinner invitation. Sure, *now* she says that!

Even so, Dad starts apologizing, too, until Quinn O'Gara insists he doesn't need to worry, that they're still working out all the rules. Yeah, it would have been nice if the Sovereign had said that upfront, before humiliating anyone.

My parents thank them like they've been pardoned from a capital crime and back away with more exaggerated bowing.

"So gracious of her," Mum says as they rejoin Adina and me. "I don't know what we were thinking!"

I try to hurry them all toward the exit, eager to get out of here. The moment we're back outside, I give vent to my feelings.

"How dare she *scold* you in front of everyone like that, when you've done nothing but support her!" I fume. "She had no right—"

"Hush, Kira," Mum says, more forcefully than I expect. "She had every right. She's the Sovereign and she's quite correct that it was wrong of us to take advantage of a chance business acquaintance with her uncle that way. Her adoptive guardians may not even know who she is—I read not long ago that they didn't. Really, what we did was inexcusable, under the circumstances."

But I'm not buying it. "You were just being friendly! Since when is that a crime? Her speech tonight was all about making friends with the locals, then she slaps you down for trying to do just that."

"No," Dad insists. "This was rather different. Don't argue with your mother," he says when I open my mouth to continue my rant. "And don't you dare repeat any of what you just said to the Sovereign, if you see her at school. You may not agree with everything she's done, but I won't have you prejudicing her against our family further."

"Then you think she's—?" Mum begins anxiously

Dad quickly soothes her. "No. She didn't seem at all angry. But we do need to be more cautious and think before we act. You girls, too."

Biting back the retort I want to make, I look away and spot Sean O'Gara crossing the parking lot with his parents—and watching me. He catches my eye and smiles again. Again I notice, irrelevantly, how good looking he is.

But this time I don't smile back.

17

Rebound

Sean

I'm not particularly surprised when Kira doesn't return my smile as we're leaving NuAgra. What her parents did was seriously uncool, from what I overheard between them and M, so she's probably embarrassed. Tomorrow at school I'll make sure to let Kira know nobody blames *her* for it.

I turn back to my parents as we cross the parking lot, ignoring M and Rigel up ahead. Holding hands. "So, Mum, how come you didn't mention one of the new *Echtran* students is Kira Morain?"

"What? Why?" My mother sounds genuinely baffled.

"Oh, I guess you wouldn't know, since you don't follow *caidpel*, but she was kind of a big deal in Nuath, a star player on the Ag team," I explain. "Made the winning shot that got them into the playoffs this year."

Molly glances at me in surprise. "Oh, is she the one you were talking about, when you were all upset she was leaving the team to come to Earth?"

"I didn't make the connection either," Dad says. "I suppose that means you'll have something to talk with her about at school, eh? You probably know the game nearly as well as she does."

I shrug. "I wouldn't say that. Besides, it's not like I can bring up *caidpel* when any *Duchas* are around. But yeah, I hope I'll get a chance to talk to her." Tomorrow, if possible. And not just about *caidpel*.

M rejoins us then and I let the topic drop.

I take the bus the next morning instead of riding with Pete, since Molly mentioned Kira might be on it...but she's not. I wait till M is talking with her friends Bri and Deb to comment about it to Molly.

"Her dad probably drove her and her sister to school again," she says with a shrug. "She didn't actually *say* she'd be on the bus today, just that she lives at Diamond View Terrace, which is one of our stops."

My disappointment only lasts until we reach the school, where I see her, her sister, and another girl getting out of a car at the curb at almost the same moment I get off the bus. I angle their way but wait until the two younger girls stop to talk to some other freshmen to catch up with Kira.

"Hey. Ready for day two?"

Her initial frown quickly resolves into a smile, though, like yesterday, I get the feeling it's a little forced. "I don't have much choice, do I?"

"Guess not," I admit. "I take it coming here wasn't exactly your idea?"

"That's putting it mildly." Her smile becomes even more brittle.

No one's close enough to hear, so I say, "Yeah, the timing *was* pretty bad, right before the playoffs and all. Guess you heard the Ags lost in the second round?"

"Yeah. I heard. Not saying they'd have won if I'd been there, but—"

"Hey, Kira, hey Sean." Alan Dempsey appears out of nowhere and sort of wedges himself in between us. "Are you guys talking *caidpel*? Every time *I* bring it up, Kira shuts me down." He shoots me a slightly irritated glance.

Is that how things are? Alan and Kira?

"I didn't bring it up," she practically snaps at him. "Not exactly the safest topic here anyway, is it?"

She's right. There are enough other students around now to make any Martian references risky. We talk about last night's Physics home-work instead until we reach the classroom. Kira and Alan go to their lab table and I go to mine, wondering if I imagined that slightly smug look on Alan's face as we separated.

And wondering why I care either way. So what if they're together? It's not like I'm over M enough yet to be interested in anyone else.

Still, when I get to AP Lit—my only class before lunch that Alan isn't in—I can't resist taking advantage of the brief lull before class starts to try talking to Kira again.

"So, are you going to the game tonight?"

She blinks at me. "Game?"

"The football game," I clarify, trying not to grin at her confusion. "Almost everybody goes. You should come. I can introduce you to some of my basketball teammates."

I usually sit with them at the games, partly to avoid watching M ogling Rigel from the stands while he plays.

"I'll, um, ask my parents. Maybe I'll see you there." Again with that smile that doesn't quite reach her gold-flecked brown eyes. Like she feels obligated to be nice to me, because of who I am. Before I can think of a discreet way to say that's not necessary, she turns away to go to her desk.

Just as well. What would I have said? *Hey, you don't have to be nice to me if you don't want to.*

Sometimes being "important" sucks. Especially since I don't feel the least bit important these days.

At lunch I keep losing the thread of the conversation between Pete, Andy and a couple other basketball players, my eyes straying to the table where all the new *Echtran* students are sitting together again. I notice how often Alan talks to Kira, and the looks he sometimes gives her when she's not looking back. Clearly, whether they're a couple or not, he'd like them to be. All the more reason I should back off.

Still, I can't help hoping she comes to the game tonight...and not with Alan.

18

Sparring match

"HEY, Kira, I meant to ask you earlier," Alan says just before we separate for our work-study shifts at NuAgra that afternoon, "are you going to the football game tonight?"

I should, since it might be a chance to start winning Sean's trust, but going with Alan is likely to have the opposite effect. Despite the way I consistently discouraged him all summer, Alan persists in behaving like he has some kind of claim on me. His jealousy could screw up my mission.

"Not sure yet," I reply. Truthfully, since technically I haven't asked my parents yet. "If I do, I'll probably go with my sister and her friends, to keep them out of trouble. That Jana always seems to be looking for ways to push the limits."

He laughs. "Yeah, I remember. Maybe I'll see you there, then." I've told him to back off enough times by now that he knows better than to push.

I join Mum at her work station but don't mention tonight's game while we're still at NuAgra for fear she might say something in front of Alan about it. When we get back to our apartment that evening, Adina brings up the subject before I can.

"Jana wants to know if I can go to the football game with her tonight. Can I? Her dad says he'll drive us there and pick us up after."

Mum frowns. "He won't stay with you? I don't know, Adina. You've barely had time to—"

"I can go along and keep an eye on them," I interrupt before she worries herself into saying no. "Most of our classmates from school will be there. It'll be fine."

My mother's frown disappears. "In that case, it sounds like a good way to immerse yourselves in the local culture, as the Sovereign has advised us to do."

"Maybe we should all go," Dad suggests. "I've seen a professional football game or two on television, but—" He breaks off at the sudden tension on Mum's face. "Or, um, maybe it would be better to let just the girls go this time, so they can make friends without us hovering. We can always go to a game later in the season."

She relaxes—and so do I. Mum would definitely make a big deal out of it if she saw me sitting with Sean, as I'm hoping to. "I'm sorry, Aidan. Last night's crowd wasn't so bad, but a sporting event is likely to be so…loud."

"I know, dear. It's fine."

A little over an hour later, Adina, Jana and I climb out of Mr. Blair's sporty red car near the entrance to the football stadium.

"You don't *have* to sit with us, do you?" Jana asks as we join the crowd going through the gates.

I suspect she's worried I'll discourage them from flirting with all the *Duchas* boys. "No, but I'll still be watching, so behave yourselves, okay?"

They both nod eagerly and hurry off to find the friends they've already made at school. I watch them for a moment, marveling at how much more easily they seem to be fitting in than I am. Not that I really want to.

Once I see where they're sitting, I head along the foot of the stands myself, scanning the people already seated in ranked rows above me. Will Sean remember he suggested I come tonight? On that thought, I spot him several rows up. He sees me at the same time. With a quick word to the boy sitting next to him, he hurries down the bleachers to me.

"Hey, you looking for a place to sit? We've got room." He sounds eager—and slightly nervous. Sean O'Gara, nervous around *me*?

"Thanks. I'd rather not sit with my sister and her friends—too much giggling for my taste." I nod toward the gaggle of freshman girls in the second row.

He looks relieved, like he was afraid I'd say no. "Come on up, then."

Grinning now, he leads the way up the stands. "Have you ever watched a football game before?"

"No, I've never watched any, ah, local sports." *Duchas* sports, in other words.

The amused glint in his intensely blue eyes shows he caught my meaning. When we reach his friends, he quickly introduces me to them. They all apparently play basketball—the one Earth sport I *am* familiar with, as it's essentially the same as Nuathan *chas pell.*

"Let's sit at the end of the row," Sean quietly suggests after introductions are over. "That way I can explain the rules and stuff during the game."

Remembering how arrogant he was at Sheelah's that time, I'm a little weirded out by how nice he's being—even nicer than his father was yesterday. To hide my puzzlement, I turn my attention to the field below and the players now running onto it from the sidelines. They all wear helmets and what looks like a lot of protective padding, especially on their shoulders.

"This must be an awfully violent sport, huh?" I murmur to Sean.

He shrugs. "Not much more than *caidpel* is." He keeps his voice low, too. "But most of these players aren't quite as, um, sturdy as we are."

That surprises a laugh out of me—my first since arriving in Jewel. "Alan wants to teach the *Duchas* to play *caidpel* and put a few teams together here. Next time he mentions it, I'll remind him how breakable they are."

Sean chuckles, too, a low rumble that unaccountably makes my mouth go dry. "They definitely wouldn't be able to compete at *your* level." There's no mistaking the admiration in his eyes, though it's only because I'm good at the sport. "I went to your very last game—though of course I didn't know at the time it would be your last."

"Neither did I."

My earlier amusement abruptly evaporates at the reminder. I'm tempted to tell him how he and his friends ruined my team's celebration that night. Instead, I turn away to watch the football game, my mission firmly in mind.

As the game progresses, Sean explains the basic rules and the various positions to me in an undertone. Unlike *caidpel,* only one team at a time plays offense while the other defends. Right now the opposing team has the football, but after two more plays they haven't advanced it far enough, so have to kick—punt—it to Jewel's team.

"Rigel Stuart is the Jewel quarterback, right?" I ask as our school's offense runs onto the field. "Liam mentioned it at lunch yesterday."

"Right. The quarterback is the only one who throws the ball, normally, though Rigel also runs it a lot. He's easily the best player on the team...for obvious reasons." There's a slight edge to his tone as he mentions Rigel, but less than I'd expect.

I watch the Sovereign's Bodyguard-turned-boyfriend vault clear over two defenders to run the ball toward the opposite goalposts—a spectacular move I've never even seen on a *caidpel* pitch.

"Obvious is right," I mutter as Rigel scores. "How does that sort of thing not make the *Duchas* suspicious?"

"Yeah, that was a little over-the-top." Sean is frowning now. "He usually holds back a lot better than that."

As the game goes on, Rigel continues to turn every Jewel possession into a quick, explosive scoring drive. Judging by the comments around us, Sean's right that he doesn't usually play *this* well compared to everyone else. By halftime, Jewel is ahead 35-10. The score would be even more lopsided if Jewel's defense wasn't so weak.

"I can't believe the Sovereign came down so hard on my parents last night but is okay with her *boyfriend* being this conspicuous!" I hiss to Sean as the crowd cheers the halftime whistle. "What he's doing is *way* more inappropriate than an innocent dinner invitation!"

Sean's frowning again. "Yeah, I don't know what he's thinking. M should say something to him. I'll tell her so, if I see her. She usually sits with her friends around the fifty yard line, but she's not there right now."

"So you agree that Rigel playing like this is worse than what my parents did?"

"Yeah, but...for different reasons. If people were using her *Duchas* relatives to get to her, influence her, she had to put a stop to it. You get that, don't you?"

I shake my head, angry all over again at the injustice. "That's not what my parents were doing! They just wanted to be nice. They'd never try to gain some unfair advantage, they're not like that. I think it was lousy of her to single them out, embarrass them in front of everybody. I thought my mum was going to cry, she was so upset."

"It wasn't just them, I don't think. It sounded like—"

"She still could have told them privately. Why did she have to—?"

"Hey." Pete, one of the other basketball players, interrupts our whispered conversation. "Either of you want anything from the concession stand? Andy and me are going. Kira?" His smile looks hopeful.

"No thanks. I'm good."

Except I'm not. I'm still pissed, not only at the Sovereign but at Sean for defending her. How can he not see her for what she really is? I'm more determined than ever now to open his eyes, win him to our side. I don't get a chance for the rest of halftime, though, because his friends all want to talk to me.

"So, Kira," says the boy sitting on Sean's other side, Tom something. "Pete says you lived in New York before moving here? Is Times Square as crazy as I've heard?"

Quickly, I recall the details of my fabricated past. "We were upstate, nowhere near Manhattan. We only went into the city once that I can remember."

"Yeah?" The guy next to Tom leans forward. "Did you go to any shows there? My brother went last year, saw two musicals. He said they were awesome."

"Um, no. We didn't go to any shows."

They all bombard me with questions then, which I do my best to answer. When Pete and Andy get back with snacks, they join in. It's a relief when the second half starts and they turn their attention back to the field.

"Sorry about that," Sean says in an undertone. "We don't get new students here very often. They, uh, probably won't be the only guys hitting on you. Not that I can blame them." His half-smile reminds me of how Alan looks at me way too often. On Sean it's not quite as irritating —maybe because I haven't told *him* to back off. Because that wouldn't advance my mission.

"Doesn't look like anyone told Rigel to tone it down," I comment a moment later. He's still dominating on the field to an almost absurd degree.

"Yeah. And I still don't see M. Wonder why she's not here?" He looks slightly worried now, though whether because of Rigel or the Sovereign's absence, I'm not sure.

We watch the game in silence for several minutes, then Sean clears his throat. "I, um, was wondering if you might want to go out with me and the guys after the game? We usually get something to eat at the Lighthouse Cafe or the burger place on the way back."

I don't see much point since it's not like I'll can do any persuading with his buddies around. But...it's also important to get Sean to trust me. Like me. So he'll listen when I *do* get that chance.

"I'll, um, have to make sure my sister and her friend find their ride first, but then yeah, I guess so."

"Cool." Like when he invited me to sit with him, what looked like nervousness fades into relief.

Jewel continues to extend their lead until they're ahead by more than forty-five points, due entirely to Rigel Stuart's flagrant superiority. By the fourth quarter they're no longer stopping the clock between plays, which ends the game quickly.

The stands erupt in cheers twice as loud as at halftime. Nearly everyone surges to their feet and people start pouring onto the field to congratulate the team, especially Rigel. He barely seems to acknowledge them, though. For a long moment he stands frozen on the sidelines, his brow furrowed, then hurries over to Sean's sister Molly, who's still cheering along with the other cheerleaders.

He whispers urgently to her and her expression changes to one of shocked concern. Giving him a quick nod, she looks up into the stands, then heads directly toward us, fighting her way through the press of people still streaming toward the field.

"Mol? What's up?" Sean says as she reaches us, her expression almost panicked.

"It's..." She glances at me, then leans over to whisper in Sean's ear.

Now *he* looks alarmed. "Right. Let's get Mum and Dad." Jumping to his feet, he takes two steps, then turns back to me. "I, uh, sorry, Kira. Change of plans. See you later!"

He and Molly rush off, leaving me sitting there with my mouth half-open. What the *efrin*? An emergency, obviously. To do with the Sovereign? What else could have galvanized them like that?

"Kira, you joining us?" Pete breaks into my puzzling. "You can ride with me if you want."

"Uh, sorry, I need to find my sister." I barely glance at him before turning back to watch Sean and Molly, now speaking earnestly to their parents near the entrance. "You guys have fun."

If something's happened to the Sovereign, the Populists could— I break off that thought, a twinge of guilt assailing me. I don't *really* want M hurt—or worse. Do I?

Feeling oddly unsettled, I head down the stands to collect Adina and Jana.

When Adina and I get back to our apartment after the game, Mum seems distressed. "Did you see tonight's MARSTAR bulletin?" she asks the moment we walk through the door.

I hurriedly pull out my phone to punch in the MARSTAR code, sure it must have something to do with why the O'Garas and Rigel rushed off after the game. Instead, it's just an addendum to last week's bulletin —something about the Sovereign and Rigel Stuart using their supposed *graell* bond to help stop the Grentl.

I'm not *disappointed* it isn't bad news, but I do feel slightly let down. "The Sovereign probably made the Council send this to legitimize them getting back together—and to keep Rigel out of trouble for the way he played football tonight."

"Don't say that, Kira," Mum admonishes me. "According to this, Rigel is a true hero. We should never have believed all that gossip or listened to those terrible things people said about him."

She and Dad keep talking about how they've misjudged him, so I go to bed before I can say more than I should. Because it's beyond unfair that Rigel's being lauded as a hero after openly inviting suspicion tonight while my parents got chastised for nothing more than being hospitable.

"Hurry, girls, or you'll be late for your very first class," Mum says from the door to our bedroom, where Adina and I are both doing homework late the next morning.

I look up, confused. "Class? It's Saturday. There's no school today, is there? Don't they follow the regular five-day *Duchas* week?"

"She means our first Taekwondo class." Adina snaps her notebook shut, looking both excited and nervous. "Don't you remember? Mum told us she signed us up."

Now I do remember. "Oh, yeah. It's a martial arts thing, right?"

Mum nods eagerly. "The instructor said it's wonderful for balance, focus and exercise, as well as for self-defense. And…" Her smile widens. "I understand the Sovereign is one of his students, which will give you another chance to make friends!"

"Lovely," I mutter under my breath.

Though if something *did* happen to the Sovereign last night, maybe the Council's keeping it quiet to avoid panicking people, like they apparently did for months with the whole Grentl thing. If my guess is right, it could be just the opportunity Crevan Erc has been waiting for. Suddenly more interested in going to this class, I close my Calculus book and start getting ready.

The Taekwondo school is close enough that Adina and I walk there. Mum comes too, supposedly in case she needs to sign anything. I suspect she really hopes to see the Sovereign again, even after what happened Thursday night.

There's no sign of the Sovereign when we arrive. I'm already mentally composing the message I'll send to Dun Cloch if she doesn't show, when she walks in. Disappointment hits me, then guilt for feeling disappointed, then anger at myself for feeling guilty.

Haven't I believed for years that the greater good outweighs that of any one individual—including myself? It's how I justified the risks I took for the Resistance. Surely the one individual we'd all be better off without is *this* girl, now coming toward me with a smile.

"Hi, Kira, hi, Adina! Welcome to Jewel Taekwondo Academy. Master Parker said we might have some new students today, but he didn't say who."

"Th-thanks," is all Adina can manage, so I take over.

Stifling my disappointment, I force an answering smile. "Yeah, thanks. Our mum thought it would be good for us—teach us new skills."

Not that I expect to get much out of it. Back in my Resistance days, I studied every self-defense move I could, in case Hollydoon was overrun by Faxon's goons again. I expect this class to be pretty simplistic in comparison.

The instructor calls us to order, has us line up by rank, then introduces the new students to the rest of the class. In addition to Adina and me, Grady is here, as well as two middle-school *Echtrans*, Sarah and Jeremy.

"Because we have so many newcomers today, we'll warm up with some basic kicks. Everyone, move to the north end of the do jang and make four rows of three each."

He asks an older black-belt girl to demonstrate front kicks and roundhouse kicks for us, then has us all kick up and down the floor for a while. We then do a stepping drill that reminds me of a warmup we used to do for *caidpel*, moving forward and backward on command. I'm starting to get bored when he announces we'll move on to simple sparring.

"Those of you with pads, put them on. You new students don't have sparring gear yet, so I'll pair you with someone experienced enough not to hurt you."

The existing students lace each other into thick red-and-blue body protectors, then add shields for forearms and shins and padded helmets. At this reminder of how breakable *Duchas* are, I whisper a quick caution to the younger *Echtrans* not to kick too hard.

Master Parker pairs us all up. To my secret delight, I find myself opposite the Sovereign, the one person here I don't have to worry—much—about hurting. "*Kyun yet!*" he calls out and we all bow to our opponents.

"Don't worry, I'll go easy on you." The Sovereign—M—grins at me. "You can kick *me* as hard as you want, though, since I'm wearing pads."

You know you want to! her expression says so clearly, I almost hear the words in my head. Like she knows exactly what I think of her and is daring me to do my worst.

"Ready, *shijak!*" Master Parker calls.

As everyone springs into action, my opponent bounces lightly on her feet, watching me. Without warning, her right foot flashes out and grazes the front of my uniform, then she's bouncing again. Startled by the speed of that kick, I involuntarily skip back a few inches, then aim a kick of my own at her chest guard.

Not quick enough. She easily dances out of the way before I make contact. Though I immediately follow up, I'm still too slow—almost like I have a mental block against hurting this particular girl. Which is ridiculous.

She grins again, then spins around backward, her heel brushing my ponytail with a kick so fast I barely see it. "C'mon," she murmurs so no non-*Echtran* can hear. "You can do better than that, can't you?"

Narrowing my eyes, I give a quick nod. *Dabhal* right, I can—and I'll prove it. Forcing myself to forget who she is, I pretend she's a *caidpel* opponent who's out of line and needs taking down a peg—or one of Faxon's enforcers. I skip sideways, then lunge in with another kick, much faster this time. But just before the ball of my foot makes contact with her chest guard, she blocks it with her padded forearm, then instantly counters with another kick of her own.

It's obvious *she's* holding back—otherwise that kick would have landed me on my backside, because I'm still not dodging quickly enough. What's the matter with me? I'm the trained athlete, here! Her belt is blue, not black. She can't be *that* good, *Echtran* or not.

I redouble my efforts to connect with a kick, using every *caidpel* and self-defense move I can adapt to the situation, but when the instructor blows his whistle, I still haven't touched her.

Master Parker gives us all a minute to catch our breath, then comes over to the two of us. "That looked like quite a match you had going there. Have you practiced Taekwondo before, Kira?"

"Not Taekwondo, sir, but some other martial arts, though it's been a while."

"It shows. I'm going to loan you a set of pads. Then we'll see what you can really do."

No way I'll admit I was already giving it my all. "Thank you, sir."

I spend the next round getting geared up, though I'm sure all this clumsy padding will just slow me down. Then I'm facing the Sovereign again.

"You still want me to hold back? It is your very first class, after all." She looks amused, which ticks me off.

"Don't you dare."

This time I put everything I have into the match, determined to give as good as I get, and more. Except…I can't. And *not* because I'm holding back. No matter what I do, she's too quick for me. Now that she's not pulling her kicks, she repeatedly knocks me back, hard. More than once, it's all I can do to avoid falling down—as any *Duchas*, or even non-athlete *Echtran*, certainly would.

The whistle blows and Master Parker has us all shake hands and bow out before getting out of our pads.

"You really are good," the Sovereign whispers as she unties the laces on the back of my chest guard. "I considered letting you beat up on me, get whatever it is you have against me out of your system. But you told me not to hold back, so I didn't."

My grudging respect for her abruptly turns to irritation at her patronizing tone. "I don't need any favors from you, okay?"

I expect my rudeness to anger her, but she just looks at me for a second, then smiles. "Okay. It's pretty obvious you don't like me much. If you ever want to talk about it, I'm willing to listen."

She moves away to help one of the younger kids out of his pads and

I stare after her. Why is she being so…*nice* to me? For a moment my resolve to hasten her downfall wavers, but then I stiffen my spine.

So what if she's nice? *Nice* is hardly a qualification for an effective leader.

"That was actually kind of fun," Adina admits as we walk back to Diamond View Terrace a few minutes later. "I saw Master Parker talking to you and the Sov…er, M. What did he say?"

"He asked if I already knew Taekwondo. I couldn't very well tell him about *caidpel* or the self-defense I learned in the Resistance, so I just said I'd done some other martial arts."

"So, is the, um, M any good?"

Grudgingly, I nod. "A lot better than I expected, yeah. Better than me," I force myself to confess.

"Hey, it was just your first class." Adina echoes M's words. "Plus there's that *graell* thing she and Rigel have. Last night's MARSTAR bulletin said it helped them fend off the Grentl. Maybe the *graell* makes her stronger and faster, too, like in the fairy tales."

"You don't really believe that, do you?"

She shrugs. "There was also that report Regent Shim sent out in Nuath last week," she reminds me. "Those Scientists wouldn't have lied about those tests they supposedly did, would they?"

I shrug. "Maybe, if the Sovereign told them to. Even if they didn't, I don't see how having some kind of mental link with her former Bodyguard will make her a better leader. It'd probably just distract her from what she—" I break off at the sight of Sean O'Gara sitting on the bench in front of our apartment complex.

He spots us at the same time and gets to his feet. "Hey. I was hoping I might catch you, since I don't have your number. I, um, wanted to apologize for rushing off like that last night, especially after asking you to, er—" He glances at Adina and hesitates.

My sister is staring at him, her mouth half-open. Not until I catch her eye and raise my brows meaningfully does she stop gawking.

"Oh. I, um, I'll let Mum know we're back, okay?" With more than one glance over her shoulder, she hurries into the complex courtyard, leaving us alone.

"Will you let me make it up to you?" Sean still sounds apologetic.

"Tonight, maybe? They have live music at the Lighthouse Cafe Saturday nights."

Instead of answering, I ask, "So why *did* you rush off last night? It looked like there was some kind of emergency."

"There sort of was, but it all turned out okay. Anyway, would you like to go? A bunch of kids from school will probably be there." I get the feeling he added that part to make it sound less like he's asking me on a real date.

Only because I still have nothing of substance to send back to my co-conspirators in Dun Cloch, I reply, "Sure, I guess so. I don't have any other plans for tonight and my homework's nearly done already."

He gives me that grin that lights up his face. "Awesome. Do you want me to swing by around seven-thirty or would you rather meet there?"

"I'll, ah, meet you there, if that's okay." I definitely don't want to risk Mum going all twittery around him. "Should I, um, call you or something if I can't go for some reason?" I can't imagine why I'm feeling so awkward. Back in Nuath, guys asked me out all the time and I never got tongue-tied like this.

"Good idea, let's exchange numbers. You have your phone with you?"

Nodding, I pull it out of my pocket, glad it looks just like everyone else's despite its special features.

"What's your number? I'll text you, then you'll have mine."

I tell him and he immediately punches it into his own phone. A moment later his text pops up and I add it to my contacts. "Cool. I'll let you know if anything else comes up."

"Thanks. Well, I, um, guess I'll see you tonight." He seems a little tongue-tied himself, which makes me feel better. "Bye till then." With a grin and a wave, he saunters off.

I stare after him as he walks away, watching his easy stride and the way his shoulders—

Shaking my head, I turn away and head back to our apartment. True, part of my mission is to get Sean to like me enough to want to spend time with me, tell me things he might not tell anyone else. But I absolutely can't afford to let that liking become mutual.

19

One-on-one

Sean

THE LIGHTHOUSE CAFE is already filling up when I get there at a quarter past seven, but I still manage to snag a small table in the corner—one with only two chairs and far enough from the other tables for private conversation. Several friends of mine come in over the next ten minutes, but though I return their waves, I don't invite any of them over. It was tricky enough convincing Dad and Molly I wanted to come here instead of accompanying them to a movie without saying why. Though it'll all be for nothing if Kira doesn't show…

For at least the fifth time, I check my phone in case I missed a text or call from her. I'm putting it back in my pocket when she walks in. Framed by the doorway, her dark auburn hair catches the setting sun behind her and glows like red chocolate. It's weird how she seems to get prettier each time I see her.

Frowning slightly, she gazes around the restaurant until I stand up and wave. Her frown disappears and she moves my way—but is almost immediately intercepted by Matt Mullins and another guy from the football team. They start talking and she nods and replies, looking slightly bored. Then, with a fake-looking smile, she leaves them to continue toward me.

"Hey," I greet her. "Glad you could make it."

Her smile is slightly more genuine this time. "Hi. So it's, um, just you after all? Or are your friends coming later?"

Oops. I forgot I made it sound like it'd be a group, for fear the thought of a one-on-one would scare her off. "Uh, they might show up later."

I wait till we're both sitting down to add, "I was kind of hoping we'd have a chance to talk a little about...well, without being overheard."

"Right."

Despite the knowing glint in her eye, I'm *not* here to flirt with her. I just want to get to know her a little better.

This week's band starts tuning their guitars, providing extra cover for our conversation on top of the general buzz of voices. I'm trying to think of a way to bring up *caidpel* that won't sound like I'm gushing when she asks a question of her own.

"So, what was your emergency last night that turned out to be a false alarm?"

Caught off-guard, I blurt out, "Not a false alarm, exactly. It could have been bad if we hadn't arrived in time. But we, um, did."

"In time for what?" She leans forward, looking interested—which is distracting.

"To stop a crazy guy from hurting M and her aunt—though it's possible she'd have managed it on her own. Hard to tell."

Her eyebrows go up. "So somebody did try to hurt the Sov—er, M—last night? Why?"

"Like I said, he was crazy—though in this case he was sort of right. He apparently overheard something M's uncle said in a bar and decided there was going to be an alien invasion. Or something. Not sure what the whole story was."

"Wait, you mean this was a *Duchas*?" It comes out a little loud, so she lowers her voice. "The—M told her *Duchas* relatives the truth about us— and now they're telling everyone in Jewel? After everything they drilled into us about the importance of absolute secrecy?"

She's clearly pissed, so I hasten to explain. "Not everyone, not even close. And it was my mum and another Council member who told M's aunt. I guess she was getting suspicious after everything that happened last week. But her uncle was drinking and blabbed to some friends and this wacko guy heard him and things just...got a little out of control. Anyway, it's all good now. He didn't actually hurt anybody and shouldn't remember anything about it after that stuff Dr. Stuart gave him."

"Dr. Stuart? Is that Rigel Stuart's dad?"

"His mother—she's a Healer. His dad's Informatics, I think. He took Shim's place on the Council a couple of weeks ago."

I'm glad tonight's band is loud, since it would be nearly as bad for anybody to overhear what *we're* saying. But even if the people at the next table were *Echtran*, I doubt they'd be able to, since we're keeping our voices down.

Kira's still frowning, but more thoughtfully now. "Doesn't it bother you that she's doling out all these political favors to Rigel's family? Making his grandfather Regent, then putting his dad on the Council? Doesn't that seem a little…inappropriate to you?"

"She hasn't—I mean—" I hesitate, remembering how upset my mum was about both of those appointments. "She, um, had her reasons. It wasn't *just* because of Rigel."

"Are you sure?" Her gold-flecked eyes bore into mine and my stomach gives a tiny lurch. "Why are you defending her, after everything she's done to you? I'd think if anyone had reason to question her judgment, it's you. I mean, you not only witnessed most of her screwups, you've suffered from some of them."

I shift uncomfortably in my chair. "It's not… Okay, yeah, she's acted impulsively a few times. But she's only sixteen, and she's been under incredible pressure since finding out who she is." I don't mention that I added to that pressure, acting so jealous of Rigel for so long. Until just recently, in fact.

"A leader has to be able to handle pressure without cracking—or turning her back on someone as supportive of her as you've been," she insists. "The feeds back home showed the two of you together constantly, up until she got Acclaimed. She sure seemed willing to ignore whatever bond she claims to have with Rigel Stuart then, when it was in her best interest to do so. When power was at stake."

"She wasn't— You don't—"

But she continues inexorably. "I guess as soon as she was secure of her position, she didn't find you so useful anymore? I'm not the only one who noticed you were hardly ever with her when she started making those speeches all over Nuath. And as soon as she gets back to Jewel, all she can think about is Rigel—again. I can't imagine that doesn't hurt, Sean."

I swallow, unnerved by how accurately she's describing how I've felt —pushed aside, after putting my all into getting her Acclaimed, keeping her safe. I even helped her restore Rigel's memory, giving him bits of the truth, making friends with him...

Yeah, it hurts. Even now, when I've admitted the two of them really do need to be together and completely backed off, it still hurts.

"It's not fair at all, the way she's treated you." Her voice is softer now. Sympathetic. "You'd be surprised how many others feel that way."

"What do you mean?" But I think I know. I saw that *Echtran Enquirer* article last week that made me out to be some chump M ditched, and I noticed the pitying glances a lot of the newcomers gave me at NuAgra Thursday night. The *last* thing I want from Kira is pity.

As though she knows what I'm thinking, she says, "Personally, I think it's admirable that you've stood by her this whole time. How you put the good of our people ahead of your own personal feelings. It's something I've always tried to do myself. Guess you got that from your parents, huh? Now *they* were actual heroes during the Resistance—you should hear my mum and dad go on about them."

I seize gratefully on the change of subject. "Were your parents active in the Resistance, too?"

"Of course, though maybe not as active as I was. It was easier for me, being a minor and traveling all over Nuath for *caidpel*. And a lot less risky, since all I ever did was pass messages."

My admiration for her increases even more. "Still dangerous, though. Good for you. I wish my folks had let me do more back then."

"Are you kidding? If Faxon had discovered who you were, you'd have been toast. I'm sure your parents knew that. Me, I was just a nobody Ag."

"A nobody?" I have to laugh. "You're kidding, right? You were, like, one of the best-known *caidpel* players on the planet."

She shrugs modestly, making her chocolate-red hair bounce. During the game and post-game feeds, she always had it in a sort of knot on top of her head. Down around her shoulders, it's a lot more noticeable. And attractive.

"Not until this season, when Faxon was already out. Last season I was still new to the co-ed league. My only claim to fame then was being one of the youngest players in years to make the cut."

"Thirty-eight years," I point out. "So you were basically a phenom even then. I still can't believe your parents made you leave Nuath right when your career was taking off like that. If the Ags had won the play-offs, you might've—"

"Hey, guys." It's Paul and Andy, two of my basketball teammates from last year. "Mind if we pull up a couple chairs?"

I definitely mind. I try to convey that with a glare, but they blithely ignore me and borrow two unused chairs from nearby tables.

"We didn't get much of a chance to talk to you last night," Andy says to Kira. "And here Sean is, keeping you to himself again. You need to give us lesser mortals a chance to impress you, too."

"Lesser mortals?" She shoots me an amused but questioning glance. I give her a tiny head-shake that they don't know anything they shouldn't.

Paul confirms that by saying, "You mean he hasn't been bragging about last year's basketball season? It's because of him we went to State for the first time in like forever. But that doesn't mean the rest of us aren't worth getting to know better." He winks at her.

"Yeah," Andy agrees. "Sean may be the best player on our team, but I've got the best car. You want to come outside and see it? Maybe go for a spin?"

"Er, maybe some other time," she replies, but with a smile that makes Andy's eyes widen and Paul suck in his breath, like they've never seen anybody so gorgeous up close before. Which they probably haven't.

They hang around for another twenty minutes, trying to outdo each other with their over-the-top flirting. Kira doesn't shut them down like I half expect, considering how stand-offish she's been at school. But she doesn't flirt back, either. I keep throwing out hints that she and I want to be alone, but they refuse to take them.

"Don't you guys have an elsewhere to be?" I finally demand.

"Not really," Andy replies with a grin, but Paul elbows him.

"Okay, okay, we get it. C'mon, dude, we know when we're not wanted."

They leave with exaggerated leers, clearly hoping to embarrass me, but I'm determined not to waste this chance to talk privately with Kira. Who knows when I'll get another one?

"Sorry," I say the moment they're out of earshot. "Like I said last night—"

"You don't get many new girls. I know."

The fact she's gorgeous has something to do with it, too, but of course I don't say that. "Right. So, tell me more about what you did for the Resistance. What pulled you into it in the first place?"

"I lived in Hollydoon."

It's all she needs to say. My family was still living in Glenamuir, just a few miles away, when Hollydoon was subjected to one of the most vicious attacks Faxon's forces ever carried out against a village.

"Oh, man." Now I'm the one feeling sympathy—even pity. "So you were there when...?"

She nods, her expression suddenly bleak. "I was one of the few that fought back—and was lucky to escape with nothing worse than a broken arm. When two girls a little older than me tried to resist, the *bullochts* raped one and killed the other. They also destroyed Hollydoon's main grain silo and half the aquaponics equipment. We were short of food for months. Most people were afraid to speak out after that, but some of us —like my parents and me—joined the Resistance."

"And you never got caught?"

"*I* didn't. But about a month before Faxon was toppled, someone tipped his people off and they snatched my mum in the night. She's... still not quite the same. But hey, enough about me." She forces a brighter tone. "Tell me what it's like having such important parents, your mum on the Council, your dad one of the Sovereign's top advisors. You must get all the inside scoop practically before it happens, huh?"

Not at all what I want to talk about, but she's obviously as eager to change the subject as I was earlier.

"Not as much as you'd think. Mum makes my sister and me leave whenever there's a Council meeting—one reason I'm here tonight. Now that M's back, they have them at our house nearly every Saturday night."

"You mean there's a meeting happening there right now, tonight?"

I nod. "Molly and Dad are at a movie."

"Wait, your dad doesn't sit in on the meetings? I'd have thought—"

"He does sometimes, but he's, um, not exactly advising M these days, after— Well, she's got her reasons," I conclude evasively. No reason Kira needs to know about the role Dad played in erasing Rigel's memory back in Nuath, not when he's so sorry about it now.

She gives a little snort. "I guess M's not big on gratitude, huh? To you or your dad."

I first noticed last night that every time she mentioned M there was a definite edge to her tone. I figured it was because of M embarrassing her parents Thursday night, but now I wonder if there's more to it. She clearly thinks I should be pissed at M, too. Not hard to guess why.

"Look, I know most people think M more or less kicked me to the curb as soon as she had a chance to get back with Rigel, but it wasn't really like that. They were together before I ever got to Jewel. Neither of them knew anything about the Royal Consort tradition, so... Anyway, she and I were never as much of a couple as it looked, even if everyone thought we should be. I decided on my own to back off once I realized she'd be happier with him." It seems important for Kira to understand that part.

"Because of that bond they supposedly have?"

"Yeah. Took a while before I was willing to admit it's real, but...yeah."

For a long moment Kira just looks at me, a tiny crease between her brows. Then, abruptly, she stands up. "Look, I really should get back. I promised my parents I wouldn't be out too late. They still get worried pretty easily."

I stand up, too, and throw a twenty on the table, more than enough to cover the sodas and fries we had. "Mind if I walk with you partway? I, uh, live in that direction, too."

She quirks an eyebrow at me, then gives a little shrug. "If you want."

I can't quite call the look she gives me as we leave flirtatious, but it's the friendliest one she's given me yet. I'll take it.

20

Play-action fake

As SEAN and I leave the Lighthouse Cafe and start walking down Diamond Street, I wonder how I can get more information out of him. That bit he let drop earlier, about the Sovereign's relatives blabbing about *Echtrans* to the *Duchas,* is definitely something I can report to Allister and Lennox, but I want more.

"I still think it's cool that the *Echtran* Council meets at your house every week," I comment before we've gone a block. "Even if you don't get to listen in on the actual meetings, you must hear lots of interesting stuff from your mum. Stuff not everyone knows."

"Sometimes," he admits. "She did give Molly and me a heads-up about all you newcomers coming to Jewel—I think we found out the same night M did. And there was the whole Grentl thing last week. They actually let Mol and me be there for some of it, since we already knew— I mean—"

The way he breaks off, like he's said too much, immediately gets my antennae quivering.

"Oh, so you and your sister knew about the alien threat before that big announcement last week?" Yep, Sean *definitely* has info I want! "How long before?"

He slants a look down at me—he seems taller than ever walking next to me—and gnaws his lower lip uncertainly. "A while," he finally answers evasively. "Not this latest threat. M only found out about that a couple days before the announcement. But that the aliens were still in touch and might pose a risk to Nuath. We couldn't tell anybody, though. They swore us to secrecy, they were so afraid people would panic. Until that announcement last week, the only ones who knew were the Council and a handful of people in Nuath."

Did Allister and Lennox know? Allister used to be on the Council...

"Was the Council okay with her releasing that statement, then? Or was it something she decided to do on her own?" Seems like the kind of thing she'd do, without thinking ahead to the consequences. "Was it really worth it to freak everybody out when that whole alien attack thing fizzled anyway?"

"It didn't exactly fizzle. If M and Rigel hadn't stopped it, it would have been every bit as bad as our Scientists predicted."

I'm skeptical. "Yeah, I saw last night's MARSTAR bulletin. I figured she made the Council send it out to get people off Rigel's back."

He blinks. "Huh. That would explain why Mum was so..." he mutters almost to himself, then shakes his head. "Whether she did or not, it basically described what happened. You wouldn't believe how relieved the Council and everybody was Friday night. What M and Rigel did was totally a last-ditch effort and the Scientists admitted the odds of them succeeding or even surviving weren't good."

I mull over that for a moment and decide it's not anything Allister or Lennox will want to hear, since it casts the Sovereign in a good light. But I'm curious about what Sean almost said about his mother, like *she* didn't want that statement to go out. I need to get further past his defenses so he'll tell me more.

"I have to admit, I've never had a particularly high opinion of Royals," I confide when we're out of earshot of a group of *Duchas* heading the opposite way. "I always had the impression they're more interested in consolidating their power than the good of our people. But you seem...different. Like you really care."

As I hoped, he looks surprised and a little flattered. "I've always cared about the good of our people, more than just about anything," he assures me earnestly. "So do my parents—you know what they did for the Resistance. I won't deny there are Royals who are more into power than they should be, but I promise we're not all like that."

I give a little shrug and smile up at him, though I can't quite bring myself to flutter my eyelashes. "I'm starting to realize that. I guess it's never good to generalize."

"I think we all do until we know better." That warm smile again, the one I can't let affect me. "It probably helps that I was essentially raised as an Ag, never got treated like a Royal until we left Mars. It's why I was at your last game—I grew up supporting the Ag team like nearly everyone in Glenamuir."

Though I knew he and his parents lived in Glenamuir for years, it had never occurred to me they had to act like Ags all that time. The experience probably *did* color Sean's attitudes—though from what I saw of him after that game, he reverted to form once the danger from Faxon had passed.

"Must've been nice to go back to Nuath and not have to hide who you were anymore."

"I dunno. I was really looking forward to seeing Glenamuir again, and all my friends there, but...they acted kind of weird around me, especially at first. I guess because I was there with M, playing the whole "future Consort" role. Later, though, I got past that and started catching up with the guys I used to hang with. That was nice."

I frown up at him. "But you spent most of your time there with other Royals, didn't you? I thought—"

"For official stuff, yeah, but not socially. I never met any Royals my age while I was there."

"Then those guys you went to that game with, and to Sheelah's, those were Ags?"

He nods. "My old friends from Glenamuir, plus a couple others. You saw me at Sheelah's? We saw your team come in, but you left before I could ask you all to join us to celebrate. Wish now I'd been quicker," he adds with a grin.

"You..." I blink up at him. "We had, um, reserved that same party room, but the owner told us your group demanded it and he didn't dare tell you no. We ended up settling for the little fish and chips place next door."

Sean groans. "Oh, man, that sucks. It was Floyd—he insisted on the best room, pretending to be important because I was with them. The owner never said a word to us about your team having it reserved. He acted all honored, probably thought the whole group of us were Royals. Floyd did sort of imply that. I'm super sorry. I didn't know."

He looks so genuinely regretful I have to believe him. Yet another preconception about Sean crumbles, along with my determination not to like him.

"I guess you're forgiven, since you didn't know."

"Thanks. Uh, this is where I turn off. Unless you want me to walk you the rest of the way home?"

I'm tempted to say I do, to give me more time to worm info out of him, but I don't want to risk him reading too much into it. "No, that's okay. I…had fun tonight. Thanks."

"So did I." His smile is warmer than ever, sparking an answering warmth in my midsection that I ruthlessly squelch. "Maybe we can do something together again soon? It's…nice to talk about stuff I can't talk about with anybody else except my own family and— Anyway, it's nice."

"I, ah, I'd like that," I make myself say, fighting an instinctive urge to run—whether from Sean or my own feelings, I'm not sure. "Er, good night."

"G'night, Kira." He reaches out with one hand, like he's about to touch my arm. But then doesn't, just grins, turn away and starts walking up Opal Street.

I swallow, irresistibly reminded of Brady and those two times he touched me, touches that almost felt like kisses. Just as well Sean changed his mind just now. My feelings are confused enough as it is.

─────────

Mum and Dad are still up when I get back, though Adina's not.

"Did you have a nice time?" Mum asks the moment I walk in. "Adina said she thought Sean O'Gara might also be at the Lighthouse Cafe tonight?"

"Um, yeah, he was. We talked some. Some other kids from school were there, too." I definitely don't want Mum thinking this was a date or anything.

Because it wasn't.

"How did Sean seem?" Mum looks concerned now. "He must be having a difficult time just now, given that business with the Sovereign and Rigel Stuart—though I thought he hid the disappointment he must be feeling quite admirably at NuAgra the other night."

"I, um, got the impression there's a lot more behind Sean and the Sovereign calling it quits than was in that *Echtran Enquirer* story. He doesn't seem nearly as upset as that reporter implied. And he and Rigel seem mostly friendly at school. So maybe their breakup was mutual."

Not sure why I want to convince Mum—or myself—of that, since it'll only make my campaign to turn Sean against the Sovereign harder.

"I told you not to put too much stock in anything that reporter writes, didn't I, Deirdra?" Dad gives Mum a knowing look. "Gwendolyn Gannett is known for the sensationalistic spin she puts on things."

"I'm glad you were right in this case, Aidan. I hated to think of Sean being hurt, especially now that it appears the Sovereign really has formed a *graell* bond with Rigel Stuart."

I'm not quite ready to believe that part, though. If I get another chance to talk privately with Sean, I'll ask why he does. No way he'll back up that story if it's not true. Not stopping to analyze why I assume that, I fake a yawn.

"I'm going to get ready for bed. Do we have anything planned for tomorrow?" Sean didn't specifically mention getting together again *that* soon, but...

"I thought we'd all go to church in the morning," Mum says brightly.

"Church?" I echo suspiciously. "Why?"

Her cheeks go a little pink. "I've been told it's an excellent way to meet the local people as they tend to be particularly friendly there. The Sovereign did urge us to become involved in the community and not limit our socializing to other Martians. Anyway, you're right, it's time we all went to bed."

I nod and head to the bathroom, eager to send my first report to Dun Cloch. Careful not to wake Adina, I lock the bathroom door and pull out my phone. On the regular screen, I see I've received a text from Trina inviting me again to come to cheerleading practice on Monday. Ignoring it, I touch the fake social media icon that will unlock my phone's secret features.

An innocuous-looking window pops up until I hold the phone to my eye for the retinal scan. A moment later, an omni-like control panel appears. I click the command Enid showed me and a holographic screen and keyboard materialize in midair. Sitting down on the closed toilet lid, I start typing my report.

Have spoken with Sean O'Gara several times now and he seems to trust me. Hope to persuade him to our cause soon. Learned tonight that Sov's Duchas guardians learned truth and let others in on our secret. Nearly caused serious incident with townspeople last night. Hope to learn more next time I talk with S.O. The Echtran Council meets weekly at his house, will try to get details on that. Will report again when I have more information. -K

The weather has turned cloudy and blustery the next morning, but Mum and Dad still insist on walking to church as soon as we've all finished breakfast. I pull my light sweater more tightly around me when a particularly strong gust buffets us. It's not nearly as cold as our last few nights and early mornings in Dun Cloch, but still a lot chillier than it ever got in Nuath.

"Are we going to St. Mary's, the church up here on the corner?" Adina asks as we take the back exit from Diamond View Terrace onto Ruby Street .

"No, I thought we'd try a different one a bit further along," Mum says.

"Why? This one's closer."

Mum again turns pink—and I don't think it's the wind. "Er, I heard that a few *Echtrans* already go to the other one. They can introduce us around, make things less awkward."

That seems to satisfy Adina, but I'm suspicious now. "Which *Echtrans*?"

"Well...the O'Garas, I believe. And, er, the Truitts. Perhaps a few others."

"The Sovereign's going to think we're stalking her, Mum. First her Taekwondo school and now her church. I'd have thought after getting in trouble for inviting her family to dinner—"

"We did not get in trouble!" Mum protests. "She was very gracious about it. Of course we won't do *that* again unless, well...unless we all really do become friends."

I shake my head in disgust—though part of me hopes Sean will be there. So I can learn more to report to Dun Cloch.

We pass two more churches before Mum turns right on Emerald and we finally reach the one she's so determined on. It looks similar to the others, a large-ish, white wooden building with a steeple on the roof. We follow a few other people inside, then hesitate, looking around.

Almost immediately, Mum spots the Sovereign. "Look," she whispers to Dad. "There she is. I...I suppose we shouldn't try to sit *too* close?"

In answer, he guides us all to one of the long benches near the back, several rows behind the one where the Sovereign and a man I assume is her adopted uncle are sitting with Sean and Molly O'Gara and their father. Embarrassed, I now hope Sean won't think I'm stalking *him*.

I learned about the major Earth religions in Earth Studies last year so there are no big surprises during the service—except when everyone stands up and sings, using the songbooks, or "hymnals," tucked into wooden pockets in front of us.

"This is lovely," Mum whispers after the first song. "Rather like our own Group Sings. I'm so glad we came!"

Even I feel a twinge of nostalgia for the closest thing to religion most Nuathans practice. Of course, the *Duchas* aren't capable of music as beautiful as the vocal polyphonics we're taught from childhood, but they're better than I expected—especially those facing us up front, leading the singing. Those include Sean's mother and the Sovereign's adopted aunt I realize, when they join the others after the singing finishes.

By the end of the service I'm in a surprisingly good mood, considering I didn't want to be here at all. Even so, I'm eager to leave. Mum, however, is happily responding to greetings and introductions from the people around us, making it impossible for me to escape before Sean, starting down the central aisle with his parents, spots me.

His face immediately lights up and he quickens his pace. "Hey," he says as he reaches our row. "If I'd known you planned to come here today, I'd have invited you to sit with us." Then he turns to my parents. "Mr. and Mrs. Morain, right? I'm Sean O'Gara."

As if they didn't already know that. Mum doesn't manage more than a muttered, "How nice."

Dad, I'm relieved to see, is perfectly equal to the situation. "I understand you and Kira have a few classes together at school?"

Sean nods. "Physics, Lit and Government. I doubt she'll have any trouble catching up."

As we finally move toward the exit, he introduces his family to mine. The Sovereign, meanwhile, is hanging back to talk with Rigel and his parents near the front of the church.

Once outside, Mr. and Mrs. O'Gara make polite small talk with my parents about their impressions of Jewel so far and Molly does the same with Adina. I stand awkwardly off to one side until Sean motions me closer.

"I was wondering if maybe you'd like to, um, shoot some hoops this afternoon?"

I stare up at him, puzzled. "Shoot some...what?"

"Sorry, I mean practice a bit of basketball. The school gym is usually empty on Sundays, so I sometimes go work on my foul shots and stuff. I thought you might enjoy...that is..."

My spirits instantly rise at the thought of doing something athletic. It seems forever since I've had any real exercise. "Is that allowed?"

"Sure. Coach gave everyone on the team the code to the outside gym door so we can keep our skills up during the off season."

"Oh, so it won't be just us?"

The twinkle in his bright blue eyes makes me realize too late I sound disappointed—and that he misinterpreted why. "Depends if I say anything to the other guys or not. Will you mind if I don't?"

"I, um, guess not." It'll mean another chance to speak privately with Sean, and sooner than I expected. Another chance to advance my mission.

"Cool. I can pick you up around three, if that works?"

I tell him that will be fine as our parents say their goodbyes. Sean and his family start walking up Emerald toward Diamond, while we head down Ruby.

By the time we get back to the apartment, I've convinced myself that the only reason I'm looking forward to this afternoon is so I can try to persuade Sean out of his foolish loyalty to the Sovereign. And the exercise, of course.

21

Incidental contact

Sean

I'M way more nervous than I should be when I ask Dad if I can borrow the car to drive to the school to shoot hoops. It's not like I haven't done it a dozen times before, though Pete usually picks me up.

"All right." He doesn't look up from whatever he's reading on his tablet. "Neither your mother or I should need it for the next few hours."

"Thanks." I take the keys from the hook by the kitchen door, wondering why I didn't mention Kira. Not that it should matter.

She's waiting just outside the Diamond View Terrace complex when I pull up a minute or two before three. I figure that's a good omen, since I more than half expected to wait—or that she'd have changed her mind about coming.

"Ready?" I ask out the passenger window.

"Ready." She gets in. Her shorts and t-shirt somehow make her look even better than the clothes she wears to school. Maybe she's more comfortable in athletic wear?

Once she's buckled in, I pull away from the curb and head toward the school. "So, how long since you played basketball? Or, um, *chas pell?*"

She chuckles—a low, delicious sound that goes right through me. "Probably not since I was ten or so. It'll be interesting to see how similar the rules are. I haven't read up on basketball yet."

"Fairly similar. According to my dad, it was an *Echtran* who introduced the game to Earth, a little over a hundred years ago. So kids would have something they could play indoors during the winter. Those kids taught it to their *Duchas* friends and it gradually caught on."

"And even adults play it here?"

"Yup. You should watch a few NBA or WNBA games—you can find them online. Those guys make serious money playing it professionally. Of course a few of the best ones are *Echtrans*."

Out of the corner of my eye, I see Kira shake her head disbelievingly, though she has to know I'm telling the truth since it's easy to check out. I've never met anyone my age who's so cynical. At least she admitted last night she might have been wrong to assume all Royals are power-hungry jerks.

By the time we reach the school, I've explained most of the rule differences between basketball and the *chas pell* she played as a kid. "College and professional ball have a few other changes, but those are the basics. You'll pick it up in no time."

"I'm sure I will." The look she gives me is amused—and slightly patronizing. I'm seized by a desire to prove to her it's no child's game I'm so good at—then remind myself I didn't bring her here so I can show off.

I park behind the gym and we get out, me with my gym bag and Kira with just a water bottle. "This way." I lead her to the locker-room door and punch the four-digit code into the mechanical lock under the knob.

She wrinkles her nose as we make our way through the boys' locker room to the gym. I don't blame her.

"Sorry about the smell. All the boys' gym classes use this locker room to change and they don't clean it as often as they should." Not that I'd really noticed before.

"I guess it's no wonder, since the *Duchas* have to rely on water for showers. I never feel quite clean after one of those, no matter how much soap I use. Give me a good old ionic sanitizer any day."

I laugh. "Yeah, I felt the same way when we first got to Bailerealta, but I got used to it before we moved to Jewel. It helps that we don't get sick as easily as they do."

As I expect, the gym is deserted. "Here." I grab a ball off the rack and hand it to her. "You'll want to get the feel of the ball before we do anything else. Go ahead and spend a little time dribbling and shooting."

We spend the next ten minutes sharing a hoop but pretending to ignore each other. I practice jump shots and layups, sneaking peeks at Kira as she does the same. For not having played in so long she's surprisingly good, though nowhere near as good as I am. I try not to feel too pleased by that.

"Ready for a little one-on-one?" I ask when she starts looking slightly bored.

"Sure, bring it on." She grins confidently, though she has to know I'm better if she was sneaking peeks like I was. Maybe she wasn't.

I put my ball back on the rack and rejoin her under the hoop. "All right. Two points for a basket, three if you shoot from outside that circle." I point at the line. "After each basket, the other person takes the ball and starts from mid-court. Let's play to twenty. You can have first possession since you're a guest."

"And a girl?" She smirks, one eyebrow raised.

Backing up to the mid-court line, she starts dribbling, pressing aggressively toward the goal. I'm a lot taller, which gives me a defensive advantage, though not as much as I expect. She's amazingly quick and, man, can she jump! Still, when she finally shoots after a few fakes, I pluck the ball out of the air before it reaches the basket and spin around for a layup before she can get in position to block me.

I toss her the ball again. "It's already coming back, isn't it? Not bad for a first try."

She doesn't reply, just backs up to mid-court, gives a quick nod and drives forward again, changing direction every time I move to block her progress. This time she comes really close to scoring, though I manage to deflect the ball just before it reaches the basket. She snags it before it bounces and starts dribbling again.

After a few feints, I dart in and steal the ball, catching her off-guard. A little hiss escapes her, but she immediately switches to defense, getting between me and the basket. Now she's getting warmed up, I can tell she's better than anyone on the Jewel boys' team—except me.

It's not easy to get past her. She's as aggressive on defense as she was on offense. As she moves to block me yet again, her hand grazes my forearm, the first time we've touched skin-to-skin. The sensation nearly makes me drop the ball—a tingle as strong as the one I get off M...or used to. It's become a lot fainter since she and Rigel re-bonded.

Kira's eyes widen slightly, the only hint she felt that little zap, too. She doesn't let it faze her, though, just takes advantage of my momentary distraction to steal the ball. Gotta get my head back in the game—which means not touching her again if I can help it. Keeping her from scoring with that handicap is tricky, but I manage it—just barely. I get the rebound and score again, but it's harder this time, even though it's obvious now she's also trying to avoid contact. Yup, she definitely felt something.

On her next possession, Kira nails a three-pointer before I can get set. The glint in her eyes shows she's enjoying herself nearly as much as I am. I take the ball to mid-court and respond with a three-pointer of my own. We mostly trade three-pointers from then on, making it way easier to avoid touching.

By the end, I'm using moves I'd never dare in front of a crowd of *Duchas* spectators, or even my teammates. So is she.

"My game, 22 - 18," I exclaim as I sink the winning goal, panting harder than I typically do after playing full-court for twice as long. "You really gave me a run for my money."

She frowns. "A run for—?"

"Sorry, just an expression. I mean you made me work for it. Well done. Let's take a break before we go again."

Together, we go sit at the foot of the bleachers.

"You know, you should go out for the girls' basketball team in a few weeks," I say, mopping my forehead with the bottom of my shirt before remembering I brought towels. "It wouldn't be the same as *caidpel*, of course, but I think you'd have fun. And you'd definitely dominate." I get two towels out my bag and hand her one.

"Like you do? And like Rigel Stuart does at football? Hardly seems fair, does it? Do you play like you were just now against the *Duchas*?"

"Nah, it'd be way too obvious—like what Rigel did Friday night. Still haven't had a chance to talk to him about that. You made me pull out all the stops, though, which was great."

My admiration apparently makes her uncomfortable because she looks away. "Guess I ought to be proud of that." Then, after a slight hesitation, "It sounded last night like you believe the Sovereign and Rigel have a real *graell* bond. How come? I've always been told it doesn't exist."

Not exactly something I want to talk about, especially after that weird touch thing earlier, but honesty forces me to admit, "I can't think what else it could be after seeing some of the stuff they can do. It's... kind of amazing."

She looks skeptical. "How can you still be such a big admirer of hers, after what she put you through? Or are all Royals required to talk her up like that?"

"Not required, no, but she *is* the Sovereign. And...I think she'll be a good one."

"Seriously?" She wrinkles her nose in distaste.

"Look, I don't get it," I blurt out. "You were in the Resistance. The whole point was to get Faxon out and the monarchy back in, right? You succeeded. So why are you so down on M now? Because she embarrassed your parents Thursday night?"

A quick shake of her head makes her ponytail bounce. "Not just that, no. Besides, the Resistance formed years before anybody even suspected she was still alive, because of all the stuff Faxon was doing. It wasn't so much about restoring the monarchy as giving power back to the people—where it belongs. Sure, when the news about Emileia broke, the Resistance used her as a rallying point. I'll totally give her credit for being a useful symbol when we needed one. But the idea of a sixteen-year-old girl actually trying to *lead* us, just because of who her grandfather was..." She trails off, probably because of the way I'm frowning.

"So...what? You think we'd be better off without a Sovereign at all?"

"Are you sure we wouldn't?" she retorts. "You said last night you decided to ignore the old Consort tradition. Maybe it's time to reconsider a few others—like the one that decrees some teenaged girl should automatically be Sovereign, no matter how inexperienced she is, just because she happened to pass a blood test."

The last thing I want to do is argue with Kira right when she was starting to soften toward me, but I can't let that go.

"If you've read your Nuathan history, you know the Sovereigns have always done well by our people. Why should that change just because this one is younger than most? Is that all you have against her —her age?"

"Not the only thing, no, but I think it's pretty important. As for the Sovereigns being so good for Nuath, that's always depended on who you happen to be, hasn't it? We've been entrenched in our archaic *fine*-based class system for so long, most people can't see past it. Maybe it's time to try something new, give *everyone* an equal voice in how things are done."

I suck in a breath. "That...sounds an awful lot like the propaganda the Anti-Royalists were putting out when M was trying to get Acclaimed."

"The Populists, you mean? I happen to think they have some good ideas. I hoped you'd be a little more open to other points of view than the average Royal, Sean, considering you grew up in Glenamuir, living like an Ag."

Her obvious disappointment bothers me a lot more than it should, considering I'm the one in the right here.

"So you're back to lumping all Royals together? That's not what you said last night."

Again, she averts her eyes. "Look, I do believe you—and your parents—want what's best for our people. But maybe you're too blinded by tradition to see what that is. Personally, I don't see how going back to the past can be the best way for our people to move forward."

"All right. I guess there can be more than one valid opinion on that. But almost everything M has wanted to do, or wanted the Council to do, *has* been for the good of our people—even if the Council doesn't always agree with her."

Her gaze snaps back to mine. "You mean…she and the *Echtran* Council don't always see eye to eye?"

I can't suppress a snort. "That's putting it mildly, from what I've overheard Mum telling Dad. Even though she's one herself, I'm not sure M trusts Royals any more than you do."

"So the Council has done things she didn't want them to do?" She's definitely giving me her full attention now. "Or is it more the other way around?"

"Both," I unwillingly admit. "I, uh, think the Council got used to calling the shots when they were the only leadership we Martians had on Earth. Early on, she still let them do that, but not anymore. Not since—"

I break off, realizing I almost said too much. That conspiracy to erase Rigel's memory isn't exactly common knowledge. And shouldn't be, if the Council wants all these new *Echtrans* to accept their leadership.

"So!" Forcing a heartiness I don't feel, I jump to my feet. "Ready to play some more basketball?"

22

Head in the game

"Sure, I'm ready for more if you are."

I'm dying to know more about whatever rift has developed between the Sovereign and the Council, but Sean clearly thinks he already said more than he should. Pushing might make him suspicious, so I drop the subject—for now.

Handing back his towel, I'm careful not to touch him. Like most girls my age, I've experienced the *taghal ardus*—that little "first touch" tingle from a guy. But the zap Sean gave me earlier was different. Stronger. Because he's Royal?

I shouldn't have to worry about a repeat, since the *taghal ardus* is only supposed to happen once. Still, it was unsettling enough I'm not willing to risk it.

Our next one-on-one game lasts longer than the first and by the end neither of us are holding back—though we both still avoid touching each other. Unfortunately, my *caidpel* skills don't translate perfectly to basketball and he's played this game a lot more than I have. Once he figures out he can block my three-pointers by jumping way higher than any *Duchas* possibly could, he beats me by a larger margin than the first time.

"I can't believe how much you've improved in just two quick games," he tells me after his winning basket. "No wonder you're such a phenom at *caidpel*." The respect in his eyes is gratifying—especially considering the hard time I gave him about his politics.

"You want to play another?" I ask as we go for more water. Working up a sweat like this feels great, even if it's not *caidpel*.

Looking genuinely regretful, he shakes his head. "Wish I could, but I should bring the van back. I said I'd only be gone a couple hours and one of my parents might need it."

"Your family only has one car?" I'm surprised. "I'd have thought such high-ranking Royals would have at least two."

"We had to leave Nuath in such a hurry, we couldn't bring much with us—not that we had a lot anyway, since we were pretending to be Ags. Whatever *sochar* my folks had before, they lost when we changed identities. My uncle helped us out some when we first got to Earth, and now Mum and Dad are making a bit from investments, but we still, um, don't have a lot of money to throw around."

Though he seems slightly embarrassed, his admission increases my respect for him. Maybe we have more in common than I thought.

"Trust me, I get it. We were only allowed one duffel apiece when we emigrated and the few Nuathan *sochar* we had weren't worth much even in Dun Cloch—and nothing at all, here."

During the drive back we chat comfortably about the things we miss most about Mars. Sean sounds nearly as homesick as I am.

"Do you think you'll ever go back?" I ask as he pulls up in front of my apartment complex.

He shrugs. "I sure hope so but...who knows? It all depends on what happens there—and here—between now and the next launch window. Mostly, I want to be wherever I can do the most good."

Again, I'm impressed in spite of myself. "Um, yeah, me too," I say, guiltily realizing I *should* have the same noble goal. "Anyway, thanks for the lesson and the games. It was a great workout."

"If you want, we can make it a regular thing, at least until basketball practice starts," he suggests as I get out of the minivan. "Maybe one night this week?"

"Maybe."

Though I enjoyed the afternoon a lot more than I expected to, I don't commit. I need to sort out my feelings, especially about that weird touch thing, before spending more time with Sean.

With that in mind, I pull out my phone before I go inside, to see if I've received any further instructions from Dun Cloch since the preliminary report I sent last night. I haven't. Maybe just as well.

"Look, Kira!" Adina exclaims the second I enter the apartment. "Isn't she adorable?"

I freeze, staring with mingled distaste and disbelief at the fluffy, wriggling white thing she's holding. "What *is* that?"

"A puppy, of course! What else? You knew I wanted to talk Mum and Dad into letting me have one. Carrie from school told me Friday she and her family were trying to find homes for the litter her dog had, now that they're old enough to leave their mother. I convinced Mum and Dad to come with me to see them while you were gone and when I begged to bring one home, they said yes!"

"Where are Mum and Dad now?"

I'm still eyeing the tiny animal suspiciously, remembering the incident with the coyote. Not that this little white fuzzball looks nearly that dangerous.

"At the store, getting food and a bed and stuff for her." Adina gazes fondly down at the thing.

Suddenly, I realize what it reminds me of. "With that curly coat, it almost looks like a miniature lamb. No wonder you wanted it."

"You're right, she does, a little." She grins up at me. "What should we name her?"

I shrug. "Your puppy. You decide."

"Aw, c'mon, Kira, don't be like that. Come pet her. She's really soft."

Reluctantly, I come forward and lean down to touch the creature. Adina's right, it's even softer than the lambs back home were. Before I can pull my hand away, the puppy turns its head and licks my hand, its tongue leaving a wet mark.

"Ew. Why did it do that?"

"She likes you. Don't act like she stinks—especially since you do right now. What have you been doing?"

"Playing basketball, like I told Mum and Dad before I left. But yeah, I'd better get a shower. Especially now." I shake the hand the dog just licked.

Adina just laughs at me as I head to the bathroom.

By the time I've showered and dressed—water showers take a *lot* longer than ionic ones—Mum and Dad are back.

"How was your outing with Sean O'Gara?" Mum asks eagerly. "You and he must be becoming good friends?"

I shrug. "We both like sports, so he offered to show me how they play *chas pell*—basketball—here, since there's no *caidpel*. It was...fun."

Before she can ask more questions, I change the subject. "I can't believe you actually agreed to let Adina keep an animal in our apartment. Aren't there rules against that sort of thing?"

"We checked on that before going to see the puppies," Dad assures me. "Small dogs are allowed, and this one shouldn't grow to more than twenty pounds, given the size of its mother."

"What about its father?"

"Carrie thinks it was the toy poodle from next door," Adina pipes up, "but she wasn't positive."

So the unsanitary little thing is the result of some genetic accident? Great.

"What's for dinner?" I ask, turning away from it. "I'm starved."

The next morning Adina and I take the bus to school for the first time. I'm not in the best of moods since I barely slept. My sister insisted on keeping her stupid puppy in our room, and it whimpered half the night until Adina moved its crate right next to her bed and slept with one hand dangling into it. That helped, though it weirded me out.

Even after the puppy calmed down, I kept replaying that unusually strong zing I got from Sean's touch yesterday. No matter how hard I tried to convince myself I'd imagined it, I knew I hadn't.

I'm still yawning as I climb into the big yellow contraption already half-filled with *Duchas* students. Adina and Jana immediately go to sit with some other ninth-grade girls near the back while I move down the center aisle more slowly, trying not to make eye contact with anyone.

"Hey, Kira! You want to sit with us?" It's Molly O'Gara…sitting next to the Sovereign.

"Oh, um, sure. Hi." I take the empty seat across from them.

Molly hops across the aisle to sit next to me as the bus starts moving. "M and I were talking just now and thought it might be cool to have a get-together with all the, um, new kids this coming Saturday so we can get to know each other better. Something informal, not like that official thing at NuAgra."

She's speaking softly enough that the *Duchas* boys closest to us can't hear her. I almost ask if Sean will be there, but I don't.

"It, uh, sounds fun. I'll let my parents know."

"Awesome. Feel free to tell your sister and any of the others you see.

We'll spread the word, too. Quietly, so other people don't feel left out." With another bright smile, she bounces back to her original seat as the bus pulls up to the next stop.

More kids get on, but no one sits next to me. I'm both relieved and slightly offended. Two stops later, in a pretty suburban neighborhood with nice-looking houses and big yards, two girls I recognize as the Sovereign's closest *Duchas* friends board the bus. Deb, the shorter one, immediately sits by me while the taller one, Bri, takes the half-seat in front of us. Ignoring the boy next to her, she turns to face me.

"Hey! Kira, right? M said you might be on our bus today. That was some football game Friday, wasn't it? I saw you up in the stands with all the basketball players but didn't get a chance to say hi." Then, turning to M, "I still can't believe you missed it. It was far and away Rigel's best game yet."

"That's what you said Saturday. I really wasn't feeling well that night, but I kind of wish I'd gone anyway." Clearly she's had plenty of practice by now lying to her *Duchas* friends.

Bri turns back to me. "Wasn't Rigel amazing?"

My nod is all the encouragement she needs to launch into a detailed analysis of the game, along with her speculation that Rigel must be getting a ton of college scholarship offers by now. I'm glad I don't have to respond much.

I assume I won't hear anything from Dun Cloch until I send them something more substantial. All I have so far is that bit about the Sovereign and the Council not seeing eye to eye, but I still don't know why. If I get a chance, I'll try to pry that out of Sean at school today, though I wish the thought of seeing him again didn't make me feel so...jumpy.

I'll just have to get past that, I tell myself as we all start filing off the but on reaching the school. I have a mission to do here, and I plan to do it, weird touch-thing or not. I'm still deep in unsettled thought when I reach Physics. Sean and Alan are already in the classroom talking together but break off to greet me when I walk in.

"Hey." Alan comes forward to put an unnecessarily proprietary hand on my arm. No tingle, of course—he's touched me plenty of times before now. "You have a good weekend? I wish you'd told me you were going to the game. I didn't see you until you were leaving afterward."

I sneak a quick peek at Sean and catch him frowning slightly, though he immediately smooths it away into a smile. "Sorry, man," he tells

Alan. "If we'd seen you, we'd have invited you to sit with us. Maybe next time."

Alan shoots a suspicious glance from me to Sean and back. "You guys sat together? That's...nice." But his tone implies the opposite.

"I came with my sister and Jana," I tell him, not sure I like the direction the conversation is taking. "They wanted to sit with a bunch of other freshman girls and Sean was kind enough to spare me from two hours of non-stop giggling."

"Yeah, I figured she'd rather meet some other seniors, so I introduced her to my teammates from last year." Sean says it off-handedly, but there's something wary about the look he gives Alan. He must be wondering, like Trina did, whether there's anything between us.

I want to make it clear there's not, but before I can think of a way that won't upset Alan too much, the bell rings.

"Guess we should get to our desks." Alan reaches for me again, this time to guide me by the elbow to the table we share near the back of the classroom.

Irritated now, I jerk my arm away. "I can get there on my own, thanks."

"Sorry," he whispers. "I wasn't—"

"Yes. You were. Even though I've told you not to."

He doesn't pretend he doesn't know what I mean, just sits down with a sulky look on his face. Refusing to feel guilty for hurting Alan's feelings when he totally should know better by now, I turn away and glance at Sean. He's not looking at me, but I get the impression he might have been a second ago. Did he see—or hear—what just passed between Alan and me? Not that it matters...

I try to focus on the Physics lesson but it's pretty elementary stuff... and I find myself uncomfortably distracted every time Sean says anything to his lab partner, or even turns his head. Which is ridiculous.

Irritated at my lack of mental control, I don't linger when class ends like I'd originally planned. I just shoot a quick smile Sean's way before hurrying off to second period.

In French class Molly greets me with a smile and motions me to sit near her and the Sovereign, like she did on the bus. Reminding myself that I should be exploiting *every* possible source of information, I comply.

There's not enough noise to provide cover for anything we don't want *Duchas* to overhear, so they both chat to me about school things.

"M and I can help you get caught up in here, if you want, and in Government," Molly offers. "I'm sure Sean and Rigel will help, too."

The idea of private tutoring sessions with Sean, especially, is so tempting I almost say no—then realize those would be perfect opportunities for private conversations. Exactly what I should be angling for if I'm going to get the kind of information Allister and Lennox want.

"Thanks. That would be great."

"We can talk some more at lunch," Molly whispers as the teacher calls the class to order.

23

Charging

Sean

THE SMILE KIRA gave me as she left the Physics classroom almost made up for her not hanging around to talk afterward. She didn't smile at Alan like that, I noticed. I also heard what she said to him when he got all possessive at the start of class.

"Given any more thought to going out for basketball?" I ask him as we leave Calculus together at the end of next period, hoping to smooth over any jealousy he might be feeling.

Pleased as I was to discover Alan's interest in Kira isn't mutual, I'd rather not alienate him if I can help it. I had way more than enough of that whole triangle thing with Rigel and M before it all got resolved.

Alan shrugs, not quite looking at me. "I'll see. Though I hope I'd do a better job of...you know...than Rigel did Friday."

"He's not usually so—" I break off with a shrug, since I still haven't said anything to Rigel about that. I should at least mention it to M. It would even be a perfect, non-stalker-like excuse to talk to her. Only... I'm not looking for those anymore. "Anyway, it would be cool to have you on the team."

He finally makes eye contact and even smiles. "Yeah, maybe it would. I'll definitely think about it."

Clearly, he's still not sure about my motives because he watches me closely as he remarks, in a deliberately casual way, "I was also thinking, maybe I should suggest to Kira she try out for the girls' basketball team, too. She'd be really good and would probably enjoy it."

"Great idea." I don't mention I've already done exactly that. I especially don't mention that she and I shot hoops yesterday afternoon, just the two of us.

I spent way too much time last night thinking about Kira, wondering if maybe I really am ready to move on, take a chance. And whether I should even want to, given her political opinions. She could have just been parroting propaganda from that "People's Network" back home, but what if she wasn't? If she's been talking with actual Anti-Royals, Kira could be dangerous...and my first responsibility should be to keep M safe.

Since Alan's not in AP Lit, I snag my chance to talk to Kira without him assuming I'm hitting on her. Because I'm not. Yet.

"Hey." I catch her before she reaches her desk, a little apart from everyone else. "I've, um, been thinking about some of the stuff you said yesterday."

"Yeah?" She looks cautiously hopeful. "And?"

"And I think we need to talk. Someplace...private."

Her chin comes up and her brown-and-gold eyes bore into mine, like she's trying to read my thoughts. "Okay. When? And where?"

"Maybe sometime after school—in the gym again? No, wait, the guys will be practicing there. We could...go for a walk or something." Crap, I *do* sound like I'm hitting on her.

Her gaze is cool now, like she doesn't quite trust me. "I'll think about it."

She continues on to her desk and I go to mine, deciding now isn't the time to push it. Not when I'm this conflicted between my responsibility to make sure Kira hasn't somehow been compromised and my desire to...what? I don't even know.

With my feelings in such a jumble, I don't try to talk to Kira again after class—not that she gives me a chance. But walking just a few paces behind her on the way to the lunchroom, it's hard not to notice how alluring she looks from behind. Then, somehow, I end up right next to her in the lunch line.

"So, um, have you had—" I start to say, when Molly, who I didn't even notice was behind me, interrupts.

"Hey, Kira, do you want to come over to my house tomorrow night for a study session, like we talked about in French class? I'd say tonight, but Trina called a meeting for after cheerleading practice and I don't know how late it'll go."

Kira looks right past me at my sister. "Oh, um, sure, I guess. I'll check with my parents and let you know tomorrow, okay?"

"Okay, or you can text me. Once we get through the line, we can trade numbers."

They continue talking across me about their school and after-school schedules. I make a mental note of Kira's. Just in case it turns out to be important for some reason.

After the cashier swipes our cards, we all head to different tables without me saying anything else to Kira. I'm just sitting down with my basketball buddies when I notice M and Molly walking over to where the new *Echtran* students are sitting. Molly catches my eye and motions me to come, too. Curious, I tell the guys I'll be back and head over, leaving my tray.

The three of us reach the newcomers' table at the same time. Before I can ask Molly what's going on, she launches into what sounds like a prepared speech.

"Hi, everyone! I've met most of you, but for those I haven't, I'm Molly O'Gara. M and I—and Sean—" She glances at me— "were wondering if you'd all like to come to Sean's and my house this coming Saturday for a kind of get-to-know-each-other party?" She looks furtively around the cafeteria and adds, more quietly, "Just, you know, us."

Everyone but Kira looks surprised, but most of them nod, some mumbling about checking with their parents.

"Great! Here's my number so you can call or text me for details." Molly hands out little slips of paper. "Oops, later."

Trina and a couple of other cheerleaders are heading our way, probably to make sure they're not being left out of anything—which, of course, they are.

"So, when did you two cook this up?" I ask M and Molly as we go back to our own tables.

"This morning at the bus stop," Molly replies with a grin.

M nods. "It was actually Molly's idea, but I think it's a good one. That thing Thursday night was so formal and crowded, and here at school we all have to be so careful. Something casual, just for us kids, will be a much better way to break the ice and really get to know each other, don't you think?"

"I do. Great thinking, Mol." I still hope Kira—just Kira—will come over tomorrow night, though. The kinds of questions I need to ask her aren't ones I want anyone else—especially M—to hear.

Though if I get the answers I'm afraid I might, I'll have to warn her.

24

Incomplete pass

NEEDLESS TO SAY, Mum's delighted when I ask if I can go to the O'Garas' house to study Tuesday evening.

"And the Sovereign might be there, too? Such an honor! I was certain she wouldn't hold our slip-up against us. So very gracious of her to help you catch up on your coursework. Of course you must go."

The O'Garas' house is a lot smaller—and shabbier—than I expect, but Molly greets me cheerfully while showing me into an equally small and shabby living room. Sean wasn't kidding about them not being rich, even though they're Royal. Molly sits in one squashy chair and I sit in another, at right angles to hers.

"M was hoping to be here," she says, "but there's a meeting out at NuAgra tonight, something about the new communication network and how to make sure it's secure enough. Mum and Dad are there, too."

"So it's just the two of us?" Mum will be disappointed, but I'm not. At least, not because M couldn't come.

"For now, anyway. Sean should be home soon but we can go ahead and get started."

Though my heart speeds up a fraction, I keep my expression carefully neutral. I'd hate for Molly to get the idea I have a thing for her brother. Because I don't. Besides, Molly might be easier to get info out of, after the way I went off on Sean about Royals and traditions on Sunday.

"We can work on French first, since Sean takes Spanish, and wait till he gets home to start on Government." She slants a look at me. "If that's what you really want to talk about?"

I blink. "What do you mean?"

Grinning, she lifts a shoulder. "Last year, when we first moved to Jewel, M used to come over to 'tutor' us." She makes quotes in the air with her fingers. "But we mostly used the time to answer all her questions about Nuath and Martian traditions and politics and stuff. You obviously know all that, but I thought you might have questions about other stuff, maybe about people at school? Of course, if you'd rather study…"

"No!" Because there's something I *do* want to ask before Sean gets home. "I mean, I'm actually okay on the French curriculum. Not so much on the Government stuff, but—"

I break off. Then, in a rush, "Molly, I've been wondering. Sean acts like it's no big deal that the Sovereign—M—is back together with Rigel. Like it doesn't bother him. But it seems like it would have to."

Molly's grin disappears and she suddenly looks more serious than I've ever seen her. "It does. I know it does. Maybe not as much as it used to, and he's gotten better at hiding it lately, but…yeah. When it *does* show, I never let on I notice. Because he really doesn't have a choice, you know? And he's trying so hard…"

"Are *you* upset about it? For his sake, I mean. Plus…other reasons, the ones everyone's been talking about."

"I was last year, when we first got here. Nobody told us in advance— told Sean—that M was dating anyone, so it was kind of a shock when we found out. He…didn't take it very well, especially at first. Gave Rigel a really hard time. The two of them nearly got in a fight at least once. But that was before Uncle Allister spilled the beans about the whole Consort thing at Rigel's birthday party."

"Allister Adair?" I couldn't imagine him being that careless. "In front of *Duchas*? Or was it just—?"

"Oh, no, he waited until they were all gone, but it was still a huge thing to spring on M and Rigel, that she was expected to pair up with Sean instead. Mum was really ticked at Uncle Allister for his timing, and being so tactless. Now I think of it, he was probably lucky M and Rigel didn't accidentally hurt him, as upset as they were."

"Hurt him? What do you mean? How?"

"Oh, um…" Like I have with Sean a couple of times, I get the impression she said more than she intended. "I just meant—"

She's interrupted by Sean's voice, from the back of the house. "Anyone home?"

"In here," Molly calls back, looking relieved.

A moment later he ambles in, his copper hair windblown. The look suits him. When he sees me, he freezes for a second.

"Oh, um, hey." He smiles at me but his ears go a shade pinker than they were.

"Kira just got here a couple minutes ago," Molly tells him. "We haven't started on any school stuff yet."

He pulls the wooden desk chair over and sits facing both of us. "Good, because I, um, wanted to talk about something else before Mum and Dad get back. Kira, on Sunday you almost made it sound like you thought we'd be better off without the monarchy. Is that what you really meant?"

Molly's eyebrows go up, her gray eyes snapping back to me. I try to choose my words carefully, determined not to mess up such a perfect opportunity. If I can open their eyes, get them to see past their preconceptions, they both could be a huge help in changing other people's minds.

"I, ah, just meant that we owe it to ourselves to explore all the options before assuming the way we've always done things is automatically the best way. You have to have noticed none of the more advanced Earth civilizations still have hereditary rulers. There's a reason. Democracy, with leaders popularly elected by the people, almost always makes a country more stable and prosperous."

To my surprise, Molly chuckles. "Wow, you sound just like M. When we first explained about the Nuathan monarchy last year, she thought it sounded impossibly archaic. Couldn't believe a society as advanced as ours still had one. We had a time convincing her the Sovereigns had done a great job for centuries, before Faxon came along."

"But did they, really?" I counter. "We were obviously better off under Leontine than we were under Faxon, but a lot of people must have been dissatisfied with the status quo even then. Otherwise, why would they have started following Faxon in the first place?"

"Because he fed them lies." Sean's tone is uncompromising. "He did everything he could to stir up dissension by telling people they were being denied their rights by the Royals. Which they weren't. Everyone already had a voice in our government, through the *Eodain*. And no one ever went without food or shelter or any other real necessities under the Sovereigns."

Luckily, I have a Populist talking point for exactly this. "Maybe not necessities, but you can't pretend those in the lower *fines* enjoyed the same luxuries those in the Royal and Science *fines* did."

"You're sounding like M again." Molly's grin widens. "Remember, Sean, at that dinner with all the Royals on the *Quintessence*, when we were on our way to Mars?"

"Yeah, but Dad set her straight."

I look from one of them to the other. "What do you mean? The Sovereign *herself* suggested—?"

"She wasn't Sovereign yet, but yeah," Molly confirms. "Honestly, if she weren't, well, who she is, she might have joined the Anti-Royals herself. Before they started getting violent, anyway. You should have seen how upset she was when those protesters in Bailerealta were hauled off."

"Protesters?" I don't remember that from the news feeds. "Populist protesters, you mean? The Populists have never been violent."

Sean huffs out a breath. "*Those* weren't violent, no. They just shouted anti-Royal stuff from the back of the crowd while she was trying to give a speech. But others are, like that guy they sent to kill her a few weeks back."

I shake my head, frowning. "That can't have been a real Populist. He was probably some Faxon supporter who claimed to be a Populists after he was caught. Maybe even a rival Royal. I've read the whole Populist platform and it doesn't condone any kind of violence."

"Of course they don't condone it *publicly*," Sean says patiently, like I'm an ignorant child. "That doesn't mean they're above using it covertly, if they think it's the quickest way to achieve their ends. Every movement has its radicals. The Anti-Royals seem to have more than most."

His piercing look implies he suspects I might be one of those.

"I'm no radical," I quickly—and truthfully—assure him. "I'd *never* want M physically harmed. Especially if it's true that she holds views I agree with." My expression must show I doubt that, because Sean leans toward me earnestly.

"Kira, you *have* to believe M only wants what's best for our people. She would never have agreed to become Sovereign in the first place if the Council hadn't convinced her Nuath could end up in a civil war if she didn't. Different factions were already starting to form, to fill the power vacuum created when Faxon was ousted."

"He's right," Molly chimes in. "I don't know how many times I've heard her complain about all the pomp and ceremony and privileges that go with being Sovereign. She even hated wearing all those gorgeous clothes she got to wear in Nuath—said they were impractical and pretentious."

By now I'm not sure what to believe. "Then why did she work so hard to get Acclaimed? Why didn't she try to hand over leadership to someone like Crevan Erc, if everything you're telling me is true? He's the one most in line with what you claim she believes."

Sean and Molly exchange a glance, then Molly gives a little shrug. "I guess it's not really a secret anymore, is it?"

"That part is, I think," he replies just as cryptically, a crease between his brows as he looks at his sister.

"I don't see why," she argues. "There can't have been any more, um, hiccups, or we'd have heard about it."

"Hiccups?" I echo, looking back and forth between them. "Like that kiss caught on camera that nearly derailed her Acclamation?"

Sean flicks a glance at me. "No, nothing like that." Then, to Molly, "If the media found out and publicized the whole story, it could still cause panic in Nuath."

"I won't tell the Nuathan media anything. I don't even know how to contact them. What's this big secret?" I demand.

Sean doesn't reply, still frowning thoughtfully at his sister. Too curious to think better of it, I reach over and touch his forearm to get his attention.

It definitely works. Even as I snatch my hand back, he whips his head around to stare at me. Because that was no regular *taghal ardus*! Not only wasn't it our first touch, this zing was noticeably *stronger* than the last one was.

"The, um, reason M needed to get Acclaimed when she did," Sean says. Though he's clearly trying to hide his instinctive reaction from Molly, her interested gaze flicks back and forth between us.

"I still think we should tell her," she says, getting to her feet. "But you'll have to do all the explaining yourself, Sean, because I just remembered I need to make some phone calls. Cheerleading stuff." With a bright smile, she hurries out of the room, leaving Sean and me alone.

"So, are you going to tell me?" I prompt, determined not to let him see how freaked out I was by that touch.

He looks at me warily. "Don't you think we'd better talk about that, er, other thing while Molly's busy?"

I can feel my cheeks warming. I'm tempted to say, "What other thing?" but that would be cowardly. "I guess you felt it in the gym, too?"

"Yeah. I tried to convince myself I imagined it, but—"

"So did I. Or at least that it was no more than that first touch thing people our age sometimes get. Just now, though…"

He looks more uncomfortable than ever. "Definitely different. The, um, only other person who's ever given me a jolt like that is M."

"The Sovereign? Oh, because you and she were supposed to—?"

"That's what I assumed. In fact, I sort of expected it the first time we touched, though *she* obviously didn't."

No reason she would, if she didn't know anything about the Consort tradition yet.

"She felt it, too," he continues, "but because of Rigel she tried to pretend she didn't. When she finally did admit it, she claimed what she got from him was way stronger. I didn't believe her for a long time, but…I guess it was true. Especially since lately—since getting back to Jewel, I mean—whatever she and I had keeps getting weaker. Probably because she's back with Rigel."

I regard him uncertainly. "So…is this some Royal thing?" I'd wondered, on Sunday.

"No, I don't think so. At least, I've never felt it off any Royal except M, and I've been around lots of Royals."

"Royal girls your age?"

"Well, no," he admits. "But it's not like *you* have any Royal blood…do you?"

I shake my head. "My parents are pure Ag for at least four generations, maybe longer. Are…are you *sure* we didn't imagine it?"

"Let's find out." With a half-daring, half-apprehensive grin, he reaches across and puts his hand over mine.

It's all I can do not to jerk away again because this third touch is even stronger than the second, sending what feels like an electrical current up my arm to ricochet through my whole body.

"I definitely didn't imagine that." He looks almost worried now. "But I still have no idea how or why it's happening. Even with M, our first touch was the most intense, but this felt like the strongest one yet. Didn't it?"

Honesty forces me to nod. "Is that...is that how—?" But I can't say it. Pretending a *taghal ardus* tingle is the *graell* is such a tired, pathetic come-on line it's laughable. In fact, the last time a boy tried it on me, I actually did laugh, right in his face.

"No clue," he replies as though I'd used the word anyway. "As far as I know, the only people to have a real *graell* bond in the last few centuries are M and Rigel. We can't infer much from a sample size of one."

"Besides, like you just pointed out, I'm an Ag and you're... I mean, that should make it even *more* impossible, right?"

Sean shrugs. "You'd think so, but Rigel's not Royal, either, and M's Royal blood is purer than mine—more closely related to a recent Sovereign, I mean. Rigel's not pure anything. His mother's a Healer and his dad's Informatics—whole separate *fines*. But whether it's possible or not, I...I hope that's not what's going on here. You should, too."

I happen to agree, since I hardly want to be bonded to some Royal. But I can't resist asking, "Why? Other than how much it would upset your parents, I mean." I force a grin, trying to make a joke of it.

He grins back. "Yeah, well, there's that, too." His agreement bothers me more than I expect. More than it should, for sure. "But the *graell* has other drawbacks. Like that *tinneas* M and Rigel get when they're apart."

"They actually get sick? I figured that bit was added to the fairytales later, for dramatic effect."

"Nope. It's why I had to stick so close to M when she was doing all those appearances, trying to get Acclaimed. Rigel's grandmother wouldn't let him anywhere near M, so she got really sick. My touch was the only thing that kept her upright most of that time. I guess we...still had enough resonance then that it was the next best thing to Rigel's."

He's clearly still bothered by it, and no wonder. Like Molly, I'm careful not to draw attention to whatever pain he's still feeling.

"What about afterward, though? Once she was Acclaimed, she seemed fine whether you were with her or not. Is that *tinneas* thing just temporary?"

"No, Rigel's grandmother had the Healers do a bunch of tests on him until they came up with an antidote, since he apparently got just as sick as M did."

"And didn't have anybody like you to help him."

I'm suddenly struck by how hard that must have been for Sean. Knowing M was bonded with—in love with—someone else while having to pretend everything was great between them. So he could stay close enough to keep her healthy. I'm abruptly furious with her all over again for *using* Sean like that.

"There are other downsides, too," he says. "Like their electrical thing."

Confusion briefly replaces my anger. "Electrical thing?"

"Yeah, when they're together, especially if they're upset, they can sort of…shoot lightning bolts. That's how they destroyed the Ossian Sphere Faxon's followers had before they could use it, and how they stopped the Grentl's EMP from reaching Earth. It's gotten a whole lot stronger since they, um, re-bonded. Scary strong. That's why it wasn't mentioned in any of the reports, so people wouldn't freak out about it."

"Scary strong?" So *that's* what Molly meant about Allister being lucky they didn't hurt him. "How well can they control it?"

He shrugs again. "Nobody really knows, according to Mum, which is why some members of the Council think they should be kept apart."

"Except then there's that *tinneas* thing. I see what you mean. I guess having a bond like that *would* suck. So are those lightning bolts the big secret you said would panic people?"

"Um, not exactly. But you shouldn't tell people about those either. There's been plenty of ugly gossip about M and Rigel already, without adding that to the mix. It might scare a lot of people if they knew. You won't spread it around, will you?"

"No. I won't spread it around. I promise."

"Thanks. I…didn't think you would." He continues to hold my gaze, his blue eyes warming, his expression softening.

Something inside me warms and softens in response. Though I've tried to fight it, I've been attracted to Sean from the start—well before that first touch. That attraction is a lot stronger now. He reaches for my hand again, leans in closer. I sway forward, too, ignoring a tiny voice in the back of my mind shouting that this is crazy. Stupid.

A car door slams outside and Sean jumps to his feet, his ears red. Not looking at me now, he runs a distracted hand through his hair. "I, um… Mum and Dad must be home."

Half a moment later, Molly comes clattering into the room, slightly out of breath. "Mum and Dad are back! I wanted to make sure you—oh, never mind." She looks from one to the other of us, her expression relieved, then disappointed.

For a second I can't decide whether I'm more disappointed or relieved either—then firmly tell myself I'm relieved. *Definitely* relieved. Kissing Sean would have created a complication I absolutely don't need in my life right now. Or ever.

I manage to get my heart rate and hopefully my color back under control before Mr. and Mrs. O'Gara come into the living room.

"Well, it does sound as though it won't be much longer before we have a secure and reliable communication network in place that will—" Mrs. O'Gara is saying, then breaks off when she sees me. "Oh! I'm sorry, I didn't realize you had a guest."

Sean immediately steps forward. "Mum, Dad, you remember Kira, don't you? I introduced her to you at church Sunday."

Mr. O'Gara nods, smiling. "I also drove her and her classmates to NuAgra on Thursday for their work-study program. Hello again, Kira."

Mrs. O'Gara's frown of alarm disappears—she probably assumed I was a *Duchas* classmate who might have heard more than I should have. "Welcome, Kira." Her lilt is more pronounced than Sean's or Molly's, whose accents are only slightly more "Irish" than a typical Nuathan's.

"Kira's the one Sean told you about," Molly volunteers. "One of the star players on the Ag *caidpel* team back in Nuath."

"Oh, yes." Her mother's smile widens, though she rakes me with an assessing glance. "You're from the Agricultural *fine*, then, dear? That will be nice for Molly, to have a friend with that in common."

Confused, I glance at Molly. "What do you mean? I thought—"

"I'm adopted," Molly explains with no trace of embarrassment. "I figured everyone knew by now—it's not exactly a secret. My real parents were killed when I was a baby, in Glenamuir. Mum and Dad took over their identities when Faxon's forces started wiping out Royals, and they took me in, as well. But yeah, I was born an Ag—not that I'm a very good one."

"What do you mean?" I ask again.

She shrugs. "I've never been very good with plants, like I ought to be."

Mrs. O'Gara smiles fondly at her. "Now, now, Molly. You have other talents to compensate. Emileia quite depends on you, both as a friend and as *Chomseireach*."

I'd known Molly acted as the Sovereign's Handmaid in Nuath—one reason I'd assumed she was Royal. But what use would M have for a Handmaid here in Jewel? So much for pretending to be the same as everyone else.

"Maybe next time you come over, Kira, you can show me some Ag tricks before I kill any more houseplants," Molly suggests.

Though I suspect it would be safer for me to stay well away from the O'Garas' house after what almost happened with Sean just now, I nod. "Sure thing. I'll get Alan and Adina to help, too, since they're also Ags."

Molly looks delighted—maybe at the prospect of spending time with Alan? I should definitely nudge him her way, if so.

"Well, um, I should get home," I say before things get awkward again. "Thanks for the homework help."

We say our goodbyes, Molly promising to have me over again soon. I notice Sean doesn't echo her on that.

Walking back to Diamond View Terrace a few minutes later, I resolve to keep my distance from Sean in the future. Already, he's making me doubt some of what I've believed about the Sovereign and even the Populists, instead of me persuading him to our side. If some kind of bond *is* trying to form between us, I don't dare let it get any stronger—which means never giving him a chance to touch me again.

Congratulating myself on making such a mature, rational decision, I walk faster, refusing to acknowledge the sudden, hollow ache in my chest.

25

Technical foul

Sean

"THAT WAS VERY nice of you two, to invite one of your new classmates over to help her with schoolwork," Mum says as soon as Kira's gone. "I know it's been difficult for both of you, having so few *Echtran* friends here in Jewel, but I'm sure that will change as you get to know all of these new students better."

Molly nods happily. "Kira's really nice. She didn't seem too friendly the very first time I met her, but that was probably because I was with M and she felt awkward because of her being the Sovereign and all. She was fine tonight, though, wasn't she, Sean?"

She shoots me a sly grin, which I ignore. "Yeah, she seems friendly enough to me. I'm, er, trying to talk her into going out for the girls' basketball team next month, since she'd obviously be great."

"Oh, is *that* who you were shooting hoops with Sunday afternoon?" Molly's grin gets bigger. "I should have guessed. I saw you two whispering together after church."

I feel my ears getting hot again and have to work hard to keep my expression neutral. Mum is already giving me That Look.

"I figured she misses being involved in a sport, and basketball is almost the same as the *chas pell* kids play in Nuath. So, yeah, I asked if she wanted to come out to the school and practice since the guys and I do that most Sundays." I carefully don't mention the guys weren't there *this* Sunday.

Mum's slight frown relaxes. "That was quite thoughtful, Sean, and I'm sure she appreciated it. Just…don't forget that you two are from very different *fines*."

"What's that supposed to mean?" Molly demands indignantly, though she has to know as well as I do. "Didn't you just say we both need more *Echtran* friends?"

One of Mum's eyebrows goes up—always a danger sign. "Of course I have no objection to you—either of you—becoming friends with Kira, or any of the others."

Molly immediately jumps on Mum's slight emphasis on the word *friends*. "You mean as long as it's *just* friends? What if Alan Dempsey, that other Ag Kira mentioned, asks me out once I get to know him? Would you have a problem with that?"

"Of course not," Mum says a little huffily. "We allowed you to go to Homecoming with that *Duchas* boy, didn't we? You're sixteen. If you want to date one of these *Echtran* boys, particularly one from the Agricultural *fine*—"

Molly lets out a snort. "I thought that was it. You're okay with *me* dating an Ag, or even a boy from a different *fine*, but Sean's only allowed to get serious with another Royal? Well, in case you haven't noticed, there *aren't* any Royal girls in Jewel except M. Maybe not even on Earth. Is that fair?"

To my relief, Dad steps in. "Molly, that's enough. Your mother simply doesn't want to see Sean hurt again. See either of you hurt. Surely there's no need to rush into anything?" He glances at me questioningly.

"I have no intention of *rushing* into anything," I assure them all emphatically. "I never did. I appreciate you defending my rights or whatever, Mol, but it's totally not necessary. Kira and I are just friends—and barely even that. I haven't even known her a week yet!"

"But—" Molly looks at me accusingly and I give her a tiny head shake. "Fine. Whatever. I just hoped—"

"I know. But it's too soon, even if I was interested in…something more than friendship. Okay?"

Reluctantly, she nods. "Sorry."

I smile to let her know she's forgiven and Mum and Dad change the subject to the meeting they just had at NuAgra. Dad tells us about the communication network Rigel's dad is putting together that will eventually be the equivalent of a whole separate internet accessible only to *Echtrans*, but I barely listen. I'm too busy trying to sort out my wildly conflicting feelings about Kira.

I'm more attracted to her than ever after tonight, especially after those additional touches. So attracted I was incredibly frustrated when Mum and Dad got home, right when I was on the point of kissing her. Or, I should say, we were on the point of kissing each other. I don't think I imagined her tilting her face up to mine...

Quickly, I break off that thought. Because as soon as she left I realized how dumb that would have been, no matter how much I wanted to. During our conversation earlier, she all but admitted she considers herself a Populist—an Anti-Royal. And I happen to know at least some of those want M out of the picture permanently, no matter how much Kira tries to deny it. If she's a threat to M, there's no way I can let myself get involved with her. No way I'd *want* to get involved with her.

Mum doesn't have to worry at all.

And if resolving to keep my distance from Kira makes my chest ache a little, well, that's just tough. I'll live.

26

Out of bounds

When I get home, Adina and my parents are just leaving to take the new puppy for a walk so it can do its business before bedtime.

"I'm still working on getting her to understand that she needs to always do it outside, so I'm trying to give her lots of chances," Adina explains as I try to fend off the fuzzy thing's effusive greeting.

"Okay if I don't come along to watch?" I try to control my instinctive grimace. "I still have some homework to do."

I wait until the door closes behind them, then go into the bathroom and lock the door. Opening the secret app, I type in a message.

Sean O'Gara proving harder to persuade than I expected. Do we have a backup plan?

There. With any luck, they'll message me back with a different mission so I can avoid Sean and still be useful to the cause. I'm about to exit secure mode when I see a notification of an incoming voice call. Hurriedly, I activate the aural dampening field, in case Adina and my parents get back sooner than I expect.

"Your location is secure?" Allister says the moment I answer.

"Yes, but I may not have long."

"Very well. Please elaborate on the message you just sent."

I swallow. I hadn't expected this. "I, ah, I'm afraid I might not be able to convince Sean O'Gara to join us after all. He still seems to be completely loyal to the Sovereign, even after everything she's done to him."

"Are you sure?" Allister sounds disappointed but not surprised.

"Pretty sure. He's not spending much time around her these days, but he defends her every time I mentioned a mistake she's made. Not only that, he keeps arguing her case, trying to talk *me* into becoming one of her supporters."

Lennox's voice cuts in—he must be right there with Allister. "I told you this was likely, but you were determined to try with your nephew. If Sean won't be swayed and is no longer close to the Sovereign, we'd do better to return to our original plan."

"For me to work at convincing all the other *Echtrans* in town, you mean?"

"Not just yet," Lennox replies. "We still need you to get close enough to the Sovereign and her friends to discover more weaknesses we can exploit."

"I did find out from Sean and his sister that the Sovereign and the *Echtran* Council don't always agree on things. Maybe we can use that somehow?"

Allister breaks back in. "Do you know what they disagree about? Does it have anything to do with us?"

"Um, I don't think so. Sean told me most of the Council isn't happy about ceding their power to an upstart teenager…not that he put it that way. Can't really blame them. It sounds like she doesn't always trust the Council, either."

"Excellent," Lennox says. "If there is already a rift forming, the Council is less likely to present the obstacle we feared. We must consider ways to deepen the conflict between them and the girl. Meanwhile, Kira, use any means necessary to insinuate your way into the Sovereign's inner circle. Win the trust of her closest friends, particularly Rigel Stuart." He says the name like it leaves a bad taste in his mouth. "Once you've done that, we'll be able to proceed."

That will mean working harder than ever to conceal my real opinions, but it shouldn't force me to spend time with Sean, which is a relief.

"Molly O'Gara already seems to like me, so that's a start," I tell them eagerly. "She and the Sovereign are really close. I also have two classes with the Sovereign every day, plus Taekwondo on Wednesdays and Saturdays."

"Yes, a very good start," Allister agrees. "Message us when you've gained enough trust to spend time alone with the Sovereign and her cohorts. Then we'll arrange a lengthier conversation on ways to effectively undermine her influence. Have you any other information to give us before we close?"

I wrack my brain, thinking over everything I heard this evening. "Molly let slip that you were lucky the Sovereign and Rigel didn't hurt you when you first told them about Sean being her *Cheile Rioga* last year. I asked how, but she wouldn't say."

"Hurt me?" Allister's voice is sharp. "Do you mean—?"

Even through the aural dampening field, I hear a door slam. "Oops, I think my parents are back. I should go."

"Very well," Lennox says. "If we wish to speak with you before your next report, we will message you. Remember to keep your device with you at all times."

They break the connection without saying goodbye. I deactivate the dampening field, close the secret screen, then flush the toilet before emerging into the living room.

"Good walk?" I ask brightly.

At school the next day, Sean seems nearly as eager to avoid me as I am to avoid him. We exchange no more than stiff smiles in our Physics and Lit classes, and give each other a wide berth whenever we pass each other in the hallways. I tell myself I'm relieved.

At lunch, he again sits with friends from the basketball team. Mindful of my new instructions, I only pause briefly at the newcomers' table with my tray of food.

"Hey, guys. Molly O'Gara asked me to sit at her table today, so I probably should. See you all later, okay?"

A couple of them look impressed, even envious. Only Alan seems disappointed. In Physics, he acted a little too pleased when I didn't talk to Sean. Another reason not to sit here and risk Alan thinking it's because of him.

Gathering my courage, I walk over to the table where Molly O'Gara is sitting...right across from the Sovereign. "Er, hi. Do you have room for one more?"

"Of course!" Molly exclaims delightedly, snatching her backpack off the chair next to her. "I actually saved this seat for you—I was just about to invite you to join us."

Smiling tentatively around the table, I sit down. "I, ah, thought it would be nice to, er, branch out, especially since I've already met most of you." Bri and Deb smile back and I glance at M, across from me. She and Rigel seem a little preoccupied, but then their serious expressions relax.

"That's great, Kira," M says. "I hope the others will start mingling more, too. Have you had your interview for the school paper yet?"

"Yes, Becky called Monday night and asked about a million questions, plus some follow-up ones before Statistics yesterday." It was like getting an intensive pop quiz on all the background info I memorized in Dun Cloch, but I'd only stumbled once or twice—and not in ways that would make her suspicious.

Rigel chuckles. "Angela, the editor, has really been riding us to get those stories in. She wants our first drafts this afternoon. M and I are doing the Walsh twins. Yours is ready, right?" The look he gives her is so intimate it makes me a little uncomfortable, especially after what Sean told me last night.

I'm curious to know more details about their bond but with Bri, Deb and a few other *Duchas* at the table, we obviously can't talk about anything *Echtran*-related. Instead I ask about school sports, claiming I'd played soccer —a common *Duchas* sport slightly similar to *caidpel*—at my last school.

"Jewel used to have a girls' soccer team," Bri tells me, "but it fizzled a few years back. All we have now in the fall is cross country, then basketball after that."

Molly gives me a knowing grin. "You should totally go out for basketball—unless Trina has talked you into joining the cheerleading squad?"

"She's tried, but I, um, don't think it would be my kind of thing." Again, I don't commit about the basketball.

The conversation moves on to school gossip about some cheerleader's breakup with some football player. I don't take part, since I don't know either of them. Still, by the time the bell rings I feel like I've taken a decent first step toward following my latest orders.

I take another at the end of Economics, when I hang back to talk to Trina after the Sovereign leaves for her next class. If anyone can tell me about M's weaknesses, I reason, it's likely to be Trina, who seems to dislike her at least as much as I do.

First I make some comment about the class, then say, "Last week you warned me to watch out for Marsha Truitt. Is there anything I should worry about other than boyfriend-stealing, since I don't happen to have one of those?"

Her eyes instantly light up, a malicious little smile curving her lips. "Oh, where do I begin? She's been a total pain since elementary school, so there's a lot. One thing you *definitely* want to be careful of is her tendency to get violent for no reason."

"Violent? Really?" I did read a mention of her starting a fight last year. Details on that would be great. "Like, who has she gone after?"

"Me, among other people," Trina replies smugly. "She's *always* had it in for me, though I can't imagine why. The last time she got pissed at me, she actually broke my nose, believe it or not! And never even said she was sorry afterward."

So it was *Trina* she attacked? Jackpot.

"Wow, that's awful!" I squeeze every ounce of sympathy I can into my voice. "Why would she do that?"

"I honestly have no idea. Afterward she claimed it was because of something I showed her on my phone, but since she also broke *that*, of course she had no proof."

By now I've seen enough of Trina to suspect she did *something* to deserve it. Still, considering how good Marsha Truitt is at Taekwondo, completely apart from her being an *Echtran*—and the freaking Sovereign —*nothing* could possibly justify a physical attack.

I'm about to ask more questions when Trina notices the time. "Oops! I've already been late to Government twice this quarter. I better hurry if I don't want to risk detention. Later, Kira!"

I don't particularly need to hurry. Wednesday's not one of my NuAgra days, so I spend seventh period in study hall, then take the bus so I can attend Taekwondo after school. On the way home, Adina tells me she's thinking about dropping out at the end of our two-week trial period.

"I'm not very good at it and I want to spend more time with Aggie." That's what she decided to name her puppy. "She already gets left alone too much."

"I'm sure the dog will be fine." I roll my eyes. "Don't most people with dogs have to work or go to school?"

"Well, yeah, but she's still so little…"

In class, I try much harder than I did on Saturday to act friendly toward M. I'm not sure she's buying it, though, no matter how much eagerness I force into my voice when asking about Taekwondo terms and moves.

"How long did it take you to get your blue belt?" I ask her as we're changing out of our sparring pads at the end of class.

"Longer than it should have because I was gone for almost six months," she replies with a too-penetrating look. "I was in a study-abroad program in Ireland spring semester, then got into an accident there, so I didn't get back to Jewel until mid-August."

Like every other *Echtran*, I know exactly where she really was all that time, as well as the story given out in Jewel to account for her prolonged absence and Rigel's supposed memory erasure.

I nod, mindful of all the *Duchas* students nearby. "Did you have fun in Ireland? Before your accident, I mean."

"Oh, yeah, it was great." Her smile doesn't reach her eyes—in fact, there seems to be a lot of pain reflected in those green depths. I feel my first stirring of sympathy for her—but quickly squash it.

"I'd love to hear about it sometime." I force a light tone as I avert my gaze to look over at Adina. She's talking to two *Duchas* students around her age. "Well, um, I should go collect my sister. See you at school."

Molly did say M disliked the trappings that went with her position, but what I just saw in her eyes went way beyond that. Like she had some seriously bad memories of her time in Nuath. Maybe I can convince Molly to tell me why.

"Ready to go, Sprout?" I say once I've turned in my borrowed pads. Adina nods and jumps up and we go change.

"You seemed to be having a good time today," I comment as we leave to walk home. "Think maybe you'll stick around after all? It'd be good to at least learn more self-defense moves."

She slants an amused glance up at me. "What, like I'm going to get attacked in Jewel? Not likely. I was hoping you wouldn't be so over-protective here."

"I'm still a big sister." I ruffle her hair with a laugh.

Just then, I hear a voice—the Sovereign's voice—calling our names. We turn and she hurries down the block toward us.

"Hey, sorry, I didn't have a chance to tell you guys in class where no one would hear, but we decided to have Saturday's party at Rigel's house instead of the O'Garas.' Less chance of other kids from school hearing about it that way, or maybe even dropping by."

"Oh, um, okay." I glance at Adina, who's nodding eagerly. "Where does he live?"

She pulls a sheet of paper out of her gear bag. "Here's his address and phone number. Or you can call me, I put my number on there, too, even though Cormac didn't want me to." She grins conspiratorially and glances over her shoulder at her Bodyguard—who also happens to be the Vice-Principal at Jewel High. He's hovering half a block away.

"Wow, I can't believe she gave us her personal phone number," Adina gushes once we're well out of earshot. "She must really trust us, don't you think?"

I just nod, pushing away the uncomfortable thought that I'm the *last* person in Jewel she should trust. What would her Bodyguard do if he knew I was reporting back to the Populists about her? I'm not sure I want to find out.

The next day in French class, Molly asks if I can come over again that evening after dinner. "We can work on some of this stuff." She jabs a finger at the textbook, then lowers her voice. "And maybe you can give me some tips on growing plants, since mine always curl up and die."

"Oh, um, okay." Now that I'm avoiding Sean, Molly is likely to be my best source of inside information. I want to ask if he'll be there—I do *not* want a repeat of last time!—but I don't dare with the Sovereign sitting right there.

Then, as we're leaving the room after class, M surprises me by stepping close the moment Molly's too far away to hear.

"When you go over to Molly's, don't make fun of her about the plant thing, okay? She's kind of sensitive about it."

"Of...of course not. I'd never do that."

Her concerned frown disappears. "I didn't think you would but...it's hard for her sometimes, not feeling like she belongs in either world, you know? Maybe being friends with you will help."

With a genuine-seeming smile, she heads off to her next class and I head to mine, thinking hard. A *Chomseireach* is basically a Sovereign's personal servant, but she sounded as protective of Molly as I'd be of Adina. Conflict wells up in me again but I firmly remind myself that being *nice* isn't enough to make her an effective Sovereign.

As the day goes on, I find it harder and harder to ignore Sean. In Lit class, I force myself to concentrate on *Fahrenheit 451* and the essay I'm supposed to be outlining on its themes. The book is interesting, parts of it reminding me of Faxon's regime and the Resistance, but I'm distracted by Sean's presence two desks away. The third time I sneak a peek at him, I catch him looking back. I quickly avert my eyes.

The thought that he might be having trouble ignoring me, too, creates a tiny bubble of pleasure that I immediately try to pop. My mission no longer involves trying to persuade Sean, so there's no reason for me to get to know him any better. No reason at all.

Over lunch, I take the added precaution of asking Molly if she can come to my place tonight instead of me going to hers. Though she seems surprised, she quickly agrees.

"Great!" If my relief at eliminating any chance of seeing Sean tonight is marred by a tiny thread of disappointment, I ignore it.

27

Fadeaway

Sean

I WAS WORRIED my resolve to stay away from Kira would be hard to keep once I saw her again. Not so much, it turns out. Since that unplanned almost-kiss, she seems as determined as I am to maintain our distance.

Unfortunately, I'm more hyper-aware of her than ever whenever we're in the same room, my eyes straying her way when I should be paying attention in class. And it bothers me much more than it should when Alan uses my backing off as an opportunity to move in on her himself. I don't notice her giving him any real encouragement, but that doesn't stop him trying.

When he again hurries to her side as we're leaving Government class Thursday, I feel a surge of jealousy similar to what I used to feel toward Rigel. Which is crazy. Then, at least, I had tradition as an excuse, and what I considered the good of our people.

Now? More like the exact opposite. Still, I speed up until I'm close enough behind them to hear what he's saying to her.

"Hey, Kira, I was wondering if I can give you a ride to the football game tomorrow? Oak Hill isn't far, so my folks said I can borrow the car."

"Um, thanks, Alan, but I wasn't really planning to go. If I do, it'll be with my sister again and this time I'd have to sit with her since my parents are a little more nervous about us attending away games."

She gives him a smile that I tell myself doesn't reach her eyes, then turns down a different hallway. Alan watches her for a moment before he continues on, looking disgruntled. I slow down so he can get well ahead of me, trying hard not to gloat. Because I have no business being so pleased she shot him down. Besides, their conversation just reminded me of something.

My next class is Weight Training, which I have with Rigel and, as of last week, Liam Walsh. Rigel and I have been answering a lot of Liam's questions about our respective sports when none of our *Duchas* classmates are listening, but today I watch for a chance to catch Rigel alone.

"Hey," I whisper when Liam moves to the other side of the room to spot Andy on the bench press. "Got a sec?"

Rigel shoots me a curious glance. "Sure. What's up?"

Together, we go to the leg press and I start loading weights for him—less than half what I know he can manage these days, his bond with M has made him so much stronger.

"Last Friday. The game. I kept meaning to ask you—?"

His mouth twists in an amused grimace. "Yeah, I know. I went way over the top. Believe me, I've heard plenty about it from my parents. They even got a call from somebody on the Council who saw the highlights on the local news."

"So I, uh, guess you'll be scaling it back tomorrow night?" That had been my main concern.

He takes his place on the bench and starts pushing with his legs. "Definitely. Even though M's planning to be there."

"Yeah, that's another thing. How *did* you manage to play like that without her there? I thought—"

"Pure adrenaline, I think. She, um, told me I had to play really well, that it would help keep her safe. Keep the, er, secret safe. Because of that crazy dude, Farmer."

I stare at him. "Wait, she told you *before* the game? But you waited until after to tell anyone else, so we could go help her?"

"She didn't give me a choice. She wouldn't tell me *where* she was until the game was over—said if I didn't play at all, Farmer would claim that proved his theory. That's why I tried to make the game go as fast as possible. I knew they'd run a continuous clock if we were up by over forty points, so…"

That had definitely ended the game sooner, though I can't imagine how he'd played so well when he had to be out of his mind with worry.

But— "How did she tell you all that? You said you didn't get her text until... Oh."

The look he gives me is answer enough. Since the two of them re-bonded or whatever, and he got his memory back, they've been able to communicate telepathically across even greater distances than those Scientists reported. A whole *lot* greater, apparently.

"Um, don't mention that part to anybody else, okay? We figure it might come in handy someday if no one knows how much our range has increased. You know, just in case."

I promise I won't, but now he's got me thinking about the *graell* again, a subject I've tried *not* to think about since Tuesday. And wondering—again—what it would feel like to be bonded to someone the way he's bonded to M.

28

Double coverage

WHEN MOLLY SHOWS up at our apartment that evening, Mum's greeting isn't quite as over-enthusiastic as I feared. Maybe because I told her Molly's not Royal, just an Ag like us?

"It's very nice of you, Molly, to offer to help Kira with her school-work. We've been hoping she would make friends in Jewel, especially as she was initially so reluctant to come."

Molly smiles up at Mum from where she's crouched down, petting Adina's puppy as it scrabbles at her knees. She won my sister's allegiance first thing, by cooing about how cute it is.

"It *is* a pretty big adjustment," Molly admits. "I especially missed ionic showers when we first moved to Bailerealta from Nuath. And recombinators—though now my mum cooks way better than our old recombinator ever did. I'll have to bring you some of her scones sometime."

After a few more minutes chatting with my family, I suggest we go out to the courtyard to study, where it will be quieter. Mindful of the Sovereign's warning this morning, I didn't mention Molly's difficulty with plants to my parents.

"Your family's nice," she comments as we walk down the one flight of stairs, backpacks over our shoulders. "They seem to be settling in here really well."

"Yeah. Of course, they were all excited to come in the first place."

"And you weren't."

I try to turn my snort into a laugh. "Not so much."

She nods sympathetically. "Sean hated leaving Nuath, too, not that we had a choice. I didn't mind so much. Maybe because I was younger, around Adina's age."

"Does he still miss it?"

"Sometimes. Especially when it rains or, worse, snows. He still has issues with stuff falling from the sky."

She chuckles but I don't. I know exactly how he feels.

"So, um what do you want to do first?" I ask when we reach the courtyard. "I really suggested coming out here because of the gardens and trees. You said—"

"I need tips, yeah. Though they may not help much, since I'm probably the worst Ag ever born into our *fine*."

I can't help laughing a little. "Come on, it's not *that* bad."

"No, it is. I have *Duchas* friends who are a lot better with plants than I am. So…what's the secret? What do you actually *do* to make them grow —or at least not die?"

Realizing she's serious, I stifle the urge to laugh again. "Um, it's kind of instinctive, but I'll do my best. There are some rosebushes around the corner, let's try there."

She follows me to the tiny, sheltered rose garden I discovered our second day here. It's set well back from the main walkways, next to the lattice that screens the heating and cooling equipment. There's a white wooden bench next to it but, as I expect, it's deserted now.

Though it's nearly dark, there's enough light for me to find a bush with three unopened buds.

"Okay, here. This one." Tossing my backpack onto the bench, I kneel down and she does the same. "Watch, I'm just going to run a finger along the leaves nearest this bud, barely touching them. You do the same on that one there."

Watching me closely, she mimics my hand motion. "What am I supposed to— Ouch!"

"Um, avoid the thorns." Again I have to swallow a laugh. "Just brush the very top leaves, then move your finger up the pedicel toward the sepals. At the same time, try to feel the life inside the stem, flowing up to the flower." A moment's focus and I sense it clearly, rising from the roots deep in the ground through the body of the plant to the bud I've chosen. "Can you feel it?"

"Er… Maybe?"

Out of the corner of my eye I see her clumsily stroking the base of her bud, her brow furrowed with concentration. Closing my eyes, I turn my attention back to my own flower, enjoying the flow of its life force and my connection to it. For the first time since leaving Nuath I start to feel grounded in a way I've missed more than I realized. The seed work I've been doing with Mum out at NuAgra isn't nearly as satisfying as connecting with an established plant.

"Oh, wow!" At Molly's exclamation I open my eyes and see that my bud is already more than half open. Hers, unfortunately, is as tight-shut as ever. "How did you do that?"

I shrug. "Like I said, it's hard to explain. I sort of tap into the life inside, then add a bit of my own energy, speeding things up a little. I'm sure with practice you can do it, too."

"Okay, let me try again."

This time I watch as she brushes her fingertips up the top of her rose stem. After five minutes or so, she's clearly growing frustrated.

"I'm sorry," she finally says. "I just can't seem to do it—or even sense it."

"Hey, don't worry about it." I pat her on the shoulder. "Maybe you're like Adina and have more affinity with animals than plants. Some Ags do." I don't mention that even Adina would have had no difficulty coaxing that bud to open.

"Yeah. Maybe." She turns her back on the roses to face me. "So, what's the deal with you and Sean?"

Startled, I rock back on my heels. "What do you mean?"

"I can tell he likes you, and I sort of thought you liked him, too. Was I wrong?"

Averting my eyes from her too-knowing gaze, I shrug. "I don't *dis*like him. But we don't have anything in common."

"You both like sports," she points out. "That's a good start. And you're both interested in politics, even if you don't agree about everything."

"That's putting it mildly," I respond before remembering I'm supposed to be winning Molly's confidence. "I mean, it's admirable that he's so loyal to the Sovereign after, well, everything, but—"

"But you don't get it."

I shake my head. "I really don't."

For a long moment Molly looks at me, her brow furrowed like it was with the rosebush. Then, "Why are you so determined not to like M? No, don't deny it. She can tell, and so can I, even though you're trying to act friendlier to her now."

I'm obviously an even worse actress than I thought. So much for my mission.

"It's...not her *personally*," I say, though that's not exactly true. "I just happen to believe the monarchy has outlived its usefulness. Especially with more and more of us leaving Mars."

"I know. And like I said before, she basically felt the same way— probably still does, though now she knows better than to say so out loud. But in a year's time she's done more for our people than most other Sovereigns did in their whole lifetimes. If she hadn't—"

She breaks off, looking at me doubtfully.

"Hadn't what?" I prompt.

"Sean didn't tell you? I was afraid he wouldn't. Guess I shouldn't either, without checking with him first. But you have to believe me when I say she's proven she's willing to sacrifice, well, pretty much everything for the good of the rest of us. Even if most of those sacrifices never made the news."

Her gray eyes are so earnest, so sincere, I have to believe she's telling the truth. Or, at least, what she thinks is the truth.

"So...she and Rigel really did risk their lives to stop that alien EMP?"

"More than risked. The Scientists told them upfront that even if they succeeded, they'd almost certainly be vaporized. But...they were our only possible hope. I was right there when the odds were explained to them, and they both insisted on trying anyway. Then there was the time—"

More unsettled than I want to admit, even to myself, I interrupt before she can continue. "Okay, but what about some of the stuff she's done that *wasn't* for the good of our people? Like getting caught on camera kissing Rigel on their way to Mars? Or before that, when she attacked a *Duchas*—Trina. I'm surprised the Council still let her go to Mars after that!"

To my surprise, Molly laughs. "Is that what Trina told you? That M attacked her?"

I nod, frowning. "She said it was unprovoked, though from what I already know of Trina—"

"Trust me, it was provoked—but M didn't attack her at all. She just tried to grab Trina's phone when she threatened to publish a nasty photoshopped picture that made it look like M...anyway, it was fake.

Something Trina did to make Sean and Rigel even more jealous of each other, and to get M in trouble. Trina's the one who tried to attack M —and then broke her *own* nose when M ducked. I saw the whole thing on the video Amber took with her phone. Ask Amber to show you. I'll bet she still has it."

Though I'd already had trouble imagining the Sovereign doing what Trina described, it rankles to learn M was in the right. Quickly recalling some of the other stuff I've read, I try again.

"All right, how do you explain her trying to elope with Rigel the moment Faxon was finally toppled, if she supposedly cares so much for our people?"

Molly's eyes go wide. "How...how did you know about that?" she gasps.

Aha! "I have my sources," I say evasively, triumphant now. "So it's true?"

"Not exactly. They weren't eloping. Just...escaping."

"Right, from her responsibilities. The first time our people needed her, if only as a symbol to rally around, she ran away."

But Molly's shaking her head. "No, she ran away because the Council was about to separate her from Rigel, probably permanently. Nobody here on Earth had even heard about Faxon's downfall yet—she didn't find out until after they brought her back. She and Rigel ran because they were scared. If you saw how sick they get when they're apart..." Her expression pleads with me to understand.

"Did the Council know about that?"

"They did—so told the Healers to come up with an antidote for the *tinneas*. The plan was to separate them to test it, but M didn't want to wait around for that. I can't blame her, since I seriously doubt Uncle Allister would have let Rigel come back to Jewel, even if it didn't work."

Her mention of Allister is jarring—it's the second time she's implied her uncle wanted Rigel out of the picture from the very start. Then I remember something else.

"Wait. Couldn't Sean's touch have kept her from getting sick?"

At her startled glance I feel my face warming, remembering why he told me about that.

"It does help some, but not enough. I think for a while he hoped he could eventually form a *graell* bond with her, too, but...that never happened."

"Because she was already bonded with Rigel?"

She nods sadly. "Sean never really had a chance." Then her face brightens. "Lately, though, I have a feeling he's finally ready to move on. Maybe once you and he get to know each other better…" She leaves the sentence hanging.

"How do you think your parents would feel about that?" I remember that assessing look Mrs. O'Gara gave me when she found out I'm an Ag, right before encouraging me to be friends with Molly. *Just* Molly.

Her eyes slide away from mine, confirming my suspicion. "They want him to be happy as much as I do. If they knew he really cared about you—"

"Whoa! Slow down. We hardly know each other." No way I'm going to tell her about that weird touch thing, especially since I'm determined not to let it happen again. "Anyway, enough about Sean. Can't you tell me the real reason Emileia worked so hard to get Acclaimed when she supposedly didn't want to?"

For a long moment she hesitates, clearly torn, then springs to her feet. "Um, it's getting kind of late. I promised my parents I'd be home by nine and it must be after that now."

"So you really won't tell me?"

"Not tonight but…I'll try to convince Sean to. He can explain it better anyway. What he *won't* tell you is that he was nearly as much a hero as M was. If it weren't for him… Anyway, I should go. Thanks for the, um, lesson, Kira, even if it didn't take."

With a lopsided grin, she scoops her backpack off the bench, slings it over her shoulder and walks away, leaving me to frown after her, thinking hard.

After everything Molly told me Thursday, I feel more awkward than ever trying to make small talk with M and Rigel Saturday night, at the newcomer get-together.

"So, what sort of stuff did you have to do in those orientation classes?" Rigel asks the group. "You were all in Dun Cloch before coming here, right?"

The Walsh twins explain that they and Erin did their basic Orientation in Bailerealta, then joined the rest of us in Dun Cloch once they knew they were coming to Jewel.

"Oh, I wondered about that," M says. "The Council told me everyone coming here got extra instruction but they didn't say where. Was it super tedious?"

That startles a laugh from me. "Kind of, yeah," I admit. "Most of it was pretty obvious stuff."

She wrinkles her nose in sympathy. "I think they just wanted to be extra cautious after some of the clueless *Echtran* tourists we've had here."

"Not to mention that Anti-Royal dude who tried to kill you." Rigel puts a protective arm around her shoulders. "It only made sense to do some extra screening before letting people actually move here."

Though they hadn't screened *me* out...because they only interrogated the adults. I'm still trying to come up with a polite response, instead defending the Populists like I want to, when Sean and Molly walk in.

Sternly ordering my color not to rise, I return Molly's effusive greeting before sending a carefully casual smile Sean's way. His ears look slightly redder than usual as he returns it. At school it was fairly easy to avoid talking with Sean by pretending to pay attention in class, then hurrying off to my next one. I suspect it'll be harder at a party.

I realized then that Liam's saying something about *caidpel*, which gives me an excuse to turn away.

"—know Brady well?"

"What? Oh, um, yeah, I guess so." I'm startled to realize I haven't even thought about Brady for several days. "I mean, we were on the team together for almost a year."

"Cool. I figured you two must be friends, you played so well off each other those last few games of the regular season. I can't really ask you about *caidpel* at school, obviously, but I've always—"

The Sovereign clears her throat and he breaks off.

"Thanks so much for coming tonight, everyone. No, don't worry, I'm not going to give another speech," she adds with a grin. "This is a party, not a meeting. I just wanted to remind you that if you've got questions you can't ask at school, tonight's a good chance to do that. Rigel and I— and Sean and Molly, too—will tell you whatever you want to know. But the first person who bows to me is going to get smacked, got it?"

That gets a laugh, and a moment later Rigel's dad comes in with a stack of pizza boxes. Everyone relaxes noticeably and it starts to feel like a real party. Soon people take M at her word and ask her questions, some about topics she avoided during the meeting at NuAgra a week ago Thursday.

I make a point of staying close enough to hear her answers. As an added benefit, Sean seems to be deliberately keeping his distance from her.

The downside is Alan. Like at school the past few days, he interprets my coolness toward Sean as encouragement to flirt with me, despite how many times I've shut him down in the past.

"Having fun?" he asks, sidling over. "Can I get you another soda?"

"I'm fine, thanks." I stop short of telling him to go away, even though he made me miss whatever M just said about the Grentl.

Alan inches closer. "You sure?"

"Yes." I take a step away from him, more irritated than usual by his persistence. I tell myself it's not because Sean is watching, from the opposite side of the room. "Just...don't, okay?" Alan's quick scowl proves he knows exactly what I mean.

"I just... Fine. Sorry." He moves off, his feelings clearly hurt. I wish it would make him give up permanently, but I doubt it.

M is still being bombarded with questions, so I quickly turn my focus back to her.

"So...Rigel's memory really was erased, like Morag Teague told everyone on the feeds?" Erin asks hesitantly at one point.

M nods, though she looks slightly wary now.

"But how...how could he get it back? My parents are Healers and they said it should have been impossible."

"It probably would have been, if not for our *graell* bond." I inch closer. "And yes, it's real. Even the *Echtran* Council finally admitted it."

"Wow, so it was your *graell* bond that cured him?" Jana asks, wide-eyed. "What's it like, being bonded like that? It sounds so romantic! My parents always said it was only in fairy tales, but I think even they believe it's true after that last MARSTAR bulletin."

"Mine, too," Erin chimes in. "Then I went back and reread the report Regent Shim sent out, about those tests the Scientists did. I'm not sure I'd want someone reading my mind like that. Is it weird?"

M and Rigel both laugh, exchanging one of those too-intimate glances. "Sometimes," Rigel admits.

"It helps that we're getting better at shielding—keeping our thoughts to ourselves when we want to," M adds.

"Most of the time it's great, though." The smile Rigel gives her makes even unromantic me catch my breath.

Sean mainly focused on the drawbacks of a *graell* bond when he explained it to me, but now I wonder if the benefits might possibly outweigh them. To have Sean look at me like that…

Nope. Nope, nope, nope. I don't want that at *all*.

Sean's no longer part of my mission, I remind myself. The last thing I need is to start seriously crushing on him. That would only distract me from what I'm supposed to be doing.

I keep listening, hoping to pick up some new detail I can report back.

29

Turnover

Sean

"WHAT'S up with you tonight, Sean? Why aren't you talking to anybody?" Molly asks midway through the evening. "This is supposed to be a party, you know. Did you and Kira have a fight or something?"

"A fight? No. We've barely talked to each other since Tuesday night." Which is perfectly true.

Out of the corner of my eye, I see Alan leaning in close to her right now, like he's been doing way too often at school. Again, I have to tamp down a totally inappropriate twinge of jealousy.

"Why?" Molly demands, snapping my attention back to her—though I still keep half an eye on Kira and Alan. "Because of what Mum said? Don't be stupid. You like her, I can tell. And she likes you. Why are you both so determined to fight it?"

I huff out a breath. "Because—"

"Don't give me that line about it being *too soon*. You told me you took Missy Gillespie to Homecoming because you were trying to move on, get M out of your system. If you were willing to go out with a *Duchas* girl to do that, why not an *Echtran* girl you obviously like a lot better? You claim you're sick of people feeling sorry for you. Maybe you've decided you like it after all?"

I turn to glare at her. "What? Of course I don't like it. That's not—" I break off at Molly's knowing smirk. "Why don't you go chat up one of the new guys yourself, and leave me alone?"

"Maybe I will. Meanwhile, go talk to Kira. You know you want to."

"She seems to be busy at the moment." I hook a thumb over my shoulder in her direction.

Molly glances that way. "You're kidding, right? I can tell from here she's giving him the brush-off—again. But he obviously doesn't give up as easily as you do."

Against my will I look and sure enough, Alan's walking away with a sulky look on his face. My spirits lift despite myself. Still, I'm not about to—

"Tell you what," Molly says. "How about I go distract Alan—he *is* kind of cute, after all—and you go talk to Kira. Or would you rather I nag *her* to talk to *you*…?"

Shaking my head in exasperation—because Molly's just interfering enough to do that—I turn my back on my sister and slowly make my way to where Kira's standing, a little apart from everyone else. Kind of like I've done all evening.

"This is supposed to be a party," I say from behind her, trying to ignore the way her *brath* seems to reach out and surround me. It's the closest I've been to her since Tuesday night. "You don't look like you're having much fun."

A tiny shudder seems to go through her as she pulls her gaze away from the group around M and Rigel to glance up at me. It makes me wonder if my *brath* feels extra strong to her, too—not that I plan to ask.

"You don't seem to be doing a lot of mingling, either," she points out, one brow raised. Apparently she noticed me avoiding everyone, too, though I haven't noticed her looking my way.

"Yeah, well, I'm not a big party person," I reply with a shrug.

"Especially lately?" she asks shrewdly.

I shift uncomfortably. Molly's taunt just now about people feeling sorry for me was bad enough. Kira alluding to it is worse. To avoid her knowing gaze, I watch the group surrounding M and Rigel.

People have apparently talked them into demonstrating their *graell* telepathy, because Erin Campbell is scribbling notes she only shows to one of them. Everyone claps when the other one recites it perfectly.

"Nice party trick," Kira comments.

That forces a snort of laughter from me. "Yeah, they should take it on the road, do children's birthdays."

She chuckles, too. "Too bad it would make the *Duchas* suspicious. Otherwise it could be a great alternative career if the Sovereign gig ever falls through."

Her words are an abrupt reminder of why I decided to cool things with her before they could get serious. "It's not going to fall through," I murmur. "You may as well give up on that idea."

"Maybe if you told me why it was so important for her to be Acclaimed in the first place," she replies so softly even I can barely hear her. "You never did get around to that, remember? I'll bet it was some lame reason having more to do with putting Royals back in power than improving things in Nuath."

"No. You're wrong."

"Prove it."

For a moment I struggle with myself, weighing the risk of her spreading the story of how close Nuath came to annihilation against the risk of her continuing to agitate against M's Sovereignty. Finally, I nod.

"Fine. I'll tell you. Tomorrow. We can go shoot hoops again and...and talk. Okay?"

She stares up at me, skepticism clearly warring with curiosity. Curiosity wins. "All right, then. Tomorrow."

The small crowd around M and Rigel finally breaks up and one or two people drift our way. Molly, I notice, is chatting animatedly to Alan, just like she promised.

"That's so cool. They really *can* read each other's minds," I hear Kira's sister exclaiming to the other two new girls, Erin and Jana.

Both nod enthusiastically. "I just wish the *graell* wasn't so rare." Jana heaves a melodramatic sigh. "It's *so* romantic. I wish it would happen to me."

I have to bite my tongue to keep from snapping, "No. You don't."

30

Double reverse

IF I FELT self-conscious at last night's party, it's nothing to how I feel waiting for Sean to pick me up again the next afternoon.

At church this morning, Molly insisted our family sit with theirs, though with the Stuarts and Truitts already there, Sean and I were on opposite ends of the pew. The worst was when the service ended and Mrs. O'Gara and Mrs. Truitt, the Sovereign's "aunt," invited Mum to join the church choir. Of course she agreed, acting so incredibly honored it was downright embarrassing.

I'm still thinking about that when Sean pulls up in his family's battered maroon minivan.

"Ready?" he calls out the window, just like last Sunday.

In answer I climb in, my smile feeling stupid on my face. What is it about this guy that makes me feel so awkward? Even Brady didn't affect me like this. Come to think of it, neither did Sean...until those weird touches. As he pulls back out onto Diamond Street and heads toward the school, I'm grateful for the center console between our seats.

"So," I say after two or three minutes of uncomfortable silence, "are you still planning to tell me what it was that convinced the Sovereign to work so hard to be Acclaimed?"

He slants a sideways look at me out of those startlingly bright blue eyes. "Didn't I say I would?"

I shrug. "People don't always follow through on what they say." Like my old *caidpel* coach promising he'd keep me in Nuath. "Especially if it's something they don't particularly want to do in the first place."

"I keep my promises." Another glance, this one accompanied by a frown. "I figured we'd talk after shooting some hoops, but if you'd rather talk now...?"

"Now works for me." I don't want to give him time to change his mind. "You and Molly have made me so curious with all your cryptic hints, I doubt I could keep my head in the game anyway until I hear the rest."

His frown deepens, but he remains silent until we're nearly to the school. I'm about to accuse him of going back on his word after all when he heaves a sigh.

"All right. But I hope once I tell you, you'll understand why it shouldn't be made public, at least not yet."

I prefer to reserve judgment on that, but don't say so. I just wait until he pulls into the back lot and parks before saying, "Go on."

With a quick nod, he turns to face me. "It...has to do with the Grentl, those aliens that tried to blast Earth with an EMP."

"Huh?" This is totally not what I was expecting. "What about them?"

"Remember I told you only a few people knew about the Grentl before this latest threat? Well, it turns out the Sovereigns have actually been in contact with them since Sovereign Aerleas. Way longer than M made it sound in her speech about taking precautions. It also wasn't the first time the Grentl have posed a threat, though I think it was the first time they threatened Earth."

Now I'm totally confused—and a little scared. "What...what do you mean?"

"Remember those power outages in Nuath last spring?"

Ignoring a trickle of fear, I nod. That last blackout was borderline terrifying. "Governor Nels said it was because of maintenance they were doing on the power grid. He said—"

"He only said that to prevent a mass panic. How do you think people would have reacted if he'd told them aliens, light years away, had the ability to shut down our power permanently?"

A gasp escapes me, the trickle becoming a flood of horror. "Without power, Nuath—"

"Wouldn't last an hour," he finishes grimly. "Exactly. Gone. Poof." He snaps his fingers and I flinch.

"But...what does that have to do with M?"

"She's the only one who can talk to them. As I understand it, Aerleas sort of imprinted on their communication device when it was discovered three centuries ago. After that, they refused to talk to anyone but her…or a direct descendant. Thanks to Faxon, M is the only one still alive. Those power glitches happened because the Grentl didn't get an answer the last time they tried to contact the Sovereign—after Faxon tried to use their device. That's how he was ousted so quickly, by the way. The Grentl zapped him unconscious for messing with their device and loyalists in the Palace seized the opportunity to lock him up. The Resistance did the rest."

All I can do is stare at him, trying to wrap my mind around everything he's telling me. I'd think he was making it all up if it weren't for that incredible light show I saw in Dun Cloch a few nights before we left.

"Anyway," he continues, "when the Grentl didn't get any response to their calls, they interrupted Nuath's power, a little longer each time, to get the Sovereign's attention. Unfortunately, the only person who could answer them was still on Earth—which meant we had to get M to Mars in a hurry. Because the device was hidden in the Palace, she couldn't get to it until she was Acclaimed. That obviously needed to happen before they cut power long enough to completely destroy Nuath. It was…a close thing." The echo of terror in his eyes forces me to believe him.

"And she…knew this all along?"

He nods. "Molly and I only found out the day before she was Acclaimed, the day we had that last, long blackout. Before that, I thought the biggest thing at stake was political stability. Which was important, but not like—"

"Not like the lives of every single person in Nuath."

"Yeah."

I think about that for a moment, more preconceptions about the Sovereign crumbling, my sense of purpose wavering—until something occurs to me.

"Then what she did on board the *Quintessence*, with Rigel, was even more irresponsible than everyone thought! If she *knew* all our lives depended on her getting Acclaimed as quickly as possible, how could she take a risk like that?"

To my surprise, something like guilt flickers across Sean's face. "They obviously didn't know about the cameras yet. That…that kiss happened just a couple hours after liftoff, M told me. They hadn't had a moment alone for days by then. I'd made sure of that. I sort of threatened to get Rigel in trouble if they didn't keep their distance, hide their feelings. So when they finally got that brief moment alone...I guess they couldn't help themselves."

His eyes linger on me with a warmth that implies he understands why, now. A blush threatens and I look away—and remember something else.

"When I tried to get Molly to tell me all this, she insisted you could explain it better. She also said you deserve as much credit as M does. That if it weren't for you..." I swallow.

Now Sean's the one who won't meet my eyes. "You already know what I had to do to keep her healthy enough for all those appearances, after Rigel's grandmother took him away."

His evasiveness tells me that can't be all. "What else?"

He heaves a sigh. "Molly probably meant what happened the day after M was Acclaimed. When she heard Rigel got his memory erased and left Nuath without her, M...sort of lost it. Went into a complete meltdown. Molly and I managed to pull her out of it enough for her to do what she needed to do—to talk to the Grentl before...you know."

I swallow. "Good thing you were there to keep her obsession with Rigel from killing us all," I say, my earlier disdain for her rushing back.

Sean frowns at my tone. "It wasn't her fault. Devyn Kane and Gordon and...a few others, *they're* the ones who nearly got us all killed. Once Molly and I snapped her out of it, M was totally committed to doing whatever she had to. Bottom line is, if it weren't for her, they'd— we'd—all be dead right now."

I raise a brow at him and he hurries on. "It's true. She not only answered them in time to prevent a disastrously long blackout, she also talked them out of destroying Nuath because of what they'd learned about Faxon. Apparently that's when they shifted their focus to Earth, deciding this is where the problems started. The Grentl really would have zapped this planet back to the Stone Age with that EMP if our Scientists hadn't figured out a way to harness M and Rigel's electrical ability to stop them. They've apparently backed off now, but what if they change their minds later? If they do, M will be our only hope. Again."

I don't say anything at first, still trying to absorb everything I've just learned—especially the fact that, if everything Sean just told me is true,

M *didn't* have a choice about becoming—and staying—Sovereign. Still, I can't let go of my Populist ideals quite so easily.

"If…if the Grentl do come back someday, she could talk to them even if she weren't Sovereign, couldn't she? I mean, if the people elected a different leader in her place she could still be, I don't know, Head Alien Liaison or something."

Sean grimaces. "Maybe. She'd probably rather do that than be Sovereign, actually. But totally apart from the Grentl thing, she's already done a lot more good than you give her credit for. Persuading people to emigrate to Earth, for instance, to lessen the strain on Nuath's power, which really is running out. When we left Mars, her approval ratings were sky-high—and that was before anybody had even heard about the Grentl. What makes you think our people even *want* a different leader?"

"Maybe they don't." Unfortunately, he has a point, which puts me on the defensive again. "Not yet. But they should still have that choice."

"If M gets her way, one day they will. For now, though, she's the best thing we've got, even if you refuse to see it." Clearly exasperated by my attitude, he unsnaps his seatbelt and opens his car door. "Come on. Let's go shoot some hoops."

I don't argue. Sean clearly doesn't want to talk about this anymore and I need a break, too, to sort through my wildly conflicting thoughts and feelings.

The gym is empty again when we go in, which means neither of us have to hold back. I'm glad, since Sean and I both need to blow off some steam. I give it my all, playing even harder than I did last Sunday, fueled by the anger I feel at myself—and Sean—for my current inner turmoil.

Sean's playing harder, too. He drives toward the basket, a determined gleam in his eyes, watching for an opening to shoot. I watch him just as closely. The instant he starts to release the ball, I launch myself upward, drawing on all my *caidpel* training, and bat it away long before it reaches the basket.

"Nice block!" he exclaims, lunging after the ball.

I sprint after it, too and we reach it at exactly the same moment. His reach is a lot longer than mine, but I turn on the speed and dart between his outstretched hands for the ball—only to feel his hands graze both my shoulders. The double jolt I get from the contact startles me breathless and I have to strive mightily not to let my reaction show.

Snagging the ball, away from him, I spin back toward the basket, my eyes narrowed in concentration. Sean's face showed a trace of the same shock I felt, but he's also quick to hide it. He gets between me and the basket, as determined to keep me from scoring as I was to prevent him doing so.

We continue to play for another forty-five minutes, by which time we're both breathing hard and desperately in need of a water break. Thirsty as I am, I almost hate to stop. The concentration required by the game has kept me from dwelling on the conversation we had in the car and the doubts it raised. Doubts about everything I've believed about the Sovereign since before her Acclamation.

"Here." Sean hands me my water bottle as I join him on the next-to-bottom bleacher. "You have to need it as much as I do." His grin is approving, even admiring.

"Thanks." If he's not going to mention that touch, even stronger than our last one on Tuesday, neither am I—though the sense-memory still makes my upper arms tingle. I'm more aware of Sean, his nearness, than ever.

My thoughts shy away from that awareness as I take a big swig of water, only to land on another, even scarier one—that two worlds owe their continued existence to a sixteen-year-old girl and her diplomatic skills.

Allister and Lennox, and especially Crevan Erc, can't possibly know. They'd never be so determined to bring down the Sovereign if they knew what a huge risk that could pose to both Nuath and Earth.

I have to tell them, I realize. Sean asked me not to make the information he shared public, and I won't. But Allister and Lennox need to know. Then they can pass the info along to Crevan Erc and the Populists can adjust their plans accordingly.

The hard part will be making them believe me.

Eager as I am to pass along what I've learned to Allister and Lennox, I don't get a chance until late that night. When I first get home, Mum and Dad want me to join them on a walk around Jewel, even when I remind them I've already had plenty of exercise.

"It will be a perfect cool-down," Mum says. "The weather is lovely and rain is predicted later this week. We should take advantage while we can. The winters here may not be as severe as Dun Cloch's, but—"

"It's still September!" I protest. But she won't take no for an answer.

Then, after dinner, Adina insists I watch all the tricks she's taught her puppy. I *am* grudgingly impressed when the baby animal sits, lies down and rolls over on command. Adina really does have a remarkable gift with animals.

"Now hold out your hand and tell her to shake."

I draw back in distaste. "What?"

"Oh, come on, Kira, she won't hurt you. Don't be a wimp."

"I'm not… Fine." To humor her, I kneel down and extend a hand toward the dog. "Shake."

To my surprise, the puppy immediately puts a paw into my hand, watching my face as though for approval.

"Good girl, Aggie," Adina croons, patting its head. "Tell her what a good girl she is, Kira."

Giving my sister an impatient glance, I mumble, "Um…good girl."

The thing immediately gives a yip of delight and proceeds to crawl into my lap, its whole back end wriggling as it tries to wag its nub of a tail.

"Wait…don't…" I protest feebly as it butts its head against me and tries to lick my face.

"Aw, look how much she likes you! I knew she would if you just gave her a chance." Adina seems even more pleased than the puppy does.

I hold it slightly away from my body preparing to scold it for climbing on me like that. But then I look down into its eager little face and…I can't do it. It's so guileless, so happy, and for so little cause. And…it does act as though it likes me. Instead of a reprimand, I give it a reluctant smile instead.

"I guess she *is* kind of cute." I hand her back to Adina. "But I still don't think she should sleep in our bedroom."

Adina grins at me, clearly savoring the victory she and Aggie have achieved over her grumpy big sister. "Can you help me with my Algebra homework?" she asks then. "I'm having trouble with some of the word problems."

Not until Adina and my parents are all asleep, more than two hours later, do I finally have the privacy I need to call Dun Cloch. Locking myself in the bathroom, I again activate the aural dampening field. I decided earlier that a text message won't do for something this big and unbelievable. I'm also curious to hear what Allister and Lennox will say about it.

Fortunately, Allister answers almost immediately. "Kira? I didn't expect to hear from you again so soon. Dare I hope this mean you've already won the Sovereign's trust?"

"Um, I'm still working on that, but I learned something today that I thought you both should know about."

I relay what Sean told me about the Grentl and how they would have killed everyone in Nuath if the Sovereign hadn't stopped them in time. Also that, according to Sean, nobody else could have done it.

"So convincing our people to remove her from power might not be a great idea after all. Not if she's the only one who can respond to them if they threaten us again. Right?"

There's such a long pause on the other end after I finish, I wonder for a moment if I've lost the connection.

Then, "Thank you for telling me this, Kira. As it happens we've already been told about these claims. We have reason to believe they are greatly exaggerated."

"But Sean said—"

"Yes, well, you said yourself that he is still almost blindly loyal to Emileia. Still besotted with her, no doubt. Of course he would be predisposed to believe her actions were purely for the benefit of Nuath. Our source believes it was in fact merely a political ploy to convince her most serious rivals to withdraw their opposition."

Though I have reason to believe Sean's no longer "besotted" with the Sovereign, as his uncle puts it, I'm not about to tell Allister that. "What if he's right, though? What if she *is* the only one who can talk to those aliens if they come back?"

"Unlikely. Our associate believes anyone of similar ancestry could do the same. Myself, for instance, or my sister. We are, after all, direct descendants of Sovereign Nuallan, Aerleas's father. Furthermore, my sister and I both have far more diplomatic experience than a teenager possibly could. Should any future negotiations prove necessary, either of us would of course be willing to step up."

"I'm...I'm sure you would, sir. But, um, since neither of you were in Nuath last spring, she really was the only one who could have used the device to prevent the Grentl from destroying us."

Whether I like M personally or not, I have to be grateful to her for that. I also wonder how a virtual prisoner in Dun Cloch could "step up" if needed. Maybe Allister figures he'll be released if the Sovereign is deposed?

"You assume the Grentl would have done so. Personally, I take leave to doubt it. Why should they? What harm had we ever done them?" His tone is completely dismissive. "In any event, the Council has assured us that we no longer have anything to fear from them, as they are unlikely to return in our lifetimes."

The Council also gave the Sovereign—and Rigel—credit for that, but I don't risk pissing Allister off by pointing that out. "Um, good point, sir. Anyway, I'm sorry to have bothered you. I...I thought you might not know."

"Kira, you *are* still committed to our cause, are you not?"

I hesitate for an instant, then reply, "I'm as committed as I've always been to the best possible future for our people, sir. *All* of our people."

His hesitation is longer than mine. Then he says, "These discoveries about the Grentl have clearly unsettled you, Kira, which is most understandable. I'd very much like you to hear Governor Lennox's thoughts on the matter. Unfortunately, he is not available at the moment. Can you arrange to be alone—completely alone—for a somewhat longer conference later this week?"

"Um, yes, I think I can manage that." Though I'll have to find a better place to talk than this bathroom I share with my sister.

"Excellent. I'll message you with a day and time after I speak with Lennox. Farewell until then." He breaks the connection.

For the first time, I wonder if he's truly committed to the good of our people—or just to what would be good for Allister Adair.

31

Bounce pass

Sean

CONSIDERING I talked twice with Kira over the weekend and spent Sunday afternoon shooting hoops with her, it seems pointless to ignore her at school Monday. So I don't.

"Hey. Good weekend?" I greet her when she arrives in Physics class.

To my relief, she seems to have come to the same conclusion. At least, she stops and smiles instead of just nodding as she passes me.

"Mostly the same weekend you had, I think." Her smile is almost a grin now—though I detect a certain wariness in her eyes. "How was yours?"

"Better than most, actually." I hold her gaze so she'll know I mean because of her.

A tiny crease forms between her brows but before she can reply, Alan comes in looking irritated.

"I thought you were going to wait, Kira." His peevish expression encompasses both of us. "I only needed to stop at my locker for a second."

Kira keeps looking at me for a heartbeat before turning to Alan. "What difference does it make? We're both here now."

He shrugs. "So you two are talking again?"

"Yeah, we ironed out our little...misunderstanding over the weekend." I can't resist slanting a smile down at Kira as I say it, earning a

235

positive glower from Alan. I shouldn't enjoy needling him like this, but he ticked me off last week, trying to move in on Kira while I was keeping my distance.

"Did we?" She arches an eyebrow at me but looks more amused than upset.

"I hope so." Again, I try to imbue my words with extra meaning. By now she's had time to think over everything I told her yesterday. If I succeeded in changing her Anti-Royal attitude, I won't feel so guilty about the way she affects me.

Her expression doesn't give anything away, though. After watching me for a long moment, she just turns away with a tiny smile. Alan follows her to their lab table, though with a quick frown over his shoulder at me.

Our next chance to talk is in Lit class, though we carefully limit our conversation to schoolwork. Even so, her comments are interesting. So much so that I catch up with her on the way to the lunchroom afterward.

"Are you as frustrated by this assignment as I am?" I murmur too softly for any *Duchas* to overhear. "Comparing the stifling of information in *Fahrenheit 451* to what went on under Faxon's regime would make an excellent essay, don't you think?"

She glances up at me in evident surprise. "I've been thinking that exact same thing! I guess all dictators realize at some point that they have to control what people are allowed to know if they hope to maintain power over them. Do you remember how—?"

"Ooh, what are you two whispering about?" Molly pops up next to me out of nowhere, grinning. "Or shouldn't I ask?"

I give her a quelling look. "Just the book we're reading in Lit. Drawing some parallels to stuff we can't talk about in class."

"Oh." Her grin gives way to disappointment, but only for a second. Then, "Why don't you sit at our table today, Sean? Then you can continue your, um, discussion."

"Right. Because Bri and Deb and the other *Duchas* at your table won't think it's weird at all if we start talking about Faxon and Mars."

Kira chuckles at my sarcasm. As always, the sound sends a not-unpleasant shiver through me. "It might be interesting to see their expressions if we did."

Molly gives us both a wry smile. "Okay, so I didn't exactly think that through. But you can still sit with us. And Kira, maybe you can come over again tonight or tomorrow so you guys can finish discussing *that* topic."

"Er, maybe," she replies noncommittally, shooting me a quick, sideways glance. "I'll, um, let you know."

Pete Griffin joins us then to talk basketball, though I notice him sneaking looks at both Molly and Kira while we chat. When we reach the cafeteria two other teammates from last year waylay Pete and me, while Molly and Kira keep walking.

When I finally have my tray, I take a couple steps toward Molly and M's table before noticing Bri and Deb are sitting between Kira and the only empty seat. Stifling a pang of disappointment, I head to my usual table instead.

Probably just as well. Molly doesn't need extra ammunition for her transparent attempts at matchmaking.

With that in mind, I don't go out of my way to talk to Kira in Government, where Molly's watching us a little too interestedly. In fact, I don't get a chance to talk to her again at all that day. And when Kira gets to Physics the next morning, Alan is with her and sticks too close before and after class to allow us to say anything to each other without him hearing.

I'm resolving to snag a word with her before Lit class when Molly catches me in the hall between second and third period.

"I talked to Kira in French class just now and she says she can come over tonight! Thought you'd like to know." A mischievous wink accompanies her words.

I respond by frowning. "Why are you doing this, Mol? You heard what Mum said last week. What if—?"

"Oh, pssh." Molly waves a dismissive hand. "Mum will come around once she sees how much you and Kira like each other."

"How much—? Molly, I keep telling you we hardly even know each other yet. If you convince Mum it's more than that, she might try to discourage Kira from visiting our house again."

Molly looks startled. "She wouldn't do that! She said herself we should be making friends with the new students."

But she looks slightly worried now—enough, I hope, to keep her from doing anything too embarrassing while Kira's at our place tonight. Molly knows as well as I do that our mum is completely capable of freezing somebody out without technically being rude. She does it to Rigel every time she sees him—and he helped save the planet.

Sure enough, when Kira arrives that evening, Mum's greeting is noticeably less warm than it was a week ago.

"Oh, hello, Kira. Molly said you'd be stopping by again so she can continue helping you to catch up in French class."

"And Government," Molly says from behind Mum. "Sean's in that class, so he can help, too. And don't you two have a couple of other classes together?"

Despite the sharp look Mum gives me, I reply, "Physics and Literature, yeah."

"I see." There's no mistaking our mother's coolness now. "I was about to suggest Molly and Kira go up to her room to study, but I suppose the living room—"

"We can all study in my room, it'll be fine," Molly interrupts. "Why don't you two go on up and I'll get us some tea and cookies."

Mum turns The Look on Molly. "Nonsense. All three of you can go upstairs and I'll bring up a tray once the tea is brewed—though I can't help thinking you'd have more space to spread out down here in the living room."

"It'll be quieter upstairs," Molly counters, looking slightly disappointed. "Come on."

Kira and I follow her up the stairs, keeping enough distance between us there's no risk of accidentally touching. Until I find out whether I've changed Kira's mind about M and the monarchy, I absolutely need to avoid that extra complication.

32

Field goal

Molly's room is small but pretty, decorated in shades of green with posters of flowers on the walls. The only off-note is the row of houseplants on the window sill in various stages of distress. She wasn't kidding about lacking the usual Ag skills.

Unfortunately, the only places to sit are the single desk chair and the bed—and Molly's already reaching for the chair.

Sean is quicker. He practically pulls it out from under her and sits in it himself, forcing Molly and me to take the bed instead of Sean and me, as she clearly intended.

I'm relieved. Friendly as Sean has been at school this week, he's obviously as eager as I am to avoid any more disturbing touches. I wonder if there's a subtle way to make Molly back off—though I suspect Sean's already tried that.

"I guess we should get our books out before Mum comes up with that tray," Molly says, settling herself cross-legged on the bed. "But we can totally talk about other things than school if you want, Kira. Sean says he finally told you why M needed to get Acclaimed so quickly last spring?"

"Um, yeah. Pretty mind-boggling to think those aliens can control Nuath's power supply from who knows how many light years away—and that the only person who can talk to them is the Sovereign." Though Allister disputed that last point…

Sean leans toward me, a tiny crease between his eyebrows. "Now you've had time to think about it, you get why it's important to keep that a secret, right?"

I nod, my eyes not leaving his. "You're right that it would scare everyone in Nuath half to death to find out what the Grentl can do—especially since there's apparently no way to stop them if they change their minds again."

"And M? Are you willing to agree now that it would do more harm than good to stir up opposition against her? Opposition that could conceivably become violent?"

This time I hesitate. Over the past six months I'd become increasingly convinced that Emileia is the worst possible leader for our people. Admitting I was wrong feels like a betrayal—not only of the Populist movement, but of myself.

"I still can't believe real Populists would resort to violence," I finally say. "But it's possible she's not *quite* as unqualified as I thought. She seems to have picked a good Regent, at least."

Sean's lips quirk up in a little smile, causing an unwelcome warmth to seep through me.

I remind myself that the approval of some high-ranking Royal shouldn't matter to me at all even though I know, deep down, that liking to see him smile has nothing to do with his rank or *fine.*

"I guess that's a start," he says. "By now I hope you know me well enough that—"

Molly cuts him off. "—the Constitution. Those projects we just turned in were all about— Oh, hi, Mum."

Mrs. O'Gara appears in the doorway. Molly obviously heard her coming up the stairs...and doesn't want her to know Sean shared that huge secret with me.

"I've brought a little something to help you keep up your energy while studying." She casts an approving glance at our seating arrangement as she sets the tray she's carrying on the edge of the desk. "Molly, don't forget to bring the empty dishes back to the kitchen. I don't want to find them stacked on the floor tomorrow."

Molly grimaces. "I only did that once." Then, at her mother's penetrating look, "Okay, maybe three times. But I won't do it again, okay?"

Mrs. O'Gara nods, one eyebrow still raised, then leaves. Molly waits till she's had time to get all the way back downstairs before saying anything else.

"I hate when she does that." At my look of confusion, she adds, "Our mum *always* knows if someone's lying to her. An inconvenient little talent she has. Which means we'd better spend *some* time on actual schoolwork, in case she grills one of us about it later."

We spend the next hour on Government, the subject I need the most help with. Good thing, too, since Mrs. O'Gara comes back twice more during that hour to "see if we need anything else," though I suspect it's really to make sure Molly hasn't left Sean and me alone.

At nine-thirty I reluctantly tell them I should get home. They both come downstairs to see me to the door and Sean opens it for me.

I involuntarily start back at the sight of rain coming down in sheets just past the porch overhang. "Ew. I'm still not used to it doing that, even though the *Horizon* landed right in the middle of a thunderstorm. Luckily a lot of Dun Cloch is shielded, so we didn't have to deal with *too* much of it after that first night."

Molly laughs. "Sean's not a big fan of Earth weather, either. You should have seen him the first time it rained in Bailerealta—only their central square is climate-controlled. Do you even own an umbrella yet?"

"You mean those upside-down bowl things on sticks the *Duchas* use to stay dry?" I've seen them on television but never used one.

That gets another laugh, this time from both of them. "Good description," Sean says. "We have one, but they do about as good a job as you'd expect. Why don't I walk you, instead?"

"Good idea." Molly grins, then glances over her shoulder toward the back of the house. "I'll handle Mum if she asks where you are," she whispers.

"It's not—" Sean begins, then shrugs. "Okay. I won't be gone long." He and I step out onto the porch and Molly quickly shuts the door behind us.

The rain looks even worse up close, though at least there's no lightning or thunder. Yet. "Do you really have something better than an umbrella? Or are you just coming along for moral support?"

"Both," he replies with a half-wink. "Molly's right that I had the hardest time of anyone in our family adjusting to the idea of stuff falling from the sky. Just wait till your first snowfall." He shudders. "It's why Mum and Dad let me get this app."

Pulling an omni out of his pocket—not just a cellphone with a few special functions, but a real Martian omni—he activates the holographic control screen and makes a selection I can't see from my angle.

"There. This'll keep us dry. The only catch is we, um, have to be touching to keep the rain off both of us."

"Oh. Okay." Pretending it's no big deal, I put a hand on his forearm. Immediately, I feel a sizzling rush of adrenaline course through me, stronger than ever.

Sean sucks in a quick breath and swallows visibly but just says, "Okay, let's go."

Together, we walk down the porch steps into the rain. Even though I expect it, I'm fascinated to see the water sheer away without touching us.

"I saw a few people using this app in Dun Cloch, but this is the first time I've used it. Nobody bothers with it in Nuath, of course, and the *teachtok* phones they gave us at the end of Orientation can't handle special apps like this."

He looks down at me curiously. "I'd have thought most of the permanent residents there would have it. Dun Cloch is huge—it can't all be shielded. And I hear they get a ton of snow up there in winter."

"I, ah, didn't meet many permanent residents, they kept us so busy." For obvious reasons, I haven't told Sean or Molly about meeting their uncle there. Luckily it's dark, so if my face gets a little pink he probably can't tell.

"Yeah, Mum said they had to process everyone through in half the usual time. Must have been intense." On that last word he glances at my hand on his arm.

Intense. That's exactly how this touch thing feels. The longer we're in contact, the harder it is to ignore, though both of us are trying.

"Er, speaking of your mum, is she going to be pissed if she finds out you walked me home?"

He gives a little twitch. "Of course not! I mean…I don't see why she would be. We're supposed to be making friends with the newcomers—you heard what M said at that NuAgra meeting." I notice he's not meeting my eye, though.

"She, ah, seemed pretty determined to keep us from being alone together this evening, the way she kept checking in on us. Probably worried I have designs on you or something." I grin as I say it, trying to make it sound like a joke. "I mean, your family *is* important. I imagine people suck up to you almost as much as they do to M."

That makes him laugh. "Nope, not to me. I don't think it's that so much as, well, Mum's always been a…traditionalist."

"So she doesn't want you making friends with non-Royals?"

"Erm… *Friends* is probably fine. I have plenty of *Duchas* friends and she doesn't mind that."

"She just wants to make sure it's not *more* than friends."

He looks uncomfortable but doesn't dispute it. Even though I've been telling myself all along it would be stupid to get involved with Sean, his lack of response stings a little. Refusing to let him see it, I quickly continue.

"She has a valid point. It's not like you and I have anything in common."

Sean stops walking to look at me, brows raised. "You don't think so? I happen to think we have a whole lot in common."

"You do?" I reply, startled. "Like what? We're from totally different *fines.*"

When he shrugs, I'm much too aware of the way his arm moves under my fingers.

"So are M and Rigel. Not that I'm saying—" He breaks off, embarrassed. "But look at the similarities between us. We both used to be kind of big shots. Now, not so much. We both care passionately about the good of our people, even if haven't exactly agreed on what that is. And we both seem driven to…to fight for what we believe in, to make a difference. First it was the Resistance. Then, once Faxon was out… I think that's why I kept trying so hard to get M to accept me as Consort, even after I knew deep down it was hopeless. Because I knew I'd be able to make more of a difference that way. And you—"

I stare at him, open-mouthed, because it hits me that he's absolutely right. "And that's why I was so drawn to the Populist cause when I no longer had the Resistance. I kept hoping *caidpel* would fill that void but…it wasn't the same."

No wonder I've been clinging so stubbornly to my belief that Emileia is a terrible Sovereign. To admit otherwise, even to myself, would leave me with nothing to fight for—or against.

"See? Not so different after all."

That sexy little smile curves his lips again and I notice how completely isolated we are, with Jewel's arboretum on this side of the street and closed shops on the other. Between the rain and the late hour, the whole area is completely deserted.

Hesitantly, I return his smile, my heart beating even faster than when we played basketball. Slowly, he lowers his face to mine and I tip mine up toward his. That voice in the back of my mind still insists this is crazy, but it's whispering now, not shouting. Sean leans in and I don't stop him, wanting this as much as I can ever remember wanting anything.

The instant our lips touch, the connection between us seems to increase exponentially. Feelings beyond anything I've ever experienced race through me from each point of contact, lips and hands. With a tiny groan, Sean fastens his mouth more securely over mine, like he's drinking in the same sensations I am. Dizzy with delight, I cling to him for balance and he does the same, wrapping both arms around me, pulling me closer as he deepens the kiss.

My hands slide up his arms to his shoulders, then around his back, further intensifying the contact between us. Time seems to stop, my heart pounding with mounting excitement. I feel his pounding, too, barely an inch away from mine, in perfectly synchronized rhythm. I'm conscious of a fleeting wish that this incredible moment could go on forever, that we'll never have to return to the real world.

Unfortunately, that's not possible.

After a long, blissful interval that's not nearly long enough, I hear a car approaching. We reluctantly break apart, Sean drawing me with him into the deeper shadow of the arboretum entrance. There, well out of sight of whoever is in the car, we stare at each other. His expression is stunned, wondering, and I'm sure mine is the same.

"I…" he finally breathes. "That was…amazing."

Mutely, I nod.

It wasn't my first kiss, and there's no way it was his, but it might as well have been. For both of us.

"I…" My voice is husky. I clear my throat. "I, uh, should probably get home."

He swallows, still staring down at me. "Right. Of course. I just—"

And suddenly I'm in his arms again, kissing him again. Not for as long this time, but every bit as intensely. Several heartbeats later Sean raises his head with a shaky laugh.

"Home. Right," he says. "Come on."

Hand in hand now, we walk the rest of the way in silence. I'm struggling to process what just happened and suspect he's doing the same. We're nearly to the entrance of my apartment complex before I notice the rain has stopped. When did that happen?

Though the contact is no longer necessary to keep me dry, Sean doesn't let go of my hand. "I, er, guess I'll see you tomorrow."

"Yes. Tomorrow. Good…good night, Sean."

For a second I think he's going to kiss me again, but we're now in a well-lit area, in full view of dozens of apartment windows, and he apparently thinks better of it.

"G'night, Kira." With a parting smile that makes my toes curl, he turns away and heads back toward his house.

I watch him for a long moment, letting myself enjoy the way he moves. Then, with a happy little sigh, I turn around and enter the courtyard.

Tomorrow is bound to bring me to my senses, forcing me to face the ramifications of what happened this evening. But, just for tonight, I'm content to relive the most amazing experience of my life and bask in its lingering glow.

33

Swish

Sean

I BARELY REMEMBER WALKING HOME, I'm in such a daze. The very first time I met her, I thought there was something special about Kira—special to *me*, I mean, not just... But I never imagined... Thoughts and emotions whirl through my mind too quickly to identify. Not until I'm on our front porch do I realize I need to pull myself together if I don't want my family to guess what just happened.

Not that I'm sure *myself* what just happened...

Pausing on the porch, I take several deep breaths. Whatever it was, I'll have to figure it out later. For now, I just need to play it cool.

Two more breaths, then I open the door to find Mum and Molly in the front hall, glaring at each other.

"Um, what's going on? Everything okay?"

They both turn to face me. "See? I told you he'd be right back," Molly says triumphantly.

But Mum looks at me suspiciously. "It shouldn't have taken you that long to walk to Diamond View Terrace and back."

Trying to act totally nonchalant, I shrug. "We got talking a bit. What's the big deal?"

Molly answers before Mum can. "The big deal is she still thinks you shouldn't like any girl but M. Though anybody with half an eye can—"

"Molly!" Mum cuts her off. "I just don't want to see you hurt again,

Sean, that's all. Jumping into a new relationship so quickly seems unwise. Rebound romances rarely end well, particularly when—"

"When they're between two different *fines?*" This time Molly cuts *her* off. "Come on, Mum, look at M and Rigel. No matter how much you disapprove of them as a couple, you can't deny what they've been able to accomplish together, as much for your benefit as anyone else's. You're being totally unreasonable and you know it. All Sean did was walk Kira home, it's not like he asked her to marry him! What do you think they could have done in less than half an hour? In the rain?"

But even as she says it, Molly's way-too-perceptive gaze examines every detail of my appearance and expression.

"I still think Molly should have gone along, if only for appearance's sake," Mum says stubbornly. "You're a prominent figure, Sean, though you don't like to admit it. I can't imagine you want to become the subject of gossip again, just when the last bit has started to die down."

I huff out a breath, my earlier euphoria slipping away. "Why don't you let me worry about that, Mum? I'll be eighteen next month. Isn't it time I started making my own decisions, especially about something this personal? And who said anything about a relationship anyway?"

"Are you telling me you have no romantic feelings toward Kira?" Mum watches me with that focus she has, waiting for my answer.

Which is none of her damned business. "Good night, Mum."

I storm past them up the stairs, then shut myself in my room. At this moment, I totally get why M sometimes says she wishes she were just a regular person. Being under a microscope sucks—especially Mum's microscope.

Sinking down on my bed I stare into space, trying to let go of my anger so I can recapture the joy I felt while kissing Kira. It was, without compare, the most incredible experience of my entire life. And there's no way in hell I'll let my mother's stupid notions of rank and propriety prevent me from experiencing it again.

My irritation gradually fades, allowing an echo of the stunned happiness I felt earlier to creep back. I used to think I'd feel something like this if M ever let me kiss her. Now I know, with sudden certainty, I was wrong. No one but Kira could ever have affected me like this. There's something special between us, something stronger than ever now, that makes everything else pale by comparison.

With a sudden, blinding insight, I finally understand what M kept trying to explain about her bond with Rigel. Sure, I was able to accept, intellectually, that they need to be together, especially after seeing what their bond can do—the electricity, the telepathy, the way his touch strengthens her. Now, for the first time, I get it on a gut-deep level. If it weren't so late, I'd call M right now and apologize for doubting her.

Instead I get ready for bed as quickly as I can, so I can spend the whole night dreaming about Kira.

Delicious as my dreams were, doubts start creeping in the moment I'm fully awake the next morning. It's totally possible Kira regrets kissing me, now she's had time to think things through. How will she act when we see each other at school today? Embarrassed? Mad? Or, worse, will she pretend nothing happened at all? Unwilling to wait until first period to find out, I decide to take the bus.

"Pete's not driving you today?" Molly asks in surprise when I head to the corner with her after breakfast.

"Nah." I sent him a quick text after I got up, saying I didn't need a ride. "He had to be at school early for something—earlier than I wanted to go."

Molly doesn't question my fib, though occasionally I've had the impression she shares Mum's gift. Which is silly, since they're not even related.

"Pete's not still pestering for me to ride with you guys, is he?"

"Nah, he only did that once."

After taking Molly to Homecoming, Pete wanted her to go out with him again. She always made excuses not to go, confiding to me he couldn't keep his hands to himself. Needless to say, when he asked me to plead his case with my sister I refused.

When I see M at the bus stop, I remember I have an apology to make. Awkward, with Molly right here, but I try—sort of.

"Hey, Sean. Slumming with us underclassmen?" M teases when we reach the corner. "No ride today?"

"That and, er, I wanted to tell you—again—how sorry I am about the crap I used to give you and Rigel," I blurt out. "The more I, uh, think about it, the more I realize how hard this last year must've been on you guys."

"Thanks." Then she looks at me more closely. "You're in an awfully good mood today," she says, smiling now. "What's up?"

I shrug, aware that Molly's watching me carefully, too. "Just slept well, I guess."

The bus pulls up a minute later and I stake out an empty seat near the front, hoping Kira will sit with me when she gets on.

As M and Molly head further back, I hear Molly whisper, "Wait till you hear why he's *really* in such a good mood!"

I hope more than ever Kira hasn't already had a change of heart.

Two stops later she boards the bus, along with her sister and the other freshman newcomer, Jana. Grinning hopefully at her, I scoot over. "Hey. I saved you a seat."

Though she's clearly startled to see me, she sits. "Hey. I didn't know you ever rode the bus."

"I, ah, felt like making an exception today." My heart is already beating at least twice as fast as normal just from having her next to me. "Did you, um, sleep well?" I murmur so only she can hear.

Dark lashes conceal those incredible eyes for an instant, then she looks at me again, her cheeks slightly pinker than before. "I...did, actually. You?"

"Better than I can ever remember."

Suddenly daring, I put a hand over hers where it's resting on the seat between us. She doesn't pull away, though her eyes widen slightly at the unmistakable thrill of connection she must feel as strongly as I do.

A giggle from behind makes us both turn to see Jana and Adina watching us from a few seats back, hands over their mouths, eyes dancing with glee. Knowing the Jewel High gossip chain as well as I do, I have no doubt the story that Kira and I are "together" will be all over the school by lunchtime. Not that I mind, particularly.

"You didn't catch any flack from your mum for walking me home last night?" she whispers then.

That memory only slightly dims my current sense of well-being. "She said something about 'appearances' but I told her it was none of her business. Because it's not."

Kira regards me searchingly for a long moment as the bus trundles along, then relaxes into a smile. "Not if you don't want it to be, I guess. *My* mum will probably be thrilled, if I tell her—which I haven't. Yet."

M's friends Bri and Deb get on a few stops later and, like Jana and Adina, immediately take note of Kira and me sitting together, hands touching. More grist for the gossip mill. Conscious of so many interested eyes, we talk about school stuff for the rest of the ride.

We have to separate to go to our lockers once we're inside, but meet again before entering our Physics classroom. That Alan has already heard the gossip is obvious from the way he glowers at both of us when he arrives—even though Kira and I are now standing a good two feet apart, discussing yesterday's lab results.

He listens suspiciously for a moment, then says, "C'mon, Kira. Bell's about to ring." When he reaches for her arm, she doesn't let him touch her, I'm pleased to note.

I take my time putting my books back in my bag after class so Kira has time to reach my table. We don't say anything but she smiles a secret sort of smile as I accompany her out into the hall. Before she heads off to second period, we lace our fingers together, just for a second. It's enough —for now.

I've only taken a few steps in the opposite direction when Alan moves to my side. "So. You and Kira? Seriously?"

I feign surprise. "Wow, word travels fast. I take it you don't approve?"

He has enough self-control to lower his voice before saying, "Oh, come on, Sean. You're Royal, she's Ag. *She* may not realize yet that you're just toying with her, but I'm not that naive."

"We're not on Mars anymore, in case you hadn't noticed," I whisper back. "*Fine* isn't nearly as important here." Still need to convince Mum of that. "I happen to actually like her and, lucky me, it seems to be mutual."

Alan snorts—*not* quietly. "Maybe you'll feel differently when I tell you about all the Anti-Royal stuff she's been spouting ever since she left Nuath. Your mum's on the Council, right? I doubt she'd—"

"Kira and I have discussed our differing political views," I assure him, ignoring a twinge of uneasiness at mention of the Council. "She's entitled to her opinions. I'm entitled to try changing them. And hey, if you think she's such a radical, why are *you* so interested in her?"

He just glares at me again and starts walking faster, leaving me behind.

I stifle a sigh. I didn't want to make an enemy out of Alan, but if my mum's disapproval isn't enough to keep me away from Kira, Alan's definitely isn't. Maybe he'll change his tune when he sees she's happy with me.

Which I plan to make sure she is, from now on.

34

Blind side

My quick hand-clasp with Sean as we leave Physics gives me such a lift I practically float to my next class.

Before seeing him on the bus this morning I was worried his mother would make him promise to stay away from me. Or that he might decide for himself that was safest, no matter how magical those kisses were last night. Because it probably *would* be safest. I was incredibly relieved to discover he'd chosen our...whatever it is...over cold logic.

I'm still smiling dreamily when I get to French—then notice the curious looks from my classmates and Molly's knowing, slightly smug expression. M, however, doesn't look happy at all. She stares at me piercingly, frowning almost like she's seeing me for the first time. Almost like she's...jealous.

Which pisses me off. Does she still consider Sean her personal property even though she threw him over for Rigel? My indignation on Sean's behalf is enough to undercut my happiness...until I see him again in Lit class.

"Hey," he greets me with that half-smile that accelerates my pulse before I even reach him.

"Hey," I respond, closing the gap between us. He takes my hand and, like always, his touch sends a pleasurable shiver through me.

There's no chance to talk during class, but on the way to lunch afterward I ask whether he told his sister about...us.

"Not exactly. But Molly's always been too observant—too nosy—for her own good, so I'm sure she knows."

"I'm sure, too. We haven't exactly avoided each other today," I point out.

"Why should we? It's not like we need to keep it a secret. Unless… you'd rather?"

I chuckle. "*You* probably have a lot more reason to worry than I do. If you're fine with it, so am I."

"I'm *absolutely* fine with it," he assures me with a smile that warms me right to my toes.

As though to prove it, once we have our lunch trays he leads me to a table in the corner where we can sit together and talk uninterrupted and unheard. Though we're still drawing a lot of curious stares, the only people who look upset are Alan…and the Sovereign. I consider asking Sean what her deal is, but I don't want to risk spoiling our first lunch together with questions about his old crush.

In Government, the teacher announces we'll be starting a new project on the electoral process. When she tells us to choose partners, Sean immediately turns to me. "Might be fun to work on that together, don't you think?"

Delighted to have a legitimate reason to spend more time together, I enthusiastically agree, barely noticing the sour looks Alan and M give us.

My good mood lasts all afternoon. Not even Adina's giggling insinuations after we get off the bus bother me—much.

"Just don't say anything to Mum yet, okay?" I caution her. "You know she'd make a huge deal out of it and I'm not sure I'm ready for that."

She laughs, but promises. "By the way, I talked Mum into letting me stop Taekwondo. I'm still not all that into it—and I'd rather spend the time teaching Aggie more tricks and stuff. I told her you'd want to keep going, though. Right?"

Given a choice, I'd now rather spend that hour on Wednesdays with Sean, but after a moment's consideration, I nod. "Yeah, I do. I enjoy it and it's almost always a good workout. It might even come in handy someday."

So when I walk to class half an hour later, it's by myself. I pause a moment by the arboretum, remembering the blissful interlude I spent with Sean right on this spot last night. If things go on like they did today, it probably won't be the last time. I hope not, anyway.

Sean may have convinced me that Emileia isn't necessarily a terrible Sovereign, but I'm still ticked at her for acting upset that he and I are together. Whether it's because she's jealous or because she considers me "beneath" him, I look forward to sparring with her again to give vent to my feelings. Unfortunately, we spend the whole class on forms and kicking combinations and never even put our pads on.

I stay after a few minutes to let Master Parker know about Adina dropping out. When I finally leave, the Sovereign is waiting for me outside.

"I think you and I need to talk," she says without preamble. "Walk together?"

Though startled, I immediately agree since I have a few choice things to tell her, too. Together, we head toward Diamond Street, her Bodyguard following half a block behind us.

"Molly tells me you and Sean are seeing a lot of each other these days. I noticed you two sitting together on the bus today, and at lunch."

I instinctively bristle at the hint of accusation in her tone. "Yeah? So? Does that break some *other* rule you somehow forgot to mention?"

"Are you still upset I told your parents they shouldn't have invited my uncle to dinner?" The look she gives me holds a trace of amusement, which only irritates me further.

"That you called them out about it in front of everybody, yeah. I guess I am."

She shakes her head. "I never mentioned them by name. Nobody knew who I was talking about until they made a point of apologizing afterward—and I doubt many people even heard that."

I frown at her, thinking back, and realize she's right. Technically. But my parents were still embarrassed, and it was her fault. "I just think you should have said something to them privately, instead."

"But that wouldn't have kept others from doing the same thing," she points out. "I thought it was admirable of your parents to immediately come forward like that. Most of the others didn't. Anyway, back to you and Sean—no, there's no rule I know of that you and he can't be together. I just...don't want him hurt again. So if you're only going out with him because you have some grudge against me—"

"I'm not," I interrupt, even if she *is* the Sovereign. "It's nothing to do

253

with you. Anyway, you're one to talk about not hurting Sean after the way you bounced back and forth between him and Rigel this past year. You knew Sean liked you, even apart from the whole Consort business, so it was just cruel to lead him on when you obviously wanted to be with Rigel the whole time."

Again, she's shaking her head. "It wasn't like that. I never, ever tried to make Sean think I liked him more than Rigel."

"That's not the way I heard it," I retort. "Everyone says you broke up with Rigel last fall, after Sean got here, and started going out with him instead, that you were still going out with him when you left for Mars. No wonder he thought you liked him back. But all along it was just some kind of...smokescreen so you could sneak around with Rigel behind Sean's back. Behind everyone's back. You even convinced the *Echtran* Council to make Rigel your Bodyguard. And we all know how *that* turned out."

She stops and I realize we're right by the arboretum. "I guess I'd better explain the whole situation. Come on, there's a place we can sit and talk in here."

But I don't want my special memory of this place tainted by the resentment boiling up in me on Sean's behalf. "Yeah, I know. It was politically expedient for everyone to think you were with Sean. You don't have to explain that to me."

"There was a lot more to it than that, I promise. Come on."

Too curious now to refuse, I follow her through the archway to a metal bench in a back corner, well away from the few people wandering along the paths. It's a lovely place—a place I'd like to visit again with Sean. Even as I'm thinking that, M gestures for me to sit, then sits down next to me. Like we're friends or something.

"The *only* reason I agreed to make it look like I was going out with Sean last year was to save Rigel's life."

It's so totally not what I was expecting, I gape at her. "To... What?"

"I know it sounds melodramatic, but it's true. You probably don't know about this—they hushed it up really well—but early last December, Rigel and I tried to run away together, to keep the Council from separating us permanently."

I nod. "Molly told me they were planning to test an antidote to your bond with him?" Running away still seemed like an overreaction to me.

"The Council—especially Allister Adair—absolutely refused to believe our bond was real until after they made Rigel leave for ten days over Thanksgiving and saw how sick we both got—and how we immediately got better once we were together again. They had to believe then, but Allister's solution was to order some Healers to come up with an antidote, then make Rigel and his parents move away from Jewel."

Though giving her the benefit of the doubt rubs me the wrong way, I can't help imagining how I'd feel if I thought I'd never see Sean again. And the connection she and Rigel had, even back then, was apparently even stronger than ours.

"So you ran."

"We ran. But the timing turned out to be terrible, because on the very same night we left Jewel, Faxon was finally overthrown. I mean, I'm sure they'd have come after us anyway, but because of that…"

"They needed you on hand as a symbol for everyone in Nuath to rally around. To make those videos, to reassure us there wouldn't be a power vacuum," I finish, recalling that chaotic time, that first video, vividly.

"Exactly. Once they caught up with us, they hauled Rigel off to Dun Cloch and me back here to Jewel. The Council claimed it was absolutely imperative for everyone on Mars to believe I was learning everything I'd need to become Sovereign, and that Sean and I were becoming a couple. They were afraid if the story of Rigel and me running away ever got out, it would undermine that impression, so they wanted to make Rigel a scapegoat. They actually charged him with kidnapping me, even though I told them that wasn't what happened at all."

Allister and Lennox definitely hadn't mentioned *that*, though they must have known. Assuming it's true. "So why did they let Rigel come back to Jewel at all?" I demand, trying to poke holes in her story. "And that still doesn't explain why you led Sean on, for months afterward."

"That was the deal I made with the Council. Sean found out from his uncle that not only was Rigel not given the antidote, but that he might not even get a trial. That they might just declare him guilty of kidnapping and treason and erase his memory before he could talk to anyone. So I called an emergency Council meeting and promised to *pretend* I was with Sean from then on, but only if they dropped the charges against Rigel and let him come back."

"And they agreed to that?" I'm still skeptical.

"Not at first. Not until I swore I'd absolutely refuse to be their Sovereign if anything happened to Rigel. Hardly anyone knows this, but…they'd just found out about the Grentl, those aliens who—"

"I remember." I don't mention that Sean told me about the destruction they nearly wrought in Nuath last spring.

"Since I'm supposedly the only one who can talk to them, that gave me a lot of extra leverage. Even so, it was…close. Finally the Council took a vote and agreed to my compromise, six to one." The shadow of remembered fear in her eyes convinces me she's telling the truth. Mostly.

"Six to one? Someone on the Council still wanted to—?"

She snorts in disgust. "Allister was the single 'no' vote. It turned out he and Lennox, the Governor of Dun Cloch, had been plotting all along to get Rigel out of the picture—and not just by erasing his memory. Rigel told me when he got back that Lennox told him to his face he planned to kill him and make it look like an accident."

I draw in a quick, horrified breath. "No way. They couldn't have—" I break off, beyond shocked. I *trusted* Allister and Lennox. "Was there any *proof*, other than what Rigel told you?"

To my surprise, she nods. "Allister incriminated himself pretty thoroughly, and there were witnesses in Dun Cloch, too. Rigel was released in the nick of time, thank goodness, and Allister got booted off the Council. Now he and Lennox are locked up in Dun Cloch—along with Gordon Nolan, who was still doing their dirty work until he got caught a few weeks ago. We haven't figured out yet how they communicated with him."

For several seconds, I'm too stunned to speak. I just know I need to get away from the Sovereign before I accidentally blurt out something that will get *me* locked up, too. I somehow doubt my accommodations would be as luxurious as Allister's and Lennox's.

"I, ah, I'd better get back." I lurch to my feet. "Thank you for explaining all this. I…I had no idea."

She stands, too. "Like I said, it was all hushed up at the time. But I promise you, Sean has known from the very start how things stand between Rigel and me, even if he didn't like it. I do think he hoped for a while if I spent enough time with him I'd change my mind, that my bond with Rigel might disappear or something and I'd fall for him instead. But I swear I never, *ever* gave him any reason to think that might happen. Even so, none of this was fair to Sean and I'd hate to see him hurt again."

"I don't want him hurt, either. I…like him a lot."

"I'm glad, because it's pretty obvious he likes you a lot, too. Sorry if I made it sound like—"

"No, it's okay. I get it. You were worried I might be using him. Like I thought *you* had, before you explained all this."

She smiles at me and I smile back—almost like we're friends.

I want to ask about Sean's touch keeping her from getting sick back in Nuath, about her bond with Rigel, and how long it took to develop, about…all kinds of things. But not now.

Right now I need to get away, be alone. And think.

35

Cooldown

Sean

"I'm going for a walk," I announce as soon as I've helped Molly load the dinner dishes into the cabinet to be sterilized.

Immediately, Mum looks suspicious. "A walk? Where? Alone?"

"What difference does it make?" Molly demands before I can answer. "Sean's gone for plenty of walks at night without you interrogating him. Now, just because he *might* like a girl, you treat him like he's six years old."

To my surprise, Dad also comes to my defense. "Molly has a point, Lili. I see no need to discourage Sean from making friends with the new *Echtran* students, or even dating one of them. Where's the harm? Either we trust Sean not to get himself into trouble or we don't."

Mum glares at all of us for a second, then shrugs and turns away. "Very well. But don't blame *me* if people start talking and you don't like what you hear."

I figure that's the closest thing to a blessing I'll get, at least until she knows Kira better. Grabbing a light jacket I head outside, then send a quick text to her:

Want to go for a walk?

It's only been a few hours since I last saw Kira but I already miss her enough that I don't want to wait until tomorrow to see her again.

Her answer comes less than a minute later.

Sure. Where do you want to meet?

I'll head your way now.

She sends back a thumbs-up and I start walking toward Diamond Street—the same route we took last night, in the rain. Tonight it's perfectly clear, though noticeably cooler.

When I reach the arboretum I pause, smiling reminiscently about the miracle that happened on this very spot less than twenty-four hours ago. I honestly hadn't believed I could ever feel this way about any girl other than M. If anything, what I feel now for Kira is stronger. It's also different, in ways I find hard to define. It's almost like Kira fills an empty spot inside me I never knew was there.

For the first time, I wonder if what I used to feel for M was really love at all. Shaking my head, I start walking again—and see Kira coming toward me.

"Hey," she says softly when she gets close. "I, ah, didn't feel like waiting."

Grinning, I reach for her hand, anticipating, then enjoying the sensations that flow through me at her touch. "I'm glad. Gives us that much longer to be together before we have to go back."

"My thoughts exactly." But though she returns my smile, she seems a little agitated.

"Anything wrong?"

She walks with me in silence for several seconds before answering. "I'm not sure. I...had a long talk with M today after our Taekwondo class."

"Oh? What about?"

Her chuckle sounds forced. "You, sort of. She was worried I'm only pretending to like you, to get back at her for embarrassing my parents. And that you might get hurt."

Though I'm touched M was concerned, it sounds enough like Mum's dire warnings that I'm also irritated. "What did you tell her?"

"That I'm not pretending." She smiles up at me, but there's still a shadow behind her eyes. "I, um, also said she was a great one to talk after the way *she* hurt you by leading you on, *pretending* she wanted to be with you when she didn't."

"Did she explain why?"

Kira nods, not looking at me now. "She said it was part of a deal she made with the *Echtran* Council to keep them from charging Rigel with kidnapping after the two of them ran away. She, um, also told me stuff about your Uncle Allister that was...pretty hard to believe."

"I'm sure everything she told you was true." I can't keep the contempt I feel for my uncle out of my voice.

"You mean if she hadn't made that deal with the Council, he might have—"

"Wiped Rigel's memory—or worse. Yeah. He and Lennox, the former Governor of Dun Cloch, were so keen to take Rigel out of the picture permanently, they tried to take what they called 'justice' into their own hands."

What I *don't* say is that I made things even harder for M and Rigel afterward with my campaign to convince M she should be with me for real. Kira doesn't need to know just how hung up on M I used to be. Even so, she seems surprisingly upset now.

"You...you really think your own uncle would have done that?"

"I found it hard to believe at first, too, but the Council launched an investigation and all kinds of nasty stuff came to light about him. I mean, he was never exactly what I'd call likable. Loved to order people around, a complete stickler for all that Royal privilege crap, but..." I shake my head in disgust. "I'm ashamed now to admit he's related to me."

She squeezes my hand and looks up at me, her expression sympathetic now. "You have nothing to be ashamed of, Sean. A cousin of my dad's used to be one of Faxon's *bullochts*. He's in prison on Mars now, and well-deserved. No one should be held responsible for what other members of their families—or *fines*—do."

"Yeah, well, my uncle and Lennox are among the worst of those overly-ambitious Royals I mentioned before. Good thing all their plotting backfired and landed *them* in prison where they belong. Being Royal is probably the only thing that kept them from having *their* memories erased."

Kira looks puzzled now. "In prison? Are you sure? I, um, saw them both in Dun Cloch."

"You saw them?" I ask in surprise. "Just...walking around?"

"Not walking around, exactly, but staying in a regular house. A nice one, too, definitely not a prison. Maybe they're not supposed to leave it?"

I snort. "Nothing like the jail cell they put Rigel in, then. I should talk to Mum about that. Seems like with that much freedom they could still be dangerous. Was Gordon Nolan running around loose, too?"

"I never saw him. Pretty sure I'd have recognized him from the feeds, since he was one of those Royals vying for Acclamation last spring. M did mention something about him working for—"

"For Uncle Allister and Lennox—at least, M thinks he was behind that attack on her last month, even though the attacker claimed to be a Populist. Guess we'll never know for sure, since the guy died in prison before they could probe his memory. He might also have sent those *Duchas* men to kidnap M in Ireland, right before we left for Mars. He's *definitely* the one who hacked the security footage on the *Quintessence* and leaked it—that video of M and Rigel kissing, I mean."

Remembering how gut-punched I felt when I first saw that video on the ship, my throat tightens for a second—but only for a second, because that memory barely bothers me at all now. What does bother me is the way Kira's staring up at me, her eyes wide, almost like she's scared.

"But most people think the Populists were responsible for both of those attacks, don't they?"

"Yeah." I'm already holding her hand but now I cover it with my other one, eager to reassure her. "But...maybe you were right about the real Populists not promoting violence. Could be people like Uncle Allister and Lennox and Gordon were just using them as a smokescreen for their own attempts to take down M." Something else to ask Mum about when I get back.

"Exactly like I suggested before." But she doesn't seem nearly as pleased about my giving her that point as I thought she'd be.

We're on a relatively deserted stretch of Diamond Street, so I pull her into my arms. "Hey, don't worry. I haven't mentioned your Populist views to anybody else, and neither has Molly. Nobody thinks *you've* done anything wrong."

She rests her cheek against my chest, though I can tell she's still tense. "Thanks, Sean. I just—"

"It's okay. Really." I tip up her chin with one finger and lower my lips to hers.

For an instant she stiffens and I'm afraid she'll pull away, but then she relaxes into the kiss, returning it with equal passion. If anything, the sensations coursing through me are even more intense than what I felt with her last night. More...binding. Which is as scary as it is exhilarating.

She's smiling again when we finally break apart, to my enormous relief—but then she abruptly sobers again.

"I should get back. And I probably shouldn't have... But thank you, Sean. You've helped. More than you know."

Startled by her sudden change of mood as well as her phrasing, I frown. "What do you—?"

"G'night, Sean." Now the smile looks forced. "I'll...see you at school tomorrow."

She turns and walks quickly toward her apartment complex without a backward glance.

36

Delay of game

I WALK FASTER AND FASTER, trying to outrun my fear. Fear that Sean will come after me. Fear I'll give into temptation and go back to him. Fear I'll lose my resolve to do the right thing.

I should never have let him kiss me tonight. I absolutely never should have kissed him back! But he felt so strong, so safe, so…right. For a moment, I almost believed he could somehow fix the awful mess I've gotten myself into. But he can't.

Less than an hour after I left the arboretum this afternoon, I received the promised message from Allister.

Tomorrow night, 10pm your time. Confirm when you've found a secure location.

I didn't answer right away, I was so rattled by everything M had told me about Allister and Lennox. All through dinner I agonized about what I should say to them—and whether I should take the Sovereign's word over theirs. When I got Sean's text, it occurred to me *he* might know the truth. Whether he confirmed or contradicted M's accusations, it could help me decide what to do.

Unfortunately, what I just found out is even worse than I imagined. Not only did Allister and Lennox try to murder Rigel, they've been using the Populist movement, maybe even actual Populists, to help them get rid of the Sovereign once and for all. Not, as they claimed, so our people can elect a proper leader, but because of their own personal vendettas against her and Rigel. With her out of the way, they probably hope they can return to positions of power.

I writhe inwardly at how incredibly gullible I was to trust them without question, even *knowing* they were basically under arrest in Dun Cloch. They claimed that was only because the Sovereign had a grudge against them—and I was so eager to believe, I never probed further. Stupid, stupid, stupid!

Oh, they were clever. I wonder now if Crevan Erc ever contacted them at all. Could be they just heard from someone in Dun Cloch how gung-ho I was about the Populist movement, since I didn't exactly keep it a secret. Then they told me exactly what I wanted to hear—that I could be an important part of things after all, that Emileia was an even worse choice for Sovereign than I already thought. And I just lapped it up, promised to do everything I could to help them.

Well, no more. I'm done. I'll tell them so when they call tomorrow night. When I reach the Diamond View Terrace courtyard, I pause just inside the entrance to send my response.

Secure location found. I'll be there.

Feeling marginally better now that my decision's made, I exit out of the "special" screen on my phone and head upstairs to our apartment.

Even though I'm positive I'm doing the right thing, I have a hard time sleeping that night. I keep remembering all that Sean told me—not just what Allister and Lennox tried to do to Rigel, but everything they're suspected of. Like sending an assassin after the Sovereign last month... and that would-be assassin's unexpected death.

How will men that ruthless react when I tell them I want out? Do they already have a backup plan to keep *me* from incriminating them? In the dark watches of the night, it seems not only possible but probable. Maybe if I promise never to mention them to anyone...

"You look awful," Adina observes over breakfast, eying my face critically.

"Thanks, Sprout. I, ah, didn't sleep very well. Couldn't seem to get comfortable."

"Really? Even after going out to meet you-know-who again after dinner last night?" She's grinning mischievously now.

Of course, Mum jumps on her comment immediately. "Did you see

Sean O'Gara again last night, Kira? You didn't mention that when you left for your walk."

"He, ah, texted me just as I was leaving, so we met up and walked together for a little while, that's all."

Mum's eyebrows go up. "Just the two of you this time? His sister wasn't with him?"

"No, but so what? Sean and I do have three classes together, after all. We're getting to be friends."

"That's wonderful, Kira!" She's clearly delighted now. "Didn't I say you were bound to make friends once we moved here? I'm so glad I was right. But goodness, first Molly and now Sean O'Gara! Their family is second in importance only to the Sovereign herself. I hope they don't think *you're* trying to curry favor now?"

She's obviously still bothered by that whole asking-M's-uncle-to-dinner thing.

"I know Sean and Molly don't. Molly's really nice and Sean—"

"Gets all goo-goo eyed around you," Adina finishes, her eyes dancing. "Don't worry, Mum. From what I've seen, Sean's at least as interested in being *friends* with Kira as she is with him."

I glare at my sister and she finally shuts up, though with another knowing grin.

Sean is on the bus again today. He holds my hand all the way to school and I draw welcome comfort and courage from his touch. By the time we get off the bus I'm nearly convinced everything will work out after all.

That certainty lasts until we have to separate in Physics, where Alan does his best to undermine it.

"You can't possibly believe he's serious about you," he whispers as soon as class starts. "He's just using you to pass the time until another Royal girl comes along. Or maybe to make the Sovereign jealous. I'm sure he's still hoping to get her back."

"Stop it, Alan," I mutter back. "It's none of your business."

"Fine. But don't say I didn't warn you."

He doesn't speak to me for the rest of the period, barely even looks at me, but his words linger. They're way too similar to what that tiny voice in the back of my mind whispers whenever I'm not with Sean.

As the day goes on I grow more and more distracted, thinking about my looming confrontation with Allister and Lennox. What will they say? What will they do? Will they send an assassin after *me* to keep me quiet?

"Are you sure you're okay?" Sean asks me worriedly over lunch when I more than once fail to respond to something he says.

For a second I'm tempted to confess everything to him—how I agreed to help Lennox and his uncle and what I plan to do tonight. Maybe, given his parents' influence, there'll be some way to keep them from— No. I'd have to tell him why I started being friendly with him in the first place and he'd never trust me again. Why should he? Why should any of them?

"I'm fine," I lie. "Sorry. I guess I just have a lot on my mind."

Time seems to speed up after that. Next thing I know, I'm out at NuAgra helping my mum, who also notices my distraction.

"No, Kira, the control group goes in this bed. Honestly, I'm starting to think Adina was right this morning about you and Sean O'Gara. Your head seems to be in the clouds today."

I don't have much appetite at dinner, I'm so nervous by now. I keep rehearsing what I plan to say to Allister and Lennox, trying out different phrasings, hoping if I can just explain my feelings well enough they'll let me off the hook. Every version I come up with sounds worse in my head than the one before.

I've just finished helping Adina with the dishes when I get a text. Half-fearful, half-hopeful, I check my phone. Maybe they're postponing tonight's meeting, maybe even canceling it...

The text is from Sean.

Want to take another walk? Get an earlier start so we'll have more time?

I'm even more tempted than before to let him help me solve my problem. I've already started texting him back that I can meet him right now when I realize if word about what I've been doing gets out, it could reflect badly on him, too. It's common knowledge at school we've been spending time together.

Quickly, I erase my unsent text and type a different one.

Sorry, can't tonight. Too much homework.

Swallowing the lump in my throat, I stuff my phone back in my pocket and glance at the clock. Barely two hours to wait...

37

Box out

Sean

I FROWN at Kira's text, my vague worries from last night and today
sharpening into real concern. Something is *definitely* wrong, even if she
insisted there wasn't every time I asked.

Yesterday everything seemed fine between us. Better than fine. I half
expected her to back off after Tuesday night. Our kissing—our connection—was so intense. But she'd let me hold her hand between classes,
sat with me at lunch, then agreed to another walk last night... Which
was when I first sensed something had changed.

Because of her talk with M? Could M have warned her away from
me? It didn't seem like something she'd do, but if she was worried I
could get hurt again... Maybe just a hint, and Kira took it as an order
from the Sovereign?

Or maybe it was something Alan said to her? I noticed him whispering to her in Physics this morning, probably saying the same stuff he
said to me the day before. Pointing out what different *fines* we are,
insisting I'm just toying with her... But Kira definitely acted off before
that, during our walk last night.

I shake my head, trying to jar my thoughts into clarity. It doesn't
help.

"Mum, Dad, I'm going for a walk," I announce, even though Kira
begged off. Walking sometimes helps me sort things out. I took lots of

solitary walks when I was so frustrated over M, then later, when I was trying to get her out of my system. That eventually worked…

Molly comes bouncing into the front hall. "With Kira?" she whispers, eyes gleaming conspiratorially.

"Nope, just me this time. Feel free to tell Mum that if she asks. I haven't shot hoops in a while and need the exercise."

I'm out the door before she can reply. Like last night and the night before, I head toward Diamond Street but this time I take my first left onto Garnet instead of continuing on toward the arboretum…and Kira's apartment.

I used to walk this way all the time, past M's house. Occasionally I'd even stand out on the street staring up at her window, imagining stuff I had no business imagining. Feeling my breath catch if her shadow passed by it while I was watching. Believing that was what love felt like.

Now I know how wrong I was. What I felt for M was some combination of youthful fantasy, possessiveness, and a righteous conviction that we were destined to be together, occasionally spiked with simple lust.

What I feel for Kira goes way, way deeper than that. I know it shouldn't be possible. I only met her two weeks ago. I kissed her for the first time just forty-eight hours ago. But I know, with bone-deep certainty, that it's true. I'm totally, irrevocably in love with her.

If she's already having second thoughts because she doesn't feel the same way, I'm honestly not sure what I'll do.

I pass M's house without so much as a glance and keep walking. And thinking.

38

Free agent

ALLISTER AND LENNOX aren't supposed to call until ten, but by nine-thirty I'm too nervous to sit still.

"I'm going for another walk," I tell my parents. They're watching some *Duchas* television show while my sister finishes her homework, the puppy curled in her lap.

"So late?" Mum asks in surprise. "On a school night?"

"I won't go far. Just...need some fresh air."

Adina looks up. "Ooh, are you meeting—?"

"Maybe." If Mum thinks I'm with Sean, she'll be less likely to worry if I'm gone a while.

As I expect, she brightens at once. "Have fun, dear, but try not to be too late."

I leave the complex through the back entrance and cross Ruby Street toward the annex they're building with more apartments. It's nearly finished already—not surprising since our people are helping with the construction to create more *Echtran* housing. No workers are here at this hour, of course, which is why I chose this location for tonight's conversation.

The annex is laid out similarly to the existing complex, with several two-story apartment buildings arranged around a central courtyard. After scoping the whole place out, I decide a stairway facing the court-yard, screened on all sides from nearby roads and sidewalks, will be my best place to sit. For ten minutes I pace back and forth, taking deep breaths to calm my nerves. Then my phone vibrates in my pocket.

My heart leaping into my throat again, I fumblingly pull it out, then unlock it with the retinal scan as I move to the middle stairway. "Hello?"

To my surprise, Allister's face appears on my screen. Our past conversations have either been texts or voice only. "You are alone and unlikely to be interrupted?"

"Yes."

"You're sure?"

"Yes."

He glances off to the side, then nods. "Excellent. If you'll touch the holo control on the lower left-hand side of your screen, we can begin."

That's a button I haven't used yet. As soon as I touch it, a thin beam of light emanates from my phone and scans me from head to toe, then surrounds my face. Suddenly, I'm back in the main room of the house in Dun Cloch where I previously met with Allister and Lennox—or that's how it seems. Both men are sitting opposite me on the couch and the woman, Enid, in a straight-backed chair behind them.

"How...how did you do that?" I gasp.

"We equipped your phone with standard holo capability but Enid has only recently enabled it to work on our end," Allister explains, gesturing at an omni on a low table in front of them. "I'm surprised you've not experienced the technology, as it's been in use for years."

By Royals, maybe, I think but don't say. I now recall Sean mentioning that *Echtran* Council members who don't live in Jewel often attend meetings this way. Cautiously, I reach down with one hand to touch the seat beneath me. I'm slightly reassured to feel concrete and not upholstery, proving I haven't *really* gone anywhere.

"Now you're here, let's get started," Lennox says briskly. "Allister tells me you're having second thoughts about the advisability of removing the Sovereign from power?"

"Er...I just said it might be a good idea to keep her around in case the Grentl come back."

Allister snorts. "As I already explained, there are others, like myself, who can deal with the Grentl should they ever return. Surely you still agree that a sixteen-year-old girl is no fit leader for our people?"

"I confess," Lennox says before I can answer, "that I was disappointed to hear your commitment might be wavering. Crevan Erc spoke so highly of your dedication to the Populist cause. Do you no longer adhere to their aims?"

I swallow, trying to remember my carefully rehearsed speech. "I definitely believe all of our people should have a voice in our government, which is the central pillar of the Populist platform. But after getting to know the Sovereign a little better, I think we might make more progress by working with her instead of against her. Especially since I get the impression that once she feels she's no longer needed as Sovereign, she'll step down on her own. So if we just wait until—"

"Don't be absurd," Lennox snaps. "The longer she is in power, the more accustomed to it she will grow and the less willing she will be to give it up. From the start, her arrogance was evident in her refusal to be guided by Allister or other members of the Council, particularly in the matter of young Stuart. Between them, she and that boy have the potential to destroy any viable future for our people, both on Mars and on Earth. Nor is that Regent of hers likely to prevent it, as he's the boy's grandfather. Time is of the essence."

Even knowing what Lennox tried to do to Rigel, the venom in his voice startles me. It must show in my expression, because Allister quickly waves Lennox to silence, then leans forward with an ingratiating smile.

"I have no doubt Emileia has been very convincing, Kira. She has, after all, managed to persuade a large majority of our people to throw their support behind her, despite her obvious shortcomings. The question is, are you still willing to help us? In our efforts to further the Populist cause, I mean."

That last bit is obviously an afterthought, which confirms what I'd already suspected. The Populist cause means nothing to them except as cover for their own, more sinister agenda.

"I'm sorry. I'm really not comfortable deceiving Emileia and her friends to dig up ammunition you'll use against her. Not when I no longer believe undermining her is the best way to achieve the Populists' goals."

Lennox turns to Allister with a frown. "I was afraid of this. We never should have trusted a child with such an important mission." He reaches for the omni on the table in front of them. "Now we have no choice but to—"

"No." Allister grabs his wrist before he can disconnect the holo-call. "Not yet." Turning back to me, he summons a not-very-convincing smile. "Not to worry, my dear." His tone is almost fatherly, though he's still gripping Lennox's wrist. "Of course we can't ask you to do anything that makes you uncomfortable. You, ah, haven't happened to mention to anyone else that you've been in touch with us? One of your new friends, or a family member, perhaps?"

I expected this question. "No. No one, I swear. If anyone suspected I was working with the Populists they'd probably kick me out of Jewel, since the Council thinks they were behind an attack on the Sovereign last month."

"Yes, well, every movement has its fringe elements." Allister keeps his smile in place. "You're likely quite correct about the consequences should anyone learn of your mission. Ah, former mission. You'd almost certainly join us permanently in Dun Cloch, though I imagine your accommodations would be rather more spartan than ours."

He lets that sink in for a moment before continuing. "If you are certain you don't wish to help us any longer—?"

"No, sir. I'm sorry."

"Ah, well. We shall be sorry to lose you. To minimize both our risk and yours going forward, we will need to remove your tracking chip and exchange the phone we gave you for your original one. Once those potentially incriminating bits of evidence are disposed of, we can go our separate ways."

I let out a cautious breath, trying not to let my relief show on my face. Can it really be this easy? "That...sounds fine to me, sir. How? And when?"

Lennox shoots Allister one last glare, then turns and whispers something to Enid that I can't hear. She nods and whispers something in response. Lennox then turns back to me with a smile that positively creeps me out, it's such an abrupt shift from the expression he wore just a moment ago.

"Enid assures me she is willing to travel to Jewel personally to take care of everything, as we are unable to do so ourselves. Where are you now?"

"In an unfinished apartment complex behind Diamond View Terrace. Nobody's living here yet and all the construction workers are gone at night."

His creepy smile widens. "Then that should be an excellent place for the, ah, extraction and exchange to take place. Enid will message you when she arrives to arrange a specific time to meet."

I nod eagerly. "That sounds perfect. Thank you all for understanding."

"We're reasonable men, not monsters." Allister's reassurance isn't quite as reassuring as I'd like. "We'll speak with you again soon, probably for the last time. Now, if you'll excuse us, we'll leave Enid to deactivate your tracking chip until it can be removed, as there is no point in keeping it functional. She will let you know when it's safe to close the connection."

Swiftly, they both stand and exit the room, leaving their omni on the low table between me and where they were sitting. Meanwhile, Enid starts fiddling with a device she's holding.

"Um, thanks for doing this, Enid," I say when the silence becomes uncomfortable. "I really appreciate it."

She flicks a glance my way, then continues whatever she's doing without replying. I got the impression when I met her in Dun Cloch that she positively idolizes Lennox. She probably thinks I've betrayed him by backing out of our agreement.

Another five minutes creep awkwardly past before she finally says, "Almost done now."

Even as she speaks, the back of my neck suddenly burns. I involuntarily clap a hand over the spot. "Ow! What—?"

"Ah. Good. I believe we're finished now."

"You mean it's *supposed* to hurt like this? Why?"

"Just a side effect of the deactivation. The discomfort will soon fade. Expect to hear from me within a few days. Ending transmission." She moves to the omni on the table and abruptly I'm alone, looking across the unfinished apartment complex courtyard.

The back of my neck has nearly stopped burning by the time I cross Ruby Street again. As the pain fades, so does my lingering anxiety. I'm still amazed by how well that interview went. I expected them to argue more, to try to win me back to their side, tell me more terrible stuff about the Sovereign. Is it possible they've realized she's not as bad a leader as they thought—or at least that she's necessary because of the Grentl thing? I can only hope.

Either way, I'm done. No more conspiring to betray people I'm starting to like. Especially Sean.

Feeling about a hundred pounds lighter than I did an hour ago, I hurry back to our apartment. I don't even mind when Aggie jumps on me, demanding to be picked up and petted. Grinning, feeling at peace with the world, I scoop her up and hold her close enough to my face that she licks my nose.

"I guess you really are pretty cute," I tell her.

Adina and my parents stare, clearly dumbfounded.

The wary look Sean gives me when I board the bus the next morning makes me realize how much my behavior yesterday must have worried him. To make up for it, I take his hand as soon as I sit down, reveling in the comfort and strength his touch now gives me, along with the pleasure I felt from the start.

"Sorry I couldn't walk with you last night. Maybe tonight?"

His happiness and relief are almost palpable, making me feel even guiltier for being so aloof and distracted yesterday. "Sure! After the game, maybe? You coming?"

"Sure." Though I'd completely forgotten there's another football game tonight, I don't hesitate. I refuse to think about Allister and company again until I have to, sometime late tomorrow. For today I can enjoy being a normal high school girl. Well, a normal *Echtran* girl, anyway, with no hidden agendas.

"Great! I'll ask Mum and Dad if I can have the van—though they may be planning to go, too. They do sometimes, what with Mol on the cheer squad and all."

"Either way, we can sit together, right?"

"Definitely."

We talk about other school stuff for the rest of the bus ride. At one point Sean suggests again I should try out for the girls' basketball team and this time I agree it sounds fun. My whole future looks a hundred percent brighter than it did yesterday.

In Physics, Alan again tries to convince me Sean's just leading me on, but I'm in way too good a mood for his snark to bother me.

"If it makes you feel better to believe that, go right ahead," I tell him cheerfully. "Personally, I think your time would be better spent getting to know his sister, Molly. Last I heard, she's not going out with anyone."

He looks startled, then thoughtful.

Smiling to myself, I open my textbook.

At lunch, Sean and I again get a table to ourselves, but only briefly. We've barely started eating when the Sovereign and Rigel plunk their trays down across from us.

"So, everything good with you guys today?" she asks brightly, though there's nothing casual about the way her eyes probe me, then Sean.

"Fine," Sean answers easily. "Why?"

She shrugs. "No reason. Yesterday you both looked a little...tense."

"I, um, was kind of distracted about some stuff going on at NuAgra. With my mum's research, I mean."

Lying to the Sovereign makes me feel oddly guilty—especially when she gives me a quick, sharp look. Crap. Does she have the same ability Sean's mother does? He never mentioned it... But then she smiles again.

"I guess it must have gone okay, though, huh?"

"Yeah, though I was probably more hindrance than help," I say, truthfully this time. "I kept mixing up the seedling containers. Luckily, Mum knows her stuff."

Rigel glances from me to Sean and back. "You guys coming to the game tonight?"

We both nod and Sean says, "You're still bringing it down a notch from that game a couple weeks ago, right?"

He laughs. "Yeah. Maybe even more than last week, we're already such favorites. Making it close might—" He breaks off, frowning at me. "Don't mention I said that, okay? Shaving points is seriously frowned on by the athletic association."

"But you kind of have to, don't you?" I ask, then glance at Sean. "Both of you? So will I, if I end up playing on the girls' basketball team." That idea has started to grow on me. "If I do, I'll need tips."

That topic dominates the rest of the lunch period, Rigel and Sean talking about the challenges of playing well without being *too* good and M about how she has to hold back in Taekwondo—not that she does it competitively.

As we gather our trays afterward, M turns to me. "I've been meaning to compliment you—all of you—on your accents. I'd never guess you were all living in Nuath just a few months ago instead of upstate New York."

Rigel nods. "The only thing slightly off is saying 'mum' instead of 'mom,' but you can pass that off as a regional idiosyncrasy if anyone questions it."

"They told us that in Dun Cloch," I admit, "but Adina could never manage it consistently, so I figured we'd better match."

As we all head to Government class together, I see Molly just ahead walking with Alan and have to smile again. It's wonderful to think that from now on I can just be *friends* with these people, with no ulterior motives. Especially M and Rigel. I now have a much greater appreciation for all they've been through and everything they've accomplished.

And...they really are nice.

39

Personal foul

Sean

MUM AND DAD are on the phone with some friends in Bailerealta when it's time to leave for the game, so they're fine with me taking the car. I text Kira and she asks if I can give her sister a ride, too. I don't mind, but I hope she doesn't sit with us. There's something I want to tell Kira tonight, without anyone else listening in.

Adina hurries off to find her friends as soon as we get to the game, taking care of that problem. Mounting the bleachers, we briefly get waylaid by M's friends Bri and Deb, then by a few of my basketball buddies, but I decline all invitations to sit with them. Hand in hand, Kira and I climb to the very top of the stands and find a relatively empty spot.

"Excellent." Grinning, I settle next to her. "I was hoping to have you to myself this evening—so to speak." I glance at the nearest group of fans, a few feet away.

"So you can explain more about football without anyone thinking it's weird?"

"That, too."

To my delight, she scoots a little closer, her low chuckle thrumming through me pleasantly.

"I'm glad that whatever was bothering you yesterday isn't anymore," I say after a brief, contented silence.

She slants a curious glance up at me. "So you didn't believe it had to do with Mum's research either? I could tell M didn't, at lunch. Made me wonder if she has same talent your mum does?"

"She's never said so, but I wouldn't be surprised. Seems like the longer she and Rigel are together—bonded—the more stuff they can do, both together and separately. Sometimes I think—"

The roar of the crowd interrupts me—the team has just run onto the field. I take advantage of the noise to face Kira more fully, lean a little closer. I hold her gaze with mine, speaking urgently. "Kira, I know we only met for the first time a couple of weeks ago and have only been... close...less than half that long, but I—"

Her hand tightens convulsively on mine, then she lets go and turns half away, breaking eye contact. "Sean, stop. Before you say anything else, there's...something I need to tell you."

All the breath leaves my body. I swallow, waiting, frightened by the sudden distress I see on her face. She doesn't continue right away—like she's trying to find the right words. The suspense is killing me.

"Go on," I finally say, my voice sounding harsh and strange to my ears. She darts a scared-looking glance my way, making me tense further.

Finally, haltingly, she says, "I...I thought maybe you'd never need to know about this, but keeping it from you feels so wrong now, I can't— That is— Remember when you said I sounded like a...an Anti-Royal, as you called them? Well, you were right. I've been one all along, since before I left Mars. I came to Jewel hoping—planning—to do everything I could to undermine the Sovereign, turn people against her."

Though she's confirming my very worst suspicions about her, I feel more relief than anything else. Because she's *not* saying she doesn't want to be with me. Or is she?

"Are you telling me the only reason you acted friendly toward me, agreed to spend time with me, was to—"

"To gain your confidence so you'd tell me things that could be used against M by the Populist movement, yes. But only at first!" She meets my gaze again, her eyes imploring me to believe her. "The better I got to know you—know all of you—the more I started to doubt everything I'd been told about the Sovereign. About Royals."

I frown at her uncertainly. "But...I thought they screened out everyone with views like that before letting them come to Jewel?"

"Only the adults, and my parents are rock-solid Royalists,

completely loyal to the Sovereign. That's why they were among the first to volunteer to come to Earth—and why they requested to live in Jewel."

That made sense. Whoever did the screening probably assumed minors would share their parents' views and loyalties. Obviously a bad assumption.

"You said you were trying to gather information for the Populists. Who, exactly? Are there others here in Jewel?"

She shakes her head but, oddly, seems more upset than ever. "That's the worst part, the part I was afraid to tell you. I've been reporting back to…to your Uncle Allister and former Governor Lennox, in Dun Cloch. They contacted me while I was there, said I'd been recommended to them by Crevan Erc, the leader of the Populist movement back on Mars. They claimed they had come to embrace those same principles and asked me to work with them. For them."

Those last words are spoken so softly I have to lean down to hear them. She looks so miserable I want to comfort her but I don't dare. Not now. Not yet.

"And you believed them? After everything—?"

"I didn't know about any of that, not then! They told me they'd only been removed from their positions and restricted to Dun Cloch because M had a grudge against them for stopping her from running away with Rigel. That they'd acted in her best interests, and that of our people, but she'd turned on them. It…seemed to fit with everything I'd been told about her by the Populists."

Her pleading expression makes me long to believe her. I stare at her, holding her gaze, wishing *I* had Mum's ability to know whether someone is telling the truth. Or, better, that whatever bond is forming between us allowed me to hear her thoughts.

"And now?"

"Now I realize how incredibly stupid and gullible I was. I wanted so badly to believe I could still be important to the movement, even on Earth. Before we left Nuath—right before I found out we were coming here—Crevan Erc himself asked me to help their cause. That, even more than *caidpel*, made me want to stay on Mars, where I could still make a difference. Like I did for the Resistance…"

She trails off, a little sob escaping her. "It's just like you said the other night—I couldn't stand the idea of being…ordinary. Relegated to the sidelines."

My throat tightens again, this time with understanding.

"I get that. I do." I put my hand back over hers and almost imagine I can feel her anxiety and guilt through the touch, along with the delicious tingle she always gives me. "The same way I thought accepting the whole M and Rigel thing would relegate *me* to the sidelines. Make me a nobody again. But maybe...maybe being on the sidelines isn't such a bad thing, after all. I mean, where would our star players be if they didn't have supporters cheering them on, helping out?"

Kira manages a shaky laugh. "Maybe you're right. I did always play my best in front of an enthusiastic crowd of fans. Anyway, I'm done, as of last night. I let Allister and Lennox know I won't be sending any more reports. That's why I was so distracted yesterday, worrying how they'd react when I told them."

"You... Wait! How did you communicate with them? They're not supposed to be able to contact anyone outside of Dun Cloch, it's part of their sentence." I double-checked with Mum about that, a couple nights ago.

"There's a woman working with them, Enid, who does all their tech stuff. She figured out how to get around the blocks on their communications. And she set up that holo thing they did last night, projecting me into their living room—they said she only just got that working."

I frown. "So last night you told them you quit? And they just let you...walk away? No threats?"

"They did argue some, but not as much as I expected. I was so relieved to be done with them, I hoped I could just forget the whole thing, never have to mention it to anyone. To you. But...I've always hated lying, to anyone. Lying to *you*, especially if— I couldn't do it. Not even if telling the truth means you don't still—"

I tighten my grip on her hand. "I do still. Very much. I think it was incredibly brave of you to tell me."

She smiles up at me, her relief so obvious now, I feel it, too.

"This explains how they sent orders to Gordon," I muse after a moment. "Everyone seemed so sure they couldn't have. Kira, can I tell M what you told me? We can't be positive you're the only person in Jewel they compromised. The Council needs to know what they've been up to, that they still have the ability to—"

"What? No!" She stares up at me in alarm. "If the Council knew I helped them, or tried to, wouldn't they consider me just as guilty? They'd probably send me straight back to Dun Cloch—lock me up and throw away the key! Allister said—"

"He just wanted to scare you, to keep you quiet," I assure her. "I can't imagine the Council punishing you for turning them in."

She doesn't look nearly so sure. And, if I'm honest, I'm not a hundred percent positive myself. What if they vote to make an example of Kira, to dissuade any other malcontents?

"Tell you what," I say after a moment's thought. "How about I just let M know the basics, that you met them in Dun Cloch and they convinced you to keep in touch. I'm sure she can figure out a way to let the Council know there's been a breach without bringing your name into it."

Kira looks at me doubtfully. "Do you really think she'd be willing to do that?"

"I really do."

Especially if I tell her how much I care about Kira and ask her to do it as a favor to me. As eager as M has been for me to move on, I can't believe she'd ruin my one chance to do so.

Slowly, Kira nods. "If you trust her that much...so do I."

Fully aware she's just put her fate in my hands, I pull her close for a kiss. Not as long a one as I'd like, since we're in public, but still incredibly sweet.

Another cheer erupts from the stands, though it could just as easily be inside my head. Pulling just slightly away, I glance at the scoreboard and see that Jewel just scored its first touchdown. Which is excuse enough for another kiss.

40

Fourth down

I ENJOY the rest of the football game more than anything I can remember, even though I don't pay much attention to the action on the field. I'm even more relieved than I was last night, knowing I've come clean with Sean and he still wants to be with me. I spend the rest of the evening in a blissful haze.

Between discreet kisses, Sean asks more questions and I give him every detail I can remember about my conversations with Allister and Lennox. He seems worried they'll send someone to silence me permanently, instead of just sending Enid to remove my chip. But I'm too happy to share his concern.

"Lennox was upset at first but your Uncle Allister talked him down. I think they just want to get rid of any incriminating evidence, so even if I *do* tell anyone about them, no one will believe me."

"Maybe." He doesn't seem convinced. "I still think I should come with you when you meet that Enid person, just in case."

"But then they'd know I told you. I should be safe as long as they think *they're* safe—and I won't feel like I'm really free of them until this chip is gone. I want it out."

He doesn't argue any more but I can tell he still doesn't like it. I'd be irritated by his overprotectiveness if I didn't know it's because he cares about me. That's enough to make up for anything else.

The next day he texts me four different times asking if I've heard from Enid yet. I text back each time that I haven't, that I might not for several more days. After the one he sends on my way to Taekwondo, I ask if he's said anything to M yet, since that might make seeing her in class a little awkward.

Not yet, he replies. *Figure I'll wait till she gets to our house this afternoon before the Council meeting and do it in person.*

Which means if Sean's wrong about her and she outs me to the Council, I could be arrested before bedtime tonight.

That thought makes it hard to focus in Taekwondo, at least at first. To make up for not letting us spar at all on Wednesday, Master Parker has us spend most of today's class doing just that. Outfitted in a brand-new set of pads of my very own, I'm again paired with M.

"Ready?" she whispers with a grin just before he signals us to begin.

I nod, reminding myself she's only talking about Taekwondo, not... the other thing.

Interestingly, now that I'm no longer angry at the Sovereign, I do a better job sparring against her. Maybe my negative emotions interfered with my reactions and strategy? More clear-headed today, I'm able to anticipate most of her moves in time to counter them. By the end of our third round, she regards me with new respect.

"Wow, you have *really* improved, Kira. Have you been practicing on the side?"

"No, but I'm in a way better mood than last time. I think it helps."

She smiles. "I noticed—and I'm glad. Sean deserves to be happy. So do you."

Before I can ask what she means by that last bit, Master Parker has us switch sparring partners for another three-round match.

Though my brief exchange with M reassured me she's unlikely to intentionally do anything to hurt me—or Sean—I'm still nervous when the *Echtran* Council meeting at the O'Garas' begins that evening. Sean texted to say he talked to M and she asked the Council to let him sit in.

That way I can help argue your case if necessary—though I doubt it will be. The second it's over, I'll let you know. You're NOT going to get in trouble.

I really, really hope he's right.

Sean warned me that these meeting usually last several hours, so I settle in to wait, trying to distract myself with homework. I know he won't be able to text me again until the meeting's over, so I'm startled when my phone vibrates less than an hour later.

The message isn't from Sean. It's from Enid.

Arrived in Jewel. Construction site appears deserted. Meet me in apartment 104-A.

I read the message through twice, looking for any hint Sean's suspicions could be justified. The text is terse, but so is Enid—at least with me. Setting my homework aside, I put on my shoes and text her back that I'm on my way.

Telling my parents I'm going for another walk, ignoring Adina's knowing grin, I leave the apartment. Because I promised, I send Sean a quick text telling him what I'm doing, even though he won't see it until after the Council meeting. With any luck, by the time Sean gets my text I'll have already sent another one letting him know his worries were groundless.

My phone back in my pocket, I walk quickly toward the meeting place, eager to have this entire business behind me once and for all. Once I enter the empty complex I have to slow down to pick my way past ladders and other construction equipment. Enid is nowhere to be seen.

"Hello? Enid?" When no one answers, I turn slowly in place, scanning the courtyard. It's not as dark as last time, since the sun only set half an hour or so ago, and I see there are numbers painted on the buildings, something I didn't notice before.

I pull my phone back out and read Enid's text again. Apartment 104-A, she said. I locate building 104 and head for its stairwell, similar to ours. Units A and B are on the ground floor. The door to B is closed and locked—I check—but unit A's door is ajar, probably why she chose it for the chip extraction.

"Enid?"

I push the door wider and step inside, peering around the unfinished apartment. The only light comes from a nearby streetlight shining through an uncurtained window at the rear of the room. "Is anyone here?"

Sean's frequently-voiced suspicions echo urgently in my head. I'm turning to leave as quickly as I came when my phone signals an incoming call on the secret app. Frowning, I unlock it and answer.

"Hello?"

An instant later Allister and Lennox are right in the room with me, standing just a few feet away.

"How—?" I begin, confused. I didn't even touch the holo button.

"This time we are generating the holograms from our end." Allister says with that fake smile that makes me instinctively mistrust him. "We said we would speak with you one last time, did we not?"

Slowly, I nod. "I just didn't expect... Where's Enid? This is the apartment she told me to come to, but she's not here."

Lennox's smile is less fake but more unpleasant than Allister's. "I'm afraid Enid is far too useful to risk. We simply had her find a suitable enclosed space before taking herself to a safe distance."

My mouth goes dry. "Safe distance from what?"

"The explosion that will shortly occur," he explains. "You should be pleased to hear we found a way for you to serve a valuable purpose after all, one that will no doubt cause most of your fellow Populists to rejoice. They may well hail you as a hero."

"What...what do you mean? What purpose?"

His nasty smile broadens. "The instrument of the Sovereign's demise, of course. In just a few minutes she will receive a text that will appear to come from your phone. With any luck, she will bring young Stuart with her and we will be able to kill two birds with one stone. So to speak."

41

Assist

Sean

M WAS SURPRISINGLY UNDERSTANDING when I told her about Kira communicating with Uncle Allister and Lennox.

"She had no way of knowing they weren't really Populist sympathizers," she said. "I've told the Council all along it was dangerous to keep what those two did secret, but they seemed to think it would undermine people's trust in Royals if they knew the whole story. Now I can say, 'I told you so.'"

"Still, if you can keep Kira's name out of it—"

"I'll try. If I do have to mention her by name, I'll make it clear she's not to be held responsible. Don't worry, Sean."

Even so, sitting here in the corner of the living room during the Council meeting an hour later, I can't help worrying a little.

"I still find it hard to believe an Anti-Royal slipped through our screening process," Connor is saying. "I assure you, Excellency, we were extremely thorough. The potential threat—"

M cuts him off. "I don't think the Anti-Royals—Populists—are nearly the threat you've believed, especially considering my would-be attacker's unexplained death. Someone obviously wanted to silence him before he could reveal who really sent him, which implies it was *not* the Populists, as he originally claimed. I consider it far more likely Gordon Nolan orchestrated that attack, acting on orders from Allister and

Lennox. If you remember, I suggested that before, but you insisted that was impossible because of the communication block that was supposedly in place. The one we now know doesn't work."

Rigel's dad, who's from the Informatics *fine*, agrees. "I did warn you, once you acquainted me with the precautions you'd used, that a skilled hacker could work around them. Their confederate in Dun Cloch was clearly able to do just that. However, it should be a simple enough matter to put a far more robust dampener in place. Particularly if we can identify that confederate to prevent any further tampering."

The discussion continues for nearly half an hour, with more than one Council member demanding to know which of the newcomers was compromised.

"You must see, Excellency, how important it is to be certain he or she poses no further threat," Breann insists. "Your safety—"

"Is not at risk," M tells her. "The person in question did admit to Populist leanings but never intended me any harm. They showed a great deal of courage in coming forward to prevent Allister and Lennox from deceiving anyone else. I won't have that person punished when no one has been hurt."

I keep expecting someone to ask *me* who it was, but they don't—probably because M is stating her case so strongly. I'm impressed all over again by how much she's grown as a leader over the past few months.

Finally, they move on to other topics. When the meeting adjourns, more than an hour later, M turns to me with a triumphant smile. I respond with a little thumbs-up, not wanting to be obvious while the physically-present Council members are still in the room. The real trick will be deflecting Mum's inevitable questions later on, when it's just us.

To delay that as long as possible, I follow M outside when everyone else leaves. "Thanks, M. You did exactly what you promised and I—"

"Just a sec," she interrupts, pulling out her phone—her first-ever cellphone. "Huh. I got a text from Kira, but it doesn't make sense." She shows it to me.

I hope you can help me. I went exploring in the unfinished apartment complex and am trapped inside 104-A.

I frown at the text, wondering why she'd have contacted M about something like that instead of me—then remember I turned my phone off for the meeting. Quickly, I pull it out and power it up. Kira *did* send me a text—but a totally different one.

Going to meet Enid to have chip removed. Text me when the meeting's over and we'll go for a walk or something. And please don't worry! Then I notice it was sent well over an hour ago.

"When did your text from Kira come in?" I ask M.

She glances at her phone again. "Just a few minutes ago. Hm." Her eyes go unfocused for a long moment, then she looks at me again, even more concerned now. "Weird. Rigel got the exact same text I did."

My earlier suspicions, which Kira managed to partially allay last night, instantly revive. "Uncle Allister and Lennox must be behind this. It sounds like they're trying to lure both you and Rigel to wherever they're holding Kira—which means it's some kind of trap. You know how they feel about you two. I'll go instead."

Already, I'm halfway down the porch steps.

"Wait, Sean! If it really is a trap, it's not safe for you to go, either. Let me send Cormac with a security detail. They'll be able to—"

"Are you kidding? If they're holding Kira hostage and a security team shows up, they'll probably kill her just like they did that guy who attacked you, so she can't implicate them."

M furrows her brow. "How do you know they won't do the same thing if *you* go, since it's obviously Rigel and me they want? How can we even be sure—?"

She breaks off, but I know what she almost said. Because the same idea occurs to me with a sickening jolt—that we have no way of knowing if Kira's still alive even now. No! I won't believe that. I can't. If they'd… If she'd… I'd know. Somehow, I'd know.

"Okay, okay, let's think," I say, though every cell in my body chafes at the delay when I want to be rushing to her side. "If we're right that they've captured her to use as bait to lure in you and Rigel, it's possible they'll do something drastic if anyone else shows up. But it would be stupid for the two of you to play right into their hands. You're both too valuable."

She stares into space again for a long moment and I know she's communicating telepathically with Rigel, probably telling him everything we've talked about and listening to whatever ideas he has. Finally, she gives a little nod.

"How about this? Rigel and I will go to the apartment annex as soon as he gets here. But we'll go knowing it's a trap and be completely on our guard, in case there's an ambush or something. Even if Allister and Lennox and whoever they're working with know about our electrical ability, they can't have any idea how strong it is now. We should be able to…incapacitate anyone before they can hurt us—or Kira."

I see a trace of fear in her expression and wonder if it's for her own safety or the chance they could inadvertently kill somebody with one of their lightning strikes. Something *I'd* be totally willing to risk for Kira's sake…but I'm not M. I'm also not staying behind.

"Fine, but I'm coming with you. No, wait, listen," I add quickly when she starts to protest. "Uncle Allister always said I was the son he never had. I'm willing to put that to the test, gamble he won't order me killed." Or, I fervently hope, have Kira killed. "If he's in charge, monitoring things, me being there might throw him off long enough for you two to use your electrical thing—though I still think it's risky for you to go at all."

"Maybe Cormac—"

"If you tell him, he'll never let you walk into a trap. It's his job to put your safety ahead of anyone else's. I get it. I'd do the same thing if…if…"

"If it was anyone but Kira?" she finishes softly. The sympathy in her eyes scares me. It implies she believes it may already be too late.

Mutely, I nod. "Yeah." My voice comes out in a whisper. "That's why I can't stay behind, not knowing if…"

"I understand. I'd feel the same way if it were Rigel."

And yet she's willing to risk him along with herself for Kira's sake. For my sake. I know I should refuse to let them do this, that I'm being totally unpatriotic to allow it. So much for all my declarations that the good of our people should always come first. Because none of that seems to matter now.

"How long till Rigel gets here?" is all I say.

42

Crunch time

"WHAT? YOU'RE CRAZY," I tell Lennox and Allister—or, rather, their holograms. "I'm not going to help you kill the Sovereign. In fact, I'm going to warn her right now to stay well away from here. And if you have Enid come after us with that bomb, I'll—"

To my surprise, both men start laughing.

"Enid doesn't have the bomb, my dear," Lennox tells me, still chuckling. "You do."

"What do you—?" I look at the phone in my hand—the phone *they* gave me. "I've been carrying a *bomb* all this time?"

Gingerly, I set it on the floor and back away. "I'll leave it here, then. And…and call a bomb squad or something."

I start to turn toward the door and feel a sharp pain in the back of my neck, like when Enid deactivated my chip. "Ow!" I look back at the two holograms. "Did you—?"

"You appear to be laboring under a misconception, Kira." Allister looks genuinely amused. "Your phone is not the bomb. You are."

I stare at him in horror. "You mean this chip is…is…"

"A powerful explosive, yes. It also allows us a certain measure of control over you, via your phone."

No wonder they told me to keep that phone on me at all times! I take a step back toward it, wondering if it would survive a good, solid stomp.

As if reading my mind, Allister says sharply, "I wouldn't. If that phone is destroyed, your chip will begin an automatic countdown to detonation. And should you leave without it, the same will happen once you're fifty meters away."

"So if I'd accidentally forgotten my phone one day…?"

"Of course we didn't want to risk such a mishap while you were still working for us. The chip was only weaponized two nights ago, when you, ah, resigned. After that, yes, the consequences would have been quite unpleasant."

I glare at them both, my mind working furiously, seeking some kind of an out. They're not here in person. They can't physically restrain me and I can handle the pain in my neck. Their only real means of controlling me is fear. My fear. And while the thought of dying without being able to say goodbye to Sean wrenches at my heart, I'll absolutely do that rather than be the instrument of M's death —and possibly that of everyone on Earth and Mars, if the Grentl ever return.

"Fine, then," I say, my decision made. "You can kill me, but you won't get the Sovereign."

With the plan of running as fast as I can in the opposite direction she's likely to come, well away from the nearest houses, I again turn toward the door—and hear rapid footsteps approaching. Too late!

"No!" I shout in my loudest *caidpel* voice. "It's a trap! Don't—!"

Searing, blinding pain radiates from the back of my neck and my jaw seizes up, silencing me. I make one convulsive movement toward the door before my arms, my legs, are similarly paralyzed, freezing me in place. I stare, horrified, at the half-open door. Was my warning in time?

Apparently not. What now sounds like more than one set of hurrying feet grows louder as M—and Rigel?—keep coming closer. With all my might, I think in their direction, willing them to hear my thoughts the way they hear each other's. *No! Don't come in here! Go get help—it's a trap. It's a trap!*

It doesn't work. Moments later M and Rigel rush in hands clasped, then skid to a stop at the sight of me, frozen, and the holograms of my two captors.

"So predictable," I hear Allister gloat from behind me. "Lennox was afraid you'd send minions instead of coming yourselves but I knew better."

M glares past me at the two holograms. "I warned the Council they were too lenient with you both before. They won't make that mistake again. You've gone too far this time, without even trying to cover your tracks."

"There was no need to do so as there won't be any witnesses," Lennox replies. "Now, Allister, finish—"

Suddenly the door slams back against the wall and Sean charges into the room. My initial rush of relief at seeing him almost instantly gives way to terror. No! Not Sean, too! Though I can't move my mouth or shake my head, I make urgent warning noises in my throat, trying to convey that they all need to leave before it's too late.

"Do it, Allister! What are you waiting for?" Lennox demands.

"Sean, get out of here!" I hear fear in Allister's voice. "Go! I'll explain later."

Instead, Sean crosses to me in three strides. "Are you okay?" he asks shakily.

I want to nod, to reiterate his uncle's words, make him leave, but I still can't move or speak. All I can do is plead with him with my eyes. Frowning, he rounds on his uncle.

"What did you do to her? Why can't she talk? M, Rigel, help me get her out of here."

Behind me, Lennox chuckles. "None of you are going anywhere, I'm afraid. Ever again. Now, Allister. Do it now. They're both in range."

"No. I'm not killing my nephew, the last of my blood. That was never part of the plan. Sean, listen to me. You have to go. Now."

"Don't be absurd!" Lennox snaps. "We can't let him go, he's a witness. You can't possibly believe he'll protect you once we've killed the Sovereign, you know how he feels about her. Collateral damage was always a possibility. Detonate the chip."

"Sean, please," Allister pleads. "You need to get as far away from that girl as possible. When I push this button, she and everyone within a thirty-foot radius will be instantly incinerated. The ceiling will likely collapse, as well."

In response, Sean wraps both arms around me. "M, Rigel, run for it! Save yourselves."

They don't move. "What, and leave you two to die? I don't think so," M says firmly.

"Sean, don't you understand?" Allister sounds desperate now. "With Emileia out of the way, you'll have an excellent chance of becoming Sovereign yourself, given your heritage. If not you, then your mother— or me. Our family can—"

"Forget it," Sean snaps. "If you kill Kira, you kill me, too. Go on, you two, get out of here," he urges M and Rigel again.

"No!" Lennox roars. "Allister, give me the detonator if you're unwilling to do it. We'll never get another chance like this."

With a mighty effort, I turn my head a fraction and out of the corner of my eye I see the two holograms struggling, Lennox trying to snatch something out of Allister's hand. M and Rigel, meanwhile, stare at each other for a moment, then point at my phone, on the floor. There's a blinding flash. Both holograms vanish and at once I can move again.

"Now let's all get out of here," Rigel says urgently.

But I'm staring at the blackened area on the floor where my phone used to be. "Yes, you all need to go. Right away, in case they can somehow explode my chip all the way from Dun Cloch. Lennox definitely will if he can. You have to get out of range, now!"

"M and I should have created enough feedback at their end to at least stun them," Rigel says. "Not positive, since we've never tried exactly that before, but any electronic devices near them have probably been disabled, at least temporarily."

"It doesn't matter. Allister said if my phone was destroyed, the chip would automatically start counting down to detonation. I don't know how long, but probably not very. I'm not worth any of your lives, you know I'm not. If you run, now, you can get far enough away before—"

Sean tightens his arms around me. "Then we need to get that chip out of you before it explodes, that's all."

"Right." Rigel glances at M. "My mom, you think?"

"We can ask, but it'll be risky for her, too."

He frowns, chewing his lip.

"I'm not risking anyone else," I tell them all firmly. "It was my stupidity that got me into this and no one else is going to suffer for it."

"Shouldn't that be our choice?" Sean asks, not loosening his grip on me in the slightest.

Meanwhile, Rigel is already calling his mother, telling her there's an emergency and to gather up her surgical equipment. I continue pleading with the others to keep their distance just in case, but they mostly ignore me, debating where the best place would be for the procedure.

"NuAgra has the best facilities," M says, "but that could put even more people at risk. Maybe we're better off staying right here. At least this area is deserted."

The others agree, so Rigel tells his mother where we are. When Sean adds his pleas to mine, M and Rigel finally agree to at least wait outside the apartment until she arrives. Sean, however, stays where he is, one arm still wrapped around me.

"I really wish you'd—" I whisper, but he silences me with a kiss.

"Not a chance. When I thought I might already have lost you tonight, it nearly killed me. If you're booby-trapped to explode, well…I'd rather die with you than live without you."

His blue eyes bore into mine, pain and sincerity in their depths, forcing me to believe him—and to realize that if our situations were reversed, I'd feel exactly the same. Though he's only been a part of my life for a matter of days, already I can't imagine living without him.

Rigel must have successfully communicated the urgency of the situation to his mother because Dr. Stuart arrives in less than ten minutes, along with her husband.

"I'm not letting her take this kind of risk without me," he tells M when she protests. "Besides, I may be able to decipher what kind of detonator they're using and help to disable it."

"Where shall we set up?" Dr. Stuart asks briskly, her manner professional. If she's scared, it doesn't show. "I've brought along everything I thought might be useful."

We end up staying in the same apartment where all the recent drama took place, partly so Mr. Stuart can examine what little remains of the phone M and Rigel zapped. While he's doing that, Dr. Stuart probes the back of my neck with her fingertips.

"Hm. I feel it, but it can't be any larger than a grain of rice."

"Even smaller," I tell her. "I saw it just before Enid injected it into me. They told me it was just to track me, to keep me safe." The irony almost makes me laugh—but not quite.

She nods. "We have tracking devices barely bigger than a speck of dust now. It's how M and Rigel were traced when they, er, attempted to evade the Council's plans last year. But this is clearly more than that. Just a moment."

Opening a large black case, she pulls out a pair of small instruments, one of which appears to be some type of scanner. She passes it over the back of my neck for several seconds, then pulls up a display and examines it, her frown becoming more and more worried.

Then she gives a startled exclamation. "Surely not. I can't believe they— Van, will you take a look at this?"

Sean has been right next to me this whole time, but now he has to shift aside slightly, though without releasing his hold on my hand. Mr. Stuart stares at the display his wife shows him, then makes a sound of surprise similar to the one she just made.

"I can't believe they were able to— But that negative energy signature is unmistakable. Somehow, they managed to get their hands on a particle of antimatter, likely from one of our ships. How large an explosion did they claim this would make?" he asks me.

"Allister said thirty-foot radius, but didn't sound sure."

Mr. Stuart gives a little snort. "No, he's no Scientist, that's certain. He greatly underestimated what antimatter, even a bacterium-sized bit like this, can do. We'd better have her moved to Dun Cloch, or at least Chicago, where the Healers have better facilities. This is far too risky for Ariel to attempt—"

"There isn't time," I exclaim. "If what Allister said was true, the detonation countdown started the moment my phone was destroyed."

"She's right, Van, look at this." She points to something else on her display. "See? The casing around the antimatter is degrading—and quickly. It's unlikely to last more than another half hour given the rate of decay."

Mr. Stuart looks more closely. "Hm, yes, that would be the detonation device. Clever, if unpredictable."

"They set it up with my phone Thursday night, when I told them I wouldn't help them anymore," I volunteer. "Enid said she was deactivating the chip but instead she weaponized it. Allister said so just now."

"Allister is—" Dr. Stuart breaks off, frowning. "In any event, we clearly don't have time to take you elsewhere, except, perhaps, the facility at NuAgra—"

"But won't that endanger more people?" I protest. "The Sovereign said—"

"We can evacuate it, if necessary, so only you and I—" she begins, but Sean cuts her off.

"If she's going, I'm going."

"And me," M, Rigel and Mr. Stuart all say together.

I'm touched—incredibly touched—but I shake my head. "No, that's crazy. If it can't be removed without the risk of killing someone else, then I'll just...have to accept that."

Sean tightens his grip on my hand. "No. There has to be a way. There has to." He looks pleadingly around at everyone else in the bare room.

M and Rigel stare at each other for a moment, just like they did earlier—using their telepathy, I assume. Then Rigel nods. "Let us try something. If it doesn't work, then…we'll try something else."

"What?" his mother asks curiously. "Electrifying the chip could make it explode immediately."

"That's why we want to try the opposite," he says. "If we can just focus well enough, small enough, we think we might be able to create a sort of stasis field around the chip, at least long enough for you to remove it. Then we can take it someplace safe before it explodes."

His father looks at him doubtfully. "A stasis field? What makes you think you can do that?"

Rigel shrugs. "We've been, um, experimenting, working on ways to control our electrical ability better. We were trying to create the smallest possible spark, but we accidentally went even further, made some kind of…force around us. It didn't register at all on the voltimeter, but it stopped the clocks on both our cellphones for nearly a minute."

"If we could create that kind of force around the chip," M continues, "you *should* be able to remove it safely, shouldn't you? Then we'll try to maintain it long enough to…you know."

Rigel's parents both frown at them for a long moment but then his mother nods. "It *could* work, yes. But if it doesn't—"

"Please!" I insist. "It's not worth the risk. *I'm* not worth the risk."

"Yes," Dr. Stuart says, her kind hazel eyes holding mine, "you are. I'm a Healer. If you die, I will take it as a personal failure. Which means I don't intend to let that happen. M, Rigel, come here. This display should show you exactly where your stasis field needs to form."

Because I can't see anything that's happening, Dr. Stuart calmly describes it for me. "The chip is clearly visible on the scope, allowing me to guide my microforceps to the exact spot. M, Rigel, is the shield in place?"

"Yes." Rigel's voice is taut, as though concentrating is taking a lot of effort. "We'll hold it as long as we can."

"You'll need to move the stasis field with the chip as I extract it," she tells them. "Now. Slowly, slowly…"

I feel a slight burning sensation in my neck, though not nearly as bad as it was earlier.

"There. It's out. Now I can apply a topical anesthetic to alleviate—"

"No, I'm fine," I quickly assure her. "Getting that thing away from everybody is what matters now."

M and Rigel move into my line of sight now, M holding a tiny instrument—the microforceps, I assume—while they both focus on it. Mr. Stuart hurries ahead of them to open the door. For several endless seconds, Sean, Dr. Stuart and I hold our breath—or, at least, I'm holding my breath. If my idiocy ends up killing the Sovereign after all—

Suddenly a nearby explosion, much sooner than I expected, rattles the apartment windows. Terrified, we all stare at each other.

43

Prayer shot

Sean

"Oh, no!" Kira gasps, her eyes wide and scared. "Do you think they—?"

Mr. Stuart's jubilant voice interrupts her. "It's all right!" he shouts. "We're all right."

A moment later, he, M and Rigel rejoin us, smiling, though M and Rigel both look a little shaky. So am I. With a sigh of relief, Kira collapses against me.

"You...you did it," she stammers. "You saved me. I don't know how to—"

"You don't need to." M comes over and gives her a hug, even though I still have both arms around her. "I'm just glad it worked."

"So am I," I tell M fervently. "Kira's right. Neither of us can ever repay you two for what you've done tonight. Ever."

She smiles at me, her eyes moist with unshed tears. "Just...be happy together, okay? That will be a better repayment than anything else you could do."

I gaze fondly down at Kira, still wrapped in my arms. "That's the plan."

While Dr. Stuart heals the tiny incision in Kira's neck and applies an anesthetic, Mr. Stuart explains what just happened.

"M and Rigel were able to keep the stasis field in place while I inserted it into a piece of scrap metal tubing from the construction site. Then Rigel flung it as high as he could over that adjacent empty lot."

"Best long bomb I ever threw," Rigel jokes, provoking a general laugh. We're all slightly giddy from the sudden release of tension.

"No doubt everyone within a mile or two will have heard the explosion," Mr. Stuart says, "but there shouldn't be any other evidence. With any luck, people will assume it was a particularly large firecracker. Still, I recommend we leave the area before the local police decide to investigate."

Everyone immediately agrees. Kira, M, Rigel and I clean up the last of the debris in the apartment while Dr. Stuart puts her instruments back in her bag.

"Shall we?" Mr. Stuart says with a last glance around.

As we all walk down Ruby Street to where both of the Stuarts' cars are parked, M turns to Mr. Stuart. "I'll need to tell the Council what happened—almost happened—just now."

"I agree," he says. "They should be notified at once about the antimatter theft and what Allister and Lennox attempted to do. I'll be very surprised if they're not both charged with high treason."

"About time," Rigel growls. "When I think of Lennox's high-flown patriotic platitudes about pinning a treason charge on *me* last year for something he knew I hadn't even done..." He shakes his head in disgust.

"I'll let you know what the Council decides to do," M promises us all.

The Stuarts head to their SUV and Rigel offers to drop the rest of us off in their other car.

"No need. Kira lives right here." I gesture to her apartment complex across the street. "I'll see her home, then walk. But thank you again, all of you. Just...thank you." I wish I could find stronger words for the overwhelming gratitude still coursing through me.

Kira nods. "I'm so incredibly sorry. Not just for making you risk your lives tonight, but for everything else, too." She looks directly at M. "I was so determined to believe the worst about you for so long... I know now how very wrong I was. From this point on, you will always have my absolute allegiance." Putting her right fist over her heart, she bows deeply to M.

To my surprise, M bows back, instead of the little tipping of the head that's customary. "Thank you, Kira. That means a lot."

Then she and Kira are hugging each other and there's a little bit of sniffling on both sides. They're both smiling when they break apart.

"Okay, let's get out of here before the cops show up," Rigel says.

"I'll See you in church tomorrow," M adds.

As they all drive off, Kira and I walk back through the courtyard of her apartment complex. It's past ten o'clock by now and nobody's around.

"Do you want me to help explain to your folks why you're so late?" I ask when we reach the stairs leading up to her apartment.

"No, I'd better make up some excuse. The truth would just scare them."

Nodding, I take her in my arms again for a long, wonderful good-night kiss. It's harder than ever to let her go after almost losing her tonight.

"See you tomorrow," I whisper when I finally do.

"Tomorrow," she whispers back, smiling tremulously up at me. "I... Good night, Sean."

Leaving me to wonder what she almost said—whether it's the same thing I wanted to tell her last night—I watch as she hurries up the stairs and into her apartment.

Kira

I'M A LITTLE ACHY in church the next day after being paralyzed and nearly killed the night before, but I don't care. What matters is that I'm here, next to Sean, his hand firmly around mine despite the occasional frown from his mother.

All through the service I sneak looks at his profile, wondering how I could have fallen so deeply in love in such a short time. Once or twice he catches me looking and holds my gaze, his lips curving in a slow smile that makes me shiver with happiness.

After church, while everyone is chatting, we make tentative plans to play basketball again that afternoon.

"It'll be better than sitting around separately, wondering what the Council will decide to do," he whispers.

I agree. Now that I've had time to think about it, I doubt there's any way M will be able to keep my name completely out of her report this time. In fact, it's possible I'll be asked to provide evidence, if Allister and Lennox are brought to trial—though I hope not. Mum would be mortified to learn how disloyally I've acted.

That concern ratchets up when Dad receives a message as we're finishing lunch an hour later.

"Look at this, Deirdra," he exclaims, showing her his phone. "The *Echtran* Council has requested that Kira attend a meeting at the O'Gara house at two o'clock this afternoon."

Mum reads the message, then looks at me curiously. "How strange that they only texted you. Kira, do you know anything about this?"

"Um, maybe?" I glance at Adina, who's understandably curious, too. "But I'm not sure if—"

"Adina," Mum says briskly, "didn't you say you were going over to Jana's after lunch?"

My sister scowls. "Well, yeah, we were going to introduce Aggie to her cat today, but—"

"That's fine. Why don't you take the puppy and go. Now," she adds when Adina starts looking stubborn.

Muttering under her breath, Adina puts her sandwich plate into the sink, picks up Aggie and leaves the apartment. The second the door closes behind her, both of my parents turn to me.

"Er, well, I was involved in an…incident last night, and my phone got ruined. That's probably what this is about."

Keeping the details as sketchy as possible and completely omitting the bit about the bomb I'd carried around in my neck for a month, I explain that there'd been an attempt on the Sovereign's life the night before.

"It was kind of scary but Sean and…and Rigel Stuart stopped anyone from hurting her. Since I was there, too, the Council probably wants to get a statement from me or something."

I seriously doubt that's all, but I see no point borrowing trouble. Surely, if the Council planned to deport me to Dun Cloch, they'd have asked my parents to come, too?

"How far is the O'Garas' house from here?" Dad asks. "It's a quarter till two now. Should we drive you?"

Quickly, I shake my head. "No, it's not far at all. I can walk there in about five minutes."

The Stuarts drive up just as I get there—all three of them, even though Mr. Stuart's the only one on the Council. M comes around the corner from Garnet Street just then, too, also on foot, her Bodyguard following several paces behind. She smiles when she sees me and motions us all into the house with her.

More nervous than ever now, I accompany the others inside.

The O'Garas' small living room is crowded, all the dining room chairs brought in to supplement the usual couch, loveseat and chairs. All seven Council members are present, three of them holographically. Glancing quickly around, I spot Sean and feel a rush of relief. We take two quick steps toward each other before his mother points him to a chair on one side of the room and me to another on the opposite side. I draw what comfort I can from the encouraging look he gives me.

Once everyone is seated, the head of the Council, Kyna, calls the meeting to order. "By now, you've all had time to read the statement the Sovereign sent you earlier, with an account of what happened last night. She requested this meeting so your questions can be answered and so we can decide how to proceed, given what we now know."

I'm pretty sure I don't imagine the censure in Kyna's eyes when she glances my way. I swallow.

"This is the girl in question?" asks one of the holographic Council members— Connor, who I recognize from Dun Cloch. "Why has she not been taken into custody?"

There are nods and murmurs of agreement from several other Council members. I swallow again.

"Because she did nothing wrong," M replies firmly. "As I told you at yesterday's meeting, she was duped by Allister and Lennox into believing she could serve the Populist cause in Jewel. She knew nothing about the explosive they implanted in her neck."

"So you claim," protests another Council member, a dark-haired man. "At the very least, she should be sent to Dun Cloch to face an inquest and possible trial."

Sean's mother nods emphatically. "I agree. We don't dare assume—"

"There's no need for that," M insists, frowning them all down. "Cormac was able to apprehend the woman working with Allister and Lennox late last night and I'm confident our Mind Healers in Dun Cloch will be able to get all the remaining facts from her. Our first priority should be to find out how they got their hands on the antimatter they used in that chip."

Though a few of them appear to agree, it's clear Mrs. O'Gara doesn't.

Because Allister is her brother? Or because she wants me as far from Sean as possible?

"This charge is even more serious than the one you made yesterday, Excellency," Connor says then. "I find it difficult to believe that Royals, particularly two who previously occupied positions of such prominence, could be capable of an attempt on your life. Can we be absolutely certain the whole story wasn't concocted by this girl, or by others in the Anti-Royal movement?"

"Didn't you read my report, Connor?" M snaps at him. "I saw Allister and Lennox *myself* last night, projected into Jewel holographically. They used a device they gave to Kira in Dun Cloch, disguised as a phone. If you doubt *my* word, Rigel and Sean are also witnesses. Because neither Allister nor Lennox believed any of us would survive, they were completely upfront about what they intended to do. Mr. Stuart and his wife arrived shortly afterward and can positively confirm the existence of that antimatter bomb. I suggest we hear what they have to say."

At a gesture from Kyna, first Mr. Stuart, then Dr. Stuart stand up and relate what happened last night, including lots of technical details about the chip and the bomb it contained. Kyna next calls on Sean and Rigel, who also confirm everything M said. With understandable bitterness, Rigel relates how Allister and Lennox positively gloated about what they intended to do.

"I doubt M and I could have stopped them if Sean hadn't come along," he adds with a half grin. He goes on to explain how Sean refused to leave when Allister told him to, and how he and M took advantage of the conspirators' tussle over the detonator to destroy my phone.

Kyna nods. "That fits. According to a report I received from Dun Cloch early this morning, both men were found unconscious in the living room of the house where they'd been secured. No one had any idea how that could have happened. Given what we've just heard, I believe both Allister and Lennox should be charged with high treason. I move that we take a vote on that."

"But...but if they're convicted, that will mean the *tabula rasa*," Connor sputters. "No Royal in Nuathan history has ever been subjected to a complete memory erasure."

"Has a Royal ever been convicted of high treason before?" M asks him.

"Of course not. But—"

Kyna raises a hand to silence him. "Shall we put it to a vote?"

They do. Connor is the only dissenter, though Mrs. O'Gara raises her hand with obvious reluctance.

"And what about this girl?" she demands as soon as Kyna records the result. "She was a conspirator, too, unwitting or not, and a self-confessed Anti-Royal. I insist she be tried as well."

Sean leaps to his feet. "No, Mum. You're not sending Kira off to Dun Cloch to make some kind of…example out of her."

"Sit down, Sean, you are out of order." She glares at her son. "If the Council feels it necessary in order to ensure the Sovereign's continued safety—"

Sean remains standing. "That's not why you're suggesting it, and you know it. Anyway, if Kira goes, I'm going with her."

Mrs. O'Gara stares at him in shock. I'm nearly as shocked myself.

"Sean—" I begin, but M waves me to silence.

"Kira's not going anywhere," she tells Mrs. O'Gara. "Last night, in front of several witnesses, she formally declared her allegiance to me. I choose to accept that allegiance."

Sean's mother is still frowning. "How do you know—?"

"Mrs. O'Gara, I suggest *you* ask Kira if she is sincerely loyal to me. The entire Council, I know, relies on your ability to know whether someone is being truthful or not."

Swallowing visibly, resentment etched in every line of her face, Mrs. O'Gara turns to me. "Kira Morain, do you promise to be *completely* loyal to Sovereign Emileia from this day forward?"

I meet her gaze steadily, noticing irrelevantly that her eyes are as blue as Sean's. "Yes. I promise to be absolutely loyal to Sovereign Emileia for the rest of my life."

For a long moment her eyes bore into mine as though she's determined to detect any shadow of a lie. Finally, with a little sigh, she turns back to the Council. "She…she's telling the truth."

"Thank you," M says to her. "Kyna?"

"Yes, thank you, Lili. Everyone, I believe this concludes our business today. I declare this emergency session adjourned."

My shoulders sag with relief.

Sean immediately moves to my side. Putting an arm around me, he faces his mother, who still looks less than happy. "Thank you, Mum. I know that wasn't easy, but…I promise you'll like Kira once you get to know her better."

She looks at me and manages a tiny smile. "I'm…sure I will. But if you'll excuse me, there's something I need to speak with Kyna about before she leaves."

Sean watches her hurry across the room, then turns to me. "She'll come around, don't worry. Meanwhile, how about I walk you home?"

"That...that sounds great."

Ten minutes later, having said goodbye to everyone else, he and I descend his front porch steps together and head down Opal Street toward Diamond—and the arboretum. It's early October by the Earth calendar and the air holds a crispness I never experienced in Nuath. Breathing deeply, I smile up at Sean.

"I think I'm finally starting to appreciate Earth's weather. It's a beautiful day, isn't it?"

Smiling down at me, he nods. "And I'm looking at the most beautiful part of it."

I feel a blush stealing up my throat. "You were...amazing back there," I tell him. "Convincing your mother you'd go with me, if they sent me to Dun Cloch—"

"I meant every word," he assures me. "I'm not sure if I could live without you, Kira, but I'm positive I don't want to. I love you."

My heart rushes into my throat. "I...I love you, too, Sean. I wanted to tell you last night but I was afraid that... I mean, I didn't think it was possible that—"

He silences me with a kiss. Though I no longer have a chip in my neck, I suddenly feel like I just might explode anyway—from happiness.

For the very earliest news about what will come next in the Starstruck universe, subscribe to Brenda Hiatt's newsletter at brendahiatt.com/subscribe.

A Martian Glossary

Acclamation: Nuathan electoral process whereby citizens indicate approval or disapproval of a proposed Sovereign.

agoid (AH-gyoyd): organized protest; opposition.

aitlean (ayt-lee-AN): airplane; primitive aircraft used extensively by Duchas; Earth's primary means of intercontinental travel.

Arregaith (ah-ree-GAYTH) (pop. 1,413): town in southeastern Nuath containing spaceport and supporting industries.

ateamh rioga (ah-TEV ree-OH-gah): a persuasive ability shared by some of Royal blood.

athshondis (ath-SHON-dis): resonance.

Bailerealta (BAY-luh-ree-AL-tuh) (pop. 412): village on the western coast of Ireland, est. circa 1575, populated entirely by Echtrans.

Ballytadhg (BAH-lee-teeg) (pop. 1,106): east-central Nuathan village known for Arts fine and industry.

beidan (BID-den): gossip; scandal.

brath: Martian "vibe" detectable by other Martians.

breag fionn (brag fin): discovery of a lie; detection of falsehood.

caidpel (KAYD-pel): predominant sport in Nuath combining elements of the Irish sports of hurling and Gaelic football.

camastall (KAM-uh-stahl): deception; deceit; falsification.

cannarc (KAN-ark): rebellion; mutiny; resistance.

chabhil (KAB-vil): negotiation; debate; (occ.) ultimatum.

chas pell (CHASS-pel): a ball game played by Nuathan children, nearly identical to the Earth sport of basketball.

Cheile Rioga (KEE-luh ree-OH-gah): Royal Consort.

chomhaerle (KOM-ahr-lee): advice; counsel.

Chomseireach (kom-SAY-rik): Handmaid; lady's maid, chaperone and companion to Princess or (female) Sovereign.

Cinnwund Rioga (KIN-wund ree-OH-gah): Royal Destiny.

cloigh (kloy): to overpower or overthrow; defeat; subdue.

comhriteach (KOM-ree-teek): compromise.

cosc damaste (kosk DAHM-uh-stay): damage control.

coslacht (ko-SLACT): appearance; impression; influence.

Costanta (ko-STAHN-tuh): Bodyguard assigned to protect the Sovereign or other members of the Royal family.

dabhal (DOB-uhl) (*slang*): damn, damned.

dhualgis cumann (doo-AHL-gus koo-MAHN): benevolent duty; royal obligation.

dilsacht (DIL-sok): loyalty; allegiance.

doolegar (DOO-luh-gahr): despondency; depression.

Duchas (doo-kas): normal Earth humans.

Dun Cloch (Dun Klok) (pop. 1,247+): largest *Echtran* compound on Earth, founded 1933 in north-central Montana. Main production hub for Martian technology.

ealu (AY-loo): to break free, escape, or elope.

Echtran (ek-tran): person of Martian birth or descent living on Earth; expatriate.

Echtran Council: governing body for expatriate Martians living on Earth.

Echtran Enquirer: unofficial news source for expatriate Martians on Earth. Tends toward the sensationalistic.

edhmiu (FEY-mew): implementation; application.

efrin (EF-rin): Hell; used as a mild curse.

Emileia (em-i-LAY-ah): current *Thiarna* (Sovereign), granddaughter to Sovereign Leontine; sole heir to the Nuathan monarchy.

fasneis (FAHSH-ness): information; intelligence.

fine (feen): genetically related subsets of the Martian population, each with certain attributes.

flach (flok) (*slang*): socially unacceptable swear word.

foare rioga (fair ree-OH-gah): ancient, traditional syringe used for blood draw to verify Sovereign lineage.

gaiscigh (GAH-sheeg): heroism; act of extreme bravery.

giola uresal (gee-OH-la OO-ree-sal): menial servant.

Glenamuir (GLEN-uh-mer) (pop. 898): largely Agricultural village in northwest Nuath; longtime home of O'Gara family during Faxon's reign.

graell (grayl): intense emotional and physical bond believed mythical by most Martians.

grechain (gree-SHAYN): Nuathan information network, both personal and mass-media; news channels within the greater *grechain*.

Grentl (GREN-tuhl): advanced non-human alien race from an unknown part of the galaxy; likely founders of underground human colony on Mars.

hiarmarti (hee-ehr-MAHR-tee): consequences; results; price to be paid.

Hollydoon (HOL-ly doon) (pop. 1,677): largely Agricultural village in northwest Nuath; suffered particularly harsh ravages by Faxon's forces.

Horizon: one of four Nuathan transport ships traveling between Mars and Earth during biennial launch windows.

Insealbau (in-SALL-baw): Installation, as of Nuathan Sovereign.

Installation: Nuathan ceremony signifying a new Sovereign's ascension to power.

Jewel (pop. 5,013): town in north-central Indiana noted for corn, artisan jewelry and annual Jewel Jewelry Festival.

Launch window: period occurring approximately every 26 Earth months and lasting approximately four months, when the distance between Earth and Mars is small enough to allow travel between the two planets.

MARSTAR: official channel for communication from Echtran Council to expatriate Martians living on Earth, generally in the form of MARSTAR Bulletins.

Miochan (mee-OH-kan): healing; curing; a major fine.

moill (mahl): delay; postponement.

naesc geaniteach (nesh gan-it-EEK) genetic affinity.

nimhic (NIV-ik): antidote; cure.

Nuath (NOO-ath): underground human colony on Mars.

omni: a small, multifunctional device developed on Mars.

orinacht (OR-in-ott): propriety; seemliness.

pleanal (plenn-UHL): advance planning; scheming.

Populists: a minority movement among Nuathans advocating equal rights and representation for all fines. (Sometimes referred to as "Anti-Royals.")

probalreith (pro-BAHL-reth): opinion poll; public opinion.

probleid (pruh-BLAYD): privilege; status.

Quintessence (kwin-TESS-ens): one of four passenger vessels used to transport Nuathans between Earth and Mars.

Rigel (RY-jel): a blue supergiant star, approximately 860 light years from Earth, located in the constellation Orion; 7th brightest star visible from Earth, its brightness (or apparent magnitude) making it an important navigational star; Rigel Stuart, son of Ariel and Van Stuart.

rundacht (ROON-dahct): extreme secrecy; classified information.

scar a cheila (scar ah KAY-lah): separated; torn asunder; ripped apart.

Scriosath: memory erasure, the most complete being the tabula rasa or "blank slate," the highest form of official punishment.

Sean O'Gara (shawn oh-GAYR-uh): son of Quinn and Lily O'Gara; destined Cheile Rioga (Royal Consort) to Princess Emileia.

shilcloas (shil-CLO-ahs): hearing another's thoughts; telepathy.

sochar (SO-kar): Nuathan credits, used to purchase anything beyond provided necessities.

spiare (spee-AH-ray): spy; snoop.

stochail (sto-KAYL): preparation, as for a battle or journey.

streach suas (stretch SOO-ahs): resist oppression; underground resistance.

taghal ardus (TAHG-ul ar-DOOS): first touch causing a "tingle" between opposite sex teens, rarely repeated on second touch.

taigde (TAG-duh): research; records.

Teachneaglis (TAK-nee-glish): small minority of Nuathans and Echtrans who prefer to do without most modern advancements, primarily found in the villages of Bailerealta on Earth, and Keary and Eriu on Mars.

teachneoc (TEEK-nee-ok): technology; gadgetry.

teachtok (TEEK-tok) (*slang*): non-omni phone.

threoirach (TRO-rok): instruction; orientation; guidance.

tinneas (TIN-es): physical illness. Rare among Martians except in the very elderly.

toachai (TO-uh-kay): future; destiny.

triail (tree-AYL): test or audition; ordeal by trial.

Tullymayne (TULL-ee-mayn) (pop. 1,993): town in southeastern Nuath containing main transportation hub and supporting industries.

twilly: obnoxious person; jerk.

udaris thusmithoir (oo-DARE-is thoos-MITH-er): parental authority.

unbaen: dictator

About the Author

Brenda Hiatt is the New York Times bestselling author of twenty-two novels (so far), including traditional Regency romance, time travel romance, historical romance, and humorous mystery. She is as excited about her STARSTRUCK series as she's ever been about any of her books. In addition to writing, Brenda is passionate about embracing life to the fullest, to include scuba diving (she has over 60 dives to her credit), Taekwondo (where she recently achieved her 3rd degree black belt), hiking, traveling, and pursuing new experiences and skills.

For the latest information about upcoming books, visit starstruck-series.com or brendahiatt.com, where you can subscribe to Brenda's newsletter and connect with her via email, Facebook, Twitter or Instagram

Made in the USA
Middletown, DE
18 January 2019